DREAM OF DESTRUCTION

Reive began to shake; behind her closed eyelids a light pulsed and words whistled through her skull—

Ucalegon. Baratdaja. Prince of Storms and the Healing Wind. The holocaust that will destroy Araboth.

And then once more the voice of the imprisoned leviathan warning her,

"*. . . in the Undercity the rift is widening: soon it will breach the open sea. . . .*"

She recalled the tremor that had shaken her room that morning, and a hermaphrodite crying *The domes moved, we saw the walls shake. . . .*

"Zalophus," Reive whispered.

He had not been mad: the city was in danger. It was all real, somehow he had sounded the very depths of the Undercity and seen it there; somehow this woman Ceryl had seen it too. It was not *a* dream that Ceryl Waxwing recited: it was *The Dream*, the Great Portent, the Final Warning that the Orsinate had been searching for so desperately with all their occult games. They had placed all their trust in the Architects, but the one thing the Architects could not do was dream.

ÆSTIVAL TIDE

Elizabeth Hand

Bantam Books
New York Toronto London Sydney Auckland

ÆSTIVAL TIDE

A Bantam Spectra Book / September 1992

SPECTRA and the portrayal of a boxed ''s'' are trademarks of Bantam Books, a division of Bantam Doubleday Dell Publishing Group, Inc.

Grateful acknowledgment is made for permission to reprint the following:

"Nick and the Candle Stick" from *The Collected Poems of Sylvia Plath*. Copyright © 1966 by Ted Hughes; copyright © 1981 by The Estate of Sylvia Plath. Reprinted by permission of HarperCollins Publishers Inc.

"Let No Charitable Hope" from *Collected Poems* by Elinor Wylie. Copyright © 1932 by Alfred A. Knopf, Inc. and renewed 1960 by Edwina C. Rubenstein. Reprinted by permission of the publisher.

"The Hymn to Demeter" from *Homeric Hymns* translated by Charles Boer, 2nd Edition, Revised, Spring Publications, 1980. Reprinted by permission of the author.

"The Court of the Crimson King" written by Greg Lake, Ian MacDonald, Michael Giles, Robert Fripp, and Peter Sinfield. Copyright © 1989 by EG Music Ltd. (Administered in the USA by Careers-BMG Music Publishing, Inc.) Used by permission.

"If You Have Ghosts" by Roky Erickson. Reprinted by permission of ORB Music Company.

ISBN 0-553-29542-X

Published simultaneously in the United States and Canada

Bantam Books are published by Bantam Books, a division of Bantam Doubleday Dell Publishing Group, Inc. Its trademark, consisting of the words ''Bantam Books'' and the portrayal of a rooster, is Registered in U.S. Patent and Trademark Office and in other countries. Marca Registrada. Bantam Books, 666 Fifth Avenue, New York, New York 10103.

PRINTED IN THE UNITED STATES OF AMERICA

RAD   0 9 8 7 6 5 4 3 2 1

FOR RICHARD GRANT:

Parcus deorum cultor et infrequens

Some minutes later a murmur ran through the crowd. Through my heavy eyelids which had almost closed at the horror of her tale, I saw gown after gown passing, and parasols, and fans, and happy faces, and accursed faces, dancing, whirling, rushing. It was like a burst of immense flowers, like a whirl of fantastic birds.

"The doors, darling!" cried Clara, "the doors are opening! Come, come quickly! And don't be sad anymore . . . Think of all the beautiful things you're gong to see!"

Octave Mirbeau, *The Torture Garden*

BOOK ONE: Ordinary Time

~~~~~~~~~~~~~~~~~~~~~~~~~~~~~~

BOOK TWO: The Feast of Fear

~~~~~~~~~~~~~~~~~~~~~~~~~~~~~~

THE LEVELS OF ARABOTH
In descending order

SERAPHIM (Level 9) The Orsinate's Level
CHERUBIM (Level 8) The Imperators' Level
THRONES (Level 7) Cabinets & Cabals
DOMINATIONS (Level 6) The Vivarium Level;
Chambers of Mercy
VIRTUES (Level 5) The Hermaphrodites' Level
POWERS (Level 4) The 'Filers' Level (Mediatechs)
PRINCIPALITIES (Level 3) The Moujiks' Level;
The Medifacs
ARCHANGELS (Level 2) The *Rasas'* Level; the
Refineries
ANGELS (Level 1) The Undercity
〜〜〜〜〜〜〜〜〜〜〜〜〜〜〜〜

Book One

ORDINARY
TIME

Prologue:

IN ARABOTH
~~~~~~~~~~~~~~~~~~~~

Inside of a regeneration vat on Seraphim, the highest level of Araboth, something wakes. Once a man and now something less than that, still it thinks of itself as *him;* still he recalls the manner of his dying, as though it were a dream.

Because, as the poets say, Death was really just a brief sleep after all. There was a smell of brimstone, and of sleet; then a wash of light the color of the sea. Then, for a timeless reach, there was nothing: that was when he was really dead. But now he is waking once more; and if he had a voice he would shriek to shatter the chamber that imprisons him.

The woman stands above the vat, staring down at the puffy white body with its net of tubes and wires running from it. She knows he is alive again. She says nothing; only leans forward a little, so that the cuff of

Dante   Hell is oneself

her crimson surgical gown trails into the vat of nutrients and tangles with a tube running into the man's mouth. Her mouth opens and she whispers a name; and almost, almost she can imagine that he might hear her.

In the tank the man tries to stir, struggles to let his arms flow through this warm pool, but if no longer dead he is still unsure if he is alive. He can feel nothing. His arms are little more than a memory of flesh and sinew, his eyes open onto the saline darkness and there is nothing there to see. He wonders if this is another nightmare—there were many nightmares, untold nightmares, once—or if he has somehow, again, failed his masters. Because if that is the case, he knows where he is. He knows that this is not Hell but a regeneration chamber. He knows that Hell is not *other people,* as a man once said; Hell is oneself, the same broken body and twisted mind doomed to return to itself over and over again, a barren country where not even Death claims dominion. And from somewhere within the softly churning ocean that is all he now knows comes the memory of another face, a charred-white skull crumbling into ruin as its voice rings triumphantly through the cold air—

" *'Look at the stars! Look, look up at the sky!—'* "

But here in the regeneration chamber there is no triumph in rebirth. There is no sky here, there are no stars. He is in a place that sees nothing of the heavens. And then suddenly it is as though a caul has been stripped from his eyes. It seems that at last he *can* see something.

He sees a face, the face of a woman hovering above his watery crucible. It is a face he recognizes. The watery surface of the regeneration chamber ripples as he flails beneath it, knowing now the truth: that even in death he cannot escape her, even in death she will make a weapon of him. She has found him, she has reclaimed the fallen one and brought him to Araboth. The grinding wheel turns once more and he is doomed again to eternal service in the War in Hell.

To reach Angels, the Undercity, one must go down, down through the nine levels of the vast stepped pyramid that is Araboth. One begins at Level Nine, Seraphim, the pinnacle of the Holy City. Seraphim, where the Orsinate Ascendancy dwell—the city's rulers, the surviving members of the deranged Orsina family who still exert their febrile will upon the ruins of the continent outside. The Orsinate, themselves subject to the whims of the true Ascendant Autocracy, who live in the slowly decaying wheels of the HORUS stations, the Human Orbital Research Units in Space, where they retreated after the mass extinctions and mutations of the Third Shining. On some evenings the skygates open in the Central Quincunx Dome. Then the Aviators return in their warplanes, the Gryphons and the great silent dirigibles called fougas arrowing down through the heavy air of Araboth to refuel. Afterward, the Aviators walk unsteadily upon the smooth white avenues, and behind their eyes one can glimpse the flames of islands burning in the Archipelago, and smell in their sweat the sweet reek of a madness that overcomes fear. On these evenings, after the Aviators are gone and the skygate remains open, the Orsinate and their cabinet gather on the viewing platforms and stare up through that little lozenge of ultramarine darkness. They imagine, some of them, that they can see the faint lights of the HORUS stations tracking across the sky—grimy stars dying an interminable silent death even as their masters continue to send their whispered commands earthward, to land with the Aviators on the ancient ramparts of the domed city. It is the only glimpse of the stars that anyone in Araboth will ever see, except for once every decade at Æstival Tide.

On Level One, the Undercity, no one has ever seen the stars. And few of the aristocracy on Level

Nine have ever seen the Undercity. To reach it one must leave Seraphim and descend to Cherubim, and thence to Thrones, and Dominations, Virtues and Powers and Principalities and Archangels, each level of the ziggurat larger and more ancient and ruinous than the one above. The levels are named for the Divine Choirs, the orders of angels. A subtle joke played by those who founded Araboth centuries before. Those founders were religious people—thus *The Holy City of the Americas*—members of two cruel and ancient faiths who joined forces after the Second Ascension and have ruled this continent ever since. And so the oldest level of the ziggurat is Level One, Angels, where once another city stood, before there were domes and mutagenic rains and space stations marking drunken parabolas across the night sky. In Araboth, Level One is the Undercity. And few people go there of their own free will.

There are ancient things in the Undercity. The Beautiful One is one of them; but for centuries the Beautiful One has been asleep. Like the man thrashing feebly in the regeneration chamber on Level Nine, the Beautiful One is somewhere between wakefulness and dreaming; though not between life and death. Because the Beautiful One is not human, and so she has never really been alive.

But now the Beautiful One is waking, too. On the lowest level of the Holy City, Level One where only Angels dwell, there the Beautiful One is stirring. Her glass eyes flicker and her metal lips part and she sees them, the others who have come to worship her. Angels, they are called ironically on the upper levels; the fallen ones. But in her twilight state the Beautiful One does not see angels. She sees a man, tall and finely dressed, and around him pale forms crouched in the darkness, white-skinned, corpselike, their eyes glowing an unearthly green. They are *rasas,* "the scraped ones," regenerated corpses set to work on Archangels' refineries and the medifacs of Principalities. The ones who are here in the Undercity have somehow managed to escape their servitude above. Even the dead, it seems, can recognize that there are degrees of suffering in Hell. Sometimes the Beautiful One thinks that she hears them call her by an ancient name, their tongueless mouths struggling over the word; and in her sleep she answers them.

But the Beautiful One does not know this, not really. She does not know because she has slept these four hundred years, and dreamed another's dream. Her mind is composed of glass and thread, of circuitry and nucleoreceptive fluids. And dreams, of course, and histories: all the memories of those who came before her.

"Mother." The words are so garbled that only the Beautiful One can understand them. "Mother, Mother. Please."

"Nefertity," whispers the finely dressed man in his crimson greatcoat. It is the sort of clothing, of archaic yet fine, even baroque, styling, that only a member of the Orsinate might wear. His hand caresses her cold glass cheek, presses gently the spot upon her lower lip, the indentation that might have been left by too rough a kiss. "Nefertity, speak to me."

Ah, she thinks. From within the coils of metal thread a flame begins to lick and preen. *Ah*.

Her eyelids snap open. From the watching *rasas* comes a sound like a hiss or a sigh, and their pallid hands move slowly.

"Nefertity," breathes the waiting man.

"Ah," she says again; and as her eyes begin to move the room flares gold with light.

"Ah," the Angels cry out, and creep closer as she starts to speak.

"Greetings, sisters and brothers," she breathes. It is a woman's voice, calm and somewhat breathless. "This is the United Provinces Recorded History project, copyright 2109, Registered Nemosyne Unit number 45: NFRTI, the National Feminist Recorded Technical Index, or Nefertity."

The voice pauses. There is a soft whir, the whicker of datafiles spinning. Then, "The intent of our project is to provide a record of oral histories of those who might otherwise be forgotten. The Albhuz Femicides, the Bibliochlasm of 2097 and the subsequent holocaust have taught us the terrible necessity of projects such as these. Together, the Nemosyne Units of the UPRH will ensure that these voices will not have been silenced forever. As the Recorded Feminist Index of the American Vatican, I represent only one portion of the vast database available through the UPRH. Your local infonet will tell you how to link with others."

The whirring stops for a moment. The waiting *rasas* remain silent, oblivious to her words. It has been two hundred years since the bibliochlasm has even been admitted as part of the Ascendants' heritage; more years than that since the last nemosyne was believed lost in the infernos of the Third Shining.

"Nefertity," the man in the crimson greatcoat whispers, "speak to me."

The nemosyne clicks; then,

" 'I am the Million,' " she begins. Even the man is heard to sigh.

The Beautiful One Is Here.

Chapter 1

A BREACH
AMONG ANGELS

The screen showed a luminous formation like the cutaway view of a chambered nautilus. At various points blinking lights signaled the presence of the Wardens, the computerized guardians of the Orsinate's special entries to the gravators that shuttled them from one level of the Holy City to the next. In the very center of the nautilus a small rectangle glowed brilliant purple—the palace where the Orsinate Ascendancy and their staff lived and ordered the systemized destruction of the world outside the domes.

It was not really a nautilus, of course. Hobi knew that, as did his father, the Architect Imperator, whose long, thin fingers traced and coded new entries onto the screen. It was a bird's-eye view of Araboth; but Hobi was doubtful as to whether any birds remained

Outside to see those radiant tiers beneath the domes. In fact, the discovery that there *were* still birds Outside would have disturbed Hobi greatly. Hobi was only seventeen. His education at the chromium hands of a Seventeenth Generation Tutorial Scholiast had taught him (as everyone in Araboth learned sooner or later) that the world Outside was a treacherous place, even a hellish one. Anything that survived Out There— birds, insects, viruses—posed a threat to the survival of humanity, humanity of course being best represented by those who lived beneath the Quincunx Domes, in particular the Orsinate and their cabinet. At any rate Hobi's education—heavily tilted toward the sort of effete skills (literature, calligraphy, computer programming) that young aristocrats had received for centuries, perhaps millennia—had fallen off in the last year, since his mother's murder. Standing now behind his father, staring at the nautilus on the bright screen, was the first time Hobi had looked at a monitor in months.

"Structural damage to Studio Ninety-seven, Grid Fourteen, Powers Level," a voice murmured. It was a mechanical voice, the voice of the Architects who had designed and now maintained the city, under his father's supervision of course.

"Very good," Sajur Panggang said softly. It was four o'clock, false morning under the Quincunx Domes. A porcelain cup of kehveh steamed on the desk at his elbow. It smelled of chocolate and bitter almonds and made the boy realize how tired he was. Sajur reached for the cup and sipped it absently. "Next level," he said.

Hobi yawned. He had been passing his father's workchambers on his way to the dining room and stuck his head in to say good morning. His father's disheveled kimono and the spent tabs of amphaze on the desk indicated that he had been up all night, again.

"Something wrong?" Hobi asked. He inhaled the

kehveh's rich smell and wondered if he should have the servers bring him breakfast in here.

"Mmm? No, no." Sajur bent forward until his nose touched the screen, squinting as a red trail spun out from Powers Level down to Principalities. The Architects were centuries old. While they constantly reassessed and repaired themselves, the image quality on the monitors had been deteriorating for decades now. "Just performing a criterion, couldn't sleep."

"Oh." Hobi leaned against the wall and rubbed the scant stubble on his chin. Sajur had not slept well since his wife's murder, many months ago. The boy rubbed his eyes, stared more closely at the screen. It looked odd: something different about the configuration of the outer walls, maybe. "Is there a problem?"

Sajur Panggang shook his head, then listened intently as the Architects recited the inventory for Principalities Level. "Now Archangels," he commanded when the voice fell silent.

"Nothing has changed on Archangels," said the Architects after a few minutes. Hobi thought of returning to bed.

"Good," murmured Sajur Panggang. "Now Angels. Level One."

The light-trail that had marked the descent to the other levels darkened to violet. The nautilus on the screen disappeared, was replaced by a seemingly random series of reticulated squares and rectangles and triangles, crosshatched with a dizzying array of blinking lights. Hobi straightened, peered over his father's shoulders. Shivering he tugged his robe tighter about his narrow chest. He had never seen an enhanced image of Angels before. As far as he knew even his father had no business down there, and certainly the Architects had never renovated it. Only escaped *rasas* were rumored to live in the Undercity—if, of course, one considered them to be *living* at all. Hobi did not. Just thinking about them now was enough to make him wish he had stayed in bed. He rubbed his arms and leaned closer to his father, staring at the display.

Even the model of the Undercity was disturbing: the frenetic lines and squares that had nothing of the exquisite order of the rest of Araboth; the black shapeless areas that showed where the ruins of the original city had decayed and even the Architects had failed to restructure them. Hobi had heard stories about people going to the Undercity. Nasrani Orsina, the exiled margravin who was a good friend of his father's, was rumored to have a mistress down there. It was just the sort of dreadful thing you'd expect of an Orsina.

The Architects hummed and whirred. "Diagnostic," ordered Sajur Panggang. Hobi was surprised at how impatient his father sounded.

Click. Click. Click. Hobi shifted his weight to his other foot, trying not to look too curious. After his mother died, his father had forbidden Hobi to spend time in his study. Before, the boy had liked to sip Amity pilfered from his father's cabinets, watching the flickers and faint jets of light stream from the Architects as they programmed renovations and repairs beneath the Quincunx Domes.

But it had been months since Hobi had slipped in here. He wondered, sometimes, just what his father was up to in his study; but he didn't dare ask him. No one disturbed the Architect Imperator. He was too important, the only person in Araboth who truly understood the workings of the Architects. Even the Orsinate's murder of the Architect Imperator's wife had been carefully scheduled to coincide with one of Sajur's interminable love affairs, so as not to unduly disturb his work. Hobi thought that perhaps the Orsinate had misjudged his father. Certainly Hobi himself had been surprised by the intensity of Sajur's grief, which had taken the form of a nearly monkish solitude. As for Hobi, Angelika Panggang had always been a somewhat mythic figure to him. He identified her more with figures from poetry—Medea, Anne Sexton, Quisa Helmut—than with flesh-and-blood women or even certain replicants. So Hobi could only assume that his father's arcane doings in his study were somehow tangled up with his grief.

Now, gazing at the flickering screen in front of him, Hobi still could not imagine what the Architects were doing. Perhaps the Orsinate had commanded a new wing be added to the palace. Perhaps the Undercity had flooded—people were always predicting that; it was a favorite sport in Araboth, along with timoring and guessing who would be the next of Shiyung Orsina's lovers to die a horrible death. The boy nibbled his thumbnail thoughtfully. His father only stared at the screen in silence, tapping one finger against his porcelain cup.

"There is a breach in the fundus of Angels," the Architects replied at last. "The rift at Pier Forty-three is spreading."

"Thank you. Indoctrinate Pier Forty-four."

Hobi glanced sideways at his father. In profile Sajur Panggang resembled his dead wife, the same fine features and sharp nose. They had been first cousins. Like nearly everyone else on the upper levels of Araboth, they were distant relatives of the Orsinate.

"A breach?" Hobi asked, a little uneasily. "What's that mean?"

Sajur Panggang started, looked at his son as though noticing him for the first time. He shook his head. "Nothing. Routine maintenance. Aren't you up a little early?"

Considering how late you were out last night, Hobi thought. He grinned and shrugged. His father frowned and flicked at one corner of the screen. The monitor went blank. Sajur leaned back in his chair, the long ornamented sleeves of his kimono brushing the floor. "Would you please ask Khum to bring some more kehveh? Or no—I'll go with you."

The Architect Imperator stood and stretched. The brocaded sleeves slid from thin wrists to show the emerald mourning bands he still wore. Hobi noticed how his father's hand shook as he picked up his porcelain cup, and how Sajur looked back at the empty screen, the banks of ancient monitors like the walls of a tomb. On one of them the image of the Undercity still lingered, its web of ruined roadways and empty channels glowing faintly. The Architect Imperator stared at it for a long moment while his son waited, puzzled. Then he carefully closed the door and turned down the hall.

Behind them in the empty chamber the other screens slowly started to glow, blue and gold and violet. The Architects began to click and whisper, doing their master's work.

Chapter 2

THE GREEN
COUNTRY
~~~~~~~~~~~~

In a rickshaw on Thrones Level, Ceryl Waxwing watched a moujik girl die. The child's arms had been pinned to the seat, the skin folded back and neatly pierced with slender spikes as long as Ceryl's finger. As the girl moaned the exposed veins and muscles quivered like taut yarn, and blood seeped onto the seat's verdigris leather. For nearly an hour now Ceryl had stared expectantly at her face, waiting for the look Âziz Orsina had told her would come—

"When the timoring is successful and they know they're dying," the margravine had said. Every word she uttered always sounded as though she were somehow managing to suck it from the air. Ceryl hated her voice, her face (the same blade of a face she shared with her sisters Nike and Shiyung and their exiled brother Nasrani, the same face that appeared on the devalued currency that Ceryl had used to buy the moujik), the way she smelled, of cunt and sweat and opium sugar—but Ceryl was too close to them now, the Orsinate, to afford such simple prejudices. "They get this look when they know, children especially . . ."

That was why Ceryl had bought the moujik girl on Principalities Level, knowing she stood a good chance of having her throat slashed while she was there. As it was three moujiks had surrounded the rickshaw, gibbering at the rickshaw driver and spitting at her as she clambered back in, the sedated girl in her arms. It was nearly two hundred years since the particular conflict with the Balkhash Commonwealth that had brought the moujiks here, peasants who were ostensibly prisoners of war but really slaves put to work in the medifacs, the great abattoirs on Principalities. Nothing went to waste in Araboth: the bodies of the dead were processed as efficiently as the vegetable and animal proteins manufactured in the vivariums on Dominations. Only members of the Orsinate and their cabinet received the honor of a funeral pyre. And so the moujik peasants proved an ideal resource, a ready labor breeding pool that did not deplete the Orsinate's own population.

Despite their centuries of servitude, the moujiks had never lost their belligerence, or their distinctive appearance. Tawny skin, flat face, round eyes the color of honey. Not as fair as Ceryl was, with her close-cropped sandy hair and blue eyes. But certainly darker than the Orsinate, although the Orsinas' long alliance with the religious fanatics from the East had left its own imprint—one could tell an Orsina bastard by its doe eyes, just a little too close-set, and its dusky skin.

No one would ever mistake a moujik for one of the ruling caste. They lacked the Orsinate's cunning and sophistication, and even the most rudimentary reading skills. But enough belligerence remained in the moujiks to impel them toward the body riots of the Third Ascension, when they had seized Principalities Level and murdered three Ascendant Governors who happened to be touring the medifacs. Since then the Orsinate maintained an uneasy truce with the medifacs. Among other things, they allowed the moujiks control of the city's black market body trade, for those on the lower levels who could not afford prosthetics. This same truce allowed for a brisk barter in moujik children for timoring, children not as highly prized as those from the upper levels, Thrones or Dominations say.

It had been Ceryl's first solo attempt at timoring, her first trip down to the medifacs. She had felt more terror taking the gravator to Principalities than at gazing upon the moujik child's contorted face. She turned to stare down at her again, then hastily looked away and groped at her pockets until she found a candicaine pipette. She broke it and inhaled, let the cold rush calm her. There had been no sublime wave of fear as she stared at the pathetic thing beside her. Oh, the child had struggled and screamed enough before the morpha set, there was no doubt that *she* was afraid. But Ceryl herself felt only disgust, and shame: the child looked so small and white against the dark leather. Blood had pooled on the seat beside her, staining Ceryl's catsuit. She leaned over to touch one of the pinions of flesh gleaming slightly in the purplish light. The rickshaw driver had pulled down the plastic shades before they went down to the medifacs. Now the smell of blood and meat filled the inside of the tiny wooden car. Suddenly she felt sick.

"Stop—" she gasped. The rickshaw shuddered to a halt. The driver turned to stare at her blankly, spat a wad of betel juice onto the pavement. "Just wait," Ceryl choked, and opened the door.

Violet light spilled onto her, the perpetual dusk of the upper levels. She smelled the warm mist heavy with the scent of the sea Outside. Despite the thousands of filters humming and doing their best to dispel it, the smell and damp of the sea still got in. Lately it seemed inescapable. Those members of the pleasure cabinet who were more superstitious than Ceryl shook their heads and whispered about bad omens— strands of kelp found floating in filtration chambers, the odd bit of mussel shell clogging a drain. Certainly Ceryl had noticed the smell more lately, but she attributed that to the fact that Æstival Tide was less than a week away.

Now it was that smell that made her feel better. She breathed deeply, eyes closed. A vague impression of warmth and green flooded her, a memory of the sound of birds. She had seen the ocean, of course, ten years earlier at the last Æstival Tide, when they finally opened the Lahatiel Gate. The sight of that restless sea had terrified her, the closest she ever came to the holy terror of timoring. Ever since then she had wondered whether you would always feel like that, if you lived near it. *Really* lived near it—on real sand and smelling real air and tasting brackish water—and not within this unimaginably vast and intricate labyrinth of a city, dying beneath its domes between the blasted prairie and the threatening sea. Maybe, if she lived by the sea, she would not be plagued by nightmares and forced to spend much of her monthly salary on pantomancers, those quack dream-merchants.

Her cheeks grew cool with mist and she sighed, opening her eyes. The rickshaw had stopped at the outermost rim of the Thrones Level Grid. The avenue here was in blessedly good repair, the surface beneath her feet smooth and cool. Only, behind one of the rickshaw's wheels, she noticed a crack in the pavement, like a thread of water running down the avenue.

"That's odd," she said aloud. The rickshaw driver cocked his head at her and shrugged.

"Something new," he said, spitting a crimson mouthful of betel juice onto the ground. "Cracks. I had to repair a wheel bearing twice in three days."

"Cracks," Ceryl repeated softly, and stared down at the ground.

Behind her were the broken spires and crooked facades of Thrones' residential neighborhoods. Like everything else on the upper levels of Araboth, these apartments were prefabricated by the Architects. Over the last few centuries the metal and plasteel structures had cracked and buckled under the weight of the levels above, until all of Thrones seemed to be caving in upon itself, albeit in a subdued, almost genteel manner. Although of course living quarters here were a vast improvement over the dayglo ghettos of Virtues, where the hermaphrodites lived, or the grim cubicles that housed the 'filers and media crews on Powers. At least on Thrones the roads had always been in good repair.

Ceryl sighed and rubbed her nose. A few yards in front of her, a shimmering heat fence crackled and sparked as moisture filtered down from the Quincunx Domes. Beyond the fence was nothing, a dizzying plunge to the next level, Dominations, and thence to Virtues, and Powers, and so on down to the lowest level of the crazily layered ziggurat that was Araboth. If one could see the city from above (but of course you could not, unless you were an Aviator), it would resemble a huge and living pagoda, its vaulted domes rearing above the nine levels like the chitinous shell of some monstrous arthropod. And Outside, the sea: smashing against the domes during the months-long storm season, whispering through the dreams of the Imperators' children as they slept in their gilded beds on Cherubim.

It was only the Architects that protected them from the horrors of the sea and the world Outside. There, an earth seeded by centuries of radiation and viral rains had given birth to heteroclites and demons. Only the tireless Architects protected them from that. On the uppermost levels, Seraphim and Cherubim, the Ascendants' robotic engineers constantly built and rebuilt Araboth's pinnacles and spires and moats. You might wake one morning and find that the outside of your chambers had been gilded. Or there might be a new place of worship where last night there had been nothing: a shining new crucifix-speared mosque, wherein the Orsinate propitiated the horrors of the ravening world with offerings of prisoners taken in ceaseless raids against the Commonwealth.

Or, if you were unfortunate enough to live on the lower levels, you might find that in a single night the Architects had destroyed your ghetto on Powers. Or they might have torched a refinery on Archangels, immolating thousands of *rasas* as the Architects' grinding machines leveled factories and apartment buildings made of polymer-strengthened paper. The next day perhaps an ice-blue lake would be there, with Orsinate bastards skimming across its surface in their azure gas-fired proas, while from its banks their replicant nursemaids stood guard with blank yet watchful eyes.

Or there might be nothing there at all, a smoking ruin such as Ceryl's dead lover Giton Arrowsmith had found once, where his chambers had been. That was before Ceryl's promotion to the pleasure cabinet. She had never thought she would look back with any fondness upon Giton's fishy-smelling cubicle on Dominations; but here she was, tearfully nostalgic in front of a heat fence on Thrones. There was no reason for it, for any of it. There was *absolutely* no reasoning behind the Architects' ceaseless construction and deconstruction of the city. Even the margravine Âziz admitted to that, and Sajur Panggang, the Architect Imperator who was supposed to monitor the great machines.

"We grew lazy and forgot how to program them," he had told Ceryl once, and shrugged. "So now they program themselves. I, um, occasionally make *suggestions* to them, and if I'm fortunate, well, they listen to me."

He was a small slender man, the Architect Imperator, with the large gentle eyes and strong chin of his Orsina cousins. Unlike his cousins, Sajur was gifted with a keen, if narrowly focused, intelligence. The Ar-

chitects had designed most of the buildings in Araboth
—for example, those dizzying residences on Cherubim that assumed such bizarrely baroque proportions
that they could scarcely be looked at by a sane person,
let alone lived in. But Sajur Panggang had created the
Reception Areas, the labyrinthine prisons that supplied the vivariums on Dominations with food. And
he had also designed many of Araboth's hundreds of
kerchief-sized parks, where the marvel of holographic
landscaping made it seem that one gazed across a
moor swept with lavender sage in bloom, or peered
up at the unimaginably distant bulk of mountains
with peaks so sharp they might have been cut from
paper—which, in essence, they were.

"The Orsinas have never been known for their
intellect," Sajur had confessed to Ceryl. This was not
long after his wife's murder. Ceryl, recalling her own
grief after Giton's death, had expressed her sympathy
for Sajur's bereavement. "It's a miracle it's all still
standing, really."

He had cast an ironic glance at the ceiling, and
stroked the elegant cobalt cylinder of a drafting man-
nequin. "A wonderful, wonderful miracle." Ceryl recalled him enviously. She wished *she* could consider
anything inside of Araboth a miracle. Because as she
stared out at the heat fence sparking a few feet in
front of her, the pale violet light that made everything
look like its own shadow, Ceryl felt only despair.

Behind her the moujik girl gasped. Ceryl's knee
bumped the open door as she turned and with one
hand brushed a tendril of greasy hair from the child's
forehead. As she watched a film covered the girl's
wide eyes, like gray silk. Then she was still. Ceryl continued to stare at her, aware that she was experienc-
ing nothing but a faint and rising nausea, the same
feeling she had if she lingered too long at one of the
promenades on Cherubim, looking down upon the
dwindling lights of Araboth's lower levels.

So, she thought, and grinned miserably. She really *was* incapable of the higher emotions. Not even

Giton's execution, not even this child dying in her lap, could move her. Only to the morphodites, the dream-mantics, could she confess what truly sickened her and haunted her dreams: the city itself beneath its shell of eternal twilight, breathing softly all around her, while its unseen Architects chattered and hummed and ordered the endless renovation of their animate hive.

She let her breath out in a long gasp and slid to the edge of the seat. A gust of hot air shot up from beyond the heat fence, heavy with the doughy smell of fermentation from one of the vivariums below. Ceryl lifted her head. She looked out over the abyss and saw a fouga, a dirigible warship, moving slowly and with a resonant wasplike hum toward the skygate in the highest of the Quincunx Domes. Behind it trailed a yolk-yellow banner, a pennon signaling an Ascendant triumph.

Ceryl sighed. The fouga would be returning from a skirmish with the Balkhash Commonwealth. She had seen last night's broadcast, showing scenes of neurological warfare played out against the calm blue reach of an island in the Archipelago. The sight of men and women writhing and howling on the beach had finally proven too much for her, and she'd switched the screen off. No one really believed in the 'files, of course. Ceryl herself had once watched an ostensibly live broadcast of a desert battle being produced in a studio on Powers Level. A number of moujiks and even a few uniformed *rasas* stood in for the Commonwealth soldiers and Ascendant janissaries. Ceryl was only mildly shocked to learn that the blood, at least, was real.

The wars were real, too. Hundreds of wars, even thousands of them. Over the last four centuries the world had shattered into a thousand parts, each with its own petty tyrant fighting its neighbors for dwindling resources. The Shining that brought about the First Ascension all but destroyed the subtle network that held the world together. The next holocaust

obliterated the faltering remnants of any telecommu-
nications systems. That Shining was followed by others, too many to count. Those who survived the
nuclear holocausts fell victim to mutagenic rains that
desolated most of this continent and its southern antipode. Of the rest of the world, only the Archipelago
and parts of the subcontinent, and Wyalong, the great
Austral island, were relatively untouched by the viral
wars. The Balkhash Commonwealth held sway over
the detritus of Eurasia; the Håbilis Emirate controlled
the Glass Continent and the Desert Lands. The vast
mutated jungles and radiation deserts of the Americas
had become the object of more wars than anyone
could count. For two hundred years now they had for
the most part been controlled by the NASNA Ascendancy—although that word "control" scarcely applied. There were huge areas of the continents where
no Ascendants had ever stepped, where those who
had survived the holocausts and viral wars had re-
verted to forms of barbarism surpassing even the excesses of their ancestors.

A few pockets of technological sophistication remained. Araboth was one of them. Ceryl could not
have pointed out any of the others on a map. She
knew that the centuries-long wars with the Balkhash
Commonwealth and the Håbilis Emirates continued,
but she could not have told you why. Something to
do with water, maybe, or the hydrofarms still active
in the western ocean.

Probably the Orsinate themselves did not really
know. In the tangled web of diplomatic intrigue and
barbarism that now constituted the civilized world,
even the Orsinate took their commands from a higher
source. The true Ascendants, the supreme military aristocracy who after the First Ascension had rebelled
against their commanders and forsaken the ravaged
earth for the network of HORUS stations circling the
planet. Since then the Ascendant Autocracy lived in
the HORUS stations, where they cosseted their ancient computers and failing stores of military hard-

ware. Only the NASNA Aviators traveled between HORUS and the rest of the world, seeding the great prairies with viral rains, poisoning the hydrofarms of the Håbilis Emirate with metrophages and burning gases.

And now here was an Aviator fouga returning to Araboth from some unknown mission. Maybe last night's broadcast had been real, after all. There might be more prisoners from the Emirate, captured to slave in the refineries of Archangels Level. Or the fouga might carry no one but the Aviators, returning for one of their periodic shows of triumph: a twitch of the long chain that stretched from Araboth to the heavens.

Ceryl heard a distant sound like the crash of waves. Slowly the shining skygate opened, like a bandage peeled away to show the wound beneath. Ceryl squinted to catch a glimpse of what was beyond, a purple sky fraught with orange flashes. The domes of Araboth besieged by enemy fire, perhaps; or perhaps nothing, perhaps some normal atmospheric disturbance—fallout from one of the HORUS colonies, or lightning. It was late spring, Outside; nearly Æstival Tide. That was the only time that Araboth opened its gates to the world: once every decade, when the city's populace would surge from the Lahatiel Gate onto the beach Outside and purge itself in the ritual of ecstatic terror known as the Great Fear. Because the world Outside was a horror. And no matter that it was a man-made horror—to look upon that world more than once every ten years would drive one mad. Everything connected with it—the color of the ocean, the hot smell of it, the roaring of the wind—had over the centuries acquired a patina of superstitious terror. Even those children conceived during Æstival Tide (and there were many; the Great Fear was a powerful incentive to lust) were believed to be contaminated. Their screams during the sacrificial hecatombs had inspired many of the Orsinate's artists.

But that was a long way off yet. The city had yet

to survive the Healing Wind. Because immediately after Æstival Tide (and sometimes earlier) the storm
season would begin, with the murderous hurricanes
and typhoons that were the ill-born children of Science as surely as were the geneslaves and the hermaphrodites and other monsters. The storms came
each year, of course, but it was commonly believed
that those following Æstival Tide were more furious
and malign than in other years. The moujiks had
names for these hurricanes. They believed that there
were really only two of them, Baratdaja the Healing
Wind and Ucalegon the Prince of Storms, and that
they returned decade after decade to batter the domes
like the hands of some monstrous lunatic. But inside
of Araboth all was safe, all was still; all was under the
protection of the softly humming Architects. And
alone perhaps among the people there, Ceryl would
awaken terrified in her broad, sumptuous, and empty
bed and feel it all shaking around her, the Healing
Wind gnawing at Araboth until the city collapsed in
upon itself like a marzipan egg.

   Leaning forward she stared at the crack in the
pavement. On the lower levels, an avenue with only
one such minor flaw would be a miracle. Here on
Thrones, however, where the members of the Orsinate's pleasure cabinet lived, Ceryl had never seen
so much as a pebble out of place. And so close to
Æstival Tide . . . The crack seemed a bad omen.

   She thought of her dream, then. Of the wall of
water green as—well, green as water—and alive,
shattering into millions of fragments, arms, heads,
bloated bodies like drumfish smashing into the crumbling seawall. She recalled the small body beside her
and shivered. From where the driver stood, waiting,
she heard the brisk snap of a candicaine pipette, a
snuffling noise as he inhaled. Ceryl kicked at a slip of
paper blowing past, stirred up by the change of pressure from the skygate's opening. *WELCOME THE
HEALING WIND!* she read. Another flyer printed illegally by one of Araboth's many doomsday cults. She

fumbled in her pockets for more of her own pipettes but found nothing, only bits of glassine and powder. Her month's narcotic ration was long spent. Her last morpha tube had gone to sedate the moujik girl.

From high overhead came the clashing of immense hidden gears. The skygate began to close. Ceryl watched as the sky was skinned to a violet sliver, until the gate clanged shut and the brief vision of the heavens disappeared in the pulsing lavender light of the domes. She turned and, gently, stroked the dank white cheek of the dead girl behind her. Then she bent until her head touched her knees and silently began to cry.

The gynander Reive sat on the bed in her little room on Virtues, the hermaphrodites' level, smoking kef and eating her last tin of krill paste. She dug the paste out with her fingers and sucked them pensively, wishing it were already evening, when at a dream inquisition she would be fed delicacies, fresh shark and sea urchin roe and prickly pears. But that thought only made her more hungry.

"Never mind, never mind," she whispered. Like most hermaphrodites, Reive lived alone, and had grown into the habit of talking to herself. But then she remembered that she wasn't really alone anymore. She smiled. Her face—rather too sharp, almost wizened—looked deceptively sweet and childlike, despite her fifteen years. "Wait!" she said softly, and pushed the krill tin away.

The empty canister rolled beneath the bed. Reive reached for her kef pipe, sucked at it vainly, and tapped the ashes onto the floor. The place was a mess, krill tins and broken morpha tubes everywhere, old kohl wands strewn beside clothes she'd received in payment for her readings, everything covered with a coat of kef ash like whitish fur. It all smelled of smoke and soiled clothing and shrimp paste, and from her bed Reive regarded it with a fastidious distaste that belied her grubby fingers and the broken rubber bands tied around the long black plaits of her hair. A room so small and narrow that if she lay on the floor she could practically touch each wall with her outstretched hands.

She sighed. If she hadn't given that diplomat a bad reading last week, he might have taken her up to Thrones with him. There she might have found a wealthy patron, some dream-buggered politician eager to have his own mantic. Instead, Reive had scryed the diplomat's dream quite bluntly, advising a change of métier, and he'd left the inquisition in a panic. Since then she was considered bad luck. She'd be lucky if she could get work scrying for some 'filer on Powers, the next level down.

"All right," she announced, replacing the kef pipe in its little sandalwood box and shoving it onto a shelf. She wiped her hands on the worn spread and stretched across the bed, reaching down the side facing the wall. A moment later and she had withdrawn something, a small glass globe that fit easily within her cupped hands. Water splashed over its lip as she set the globe carefully in her lap and stared down into it.

In the periwinkle light that glowed from the tiny room's ceiling the globe seemed to float, a softly gleaming turquoise. Within it something else floated, a shrimplike creature the length of Reive's finger. Its segmented body was a translucent coral, so that she could see the violet bead of its heart pumping, the gold and red filigree that formed its organs. Its feathery legs were a brilliant acid green, its slender tail a yellow that was nearly luminous in the ethereal light. It had long whiplike antennae that moved slowly through the water and large round eyes that were an unexpectedly brilliant azure. Beneath its thorax was a tiny pouch holding what appeared to be myriad pearls of a nacreous pink. It was a mysid, a kind of shrimp that carried its young in a brood pouch until they

were several months old. The eggs of this one were
supposed to hatch very soon.

Reive gazed transfixed at the tiny creature, murmuring. It was not a *wild* creature, of course, but
stolen from a vivarium on Dominations Level, where
the mysids were raised to feed larger animals like fish
and certain aquatic birds. A patron of Reive's, a biotech who had befriended the gynander on one of her
solitary visits to the vivarium level, had given it to her
in exchange for a dream reading. A completely illicit
transaction—if a sentry from the Reception Committee were to find it here, Reive would be executed.
Animals and plants still carried all the ominous
weight of their origins Outside, despite the fact that
every creature now living within Araboth had by this
point been so genetically altered as to bear little resemblance to its forebears. The mysid, for instance,
was descended from creatures only an inch long.
When the Hábilis Emirate took control of the Archipelago and its hydrofarms, the Ascendants engineered
the mysids as an alternative to reliance on the Archipelago's krill shrimp. But Reive didn't know that;
Reive just knew that the mysid was beautiful, and it
was hers, a secret from the prying eyes of the other
gynanders on Virtues.

"Don't be afraid, we are here, we will protect
you," the gynander whispered, tracing the curved
glass with a grimy finger. Within its turquoise globe
the mysid swam lazily, its feathery legs sending phosphorescent ripples through the water. Reive reached
one hand behind her, pulping the bedclothes until she
found a box of papery rice crackers. She crumbled the
corner of one into the globe and watched entranced
as the mysid fed, the bits of cracker disappearing between the transparent mandibles and its inner organs
deepening to royal purple as it digested its food.

Without warning a soft, bell-like tone echoed
through the room. Reive sat up in alarm, spilling a
little precious water onto her lap. She clutched the
globe, looking back and forth. The room seemed to be

trembling—she could not be sure at first. It was all so quick, a tremor so slight that it was only when she focused on her kimono on its brass hook, its faded sleeves swaying ever so slightly, that she was certain of what was happening. She took the globe and hid it behind her bed, bracing it with a mismatched pair of slippers. By the time she stood in the center of the little chamber all was still again.

"Damn," Reive breathed. She crossed her hands in the ward against Ucalegon and flopped against the bed, her heart thudding. Maybe the storms were beginning early this year. It was only a week until Æstival Tide; perhaps the winds were rising in anticipation of the great festival. Or the Commonwealth might have struck against the city; but even Reive, untutored as she was, knew that was unlikely. She took a deep breath and stood, crossed the room and opened the door and stuck her head into the corridor.

Outside, the long, curved hallway seemed undisturbed, except that one panel in the ceiling lights was flickering deep violet instead of its accustomed pale blue. After the fishy must of her chamber Reive breathed deeply, grateful for the modestly fresher air out here. Virtues Level was not considered important enough to benefit from the more advanced filtration systems of the upper levels. A complex perfume filled the corridors connecting the warren of little chambers where the hermaphrodites lived. Opium sugar and krill paste; the lemony scent of the cheap cologne the gynanders favored this season, a perfume called *Arielle;* the muskier odor of the myrrh and sandalwood chips the hermaphrodites burned during their dream-trances; and beneath all of it the harsh acrid note of the periwinkle-blue lead powder that they used as the base for all their cosmetics. The powder was poisonous, of course, and after constant use many gynanders died quite young. This was not inadvertent, population control being a constant concern of the Orsinate. The hermaphrodites were sterile, but they still ate and took up space. And then of course they aged, and older hermaphrodites were ugly and therefore useless. The toxic lead powder was a fortuitous solution to this problem. Most gynanders knew the cosmetics were poisonous, but they were a vain lot and used them anyway. There was much competition for the business of dream-readings, and patrons were often influenced by an unusual face.

Several of these faces turned to stare at Reive as she entered the hall.

"You heard that?" one called, her voice high and childish.

"We heard it," Reive admitted. "You did too?"

"We all did," Drusilla, the other gynander, replied. She stood in a small knot of six or seven, some in kimonos, one half-dressed in scarves and thin gold-colored chains. Two of them, like Reive herself, were naked except for filmy pantaloons and wore no cosmetics. She stepped gingerly from her doorway and tiptoed down the hall to join them.

"What was it?"

"We don't know, Numatina said a bomb—"

"!"

"—but Charlless said it is the storms—"

"That's what *we* thought," Reive murmured triumphantly.

"There was another last night on Cherubim! The domes moved, we saw the walls shake—"

"Well, *we* think it is Ucalegon," Drusilla finished, her lips tight. The others whispered urgently, crossing their hands across their small bud-breasts. The ones who wore no makeup looked alike: white, heart-shaped faces with almond eyes, thin mouths and high rounded cheekbones. All had the same spare build, the same black hair, the same fluting voices; the same tiny breasts and the same small bulge between their legs where they hid their twin sexes. If you were to scrub their faces clean and line them up in a room, it would be difficult to tell any difference between them at all. That was the curse of their common origins within the crucibles of Dominations.

But the hermaphrodites were too vain to spend their short lives being mistaken for each other. Thus their reliance on colored kohl wands and pots of red and silver rouge, their pride in a finely drawn mouth or eye, and also their dislike of Reive.

The first gynander gazed at Reive through slitted eyes. Drusilla had already painted herself, the periwinkle powder deepening to lavender where she had highlighted her cheekbones, her eyes drawn into elaborate wings with a stippling of scarlet dots beneath them, a full scarlet mouth pouting over her narrow lips.

"We heard you were dead, Reive," she pronounced.

"We heard that too," another gynander chimed in. Over her pale blue mask she had drawn a series of stark curves in black, outlining her eyes and mouth. "We heard your patron killed you."

Reive drew herself up stiffly. She was taller than the other gynanders, and without makeup she looked different from them too—her face sharper, almost copper-colored where theirs were milk-white; her hair black but thin where the others had thick curling plaits; her eyes round and, worst of all, the forbidden color, where the others' were black. She stared coldly at Drusilla.

"We are alive. We have a new patron," she lied, "an aristocrat troubled by nightmares. A member of the Reception Committee," she added grandly, and glanced to see if the others looked frightened.

"Oooh, Reive," whispered a pallid creature shivering in a thin kimono. "Really, Reive?"

"You liar," Drusilla spat; but Reive only tossed her hair.

"We must go to meet her now," she said airily, and turned and walked back to her chambers, ignoring the whispers behind her.

"Ucalegon will take you," Drusilla hissed, and as Reive slammed her door she heard the others giggling.

"Damn," she muttered. She kicked her cosmetic box, sending it spinning across the floor. When she heard it crack against the wall she swore again, more loudly, then got onto her knees and gathered up the kohl wands and little tubes of rouge and mascara and powder. She settled on the floor, balancing a small broken triangle of mirror on her knees, and began to paint her face.

When she was finished a simple mask peered at her from the shard of mirror, her cheeks a pale copper, her mouth demurely small and golden, her eyebrows raised to give her a look of innocent surprise. Reive drew the mirror up to her face and tilted her head so that her eyes caught the dim blue light. For years she had planned to get tinted lenses to disguise the true color of her eyes. But there was always something else to buy with her meager earnings, decent food for one thing, *anything* besides krill paste; and of course she always needed more kohl and opium sugar, though fortunately she wasn't as dependent on that as some. And, she had to admit, green *was* an unusual color, forbidden or not; and sometimes patrons liked that. Although now it seemed they wouldn't like anything to do with Reive.

The gynander sighed and shook her head, her long uneven black plaits flying. She stood and rummaged under the bedcovers until she found a new pair of orange pantaloons of pleated false silk. She pulled them out, smoothing the fabric through which the outline of her penis could barely be seen, a small shadow against one pale thigh. Three thin rings of steel and rubicore pierced each of her nipples, and she wore a tiny pouch slung around her narrow waist. Last of all, she sat cross-legged on the floor and carefully drew two wards, one upon each tiny breast: the ward against Ucalegon, the Prince of Storms, and the one against Baratdaja, the Healing Wind.

Before she left she flopped onto her bed and leaned down to peer at the glass globe. The mysid

floated tranquilly, hardly moving even when she
gently prodded it with a finger.

"Goodbye, Gato," she whispered. "We're leaving
now."

She went out shirtless, shivering a little in the
hallway. She was relieved to see that the others had
gone, no doubt to gossip about her in Drusilla's chambers. For a minute she leaned against the wall, decid-
ing where to go. It was too early to look for
inquisitors. She didn't want to seem desperate. For-
tunes changed with mercurial speed in Araboth, especially among hermaphrodites and the Orsinate's
pleasure cabinet. By evening she might find herself
with a new patron, a new chamber on a higher level.
Abruptly she turned and headed down the corridor
toward the Virtues Level gravator. It was two hours at
least until patrons would start filling the corridors,
looking for dream-mantics. For now she would slip
up to the vivarium and visit Zalophus.

"Ceryl! Is that you?"

Ceryl started, hastily wiped the tears from her
face. From around the curve of the avenue an
aardman stalked toward the rickshaw, carrying a
small woman in a long, pleated white skirt, a fez
perched unsteadily on her head. Tatsun Frizer, a taster
in the Toxins Cabal and like Ceryl a member of the
Orsinate's pleasure cabinet. She wore absurdly ornamented yellow vinyl shoes that curled under so that
she could not walk in them. In her arms she cradled a
puppet, one of the newly fashionable and more odi-
ous geneslaves designed by the legendary puppeteer,
Rudyard Planck. It licked its thin gray lips and glared
at Ceryl with swinish red-rimmed eyes.

"Don't stop," it hissed loudly into Tatsun's ear.
Rudyard Planck despised the Orsinate. He had
mocked them first with a series of bioengineered
urangutangs that strutted about imperiously and,
when asked their names, grunted "Âziz," or "Nike"

or "Shiyung" in reply. Then there had been an argala, a sexslave with Shiyung's delicate features that bellowed like a man during coition. And now these hideous puppets, all of them possessing Âziz Orsina's nasal voice. It was one of the imponderables of Araboth that Planck's escalating burlesques of the ruling family had only earned him their favor.

"Go on, baggage. Eat spit. Faaugh." The puppet drooled and gibbered at Ceryl until she had to look away. Tatsun gently cuffed the puppet's hairless skull and commanded the aardman to halt.

"We missed you at Nike's inquisition last night," she said. As she spoke the coder in her throat pulsed violet and orange—last season's accessory, still affected by members of the Toxins Cabal who claimed the coders helped them focus on the subtleties of the poisons they designed. The lurid colors made Ceryl's head ache. She rubbed her temples distractedly and glanced over her shoulder at the body in the rickshaw. Tatsun ignored her pained expression and added, "It was *lovely,* there was a new morph there who *obviously* had never scryed for the margravines before—she was so awful it was *funny,* Âziz and I laughed and laughed! And that *awful* Rudyard Planck was there with one of his new generation of puppets, aren't they just *awful*? He *gave* me this one," she added with a smug grin. The puppet continued to stare at Ceryl, working its mouth so that its long white tongue slid lewdly in and out between evil little teeth.

Ceryl sighed loudly. This was the second inquisition she'd missed this week. Soon there would be talk. But she couldn't tell the others about her nightmare, the vision night after night of the dome cracked like a limpet's shell and the sea burrowing into it like a huge green tongue. She looked up to see Tatsun gazing disapprovingly at the dead moujik girl, her aardman carrier staring into space.

"You're timoring," Tatsun said, a little primly. She had recently joined the Disciples of Blessed Narouz's Refinery, a sect that, unlike many others—

the First Church of Christ Cadillac, the Daughters of Graves—frowned upon timoring and its attendant horrors. "Is that why you weren't at the dream inquisition?"

Flushing, Ceryl shrugged. The puppet cackled gleefully, slunk to Tatsun's other shoulder, and raising one leg squirted some acrid-smelling liquid into the air. The aardman snarled. Tatsun scolded the puppet and looked again down at Ceryl, frowning.

"Nice shoes," Ceryl said at last. She started to ask about the dream inquisition, but the puppet's leering eyes stopped her. She put her hand on the edge of the rickshaw door. "I'd better go—I just needed some air, that's all."

Tatsun shook her head. The puppet hissed, "Let her rot! Go, let's *go*—" Tatsun whispered something to the aardman, who tightened his grip about her, turned, and began to stride off. As they disappeared around the curving avenue Tatsun called back to Ceryl, "Âziz is hosting a reception after the Investiture. Next week. In the Four Hundredth Room."

"I'll be there," Ceryl sighed.

"You'd better be," the puppet said, giggling wildly. In a moment they were gone.

Ceryl rubbed her forehead. It ached again, as it usually did after she had been to a timoring, or after a night full of bad dreams. She was uneasy now: it had been a bad idea to skip the inquisition.

From the front of the rickshaw the driver cleared his throat. Ceryl looked up. "Sorry." She clambered in beside the girl's corpse, grimacing. "Bring me back down to Principalities—"

The rickshaw driver nodded and headed for the gravator. Once inside, the rickshaw jounced as the transportation chamber moved, the worn-out gears turning with a deafening squeal as they dropped, level by level. Ceryl winced and covered her ears. The narrow windows darkened as the chamber passed through Dominations, Virtues, Powers. When the doors opened on Principalities, the rickshaw shuddered out onto an avenue in such disrepair that some of its sidewalk plates bounced up behind them, jangling like broken glass. A hazy crimson light suffused everything, rising from the refineries on Archangels. Here on Principalities there was the stench to contend with as well. Peering through the slats at the rickshaw driver, Ceryl saw that he had pulled a mask over his face. Ceryl covered her nose and coughed. Kef smoke, burning rubber, rancid oil, and fenugreek. Over all a thick smell of the abattoir, of death and blood and singed hair; the smell of the medifacs.

"There—" Ceryl called out, choking, to the driver. "Stop there by that bonfire—"

Around the sputtering blaze a half-dozen moujiks were gathered, toasting something on twisted metal skewers and smoking kef. Ceryl gestured at them, pointing at the seat beside her as she leaned over to open the door. As she did so they ran to the cab, pushing her aside as their hands swarmed over the corpse, gabbling in their harsh patois. Ceryl leaned rigidly against the seat, gasping as the last one darted from the cab and followed the others toward the bonfire, all of them clicking their tongues excitedly.

"Now what?" the rickshaw driver sighed as she slammed the door shut. He looked at her wearily through the slats, his eyes bloodshot, his mouth stained red from chewing betel. Ceryl twisted a strand of hair around her finger, glanced up at the Nuclear CLOCK suspended from the Central Quincunx Dome. After eighteen already. She'd skip returning to Thrones, go directly to the vivariums.

"Back to Dominations, I guess," she sighed. "To my workchambers."

The rickshaw driver spat and yawned, then hitched up his poles and began pulling the rickshaw toward the gravator.

Obviously not everyone had heard of the disaster with last week's diplomat: several biotechs solicited the gynander on her way to Dominations. Reive turned them down, hoping to find a more affluent patron from a higher level. Finally she consented to the demands of a plum-skinned young man wearing the pink fez and white skirts of the Disciples of Blessed Narouz's Refinery. He made several lewd suggestions, touching Reive's penis lightly with a finger. She shook her head—

"We are celibate," she said somewhat curtly. Gynanders were sexually immature. They sometimes enjoyed passionate friendships with each other or were adopted by lustful patrons. Otherwise they avoided sensual attachments.

"A reading then—here—" The young man fumbled in the pockets of his loose white skirt and finally came up with a parchment card, imprinted in yellow ink with an invitation to a party that evening on Cherubim Level. "I'll give you this, I can't go—"

When Reive nodded he took her hand, small and pale and limp as her penis, and kissed her palm. Then he recited his dream in low urgent tones.

Reive listened, eyes closed. The young man finished and fell silent. She breathed deeply, letting his dream speak to her in its own words. From very far away she heard a strange *plink . . . plink . . . plink*, as of water dripping. When she slipped her hand from the boy's and brought it to her face she could smell, very faintly, the refined petroleum used in Blessed Narouz's rites. The young man stared at her eagerly.

"There is a small melanoma within your brain," she began. "That is the symbolism of the burrowing worm. The girl with no eyes means that you will be refused treatment, because of your affiliation with the new cult. To prevent suffering we would suggest you offer yourself to the medifacs." She heard him stifle a gasp. "We are sorry," she added gently. She got to her feet, reaching for the parchment invitation. The young man snatched it away, cursing, and Reive turned and fled. As she ran down the corridor leading to the vivariums she heard him shrieking after her.

The Architects had left the entry to the vivariums unchanged for many years. Reive disliked it—an immense doorway of black resin, shaped like the head of an aardman with protuberant crimson eyes and fearsome teeth. She passed through its open mouth, beneath the archway where the motto of the Orsinate Ascendancy had been etched in looming block letters.

PAULO MAIORA CANAMUS!

The motto of the Second Ascension, the deranged Governors who had created the first generation of geneslaves, and released the horrors of the viral microphages across the continents. A psycholinguist in the pleasure cabinet had translated it for Reive one night after an inquisition.

" 'Let us raise a somewhat loftier strain.' " She had laughed bitterly. Reive still didn't understand what it meant, but she didn't ask the linguist to explain.

From above the curving narrow corridor long diatomaceous tubes shed waves of ultramarine light. In places the walls opened onto vast arrays of glass and cable and steel, tanks and catwalks and bubbling alembics the size of small buildings. Then the walls would close in again and the fretwork of struts and spans would disappear, but the smells rising from the labs remained. Seawater and kelp from the oceanic tanks, steam from the heating ducts, the piny resins of the Northern Pacific Diorama. The gynander approached the hallway that led to the Chambers of Mercy. There the vivisectors practiced their sanguine art upon Araboth's dead, rehabilitating them into the *rasas* that tended the refineries and performed the most dangerous of the million tasks that kept the city alive. As she hurried by its entrance three novices passed her and nodded soberly. They wore faded yolk-yellow trousers and blouses of transparent fabric, to show that they had not yet attained full knowledge

of their craft. Through the cloth she could see faint
patterns tattooed upon their breasts, prescriptive nos-
trums to guard against natural childbirth and storms
and *nerotus,* the psychic illness that afflicted those who
spent too much time among the regenerated dead.
The gynander returned the novices' cool gaze and
turned down the hall leading to the vivarium. Behind
her she could hear them, whispering.

In this hallway the light tubes flickered a paler
blue, the diatoms fed a lower algae content. Aquari-
ums were set into the curved walls, long narrow tanks
and smaller round ones, some with cracks where the
Architects had not accounted for the diurnal contrac-
tion in the polymers that formed the walls. Luminous
fish floated in black water, green water, water of
deepest blue. Anglerfish with glowing crab-shaped
lures protruding from their skulls; delicate fairypipes,
their skeletons luminous pink; lightning fish spearing
their tanks with brilliant arrows. The tanks had been
tended for hundreds of years. Many of these creatures
were extinct now, Outside. Their keepers could no
longer recall why it was they cared for them.

The gynander walked here slowly. She loved
these things, and the other half-human heteroclites
that had been engineered in the nucleovats and cellular refineries of Dominations. Strange things, stranger
than the gynander herself, things from the First Days.

Things like Zalophus.

Ahead of her the ceiling arched, and the passage
split into two wide corridors. To the right the hall
curved down to where the ghoulish aardmen were
bred, and the birdlike argalæ, and the arboretums
where sentient plants caressed passersby with slender
branches. Reive grimaced. The soft, steady pumping
of the ventilation system wafted the pungent scent of
the argalæ's excrement, nitrogen-rich and processed
for fertilizer. She took the left-hand fork.

This was the final descent to the oceanic vivariums, where the biotechnicians imprisoned the genetically enhanced whales and sirens, the white-beaked

telepathic inia and other dolphins, the manatees and orcas and half-human hydrapithecenes and, most ancient of all, sweet-voiced Zalophus, who would lure unwary visitors to his tank and devour them.

The corridor widened into a vast space, a sort of cavern that fed into the gulf Outside. Huge barred gates rose to the ceiling, allowing water to pass through the intricate system of weirs and nets and canals that supplied the open-air tanks. Mingled with the rush of waves sighing in and out were the explosive sounds of sirens breaching, the inquisitive whistles of dolphins, the soft insistent lies of the hydrapithecenes in their solitary enclosures.

"Free us," they sang after Reive as she passed. She ignored the faces gazing at her from the depths. Faces from a nightmare, some of them, gilled and bearded with long fleshy tubes, or scaled like fish. Others more like their human ancestors, but with moist skin of palest peach or blue. Their lipless mouths twisted furiously, revealing the rows of razor teeth within, the suckers oozing toxins like ink through the water.

"Free yourself," the gynander called airily; but she ran as one bearded siren smashed itself against the glass walls of its cage, blood swirling from its mouth as it screamed after her.

She met no one else. It was midnought, the middle of the thirty-two-hour day regulated by the Architects. On the levels above her, the Orsinate and their pleasure cabinet were still abroad, playing in the eternal twilight. On the levels below the workers would be rising, the 'filers on Powers readying for another broadcast day, the moujiks and *rasas* stumbling toward the refineries and medifacs. But here Reive was alone. She talked to herself, absently whispering invocations against Ucalegon, repeating the words she had replied to the plum-skinned boy's inquisition. She stopped to call to the dolphins, leaning down to graze her fingers against their smooth heads as they butted against the sides of their tank. They whistled plaintively when she left, then returned to their endless circuits of their prisons.

In the center of the chamber was Zalophus's pool, the largest in the vivarium, and the oldest. A marvel of the ancient engineers, it was rumored to plunge to unimaginable depths, to the Undercity itself, where the great whale slept and brooded, dreaming his endless dreams of hunger and escape. The Architects had designed his cage to resemble a huge grotto. Their memory files recalled such things; none of the Ascendants or the biotechnicians who toiled on Dominations had ever seen the lush green places Outside that inspired it. Boulders of molded resin and real plants—bougainvillea, honeysuckle, purple eelgrass—cascaded beneath the brilliant growth lamps. Sea urchins nestled in a cleft between strands of kelp and sea fern. On one of the false boulders a cormorant perched drying its wings. It regarded Reive with one tangerine-colored eye and snapped its beak. She wondered if it had come from the labs, then shivered at the thought that it might be from Outside. Hastily she dipped her head and touched the whorls on her breast that formed the ward against Ucalegon.

A moment later she stopped at the edge of the pool. A heat fence separated her from its occupant. The gynander whistled softly to herself, shading her eyes against the growth lights. When she inhaled, waves of warm scent washed over her: salt and sea lavender, coconut oil and almond flower, an underlying musk like semen. She shut her eyes. It made her think of the long slant of beach outside the city, the rust-colored sand and impossibly blue water that she had seen only once before at Æstival Tide, ten years earlier when she was a very small child. There was a smell like burning roses and she could hear the Daughters of Graves singing, see the Orsinate standing stiffly on their viewing platform, tossing ginger blossoms and the dried leaves of sweet cicely onto the crowd below.

Her hands had already begun to stretch through

the heat fence when a deep voice crooned, "You'll harm yourself, human child. Come here to this side, where it's open—"

Reive gasped. Her hands stung where the fence had burned them.

"Zalophus!" She tried to keep her voice from shaking, tried to smile.

In the dark water in front of her he hung suspended. All she could see was his head, like one of the gargoyles upon the facade of the Church of Christ Cadillac. Huge, grotesquely pitted and scarred by centuries of bashing against the concrete walls of his prison, his blunt snout ended in a mouth that held white teeth longer than her hand. A long furrow ran the length of his skull, hiding his blowhole. A flap of warted skin folded back from it when he breached. To either side of that knobbed dome glittered his eyes. Eyes larger than Reive's clenched fists, liquid eyes, eyes so dark it was impossible to tell what color they were, if they had a color at all. They stared at her calmly; at least she supposed it was calmly—his eyes revealed nothing, just as his voice seldom changed. So deep a voice that it seemed he moved other creatures to his will by speaking, his voice alone manipulating their frailer skeletons. But Reive believed there was something else at work there as well, some subtle telepathy by which he bent the waves of air and water and made of them a web to snare the careless.

Ancient Zalophus, sweet-voiced Zalophus: Zalophus the ever-hungry.

"There was a siren here this morning," the great cetacean boomed. Reive stepped back and covered her ears. "She wept, remembering when the seas were full of her kind, and men worshipped them and made them offerings of stillborn children."

"She lied," said Reive, dropping her hands. "The seas were never full of them, they were engineered here a hundred years ago. They have never seen open water."

"So sad, she was so sad," Zalophus moaned, sending up a plume of dark green spray. "I ate her."

Reive laughed, covering her mouth. Zalophus stared at her with huge unblinking eyes. Then, without warning he breached. With a cry Reive stumbled backward. For an instant she glimpsed the rest of him, long body like a whale's, but with narrower fins and tail, great pits gouged in his rubbery flesh by the crab-sized sea lice that scurried frantically across his back as he crashed into the water. The cormorant shrieked and flapped into the air. A headier smell overwhelmed Zalophus's sweet scent, brackish, the odor of rotting fish. He disappeared beneath the surface, the water boiling and clouded where he had been. She could just make out his form far below, like a cavern in the deep water.

"Damn!" Reive glared at the cormorant eyeing her balefully from its new perch. He might stay submerged for hours now. "Zalophus," she cried; then more loudly, *"Zalophus!"*

Nothing happened. The surface of the pool grew calm. Very faintly she could hear clickings and a deep brooding moan as the monstrous creature called out to sea, the constant and futile effort he had engaged in for centuries, seeking others of his kind.

But there were no others. There really never had been. He was the first of the hydrapithecenes, the very first of all the geneslaves bioengineered during the Second Ascension; the most grotesque of all the Ascendants' creations, and the most useless. The aardmen had been engineered as slaves, combining canine servility with human cunning and cruelty. They were guardians and gladiators, fighting human men and women for the pleasure of the Orsinate, who loved to gamble. Of the other geneslaves, the swanlike argalæ had been bred for their beauty: limbs so long and slender they snapped during lovemaking, breasts that were never meant to suckle, feeble wings that would never take flight. They had a mad witless gaze, shallow rib cages that barely contained their

lungs, tiny white teeth useless for anything but
lovebites. Once Reive had accidently killed one, during an orgy in Âziz's private chambers. She had wept,
because the argalæ were beautiful: the Ascendants'
opium dream of the ideal partner, slender and childlike and utterly dispensable. And the *rasas* were simply a solution to the problem of Araboth's dwindling
population. Too many centuries of inbreeding on the
upper levels; too many genetic mutations among the
slaves brought back from the wars. So within their
cruel alembics the Orsinate distilled a life essence, and
with it infused the corpses carried daily into the
Chambers of Mercy by yellow-robed coenobites. Thus
the Orsinate could continue to vent their murderous
caprices upon Araboth's human population, and still
be certain of a stable work force.

But Zalophus? Zalophus was the folly of those
who had hoped to create the ultimate affront to the
hated world Outside. Using human cranial matter and
cellular tissue from the preserved carcass of a
zeuglodon, an Eocene whale found in the channels of
the Empire's northernmost reach, they had engineered Zalophus. A sentient carnivorous whale, his
fellows extinct for æons, kept alive for these hundreds
of years by the ministrations of the Architects and
their human disciples. Among all the creations of the
Ascendants, he was the most grotesque and feared;
save only for the Compassionate Redeemer, which lay
mired in its decade-long sleep until awakened for
Æstival Tide.

Like the rest of the Orsinate's menagerie,
Zalophus languished forgotten until Nike or Âziz or—
more likely—Shiyung recalled him. Then the margravines might troop down to Dominations, party entourage in tow and stoned on negus or lucifer, to toy
with the great sad-eyed monster. They would command him to call forth his memories of the First Days,
the flames of the Biblioclasm, the silent holocaust of
the Third Shining. Or Shiyung might ask his advice on
some difficult piece of gene-splicing, or beg him to tell

her of the chilly Eocene seas where he had preyed on eels the size of fougas.

Reive had been at one of these reckless gatherings. Alone among the drunken guests, she had been touched by the plight of the captive monster. Since then she came here often. Zalophus terrified her. She knew he was half-mad from the ages of his incarceration and would devour her as easily as speak to her. But still she came.

"Zalophus," she called softly to the still water. A whale louse lay on its back at her feet, twitching its scorpion head. Reive kicked it into the pool. "Zalophus!"

His head erupted so near to her that she screamed and tripped as she scurried away. "Zalophus—"

"She was *sad,*" he repeated. The tolling voice was immeasurably sorrowful. "So sad."

Reive stared at him warily. "We are bored, Zalophus. Do you have any news? Do you have a dream for us?"

Zalophus rolled onto his side so that one eye glared up at her. Water poured smooth as oil across his gray flank. "You are the one brought me the bird girl."

"Reive. That's right."

"Reive." One immense flipper slapped the surface, sent up a fountain high as her head. "Bring me another one. I had not tasted that before."

Reive shrugged. "We will try. Can you tell us a dream?"

The bloated body righted itself, the huge head turned to regard her with what might have been construed as longing, or even sorrow, in a less horrible form. "A dream? I have nothing but dreams now, in my sleep I hear the icelands moving, I hear my sisters calling and the winds gathering for the great storm, I hear the voice of Ucalegon shouting in its sleep . . ."

Reive stepped back, uneasy.

". . . in the Undercity the rift is widening, soon

it will breach the open sea and I will be free! but only come with me now, human child, come with me and prise the gates open, free me—"

Reive shook her head, frightened to see the water roiling about the huge thing, the madness bleeding into his black and empty eyes. "We can't," she stammered.

Zalophus raised his head so that she could see his long jaw, the row of spike teeth where parasites raced to feed upon shreds of flesh and dripping strings of plankton.

"Free me!" he bellowed. From across the vivarium came high-pitched shrieks and whistles as the dolphins raced terrified about their tanks. "Soon the fissure will spread and my sisters will come for me, they are waiting in the icelands, they are waiting waiting waiting, *FREE ME!*"

The voice exploded in a screaming howl. Crying out, Reive fell back as he leaped, fins cutting long troughs through the water, the great body blotting out the light so that she saw only his skull silhouetted there, the prow of his jaw, the cruel mouth grinding as he fell and bellowing crashed into the pool. A wave rushed onto the walkway and she fled, while behind her the last zeuglodon roared and wept.

In the chambers of the Architect Imperator sat Nasrani Orsina and Horemhob Panggang. They were waiting for Hobi's father to return from a meeting with Shiyung Orsina and the imperious Âziz.

"I'm sorry he's not here to see you," said Hobi. He felt distinctly uneasy entertaining the exiled Nasrani alone. This close to Æstival Tide, one always sensed that something terrible might happen. Ten years ago, when he was only seven, Hobi had watched horrified as Âziz sentenced a boy his own age to death for crying during a purification ceremony. "But I'm sure he'll be here soon."

He offered Nasrani another pickled apricot. "I

think he's gone to the ceremony at the palace. The—"
He put the tray onto the floor and frowned. "The
what-is-it, the Investiture."

"Mmph," replied Nasrani Orsina. At the word *investiture* he winced. He lay on a stack of pillows stiff
with brocade and metallic trim. Not especially comfortable but sumptuous to look upon, the decor was
in keeping with Sajur Panggang's architectural theo-
ries. He took another apricot and drained a glass of
Amity-in-Occis, a rare and powerful liqueur distilled
from kelp and wormwood. "Eee s'a vern guh, Hobi."

Hobi (correctly) interpreted this to mean that the
Orsina in exile found the potent fruit to be very good.
"Thank you." He nodded politely. Like his father he
was small and slender, but more muscular. His
mother had been a cousin-german of the Orsinate.
From her Hobi had inherited slanted eyes of an amber
color and the surprising delicacy of his features—a
strong chin that still seemed childishly rounded beneath Hobi's recent attempts at a beard, high cheekbones, and long hair the color of the oak—real oak—
paneling of the sitting room. "My father is very fond
of them—I think they were something Mother liked."

Nasrani nodded. "Do you miss her?" He sipped
his liqueur, gazing at Hobi through slitted eyes. He
was not unaware that the two of them were related: it
was the eyes, mostly, that showed it. Tiger's eyes, like
Shiyung's. She was the beauty of the family, and Nasrani had always thought it a pity that she had no living heirs. There had been a child, once. *His* child, he
was certain; but the baby had been monstrous—a
morphodite, Shiyung whispered to him months afterward. But that had been a long time ago. If the child
had lived it would be nearly as old as Hobi now. Nasrani sighed and finished his Amity. The boy looked
younger than the last time he'd seen him. He supposed the scrabbly beard did that. Nasrani smiled and
said gently, "Your mother was a fascinating woman,
Hobi."

With a clumsy shrug Hobi reached for the decanter. "Yes. My father misses her horribly, I know."

Nasrani nodded. Angelika Panggang had been poisoned last spring by a woman in the Toxins Cabal. A tiny venomous frog, sleekly orange as its innocent brethren and served with flaming raisins to Angelika after her morning sauna. The taster had looked on bemused as Angelika had a seizure. Later she claimed she thought her mistress was exercising, and was acquitted by the Orsinate. Because of her husband's prominence, and her own relation to the Orsinate, Angelika was given a pyre with full funeral honors, including the sacrifice of her entire personal staff. The rumor was that her death had been a warning to her husband, whose predilection for very young girls had embroiled him in an affair with Âziz Orsina's favorite bedmaid. The bedmaid, too, ended up in a fiery eclipse, but that was some months later.

Since his wife's death the Architect Imperator had grown introspective. His attention had turned to arcane matters: divination by means of broken glass; a penchant for the nearly unlistenable form of sadist opera known as *Fasa;* an inexplicable fondness for the company of Rudyard Plank, the dwarf whose legendary bad taste had made him a favorite of the margravine Nike. Sajur had also developed a burning hatred for the Orsinate, and a taste for flouting it—for example, in his weekly *tanka* games with Nasrani Orsina, the infamous margravin now exiled (for a failed assassination attempt upon his sister Âziz) from the Orsinate's Level.

Several more minutes passed. Nasrani fiddled with the glass buttons of his crimson greatcoat and drank another tumbler of Amity in thoughtful silence. Hobi was surprised the exile did not yet appear drunk, but experience had taught him that Amity caught up with everyone, sooner or later. The thought troubled the boy and he gnawed at a fingernail.

The decanter was nearly empty. Nasrani stared at it with bemused affection, as though regarding a beloved but naughty child. Hobi leaned forward to press a button beneath the table. A moment later a replicant appeared, ram-headed and wearing the same long linen shift and trousers that Hobi did.

"Khum." The boy indicated the decanter, now empty. "Bring us more of that, please."

Nasrani watched the server, amused, as it gathered the tray and glasses and retired to the pantry. "That is a very old one," he said after a moment.

Hobi nodded, somewhat embarrassed. "I know. It was—well, it was a gift, I think, or something, I think we inherited them, my mother always said we should get some new ones—"

Nasrani shook his head. "No—it's a very good one, they don't make them like that anymore. Third Ascension: a vogue for things *Egyptienne*. And animals, of course, the fashion cabinet says that animals will be very popular this season. So your father's old replicants will actually be quite stylish." He smiled. The boy looked relieved. "Are you interested in such things?"

Hobi shrugged, started to say no when he recalled that Nasrani Orsina was an Orsina, even if an exile, and he was being kept waiting by his father. "Yes, I am."

"Would you like to see some others?"

Hobi looked startled. He glanced around the room suspiciously, as though these others might be lurking behind the priceless oak paneling. The ramheaded Khum returned bearing a new tray and several full glasses gleaming with emerald liquid.

"Very good, then," Nasrani announced. He stood, the tails of his greatcoat swirling, and swept up one of the glasses. "Khum, tell the Architect Imperator that as punishment for his tardiness I am not only drinking all of his Amity but stealing his son. Come on, Hobi."

Hobi started to stammer something by way of protest—*oh, no you needn't trouble, he'll be right back, help!*—but Nasrani was already out the door. It seemed rude to remain. And since rudeness was often punishable by death within the Orsinate's cabal, Hobi hastily decided to follow.

On the promenade outside, the pagoda-shaped houses of Araboth's Imperators shimmered in the perpetual twilight, mauve and pink and faintest gold. Here on Cherubim Level the air smelled of some warm spice, cinnamon or galingale perhaps, piped in to counteract the briny scent of the heavily filtered breezes. Only a few yards away the heat fence crackled, and Hobi could glimpse the tops of buildings on the next level down.

"Should have thought of this sooner," Nasrani was muttering to himself. "Inadequate education these days, never see anything outside their own homes. Good idea."

Hobi hurried after him. In the middle of the next block the boy stopped, for a moment losing sight of the exile's crimson coat as the older man strode on. At Hobi's feet fluttered several paper billets. He stooped and slowly brought one to his face.

10,000 PRAYERS TO UCALEGON! he read, and **PRAY FOR THE HEALING WIND!** When he looked up he saw Nasrani waiting impatiently.

"Look at this," Hobi said as he caught up with the exile. He held up one of the flyers. "Isn't this treason?"

Nasrani glanced at it and sniffed. "But there is rebellion everywhere, my dear," he said. He turned the corner near the Cherubim Level gravator. "That is why you Imperators have all those replicants with horses' heads and rubber feet. But my sisters can afford the luxury of treachery, and so they employ human help. And humans won't put up with this sort of thing forever. Public executions, children kidnapped for torture parties, people killed to be made into *rasas*, houses torn down while one sleeps. You can see how it would wear one down after a while."

"But it's religion," said Hobi. From one of the lower levels he heard watchmen hoarsely chanting the midmorning call to prayer. He looked up; the nu-

clear CLOCK said nineteen. "I mean, Prophet Rayburn said that only the children of the chosen should
be allowed to—"

Nasrani rolled his eyes. "Oh, come *on,* Hobi! I'm
an *exile,* you don't think you need to talk like that to
me?" Then, in a singsong voice, *"Here* we are—"

Ahead of them was the gravator. Nasrani made a
grand gesture and held the door open for Hobi.
"Now!" The exile beamed as the doors folded shut
and the ancient machine shuddered. "I think you will
find this very interesting, Hobi."

The gravator, while not as elegant as the one that
served the Orsinate's Level, was still quite ornate.
Elaborately carven benches ran along the walls,
heaped with pillows, and small round lanterns cast a
rosy light on the faces of the two passengers. In the
center of the moving chamber the Architects had installed a small perfumed fountain shaped like an argala, a popular motif several seasons ago. As the
gravator descended, minty-smelling water spewed
from her mouth onto the boy's feet. He hastily moved
to the other side of the room.

Nasrani sank heavily onto a bench. The gravator
gave a horrible lurch and plummeted a thousand feet,
then slowed as it passed through Thrones Level. Another sickening plunge. The chamber filled with the
musky scent of the vivariums as they passed Dominations. Then Virtues, where the dream-mantics lived;
and down to Powers, with its faint background hiss of
electrical equipment.

Then, "Did we miss it?" Hobi asked, alarmed.

The gravator pitched, water slopped from the
fountain onto the floor, and they dropped another
level. Hobi tugged aside one of the heavy indigo curtains covering a window. He looked outside and then
turned to Nasrani, his face white. "Nasrani—we're
still dropping—shouldn't we have gotten off sooner?"

Nasrani smiled, hitched up the tail of his greatcoat to scratch his leg. Hobi swallowed. Beneath his
flowing trousers the exile wore high boots of bur-

gundy leather; and tucked neatly into a flap on each one was a stiletto of gleaming steel. "No, no, Hobi," he said, flicking his fingers dismissively. "This isn't an *ordinary* visit. You'll see."

The boy shivered. It struck him that there was a good reason Nasrani Orsina had been exiled; that he was not merely the polite and epicene dinner guest his mother had been so fond of. And with a small electrical thrill of terror—because of course this was something he should have considered all along—Hobi wondered just what this man was doing with him, the son of the Architect Imperator.

"Should we—maybe we should have waited for my father—" he stammered.

Nasrani shook his head. He frowned, pulling at a stray thread on his greatcoat, then slid one of the stilettos from its sheath and neatly cut it off. He twisted his head, gazing at Hobi with studied casualness. "Have you ever been to the Undercity?"

Hobi felt his whole body freeze, as though he had walked into a replicant's holding chamber. "Level One? Angels?"

"Mmm mmm," Nasrani said absently. He glanced at the window, marbled gold and black where they passed through the refineries of Archangels. "Yes, that's right. The Undercity."

Hobi bit his lip, grabbing on to the edge of the bench as the gravator bucked and rolled. Near the door hung a slender golden cord with a small neatly lettered sign dangling from it. *Pull in case of emergency*, it said. He and his friends used to joke about it, and once Magya Electroluxe really *had* pulled it, with exciting results. But doing such a thing now would mean admitting to himself that in a few minutes the damned thing would stop at Level One, Angels: the Undercity. When he looked aside at Nasrani he saw that the exile was smiling. Hobi reddened. Abruptly he let go of the bench, straightened, and tossed his long hair. "Oh, I've been *there*," he lied.

"Really?" Nasrani looked interested. "Weren't you afraid you'd be tortured or go mad?"

But before Hobi could reply *(tortured?)*, with a sudden *boom* the gravator jolted and was still. In front of them the heavy metal doors were fanning open. And he had no choice, really, but to follow Nasrani Orsina into the Undercity.

The rickshaw driver slowed to a trot as they rounded the entrance to the vivariums. Ceryl could hear him panting. She shook her head; she should have engaged another before returning to this level. She was thinking of walking the rest of the way when she sighted the gynander strolling by. As the rickshaw rattled past her, Ceryl looked over her shoulder at the slender figure, her mind racing.

The dream inquisition she missed last night; her failed attempt at timoring; and most of all her nightmares . . .

"Stop!" she ordered the driver, leaning forward until her head peeked out from the rickshaw's bamboo shell. "Right here, please, stop—"

The rickshaw slowed to a halt. The gynander continued walking, singing to herself and not even raising her head. Ceryl stumbled to her feet, tugged at the rug covering the cab's floor, and threw it onto the bloody seat beside her as she got out.

"You—"

The gynander stopped. For a moment Ceryl thought she had mistakenly called to a real woman. But no—the slender figure had an elaborately painted face, small breasts emblazoned with colored whorls and waves; and through her diaphanous trousers Ceryl glimpsed her penis, no longer than a finger. Perhaps it was just that she was taller than most morphodites, and had done something to straighten her hair. She looked to be about fifteen. Ceryl knew she could have been twice that age, though not much older—morphodites didn't live very long.

"Yes?" The gynander's tone was haughty, and for a moment Ceryl thought of flouncing back into the rickshaw. But then the gynander tipped her head, and for the first time Ceryl got a good look at her face. She gasped. Beneath the oily plaits of lank black hair, behind their heavy swirls of kohl, the eyes she turned to Ceryl were wide and cold as the open water that crashed relentlessly through her dreams, and green. Leaf-green, sea-green, poison-green. The forbidden color; the color of death.

"You," Ceryl stammered. She would have fled, but the gynander had already stepped forward and was staring at her intently, her eyes slitted.

"You are troubled by a dream," she said softly, her tone still oddly commanding for a morphodite. Ceryl shrank from her as Reive stretched one powdered hand to touch the other woman's forehead. *"There*—we can feel it, there—"

Reive murmured the traditional greeting to a client, hoping it would calm this woman. She was accustomed to people being startled by her eyes, but this woman seemed terrified. Reive thought maybe she had heard of Reive's unhappy experience with the diplomat, but no; the woman seemed genuinely frightened.

That could be very good for Reive. If she gave this woman the right kind of reading, she might reward the gynander generously. At first, when the rickshaw passed her Reive had ignored it. She was ravenous, and wanted only to get to one of the shrimp stalls by the Dominations gravator. But then she had seen the woman leaning from the cab. Tall and pale, with yellow hair clipped elegantly short and curling about rubicore earcuffs, she wore a midnight-blue catsuit and bronze leather boots that reached above her knees. Around her neck hung a pendant with Prophet Rayburn's crucifix and another, the heraldic eye and letter ☾ that marked her as a member of the Orsinate's pleasure cabinet. If Reive could impress this woman with her scrying, she might take the gynander to her chambers; might even bring her along to one of the Orsinate's dream inquisitions.

"We are very experienced with nightmares," she murmured soothingly, "very good, very reasonable . . ."

Ceryl swallowed. It might be an evil omen—it *must* be an evil omen—but then her nightmares were evil too. Maybe this green-eyed morphodite could exorcise her horrible dreams, before she was forced to share them with the Orsinate. "Reasonable," she repeated, stalling.

Reive bit her lip, her mouth filling with the chalky taste of rouge. She hadn't had a client this wealthy in weeks, not to mention one with access to the very highest levels of the city. She blurted, "Free! We'll do it for free, for the honor of Prophet Rayburn and the Saints—"

Ceryl sucked in her breath. It *was* an omen, damn it! The venal morphodites never did anything for free. She toyed with the pendant around her neck, thinking. From behind her she could hear the traceman muttering to himself, his voice rising angrily. In a few minutes he'd refuse to take her any farther.

"Get in," she said abruptly. "My workchambers are here on Dominations. But hurry."

Reive frowned. This would be no immediate passport to Cherubim after all. For a moment she looked down the corridor, debating whether she should leave. But then Ceryl grabbed her arm and pulled her toward the rickshaw. Reive tossed her head and flopped in, making a face at the rug covering the seat. When the rickshaw jounced forward she started, drew her hand up smeared with blood. Beside her Ceryl stared through the slits in the bamboo cab, crimson light winking from her earcuffs as they headed down the avenue.

Ceryl Waxwing's workchamber was at the outermost rim of Dominations Level, near the Amazonian dioramas. It was not a coveted spot. You could see the flat gray surface of one of the domes from here, and hear the boom of the ocean rolling against it. Because of its proximity to these reminders of Outside, the chambers had been empty for years before Ceryl was assigned to them. And since her promotion to the Orsinate's pleasure cabinet, Ceryl herself should be in her new quarters up on Thrones. Every week she told herself she would move, that this would be the end of it; and every week she spent as little time as possible where the Orsinate might find her. She hated giving up her workchambers, although even she had to admit they were nowhere near as spacious or comfortable as her new quarters. When pressed, she said that she needed access to the plants and animals of the vivarium level for her work as a pharmacologist.

But the truth was, Ceryl couldn't sleep on Thrones. She would never admit it, but she missed the sound of the sea. She wondered sometimes if that had something to do with her nightmares—knowing it was so near to her Outside, that constant crash and sigh that surrounded her as she worked.

But then, even Shiyung Orsina had been stirred by it.

"Does it keep you awake at night, listening to that?" she asked Ceryl the first time they'd met. The margravine stood staring out the workchamber's strip of window, a glass of Ceryl's cheap brandy in her hand.

This was not long after Ceryl's lover, Giton Arrowsmith, had died. Shortly before his death, Giton had become involved with the cult of Blessed Narouz's Refinery. Ceryl suspected that the Orsinate had him killed, ordering the destruction of the block of flats where he and several other disciples of Blessed Narouz lived. When Shiyung suddenly appeared at her door, Ceryl was convinced she was about to be hauled off by the Reception Committee. Instead she ended up being promoted to the pleasure cabinet.

She'd heard scuffling outside, and then the sweet

yet commanding tone of the most popular of the margravines. Then someone had started banging on her door. When she'd opened it, there was Shiyung, with a full retinue of guards and 'filers following her, taping her official visit to the Amazonian vivarium for broadcast that night. In the crowd Ceryl glimpsed her supervisor, her white face belying her confident words.

". . . Waxwing is our best pharmacist, I'm sure she can do something for your migraine—"

Ceryl tried weakly to explain that she was not a *pharmacist*, but the subtleties of her work were lost on the margravine. Shiyung drifted into the room clutching her forehead, gesturing dramatically for the others to leave. They did so, casting sympathetic glances in the stunned Ceryl's direction.

The margravine was taller and even lovelier than she appeared on the 'files. As always when she made one of her highly publicized tours of the lower levels, she wore laborer's clothes—in this case, a biotech's yolk-yellow robe and high rubber boots. Her sleek black hair was pulled through a copper loop. At her throat the Orsinate's heraldic eye glittered wickedly.

Ceryl stared at her, speechless. It was as though the dreaded Zalophus had appeared at her door.

"Thank god! A pharmacist!" The margravine moaned and sank into a chair, shielding her eyes from the dim light. "Please—the migraine—help me—"

With shaking hands Ceryl had mixed a nostrum combining tranquilizing neurots and a strong anaesthetic (cheap brandy laced with alomine) along with a mild hallucinogen (datura), followed by a few minutes of massage therapy. To her amazement (and eventual dismay) the philter worked. After an hour Shiyung lifted her head, batting her eyes weakly.

"It's gone," she whispered. She fingered the pendant at her throat and gazed at Ceryl with huge black eyes. "My god, you've saved me—"

Ceryl nodded, moving quickly to help the margravine as she got unsteadily to her feet.

"That's a remarkable cure," said Shiyung, her voice a little slurred. "Amazing. Nothing else has ever worked. *You*—" She pivoted and pointed at Ceryl, the tip of one long finger resting on the pharmacologist's nose. "You are a miracle. Come."

"Come?" Ceryl stammered.

The margravine nodded. "I hereby appoint you my Personal Pharmacist and Healer."

"But—"

The margravine wiggled her fingers in Ceryl's face. "Oh, please—don't be obsequious. I can't bear it when they're obsequious." She shook her head, wincing, then turned to the door. "But I must get back to the others! There was a rumor of a strike by the Amazonian staff—I must make them feel *needed* again—"

She extended her hands toward Ceryl, closed her eyes and murmured a blessing in which Shiyung's own name figured prominently. Then she reached for the doorknob. When she hesitated Ceryl swallowed and took a wary step backward.

"A word of advice," whispered Shiyung. She cracked the door open. "Hire your own Personal Taster before you move. You'll need one up there."

The margravine's new Personal Pharmacist watched in disbelief as Shiyung floated back into the hallway, her headache transmitted to Ceryl. From her desk Giton's holoed image stared at her accusingly.

That had been six months ago. She still hadn't spent more than a few days in her new appointments. She was terrified that the Orsinate would discover she was nothing more than a low-ranking pharmacologist who sold quack remedies and bootleg narcotics to the other menial toilers on Dominations. Even with her promotion, there was no way she could afford her own food taster. Whenever possible she avoided her duties in the pleasure cabinet—which consisted mostly of attending parties and dispensing cures to hungover cabinet members—and fled back to her old workchamber. Ceryl Waxwing's apartment on

Thrones remained empty. Now she watched uneasily as the gynander stared out the grimy little window.

"What's that?" Reive pointed outside as Ceryl rummaged in her tiny refrigerator for food.

"The dome." Triumphantly she held up a jar of dulse jam and some crackers. "Hah! I knew I had something—"

The gynander continued to gaze out the window. "The sea's out there?" she asked, trying to clear a spot on the glass.

Ceryl handed her the food and looked away, embarrassed. "I guess so."

"Oh." Crumbs fell to the floor as the gynander pressed her face up to the glass. "Right there? Right outside your window? The ocean?"

Ceryl cleared her throat and pretended to read a monitor on her desk. Perhaps this had been a bad idea after all. This morph had no manners whatsoever—imagine mentioning the *ocean* to a stranger! Ceryl fiddled with her monitor, glancing sideways at the morph. She'd be wasting her credit and, worse, her time. At the thought of another night plagued by bad dreams she sighed and rubbed her temples.

The gynander ate noisily but without further conversation. Finally she dropped the empty dulse tin and wiped her hands on her pantaloons. Ceryl watched her with distaste.

"All right," the gynander pronounced. She cast a last curious look at the window. "Please tell us of your troubles."

"I—I've been having these dreams."

Reive nodded solemnly, as though she had never heard the words before.

"Nightmares," Ceryl went on quickly. "I—they're not the sort of dreams I can talk about easily at an inquisition when there're others around. I'm—in the pleasure cabinet," she added. She tapped nervously at her monitor. "You understand . . . ?"

The gynander nodded. "It is, perhaps, a *treasonous* dream?"

Ceryl raised her eyebrows at the gynander's bluntness. "We-ell," she stammered, then nodded. "Yes, I think—well, *someone* might think it was treasonous," she said lamely.

Reive stepped across the room to a chair and settled into it, drawing her feet up demurely beneath her and cupping her chin in her hands. She lowered her eyes so that Ceryl couldn't see her expression.

A treasonous dream! Better and better—if this woman proved to be a stingy patron, Reive could always blackmail her. The gynander coughed delicately. "Please," she said, closing her eyes and tilting her head so that Ceryl could see her face, painted with that mask of studied innocence. "We would like to help you."

Ceryl took a deep breath. *This is it,* she thought, then said, "For the past year I have been having these terrible dreams. . . ."

It came out hesitantly. Ceryl had thought it would be easier, telling it alone like this. Instead she found herself in a bizarrely intimate situation, sharing her worst secret with a stranger. She paused.

It wasn't too late. She could throw the morph out and never tell anyone; though that would mean suffering from the nightmares, perhaps forever. Or she could expose her secret at the next inquisition and face the consequences.

The thought made her cringe. She hated the dream inquisitions. She had of course attended them before her promotion, with other biotechnicians and once even with a group of drunken Aviators slumming down on Dominations. But these were small homey gatherings, brisk with vivarium gossip; not the perilous intrigue of the Orsinate's inner cabal. There, a faltering confession or a spiteful morphodite could result in one being dragged off by the Reception Committee.

She hated it all. The hermaphrodites with their languid expressions and voices slurred from smoking kef. The margravines watching with keen narrow

unshared dream

eyes for the merest hint of treachery, as one by one their guests recited their nighttime journeys. Diplomats confessing to fitful reigns in imaginary kingdoms; Imperators intoning childish humiliations; the tedious minutiae of countless dark inexplicable passions and coughing sounds in the dark. Then the margravines themselves would speak; and the only remarkable thing about *their* dreams was that they were just as dull and absurd as everyone else's.

Ceryl never told them about her nightmares. When it was her turn to speak, she made up dreams. So far no one had noticed the difference. She created oddly wistful scenarios—eyeless children in blue-lit alleys, sexual hijinks with aardmen—or else she repeated dreams she had heard at those simpler gatherings on the vivarium level. But after a few months she ran out of ideas. Then she had desperately gone through old cinemafiles and even crumbling books in the Orsinate's library. Anything to come up with ideas to satisfy the grinning curiosity of Âziz and Nike and the others who sprawled in the Four Hundredth Room, smoking kef or prodding each other with morpha and endope, drinking the Orsinate's wine and patting the creepily quiescent morphodites all the while.

She hated it because it was so banal; and so dangerous. The scrying morphodites could reduce the most lurid nightmare to a bad meal, twist an innocent fancy into betrayal. The angelic boy in one's arms became a herald of senility and death; the bronze-winged hippogriff an assassination plot. Through it all the margravines listened and nodded among themselves, rewarding this fantasy, condemning that. And Ceryl cursed whoever it was had resurrected this ancient mania for probing one's sleeping secrets, and prayed for another kind of game to become the Orsinate's next fad.

She kept *her* dream to herself. Because in a way it was a beautiful thing, the only beautiful thing she had, maybe. Even though she knew it was as foolish as Tatsun Frizer's account of the rubber wheel or Shiyung's recurring vision of the whistling head.

To herself, Ceryl called her dream the Green Country. That was another reason she could never speak of it. Because everyone knew what the Green Country meant: the forbidden place and color, the horror of sky and plains unshackled. The world Outside, so dreadful that it could only be looked upon once every ten years, and then only to remind the people of Araboth of their good fortune to dwell beneath the nurturing domes.

But in Ceryl's dream the world was not a firestorm of poisonous ash and viral rain. In Ceryl's dream she was walking toward the fouga hangars, the steel and plastic warehouses on Seraphim where the dirigibles waited like sullen clouds, until the Orsinate ordered yet another strike against the enemies that crouched Outside. In the dream Ceryl walked through the hangars until she found a fouga just starting to waft upward. She ran to the ladder dangling from its gondola and climbed, until the choking chemical air inside the hangar gave way to the fouga's metallic chill.

Once inside the steering cabin she was not surprised to find herself alone, or to hear the computer navigator whispering to itself as the airship floated silently toward the skygates. She stumbled as she walked along the narrow strip of uneven rubber flooring. From overhead came the insistent whine of the fouga's propeller gears.

And then she was standing by a window in front of the gondola, and the skygates were opening before her; the shields parting like the struts of an ornamental silver fan to reveal the vastness behind them. Ceryl cried out as the fouga floated free into a sky thick with smoke and soot, ashes flung against the window so that she drew back, afraid the glass would break.

But it did not break, though she saw blue lightning lash against the curved horizon of the domes beneath her, and lightning like shining water stream-

ing down the sides of the fouga as it rose up and up
through the air.

And then (and this was the part she would never
be able to tell them. It was their greatest taboo, the
sublime imago that lurked behind all the excesses of
the Orsinate, all the ordered horrors of timoring)—

And then she saw it. The darkness pared away as
the fouga rose through the sunless air until there was
nothing *but* sun, a radiance that blinded her so that
she clutched at one of the metal pillars inside the gondola, as abruptly the fouga's upward trajectory
snapped and the airship plunged earthward.

And there it was, an endless country rising
through the darkness like a mountain from the sea.
Green everywhere, from the pale yellows and nearly
blue washes of the dawn sky at Æstival Tide to the
deepest most occult shades of emerald, lanced here
and there by lakes and rivers that glowed in that painful light like the brightest of the Orsinate's numinous
sculptures. And even though there was more to the
dream—a wave like the sky crashing down upon the
city, the sight of the domes crushed and splintered
into black, a fissure splitting the Undercity like a blade
drawn through sand—even though the dream went
on until Ceryl woke shivering in her bed, it was that
color that tore at Ceryl's stunned consciousness.

Because in all of Araboth she had never seen so
much green. It was the color of death, the forbidden
color; the color worn by fainting young artists and by
the mob screaming into the surf once a decade at
Æstival Tide, the color of the sea itself as it smashed
against the Lahatiel Gate and sent the revelers laughing and screaming at the horrors of the natural world.

The color—and her hands grew cold as she stammered to a finish and stared into the mantic's face—of
the gynander Reive's eyes.

He had never seen Night before. Hobi assumed that
was what this was—an impenetrable, fetid darkness

everywhere save behind him, where the gravator glowed softly. But even as the boy whirled to dart back inside, the chamber began to rise, and the machine started its journey (longer and noisier than its descent) back to the upper levels.

"Oh," said Hobi.

Goose bumps pricked his arms and he shivered. On the upper levels it was always the same temperature, unless you were at one of Âziz's weather parties. Hobi squinted, trying to see where Nasrani waited; finally made him out more by his smell (cardamom-water and snuff) than sight.

"Damn," the boy whispered. He stepped forward cautiously, waving his hands in front of him. His eyes must be getting used to the darkness. He could see faint flickerings of red and orange that made the shadows of things, Nasrani for instance, loom even larger and more forbidding than what they portended. "Nasrani?" he called anxiously.

The exile was bent over one leg, pulling something from his boot. "Just a minute—" he cried, and turned to the boy.

A beam of light sliced through the air, blinding Hobi. He shouted and fell; then cringing waited for the exile to strike. When he dared lift his head he saw Nasrani standing in front of him, adjusting the levels on a lumiere.

"Sorry, sorry," Nasrani muttered. "Had it all the way up. I always do that here. You expect it to be dark but forget that a little goes a long way. By little I mean *light*, of course." The exile waved the lumiere impatiently, its beam now narrowed to the breadth of a finger. "Come on then. Mind the crocodiles."

Hobi stumbled to his feet, glancing around nervously. "Crocodiles?"

The exile said nothing. Hobi followed him, hoping that by *crocodiles* Nasrani referred to the ground beneath their feet, which was waffled and beslimed as some great cracked reptilian skin. More than once he stumbled, or teetered swearing on one foot when the ground seemed to give way beneath him. The lumiere served only to point out bits of things—a glittering eye, for instance, that disappeared when Hobi stopped to stare more closely. When he turned back Nasrani and his lumiere were nearly out of sight. The boy hurried after him.

They seemed to be groping down an alley. It stank of sewers and something else, a strange grubby smell. Could it be *mud*? Hobi paused long enough to stoop and let his fingers touch the ground. It felt soft and damp, and gave way to the pressure of his hand. Maybe the rumors were true, and the Undercity really was the site of the original city, and he was walking on real dirt. The thought made his stomach churn. He shuddered and started walking again. ⅗ /*

"Keep close to me here, Hobi." The exile stopped. He grabbed Hobi by the shoulder and drew him close. Then very slowly Nasrani stepped forward, Hobi trying not to trip beside him. The alley ended abruptly. They took a step down, and another; and then the exile pointed upward.

"There it is," he said.

Hobi gasped. Above them reared the immense ziggurat that was Araboth. Level after level after level it soared, so far above them that the periwinkle lights of Cherubim and Seraphim twinkled faint as stars and the fires of the refineries could be seen only as fingers of scarlet and gold clawing at the darkness. Gazing upon it like this a horrible feeling took hold of the boy: as though the city were alive and he crouched beneath it, his only hope of survival that the behemoth did not see him there.

"The Holy City of the Americas." Next to him the exile's voice rang coldly. Hobi wanted to cry out, beg him to keep silent lest he draw attention to them; but Nasrani went on, his tone bitter, almost cruel. "*Araboth* is what the ancients called Seventh Heaven, the city of god. Did you know that, Hobi? But of course you wouldn't. That is why the Prophets named each level after one of the Divine Choirs. So here you are, looking upon the celestial city. Beautiful, isn't it?"

He laughed, a miserable sound, and swept his arms out. The lumiere's beam lanced through the blackness until it was swallowed by the void. Hobi opened his mouth but could say nothing, only stare dumbly at the awful vision before him. With a last bitter laugh, Nasrani cried,

> *"When all the world dissolves,*
> *And every creature shall be purified,*
> *All places shall be hell that is not Heaven."*

Then he stepped forward once more, and Hobi had no choice but to follow.

He walked with his hands held out protectively in front of him, batting at the empty air. They seemed to be walking on the ruins of an ancient avenue. The shadows of crumbling buildings stood to either side, and openings that might be other roads leading into the darkness. There was a heavy stench hanging about it all, a smell that reminded Hobi of the scent that seeped in through the filters, the smell of the sea. But this was stronger, and there was in it too the rank odor of decay, of stagnant water and mildew.

Occasionally sounds echoed down from very high overhead, shrill noises and explosions from the refineries, and what sounded like chanting. From the shadows of the decaying buildings Hobi sometimes heard noises—a sort of slithering sound, like something being dragged across the ground, and once a murmuring like voices. But he saw nothing clearly, only occasional jots of gold, like candlelight reflected from a glass of claret.

"Sorry to bring you around this way," Nasrani called to him. His voice once more held its accustomed note of playful irony. He seemed familiar with the way. At least he did not stagger and trip against things the way Hobi did, or swear except very softly when something snagged his greatcoat. It seemed they had been walking for a long time now, an hour maybe.

Hobi's fear faded to a faint though constant anxiety. Finally he took a deep breath and said, "Um, Nasrani—this is—would you mind telling me—"

"What?" The exile turned, the lumiere showing his frown. "Did you say—"

Suddenly the man shouted and fell to his knees. With a cry Hobi reached to help him.

"Nasrani! What is it—"

"I don't know!" He clutched Hobi's hand and stood, brushing himself off, and retrieved the lumiere. "There—can you see anything there?"

He pointed the light at the ground. Hobi squinted, shaking his head. Nasrani pushed him forward a little, until Hobi felt the ground give way beneath him. He yelled and lurched against Nasrani.

"It's a *hole!*"

His heart pounded so that he gasped for breath. The thought of a hole down here, where it could plunge into the very core of the earth itself! And Nasrani had nearly pushed him into it! Hobi turned, his voice rising as he swore furiously, but Nasrani only grabbed his arm and shook him hard.

"I wouldn't have let you fall, Hobi—but it's there, right? You felt it too?"

Hobi yanked his arm free. He caught his breath, nodding. "Ye-es. There's a hole there—what's that mean?"

Nasrani's voice echoed as he inched forward. Hobi could hear him shuffling carefully to the left. "Here—" he called after a minute. "Come this way, but be careful—"

Hobi edged after him, hugging his arms to his shoulders. He heard loose stones or dirt rattle under his feet and then fall away, the sound abruptly silenced.

"Oh, god," Hobi muttered; but then Nasrani was gripping his arm and pulling him gently forward, until he felt more solid footing. He fell forward, his hands smacking against a wall as he gasped in relief.

"What does it mean?"

The exile's voice came very close to Hobi's face. The boy started, still trying to catch his breath. Something clinked; the lumiere cast its feeble light upon a handful of keys. Nasrani picked out one and held it up to the light. He said, "It means there is a fissure here that was not here yesterday."

"What?" Hobi shook his head. "A fissure, what do you mean, a fissure?"

"A fissure. A hole, a rift. A break in the earth. Now."

He raised the lumiere so Hobi could see that they stood in a recessed doorway. The brick walls gleamed damply. Tendrils hung from the corners of the ceiling. When Hobi touched them they felt wet and pulpy, and his fingers smelled of rotting fish.

"I don't understand," the boy said uneasily, wiping his hand on his trousers.

"It used to happen Outside." Nasrani rattled a doorknob. "Earthquakes. The ground would open up. Not here—I mean not in this part of the continent. I don't understand it, there shouldn't be any threat of earthquakes here. A gap like that could breach the integrity of the whole foundation. . . ."

Breach. Hobi went cold.

His father. The Architects. *A breach in the fundus of Angels.*

". . . have to ask your father if he knows anything about this. Watch that fungus there." Hobi jumped as the exile poked him. There was a loud click. "Ah, here we are—"

A gust of musty air rushed out to choke them. "Come now." Nasrani coughed, pulling at Hobi's sleeve. Behind them the door slid shut with a sucking noise. They stood in total darkness, except for the lumiere's tiny glow.

"Wait here," commanded Nasrani.

"What—" Hobi stammered, but the exile had already crossed the room. From the darkness came a faint ticking, a soft hum as of machinery. Hobi's heart throbbed painfully. He thought he might faint.

From across the emptiness came a *flltt!* A candle flared into life, so bright and sudden that he gasped. Then another, and another, until the room was ringed with light. Hobi raised his arm, shielding his eyes. Across the walls Nasrani's goblin shadow leaped and crouched. Hobi stepped forward, amazed.

"What *is* this place?" he whispered.

All around the circumference of the room were cabinets. Small ones that barely came to Hobi's knees. Tall ones that towered above him. Cases that covered an entire wall, and some so small they must have been designed for ornamental value alone. In front of a metal cabinet stood the exile, the split tails of his greatcoat curling behind him like wings. In his hand flickered a candelabrum, so encrusted with yellow wax it resembled some bizarre plant. He raised it, pointing to where a long banner draped the wall.

"Witness the wonders of the ancients," Nasrani said dryly.

Hobi walked until he stood beneath the banner. Across it spilled crude, luridly painted letters:

DOCTOR MONDO'S AMAZING CYCLORAMA!

Hobi glanced at Nasrani, then at the banner again. Ragged and charred at the edges, its colors had faded—blue to a pale shade that was almost white; red to a bloody smear; green to a pallor that reminded Hobi of the strings of moldy stuff hanging from the door outside. The corners of the banner had frayed and then been painstakingly repaired with heavy black thread that tore through the fragile cloth like a razor. It looked to be several hundred years old.

SEE! THE TITANIUM CHILDREN!
MAXIMILLIAN UR: THE BANE OF SHEIKS!
THE ANODYNE PHYSICIAN: HER SIGHT ALONE
WILL HEAL YOU!
MOGHREBI: PRINCESS OF THE SANDS!
WISE APULIEUS: WILL HE MAKE AN ASS OUT
OF *YOU*?
NEFERTITY: THE BEAUTIFUL ONE IS *HERE*!

Beneath the names was a badly drawn picture of
a woman's head. She stared straight out at Hobi with
large tilted eyes, a cool gaze that was all the more
unsettling for the crudeness of its execution. Hobi
stared back at her, then crossed the room to join Nasrani where he stood in front of a tall steel cabinet.

It held a woman; at least he *thought* it was a
woman. She stood behind the glass, regally tall, skin
black as oil, eyes closed and mouth in a tight grimacing smile. Looking at her Hobi felt distinctly queasy.
He was certain she was dead.

"She is only sleeping," whispered Nasrani, as
though he read his thoughts. The boy jumped. Nasrani held up his candelabrum so that its wavering
light cascaded across the glass in ripples of black and
yellow. "Second Ascension. Very rare." He scraped a
bit of wax from the case, shaking his head. "Be careful around her. She is very sensitive to noise and
light."

Hobi gaped. "She's alive? Who is she?"

Nasrani made a small *pfff* of disdain. "Alive? Of
course she's alive. I told you, she is sleeping. They are
all sleeping."

He swept his arm in an arc, waves of light trailing
the candelabrum and bouncing from the other cases.
He gestured at each one as he intoned their names.

"Moghrebi, the Blackamoor Princess. The Skeptic
Apulieus. Maximillian Ur, the Bladed Nemesis. The

Titanium Children, Jackie and Jane. And Nefertity: The Beautiful One Is Here.''

Hobi looked around the room nervously. ''She is?''

Nasrani tilted his head, annoyed. ''Her *name*. That's her name. Nefertity: The Beautiful One Is Here.'' He gestured impatiently toward a case at the far end of the room, then said, ''I found them when I was—exploring—down here, many years ago. There was a tunnel, the remains of a sewage system.

''It led—well, never mind where it led. I followed it, and eventually I found them, just sprawled everywhere, totally neglected. No sign that humans or Architects had been there in ages. Nothing but abandoned buildings, rusting machinery—*such* machines, Hobi! Giant wheels, immersible booths, elevated transways—they were rotting amid the ruins of a *funfair*! Obviously the idiots who had found them had no idea what they were—they must have discovered some forgotten cache of an earlier Ascension and thought they had god's own amusement arcade.'' Patting the outside of the metal cabinet he added, ''Moghrebi here was designed as an intelligence unit for the Thirty Wars in the East. But *they* were using her for''—he spat the words—''fortune-telling!''

Within her glass case Moghrebi remained motionless. Hobi stared at her, trying to focus despite the flickering light and shadows, trying to see if she was breathing. After a full minute he was certain she was not.

''She's a replicant,'' he said at last.

Nasrani looked at him as though he were mad. ''Android,'' he snapped. He turned and stalked across the room. Hobi trailed after him, chagrined.

When he reached the far wall, Nasrani put down his candelabrum and crouched to inspect a tiny cabinet. Hobi heard a soft *click;* then a figure no bigger than his hand somersaulted out, to straighten and stand at Nasrani's feet.

''Toys,'' said the exile. He extended a finger to

touch the tiny figure's head. It was a woman, a green woman. Antennae like filaments of glass sprouted from above her eyes, quivering. "That fraud Planck should see these. He'd be ashamed to peddle those pathetic cretins of his—" He snapped his fingers and the tiny woman vaulted back into her case.

There were others, many others. Hobi lost count after Maximillian Ur with his clashing knives and the Anodyne Physician, the Mechanical Baboon and her dog-faced brood who danced when Nasrani raised his arm and commanded them. A retrofitted scholiast with an eyeless face and hands like a young boy's, groping and eager as they reached to stroke Hobi's cheek. Wise Apulieus, looking surprisingly modern in his white jacket and simple gold jewelry. The Titanium Children, Jackie and Jane, their azurine eyes regarding him with detachment as they danced a silent tango across the darkened room. Moghrebi, intoning dire prophecies as she went through the motions of reading a small paper volume. Nasrani woke them all, going from case to case and opening the glass doors to release them into the flickering shadows of the great chamber, until the place was full of them: laughing, chattering, dancing, singing, silent androids and robots, tiny monads and automatons and replicants. Humanoid and animal, children of metal and monkeys spun of glass, they bowed to Nasrani and greeted him by name, then turned gracefully to his guest.

"Charmed," murmured Apulieus, stroking the boy's cheek with a hand that felt smooth and dry as wood.

"You must surrender!" roared Maximillian Ur. His three rows of steel teeth clashed together with a sound like grinding gears.

"If you will please lie down we can begin the examination," crooned the Anodyne Physician.

Hobi looked around a little desperately. "Nasrani," he called out, finally sighting him in a dim corner.

"I saved them," explained Nasrani, walking with care to join the boy. In one hand he cradled another of the tiny monads, this one with dragonfly's wings of transparent blue glass. "It took years—I watched every 'file I could find, read everything I could about them. They had all been perverted from their original uses, as weapons or medics or intelligence units. Except for these, of course."

He held up the monad. Its wings whirred and it rose into the air a few inches above his palm. "Monitors, to watch children. Or maybe they were toys. By the time they ended up here no one remembered why they had been made." He watched the graceful creature dart across the room, then sighing left Hobi among the small crowd of replicants.

Hobi watched him, curious. The exile seemed to have forgotten him: he crossed to the darkest end of the room and there stood brooding in front of a cabinet that Hobi had not noticed earlier.

"Nasrani?"

The exile said nothing. Gently the boy pushed away the Anodyne Physician's probing hands and went to Nasrani, stepping carefully over flickering candles until he reached the cabinet. Nasrani stood in silence, one hand tracing the edge of a delicate golden handle in the front of the case.

Hobi had never seen anything like it before. A kind of sarcophagus of glass and chromium, with pale blue and yellow and pink tubes curved about its crown. Nucleoceptive fluid flowed through the tubes, silvery bubbles rising in long streamers until they disappeared at its top. Behind them the other replicants and robots hissed and clattered while the candles died and the air grew soft with the scent of burning wax. In front of him the sarcophagus glowed painfully bright, vivid rose shot with deep blue highlights. But he couldn't make out what was within the case—the light had a peculiar clouded quality, as though it were heavily filtered; as though whatever was inside were so brilliant it would blind whoever gazed upon it. Still, after a moment or two his eyes grew accustomed to it. He glanced at Nasrani, but the man still paid him no notice. Hobi stepped closer to him and leaned forward to see what was inside.

Ever after, he remembered this moment as the one that changed his life: an instant when all the real sounds—Apulieus intoning to Maximillian Ur, the Automated Tenor doing scales, even Nasrani's soft breathing—died, and he heard from somewhere else a single clear note, as though a glass bell had been struck. Nefertity would tell him he had imagined it, but Hobi had never imagined anything in his life. The sound was real as the figure in the case before him.

It was a woman: a woman of glass. He could see her veins, filaments of glowing jade and cerise, twisting around joints of silver metal. Her ribs curved like two hands cupping the softly glowing air, and behind them, where a human heart would be, was a sphere of the most perfect gold. Electrical fibers chased across it, and when Hobi touched the front of the sarcophagus threads of light streamed toward him. Even her face was transparent. It was as though someone had taken a living woman and replaced all her inner atomies with ice and crystal. Everything except her eyes. They glowed through translucent eyelids, beneath lashes that were like splinters of light—orbs like globes of living water, the deepest green he had ever seen. At the corner of each was a drop of blood. As he gazed transfixed her eyelids flickered. Blood welled from each eye and spilled to the bottom of the sarcophagus.

"Only when she sleeps," whispered Nasrani. He too had outstretched his hand to graze the glass above her cheek. "Because then she dreams that she is human."

"She's beautiful," said Hobi, hardly daring to speak. And she was: in spite of the arcane array of metal and glass, her antique, almost doll-like features, she was breathtakingly lovely. "What—who—is she?"

Nasrani only stared at her without answering. After a moment Hobi asked again. Nasrani turned away, to look out at the room where the other replicants engaged each other in witless conversations. When he spoke his voice was soft, almost a whisper.

"She is a nemosyne. One of the memory units devised after the First Ascension, when people feared that the holocausts would destroy all records of humanity. They were designed and then given to various wise men and women, who programmed them to record, oh, everything. There were nemosynes for agriculture and meteorology, oceanographic units and military units and units that had entire libraries of books and films and 'files on them."

Hobi shook his head. "What happened to them?"

Nasrani shrugged. "Like everything else, they were destroyed over the centuries; most of them at least. But some must have survived—this one did— and probably they are out there now, keeping their secrets until we can find them and learn from them again."

In the silence Maximillian Ur's blades whickered and snapped, and Apulieus scolded noisily. Finally, Nasrani said, "If we could find them, we could rebuild the world. We could locate and renew the fallen cities. We could find the lost arsenals and defeat our enemies at last, and end the wars with the Emirate and the Commonwealth. We could do anything, if we could find more of these—they have blueprints for machines and computers, they could teach us how to stop the plagues, how to repair the starships, how to revive the poisoned deserts. They remember everything."

He fell silent, staring at the imprisoned nemosyne.

Hobi pressed his face against the cool glass. From inside he could hear a very faint whirring, a sound more like running water than the pulse of circuitry. She had skin of some very thin fine metal stretched across the sharp planes of her cheeks and jaw. As he stared the translucent skin shivered, and her eyelids trembled.

"How do you know?" he asked at last.

Nasrani shook his head. "I found 'files about them. I even have records of where some of them were stored. But those cities are dead now, and the nemosynes like everything else in them were destroyed. Or else they are waiting until we find and wake them once again."

His eyes as they gazed at the nemosyne were brilliant, almost feverish. For the first time Hobi noticed what an odd color they were. Nasrani's voice rose plaintively.

"But I can't even figure out how to get this one to operate correctly! All she will do is state her operating history and serial number. Sometimes she recites things at random, things from her datafiles. She was a storage unit for minority histories. Women's folktales. Poems. Useless things—she'll recite them forever. But I can't get any response beyond that. She won't answer my questions."

His annoyance faded. "She is still half-asleep, and I don't know how to wake her," he ended sadly.

"Wake her," murmured Hobi. He gazed with wide brown eyes at the glass woman, once more rested his cheek against hers to listen to her receptors softly pulsing.

"If I *could* wake her," Nasrani went on, "I could find out about the rest. They were supposed to be linked. I might even be able to access the others, if they still exist."

"What would you do with them? I mean, if you could talk to them?"

Nasrani straightened, glanced at the boy, and cleared his throat.

"The world is too large now," he said, as though addressing an audience. "Too small in some ways— how many people here, besides the Aviators, have ever been Outside? But too large as well. Too difficult

to travel Outside, too many dangers, too many enemies. The nemosynes could—*teach us*—things."

"But her?" Hobi stroked her cheek. "What could
she teach?"

Nasrani sighed. "If I could find out how to access
her interactive mode I might be able to question her,
link with the others or at least access some of her
classified files. But I just can't figure it out. There must
be a trick to it, but I've spent years trying and I still
can't wake her." With a sigh he turned and walked
away.

For a few minutes Hobi remained. "Wake up," he
whispered, his breath clouding the cool glass. Within
her sarcophagus the Beautiful One slept on, heedless
of him, heedless of all the world. He looked away,
embarrassed.

In the middle of the room stood Nasrani, surrounded by the last few guttering candles. He seemed
dispirited; even the tails of his greatcoat drooped to
brush the floor.

"Moghrebi," he called softly. "Apulieus, my good
man. Come now, Moghrebi. Be a sweet girl, Jackie."

One by one they returned to their sleep: the Anodyne Physician entering her cabinet with good grace,
bowing her golden head to Nasrani and staring out at
Hobi with unblinking glass eyes. Apulieus waved
mockingly and disappeared behind his case's oaken
doors. The monads buzzed into their tiny compart-
ments, their noise silenced as the doors snapped
closed. Last of all went Maximillian Ur, his four arms
with their glittering knives whistling through the air
as he groaned and clicked and threatened, until Nasrani slammed the door after him.

In the hollow silence that followed Nasrani's
voice echoed mournfully. "I keep them so she won't
be lonely," he said, "so that in case one day she
wakes, she won't think she is the last of her kind."

He bent to blow out another candle, then started
for the door, motioning for Hobi to join him.

For a long final moment the boy gazed at the

nemosyne, her staring green eyes with their golden veins, the sanguine tears welling up in them to spill upon the floor. His hand lingered on her face until he heard Nasrani shuffling impatiently.

As the boy went to meet him the last few candles began to sputter and go out. Nasrani fumbled for his key. The encroaching darkness frightened Hobi, and he stepped a little closer to the exile. It was silly, but when the replicants had been moving about, the place didn't feel so desolate. At home he had often been in a room full of servers and tutors and scholiasts, but he had never felt like this, as though the replicants had characters of their own. The nemosyne most of all, of course: beautiful and tragic, trapped within her glass coffin. But the others too, although he had known them only briefly. Wicked Maximillian. Sarcastic Apulieus. The gentle Physician. His own robotic Physician had about as much character as his toothbrush.

But here for a little while, he had felt as though he were in a crowd; almost as though he were at a party. And he remembered something his mother had once said about Nasrani Orsina.

They had been at a gathering in the Orsinate's sanctuary, the Four Hundredth Room. It was several years before Nasrani was exiled for his attempted murder of his sister—

"Look at him." His mother raised her glass, a tiny bell-shaped tumbler dancing with the emerald spirits of Amity-in-Occis, and peered through it as though it were a spyglass. "Your father's friend, Nasrani Orsina." The name sounded like a curse in her mouth. "He's like a clockwork man. Nods and talks and laughs on cue, bows to his sisters and smiles as he slices out your liver. A perfect gentleman. A perfect clockwork man."

His mother was given to such blunt pronouncements. She had once, to her face, called Nike and her sisters "inbred swine," a slur that had caused Nike to laugh with her hooting voice. The truth was that Angelika frightened her: Nike thought she was a witch. But now Angelika was looking not at Nike but at her brother Nasrani. Hobi wondered what it could be about this tall man, elegant in lavender moleskin trousers and crimson greatcoat, that reminded his mother of an automaton.

"His eyes," she'd said. A drop of Amity clung to her upper lip like a petal of lime blossom. "His hands, his feet, everything. He has everything that a real person has, except a heart. Even that sow Âziz has a heart, although it's a sick rotten thing." She'd turned then to greet Âziz, kissing her and leaving a carnal smear of red across her cheek.

Hobi thought of that now as he watched Nasrani stoop to retrieve the failing lumiere. A clockwork man.

"What brought you down here? The first time, I mean."

Nasrani turned to him, brandishing the lumiere so that Hobi shrank from him. But then he realized that Nasrani's expression was not angry but tormented. Without a word he yanked the door open and stepped outside. Sudden terror seized the boy: that he had offended the man and would be left here alone. He started after Nasrani, stammering apologies.

"No, no," said Nasrani. He held the door until Hobi stood beside him. Behind them something squeaked and chittered. Hobi looked over his shoulder in time to see a tiny form dart out to seize a bit of tallow. "I'm not angry, my dear. It's just that—"

The exile's eyes were immensely sad. "It's just that I come here to forget. About all that—"

He shook his hand, indicating the ceiling and what lay beyond, level after level of misery and tumult and twisted steel, humans reduced to living in the ruins of monstrous machines and computers endlessly designing unlivable new habitats. "All that up there. The Holy City; the family curse." He drew a hand to his face as though he were in pain.

In the doorway Hobi hesitated and looked back. For a moment he glimpsed the room, lit by a single pallid flame. In their cabinets the replicants and androids stood, gazing blindly or else with eyes closed, returned to that terrible dreamless state wherein they would wait forever until someone came to rouse them. He stared at the nemosyne, her body shimmering blue and rose as the last blue flame leaped and tossed its feeble light upon her frozen smile. Then the flame went out. He heard tiny voices twittering, small feet pattering from the corners, and looked away as Nasrani locked the door.

Outside of Ceryl Waxwing's chambers the nuclear CLOCK clanged twenty. Reive waited to see if this woman would say more. She had already said too much. But Ceryl was silent, her face pale as she stared at the window.

"That's all," she said at last. She would not look at Reive.

In her chair the gynander nodded and bit her lower lip, her brow creased as she debated how best to answer. Her breath felt heavy inside her; her head spun as she gazed at Ceryl and thought, *She is mad, to have even dreamed of telling this to anyone, she must be crazy. . . .*

But Reive said nothing; only closed her eyes and wished she had brought the little brass case that held her joss sticks and incense burners, anything to gain a little more time, a few more minutes before Ceryl grew tired of waiting for her answer.

The meaning of the dream was clear. Reive had never before heard of a dream so obvious in its portents. Usually she had a little more trouble than the other mantics; just as she looked subtly different from them, so it was more difficult for her to scry the truth behind the mundane fantasies of bored technicians and anxious diplomats. The hermaphrodites had been bred for their sensitivity to the unconscious whims of others, but somehow Reive lacked their insight. She even wondered if she was a true hermaphrodite at all; but of course the physical evidence was unmistakable. It was simply that she had no gift for scrying. Often she just sat there, listening to the tiresome recitative of a nervous aristocrat while a yellow plume of smoke rose from her incense burner. When her patron finally grew silent, waiting for her to interpret the dream, Reive would make something up.

This time that would not be necessary. The back of her neck prickled, excitement burgeoned inside of her like a drug as she realized that this must be what it was like for the others, this certainty that she could read Ceryl's sleeping thoughts like a map. As sure as she knew her name she knew what this dream portended. She took a deep breath and opened her eyes.

"You have dreamed of the holocaust that will destroy Araboth."

Her voice sounded too deep, hollow as though it boomed up from some great depth. Across from her Ceryl Waxwing blinked.

"It is the dream of Ucalegon the Prince of Storms, and Baratdaja the Healing Wind." Inside of Reive's head was a pounding that threatened to drown the sound of her own voice. She gasped, "It is growing Outside; it is waiting for the gates to open. . . ."

Ceryl nodded slowly. Her hands shook as she drew them to her face. "What else?" she whispered.

Eyes wide, the gynander shook her head, unable to speak. The thudding inside her head became a roar. She heard the voice of Zalophus shrieking—

I hear my sisters calling and the winds gathering for the great storm, I hear the voice of Ucalegon shouting in its sleep. . . .

The gynander began to shake. Behind her closed eyelids a light pulsed and words whistled through her skull—

Ucalegon. Baratdaja. Prince of Storms and the Healing Wind. The holocaust that will destroy Araboth.

She recalled the tremor that had shook her room

that morning, and a hermaphrodite crying *The domes moved, we saw the walls shake. . . .*

And then once more the voice of the imprisoned leviathan warning her,

". . . in the Undercity the rift is widening: soon it will breach the open sea. . . ."

"Zalophus," Reive whispered.

He had not been mad. The city was in danger. It was all real, somehow he had sounded the very depths of the Undercity and seen it there; somehow this woman Ceryl had seen it too. It was not *a* dream that haunted Ceryl Waxwing. It was *The Dream*, the Great Portent, the Final Warning that the Orsinate had been searching for so desperately with all their occult games. They had placed all their trust in the Architects, in things that could be measured and quantified and engineered, but the one thing the Architects could not do was dream.

They had thought to keep the world Outside at bay, and had, ever since the Long Night of the First Ascension, when the prairies turned to glass and the sky choked beneath black and frozen rain. After that Araboth had been raised, the Architects set to guard the people who fled the poisoned world Outside the domes. In all those centuries they had never left. The ruling families retreated to the upper levels, where they bred with each other like mad wary spiders. And gradually the world Outside faded to nothing but children's stories, a green monster resurrected each Æstival Tide and ultimately defeated when once more the Lahatiel Gate clanged shut. An emerald nightmare; the dream of the Green Country.

She saw it now as though it were etched upon her brain. A fissure splitting the Undercity like a wound, prying apart the monstrous colonnades upon which the city rested. Outside, the Green Country overtaking the city. Araboth crushed beneath the wave, a wave like a verdant cape covering the spires and struts and domes of the Holy City.

Reive's eyes flew open. Ceryl cried out at the

sudden flash of color in the gynander's masklike face. They stared at each other, neither one daring to speak as they thought the same thing.

Treason. Torture. Execution. Death.

Ceryl spoke first, her voice trembling. "There is no other meaning?" Her tone was without hope.

The gynander shook her head. "No. But this is not the only sign. There have been other things," she said slowly. "We have seen them—on Virtues Level the ground shook, and we heard a warning, from—"

She fell silent, reluctant to speak of Zalophus.

Ceryl nodded. She kneaded the sleeves of her catsuit, her palms leaving damp stains on the fabric. "I have too," she said hoarsely. "Now that you mention it. A crack in the pavement . . ."

Such a tiny thing, it had seemed a few hours ago; now Ceryl stared at the floor of her room, terrified that she would see something there, a rift that would widen until it swallowed them all. She looked at Reive.

"You can't tell anyone," she said. Her hands tightened as she clenched her arms. Reive said nothing and she went on, desperately, "You know what will happen if you do—they'll take me, the Reception Committee will come and take me away. This close to Æstival Tide, they'll give me to—"

"The Compassionate Redeemer," Reive said softly.

Ceryl nodded. She looked around her room at the alembics and vials of dried herbs, the weights and measures she used in her work. She could hear the steady crash of waves against the outer domes, a sound that thrummed counterpoint to the panicky beat of her heart. It all seemed tainted now, as though her dream were a sickly odor that had seeped into all her things. When she glanced back at Reive she saw the gynander watching her with wide frightened eyes. A pang shot through Ceryl. A feeling she had not had since Giton died: that there were other people in the world beside herself, and somehow she might be held responsible for them.

She took a deep breath. "I think I'd like for you to come with me. To my chambers on Thrones Level. It—I think we might be safer there. At least the rooms are larger than here, there would be room for both of us."

On Thrones they would be closer to the Orsinate, and that was dangerous. But if the city was really threatened with destruction, it seemed they might be safer on the upper levels than here. And there was something to be said for hiding in plain sight. "Will you come with me?"

Reive crouched into her chair, looking more like a child than ever. For a horrible moment Ceryl thought she would refuse. And Ceryl couldn't risk that; couldn't risk letting the gynander return to her own level, where she might betray them both. The thought of killing Reive sickened her; but she would have no choice. She looked at the gynander beseechingly.

Reive lowered her head, drew her hands to her ears. She wished she'd never come here; wished she'd not been so greedy for food and a new patron. But it was done, now.

And Ceryl's quarters *were* on the upper levels. There would be no other hermaphrodites there to snigger at Reive behind her back. She would be well fed, and, if she could trust Ceryl, well cared for. Very slowly, Reive nodded.

Ceryl let her breath out in a long *whoo* of relief. "Good," she said, and paced to the door. "I think we should go now—"

Before you change your mind, she thought—

"Before it gets any later. I've got everything we'll need up there, the kitchen's full, I've never even spent the night—"

She practically dragged Reive after her, the two of them hurrying down the corridor to the gravator that would bring them to the pleasure cabinet's level.

It wasn't until they reached Ceryl's chambers and locked the door behind them that Reive realized that she had forgotten the mysid in its globe.

Hobi grew increasingly nervous as they waited for the gravator to arrive in the Undercity and bear them back to the upper levels. His eyes ached, striving to give sharp edges and angles to this shapeless night. Phantom pyramids and cubicles appeared before his eyes, ghostly well-ordered images that begged for substance; but Hobi knew there was only this inchoate blackness, this dank and primal air, this soft *earth* beneath his boots. He shuddered, longing for the cool blues and whites of Cherubim, the sterile and vivifying scents from the air ducts.

"Because of the Architects," Nasrani was saying. Hobi started. He hadn't been listening; a soft labored sound, like something breathing, had diverted his attention to a heap of rags near the gravator entrance.

". . . back then they were training me to be the next Architect Imperator—"

Hobi looked up in surprise as Nasrani continued, "Before you were born. I had the finest tutors. The Kray Nine Thousand and Natambu Bellairs. I'm the oldest in the family, you know. Âziz comes next, but she's three years younger and . . ."

Hobi nodded, fidgeting. Far above the gravator could barely be discerned, a square of violet light floating down, cables wrapping it like black velvet ropes.

Nasrani continued, ". . . and really she's the least intelligent of all of us. That's why she relies so utterly on the Architects; why for generations they have all enslaved themselves to the Architects. Because they were stupid; because no one had the education or temperament to question the machines."

"But you did." Hobi nodded. It seemed the right thing to say.

"That's right. I did. I was researching the western

storm system, what the moujiks call Ucalegon. Did you know there was another city here once, before Araboth?"

Hobi shook his head.

"There was. It was called Indianola."

With a grating noise the gravator finally stopped in front of them. They stepped inside and sat down. Hobi practically groaned with relief as the doors closed and the machine began to rise once more, but Nasrani went on as though nothing had changed.

"We've found evidence that this site was settled nearly a thousand years ago. It was a port then, feeding into the Gulf—"

"The Gulf?"

"Yes, the Gulf! All that water out there? The *sea*?" Nasrani glared at him. "You've been out at Æstival Tide?"

Hobi looked offended. "I just never heard anyone call it that."

Nasrani raised his eyebrows triumphantly. "My point exactly. That's because nobody *knows* anymore. The Architects clean their files periodically and purge them of old data, and then no one remembers the original names of things. But there *was* a city here, quite a large one. Indianola. The Gateway to Texas, they called it. It was a trade center for petroleum and metals and other things. Cattle, in the very beginning when there were farmlands here. A pleasure city for a while. Then a port again, for trade with HORUS and the Commonwealth, before the Long Night destroyed most of the cities and there was no one left to trade with. Then when things were restored somewhat after the Third Ascension, it became a port for the slave trade."

Hobi tilted his head. "So was this city destroyed by the Commonwealth or the Emirate?"

"It was destroyed by a storm. By several storms. Hurricanes, tidal waves, typhoons. The first time—the first time we have records—was in the nineteenth century. Then again in the twentieth, and again in the twenty-first. Each time they rebuilt the city, and each time it was wiped away as though it had never existed. The last time was the worst—by then the storm systems had grown terrifically—the weather had mutated like everything else. Afterward the Long Night came before they had a chance to rebuild it. When the Prophets of the Two Faiths finally joined forces a hundred years later, they raised the Quincunx Domes atop the ruins of those earlier cities, and named the new city Araboth. Seventh Heaven."

Hobi glanced out the window. Outside the glow of the refineries faded as they rose another level. "Is it a secret, then? That this was Indianola once?"

Nasrani took a snuffbox from his greatcoat and did a pinch, sneezed, then tucked his long legs under him. "No. No secret; just forgotten history.

"I learned other things, too. Especially later, when I started to try and find out about the nemosynes. I told you that the weather has been changing outside—the Shinings did that, and then some of the HORUS projects had an unanticipated effect. In the last few years it's gotten worse—the Aviators bring back reports of storms in the Archipelago that wipe out entire islands in a single night. I myself have seen images from the HORUS satellites that show that the very shape of some of the continents has changed. There is a new storm system that builds in the seas to the east of Araboth. Every year for the last six or seven years at least one of these storms has come near enough to alter the topography of the coast a hundred miles south of here."

Hobi stared openmouthed, but before he could say anything the exile cut him off.

"But did the Architects see this? They did not! Storms like these—if one of them were to strike here it could destroy us—"

Hobi protested, "But it would never break through. The domes . . ."

"The domes are hundreds of years old! And the Architects are even older. I believe they are starting to fail us—they are not as reliable as they once were. In the last year they have been giving the wrong data. Nothing anyone would notice during routine use; but as I told you, I was trained to be the Architect Imperator, so *I* noticed. Little things, like that hole we saw in the Undercity. . . ."

Hobi cried, "But—but what does it mean?"

Nasrani took a deep breath. "It *means*, either the Architects are malfunctioning or—or they're malfunctioning, that's all."

Suddenly he looked tired, not the margravin in exile but a haggard man no longer young. He looked at Hobi almost desperately. "That is why I'm trying to wake the nemosyne, to see if she can access others Outside. Perhaps there is a master diagnostic that could repair the Architects. Or one of the meteorological nemosynes that could track the storm systems accurately. Because otherwise . . ."

He spread his hands, shrugging, and said nothing more.

Hobi looked away, brushing his long hair from his face. Periwinkle light filled the gravator, and the smell of lemons. They were approaching Cherubim. He thought of his father sitting up all night, talking to the Architects. He thought of all those other nights since his mother had been murdered, his sleepless father bleary-eyed and grim in his study. He thought of the fissure in the Undercity, and of a clear voice intoning *The rift at Pier Forty-three is spreading.*

"How do you know all this?" he asked at last, his voice cracking. "Why haven't the Architects said anything? Why doesn't my father know?"

Nasrani threw up his hands, falling against the wall as the gravator lurched to a stop. "Because the Architects are wrong, that's why! They've been relying on old data, the lines from HORUS have been skewed, *I* don't know! But they're wrong, there *is* a new storm system. And *I* know, because I've seen it."

Hobi swallowed. He remembered what the exile

had said earlier, about the tunnel that had led him to the replicants. "You've been Outside?"

Nasrani nodded. Without looking at the boy he stood and started for the door. Hobi followed, shaking his head.

"But you're alive. They say you can't go Outside, except at Æstival Tide. They say you'll go mad. They say you'll die."

With a grinding clang the doors slid open. "Well," said Nasrani as he looked down at Hobi with his clear pale eyes. "It's like I told you:

"They're wrong."

Chapter 3

THE INVESTITURE
~~~~~~~~~~~~~~~~~~~~~~~

It had been some time since Ceryl had been to her chambers on Thrones. When she opened the door a musky smell greeted them, amber essence and patchouli, but everything was neat and considerably more luxurious than what Reive was accustomed to.

"You can sleep here." Ceryl pointed to a long divan plumped with yellow velvet pillows. "I'll be in the next room if you need me—help yourself to anything you can find." She was exhausted. Not even the threat of more nightmares could keep her from sleeping. She drew a bolt on the door, then retired to the bedroom.

Reive collapsed on the divan and stared at the ceiling. She found herself listening for the sound of gynanders whispering or running down the corridors. But it was quiet here, quieter than any level she had ever visited. None of the growlings or splashes of the vivariums; no chatter of recording equipment as on Powers. With a sigh she fingered a plait of her hair, chewing the end wistfully. She had none of her own clothes with her, of course. Worse, she didn't have her cosmetics. She would have to make do with whatever she found here, which (she had peeked in a closet) looked to be mostly somber blue and brown catsuits and heavy leather boots. But Ceryl's quarters were large and comfortable. There were stacks of 'files along one wall, a huge viewing monitor on another; and the promise of parties to attend. Sinking into the divan's plush cushions with the rich smell of amber wafting over her, the soft warm glow of a night-light nearby, it seemed to Reive impossible that anything could go wrong here on the upper levels. Ceryl's dream was probably just that, a dream; the tremor she'd felt earlier some minor disturbance—maybe one of the Architects' grinding machines at work somewhere below. And everyone knew Zalophus was mad. The gynander quickly fell asleep, her own dreams peaceful and utterly forgettable.

Until without warning she was tearing at the coverlet, her heart thudding as she staggered from the divan, crying out softly as she tried to recall where she was.

The woman with the dream. The upper levels. Reive grabbed the edge of a table, breathing deeply until she felt calmer, and then she recalled what had awakened her.

The mysid. She had given it no thought until now, but suddenly she was torn with visions of the frail thing floating dead and gray in its bowl. Left alone in her chambers it would die; might already be dead, if another tremor had shaken Virtues Level and sent some bit of rubbish falling onto its fragile globe. Or—and this would be worse—someone might find it, a snooping guardian or the awful Drusilla, and then it would be traced back to Reive, or else tossed with the day's slops into one of the level's septic tanks.

Tears burned at the gynander's eyes. How could she have forgotten it? Her prized possession, the secret living thing she had hidden and protected all these months. Before she could think better of it she was at the door, sliding back the bolt with a soft whicker and padding into the hallway, headed for the gravator that would bring her back to Virtues.

She met no one on the way. It was too early for shift-change, and there was seldom much traffic between her own level and Ceryl's, especially at this hour. Once in the pale blue and pink corridors of the hermaphrodites' quarters she raced silently to her room, scarcely waiting for the sentry to bid her enter. Then she was inside.

All was as it had been, the same tangle of clothes and cosmetics, the same thick smell of unwashed bedcovers. A few flecks of plastic had peeled from the ceiling, and the dim lighting flickered as though the current had wavered in the last few hours. Otherwise there was no sign but that this was any other evening, with Reive returning late from an inquisition. She stepped breathlessly to where she had hidden the mysid's globe behind her narrow bed, reached down and withdrew it.

Inside the orb of dusty glass the little creature floated, its translucent skin almost silvery in the uneven light. When Reive touched the globe with one eager finger the mysid stirred, darted to the bottom of its tiny cage with legs beating fiercely.

"It's all right," Reive whispered, hugging the globe to her breast. "We didn't forget you, we came back. . . ."

In a pile by the door she found a long scarf of iridescent blue cloth. Carefully she wrapped the globe in this, then gave a last look about her room. Her cosmetics box lay on the floor where she had left it, and there were her favorite gold chains, the little tin where she kept rings and earrings and odd bits of cloth for binding up her hair. She had a strange certainty that she would not be back here, but if she carried the mysid in its globe she would have room for nothing else. Finally she headed for the door, trying to hold the glass bowl tightly but casually, as though she carried nothing but a wad of cloth.

The hallway was still empty, but as she rounded the corner where the gravator waited she heard voices, shrill laughter, and Drusilla's nasal squeal—

"—must have found somebody! Let's bang on her door and find out—"

With a smothered cry Reive ran the last few feet to the gravator, moaning softly as precious water spilled from the globe to soak her chest. Then the doors were opening, nearly blinding light poured from the conveyance as she stumbled inside and, gasping, bade the gravator return to Ceryl's level.

"Where the hell have you been?"

Ceryl stood inside the doorway, her eyes wild, smelling strongly of cheap brandy. "I've been up for an hour, I—"

Only of course she couldn't admit just what had terrified her—the thought that the gynander had left to betray her and her treasonous dreams to the Orsinate. But here was Reive, disheveled as Ceryl herself, clutching a sodden knot of blue cloth and panting.

"We—we are sorry, we forgot something—"

She stepped into the room. Ceryl closed the door behind her and reached for a tiny glass of some bronze liquid. She took a sip, staring at the bundle in Reive's hands, then asked, "Well, what is it? You know you could have been detained if you'd been stopped—"

"We saw no one," Reive replied sullenly. She had thought she could return and find a new hiding place for her treasure. That would be impossible, now.

"Well?" Ceryl shook her glass impatiently, sending the spirits inside whirling in a diminutive vortex.

Reive sighed, defeated, then slowly unwrapped the globe and set it on a table.

"What the hell is *that*?" Ceryl bent over the bowl, her tone more bemused than angry. Moisture pooled down the sides; it seemed to be half-full of cloudy water, and something like a bluish tear hung suspended in its center.

"It's a—our—it's a mysid. A shrimp."

"A shrimp," Ceryl repeated. She glanced at the gynander, her childish face pale and nearly tearful, then back at the globe. "Is it—wherever did you get it?"

"The vivariums," Reive said miserably. "A patron gave it to us, as payment for a reading."

Ceryl stooped so that she could peer more closely into the small bowl. Inside the frail creature darted about, its feathery fins beating the water to a reddish blur. "You've kept it? As a—as a pet?" When she looked up the gynander was staring at her, terrified. With a pang Ceryl realized that Reive thought she would get rid of the thing—toss it down the septic line or turn Reive in for illegal possession of vivarium property.

Reive nodded, rubbing her eyes. "It needs more water. Some spilled on the way here." She pointed at the scarf leaving a sodden blot on the floor at her feet.

"Yes—well, there's water in the kitchen reservoir, let's refill it."

"No." The gynander shook her head. "That would kill it—the water has to stand for a few days. That's what the woman told me."

Ceryl sipped thoughtfully at her brandy. "Of course. Well, I can get you the right kind of water," she said at last. "From my workchambers on the vivarium level. How long have you had it?"

"A few months. It's going to have babies—see? That's an egg-sac." She stuck a grubby finger on the edge of the globe, then said shyly, "Its name is Gato."

Ceryl gazed at the clot of tiny pearls beneath the mysid's thorax, then back at the gynander. Sudden pity washed over her—to think of anyone, even a hermaphrodite, keeping such a pathetic thing for a pet! and completely forbidden, as well. Unaccountably she thought of Giton, the trouble he took with his few belongings, his prized holo showing himself and Ceryl outside the Cathedral of Christ Cadillac one festival day.

After a moment she said, "We'll have to find someplace to keep it. Where it won't be seen. What does it eat?"

Reive looked up at her, her pale eyes wide with relief. "Anything. Rice crackers, mostly. Sometimes krill paste."

"It would probably prefer some kind of fish nutriment." Ceryl stood, a little unsteadily, and placed her empty brandy glass back on a shelf. "Tomorrow, I'll bring some water back, and something for it to eat."

At the door to her bedroom she paused. The gynander still knelt beside the globe, looking more childlike than ever with her thin dark hair unbound, her white face pressed close to the glass. Ceryl nodded, once, to herself, then said, "Would you—would you like to sleep in here, with me? There's more room, I mean you could probably sleep better—"

Slowly the gynander raised her head, brushed a tendril of hair from her cheek. She nodded, shyly, and reached to stroke the glass a final time.

For a few more minutes Ceryl waited, until at last the gynander rose and crossed to join her. Ceryl looked back at the globe, gleaming pale green and blue in the half-light, the mysid floating dreamily in its clouded center. Then she turned to Reive and shut the door behind them.

By next morning Reive had settled in. Ceryl wouldn't let her go back down to her own room to retrieve her belongings. Reive didn't care about the clothes; she found a few scarves among Ceryl's things, some understated jewelry, and a pair of sandals that almost fit. But cosmetics were another matter. After a heated discussion, Ceryl arranged to have a box sent over from the pleasure cabinet's private spa. Reive squealed and hid behind a mirror for the next few hours, delighting in expensive powders and liquid maquillage, kohl and real gold dust that she applied liberally to her cheeks and shoulders.

Best of all, there was a gravator that went up to Cherubim and Seraphim, the highest levels of Araboth. She removed the wards she had drawn upon her breasts and painstakingly outlined the Orsinate's heraldic eye and Prophet Rayburn's crucifix.

Ceryl watched her, smiling. She too felt better today. The gynander seemed genuinely happy; betrayal seemed as unlikely as the sudden destruction of the city. Her sleep had been untroubled for the first time in weeks. Maybe her luck had finally changed. Maybe she had just needed to share her fears with another person.

Still, before she left to go back down to her workchambers she warned Reive against going out alone.

"You don't know your way around here yet." She felt a slight twinge, knowing that the real reason was her doubts as to the gynander's loyalty. "And sentries can be aggressive about checking newcomers."

"We want to go see the palace."

Ceryl sighed in exasperation. "The palace! But surely you've seen it on the 'files—"

Reive tossed a kohl wand into her cosmetics case. "It's not the same." She took a mango from a basket and peeled it sullenly. "We've never been to the upper levels before, why should we stay cooped up in here all day?"

"But if you're not registered for this level, the gravator won't let you in. They could do a trace on you, which means you'll be detained by the Reception Committee—"

"We're registered under the Orsinate," Reive said. "We're allowed free commerce on all levels, as long as we're somebody's guest." Her tone turned pleading but her eyes held a trace of belligerence.

Ceryl turned, defeated, and went to gather her things. "If they detain you I can't do much to help. . . ."

Reive shrugged and took another bite of mango. At the door Ceryl paused and said, "I'll be back—I don't know when. This evening, probably. *Please* don't go out alone—"

As soon as she was gone the gynander dressed, sprinkled a few flecks of rice cracker into the mysid's bowl, and headed for the gravator.

Ceryl's chambers were in a block of affluent residential buildings, pagoda-shaped and shining with blue and red lacquer. The air smelled of lemons, and banners proclaiming an Ascendant triumph over the Commonwealth hung limply from the corners of the pagodas. Between each block ran spacious avenues, crowded with rickshaws bearing members of the pleasure cabinet to and from the gravators. Everyone seemed short-tempered, even more so than one might expect bored aristocrats to be. This close to Æstival Tide, the competition for invitations to purification ceremonies and the more elite parties grew intense. In a day or two the scroll listing those who would join the Orsinate on their private viewing platform would be released. Until then, cabinet members and advisers, lesser relatives of the ruling family and even a few ambitious interlopers from the lower levels would all be scrambling for the opportunity to gain access to the margravines and Imperators.

Some members of the pleasure cabinet already wore the slender fillets of brass and malachite that were one of the first heralds of the Feast of Fear. They elbowed their way past the others disdainfully. Reive recognized a high-ranking diplomat who had been briefly famous during the Archipelago Conflict, and a woman who was lead soprano in the sadist opera

Fasa. No one seemed to find it curious that a gynander wandered about unchaperoned. Once Reive saw another hermaphrodite, bouncing around in the back of a rickshaw with an austere-looking man whose black gowns marked him as a vicar in the Church of Christ Cadillac. Reive waved discreetly, but the other hermaphrodite looked through her with slanted agate eyes. After that Reive cultivated a cool expression, following the traffic and trying not to stare.

There was a bottleneck at the gravator that serviced Seraphim, the uppermost level where the palace stood. Diplomats clambered from their rickshaws, waving invitations at each other as they argued over who had seniority and their drivers demanded payment. When a scuffle broke out between the vicar and one of the eunuch followers of the Daughters of Graves, Reive slipped toward the front of the queue unnoticed.

The line moved quickly as the gravator's sentry processed each person. When her turn came Reive approached it nervously. Sentries were unknown on the lower levels, since gravators there did not ordinarily service the rarefied reaches of the Orsinate and their cabinet. An awning of faux bamboo hung above the entrance, yolk-yellow military banners stirring in a breath of breeze emerging from the chamber's vents. The sentry was a smooth cylinder of yellow metal, faceless. It beckoned Reive with a long metal arm containing a tiny optic that glittered as it made a pass across her face. A long moment while she heard it whirring as it accessed her retina print. Then it sighed, "Reive Orsina. Pass."

Inside, the gravator was opulent, but so crowded that all Reive glimpsed of it was a marble floor, scuffed and rather dirty, and overhead a chandelier made up of myriad holograms that showed the margravines' faces shimmering and smiling down upon their disgruntled staff. Reive squeezed in between a member of the Toxins Cabal, a plump woman whose sweat smelled of fenugreek and bleach, and a Disciple of Blessed Narouz, the Orsinate's heraldic eye dangling conspicuously from his neck. When the gravator began its smooth ascent he leaned against Reive, leaving a smear of petroleum along her arm.

In a few minutes they had reached their destination. Reive was expecting something—music, an announcement—but the doors only slid open and everybody walked out, with a little less shoving than on the lower levels but a few more sidelong glances. The Disciple of Blessed Narouz tried to push a flyer into her hand as he left, Blessed Narouz's swarthy face scowling and gesturing from its surface, but Reive hurried past him.

At the apex of Araboth's ziggurat, Seraphim was the smallest of the city's levels—though still vast—and more wonderful than Reive could ever have imagined. She blinked, stumbling as she tried to find a place to stand and gape. Brilliant light filled the air, a light that was truly golden. Looking up she saw huge curved banks of lamps set within the domes, so near that the reflections of things on Seraphim could be seen faintly, like flaws in glass. A faint tinkling sound filled the air, ambient music commissioned from one of the countless artists the Orsinate retained as permanent guests of the Reception Committee. A heady, complex smell wafted up from vents in the walkway —lavender essence and amber musk, an underlying note of oranges and the faintest wisp of opium smoke. Reive stood a few feet from the gravator, trying to catch her breath. After several minutes she felt even more dazed, and happier than she had ever been in her life.

"Are you engaged, holy child?" A soft voice crooned beside her. Reive started, looking up into the violet eyes of the *galli*, the eunuch who had been in the gravator a few minutes before. His hair was dyed the same shade of deep blue as his robes, his palms stained red.

"Oh! Ye-es, yes, we are meeting someone—" She rubbed her eyes as though she had just awakened, then stared perturbed at the kohl smudged on her hand.

"Ah." The *galli* nodded, his high voice betraying a giggle. "I understand. You are here for purely social reasons."

He smiled kindly, then taking Reive's arm pointed to where a path of stones and glass laid in an intricate mosaic twisted into the distance. He lowered his voice to a shrill whisper and said, "Many people find the Walk of Memorable Incidents to be an instructive way to begin their visit here."

Reive stammered her thanks, but the *galli* only placed a finger to his rouged lips, murmuring, "Keep your eyes lowered here, holy child. Remember our margravines are sensitive to eyes like yours—"

He drew up his blue robes and raised one hand, exposing a scarlet palm. "May you come safely through the Feast of Fear," he said, and walked off.

Reive waved at him limply. Her exhilaration began to fade. She yawned. A heavy tiredness seeped into her, like smoking kef or inhaling fine incense at one of the better sort of dream inquisitions. She started in the direction the *galli* had pointed and began to wander along the Walk of Memorable Incidents. Apart from several scenes depicting carnage from the Commonwealth and the Hâbilis Emirate, the most memorable image on the mosaic path showed Roland Orsina embracing Melissa Sirrúk, his wife and partner in founding the Orsinate dynasty. Reive kept her head down, absorbed in the bright pictures. After a few yards the mosaic depicted another scene, this one of Sirrúk's funeral pyre, the masses mourning her bizarre and untimely death by choking on a whole pear. A few feet farther on Melissa's first successor appeared, her face picked out in chips of chalcedony and tourmaline, but by then Reive had lost interest in the path.

There was so much more to see. All of Seraphim was laid out atop a pavement of smooth marble, with pathways like brightly colored channels sweeping through it. Here and there were grids of intricate geometric shapes, blue and yellow and purple tiles, or expanses of highly polished stone, agate and obsidian and tiger's eye, white jade and rounded steps of soft cinnabar. Sculptures from the Orsinate's famed collection were everywhere, and fountains spewing jets of scented water into pools where pop-eyed koi swam languidly, waiting to be fed. In the distance Reive saw men and women in beautifully tailored cutaway suits and robes of silk jacquard. They seemed to stalk about purposefully, like figures in a puppet opera. Compared to the rancid air and garish neon of Virtues Level it was all quite stunning, miraculous in fact. She marveled that Ceryl ever returned to Dominations.

But after a little while Reive slowed her walking. The daylights hurt her eyes. Brilliant reflections bounced from the polished walkways, too bright and too hot. When she stopped to admire one of the fountains, its scent seemed harsh, the smell of jasmine cut with an unpleasant chemical odor. The ambient music grew annoying as well. Reive found herself missing the sudden shrieks and whistles that greeted her when she visited Dominations, the brackish smell of the oceanic tanks and Zalophus's bellowing. Even the koi, with their golden scales and extravagantly furbelowed fins, seemed demanding, rushing to nibble at her fingers dangling in the water.

She was thinking that perhaps she might return to the gravator, when a long electrified wail drowned out the plashing fountains. It was a sound Reive recognized from the evening 'files: the signal for the arrival of new prisoners. She looked around and saw that most of the other strollers were pointing in the direction of the siren. They gathered in small excited groups, then began walking more quickly, all heading for what seemed to be a broad white avenue. Reive flicked one of the greedy koi from her hand and hurried after the crowd.

At first she kept her eyes downcast, remembering the *galli*'s advice. But it soon became apparent that no one was paying Reive the slightest attention, and so she looked around.

The boulevard was wide, nearly as wide as whole residential blocks on some of the lower levels, and made of a false marble cool and smooth and golden-veined as the real thing. Vents in the pavement released the scents of lemon and frangipani. But beneath the strong citrusy tang was another odor—the smell of the sea, stronger here than it ever was below, even in the vivariums. For a moment Reive shut her eyes, trying to imagine herself back on Dominations. When she opened them again she stopped in amazement.

Once Reive had met a poet from the pleasure cabinet who carried with him a beautiful piece of ephemera, a pagoda of brass and bamboo that housed a copper-jointed cricket that sang like a lark. That cricket-house had been a model of the building that loomed before her now. Gates of gold and vermillion and lapis rose behind snowy arches. Huge winged telamons upheld each of the palace's nine levels. From every corner spun glittering spires of blue and gold, so long and fine and shining it was a wonder they did not dissolve into mist. At its very peak, seemingly inches from the central of the Quincunx Domes, two statues soared. The first was of gold, a winged figure holding a trumpet. It had been salvaged from the Or-sinate's ancestral city after the Long Night. Beside it reared a second statue, the golden crucifix upon which Prophet Rayburn hung, smiling beatifically. Reive had always been confused by this symbol, since it was well known that Prophet Rayburn had been garroted by his own daughter Livia, and it was *she* who had actually been crucified, by her cousin-german Sejanus Orsina, nicknamed The Unruly. The twin statues made a stirring site, seeming to impale the very roof of Araboth, so near that Reive's head pounded to look at it. By means of the Architects' arcane machinery, spectral lightning lanced down from the domes to strike the winged figure and the smiling Prophet, sending waves of blue and violet rippling across the boulevard.

For the next hour Reive did nothing but watch the lightning play about the palace. She was afraid to go any nearer; afraid that some of the calm-looking men and women walking up and down the palace steps might actually be members of the Reception Committee alert to the presence of an uninvited guest. When she grew tired of standing she found a bench of hammered copper and sat there by herself, wishing that she had brought some mangoes with her.

That was Reive's first day on Seraphim.

"No one questioned you?" Ceryl asked, astonished, when she returned that evening.

Reive shook her head. "No one paid any attention to us."

"No sentries?"

"Only in the gravator, and it let us pass. They have fish there that will eat from your hands. But it is too bright, it gave us a headache."

In spite of that she returned the next day. This time she remembered to bring mangoes, and a small bottle of aqua vitae she found in Ceryl's liquor cabinet. Again the gravator sentry whispered, "Reive Orsina. Pass." Again she was ignored by everyone, save a small girl walking with her replicant guardian. The child spat at Reive and made the sign against Ucalegon when she passed.

When Reive awoke the third morning, Ceryl was already dressed, in a severe suit of black satin with tiny buttons of green jade down the front. Upon her brow she wore a brass and malachite fillet, her sole concession to the upcoming festival.

The somber clothes matched her mood. When Reive yelled to one of the servers to bring her kehveh and fruit, Ceryl hushed her impatiently.

"I'll probably be late today," she said, rifling through a stack of credit disks and several invitations on parchment and allurian cards. "There's a ceremony I have to attend. There'll be some kind of reception afterward, and Shiyung always gets a headache after a party."

"Can we go with you?" Reive pulled a sheet close about her and cocked her head. "It's nearly Æstival Tide, no one will notice us—"

"No!" Ceryl shoved credit disks and cards into a pocket. "It's too dangerous, Reive. It's a military ceremony, the margravines will be there. You'd be bored. And look, there's 'files here neither of us has ever seen, and—"

Reive glowered. Ceryl hesitated, then said, "And I'll get you an invitation to something—something special, I promise."

Reive glared as Ceryl hurried out the door. For a few minutes the gynander lay on the divan, staring balefully at the ceiling. A military ceremony, with the margravines. The Feast of Fear was practically here already, and Ceryl wanted to keep her imprisoned. She sulked for a quarter hour, then throwing the sheets on the floor she slid from the divan. She dressed quickly, painting her face cursorily and braiding her hair into a single long plait. She thought of leaving Ceryl a disdainful note, something along the lines of *See You At The Palace*, but decided against it. She was in such a hurry that she forgot to take anything to eat or drink.

There was not much of a crowd at the gravators that morning. Many of the cabinet members had finally obtained their invitations and found temporary lodgings as palace guests, or within one of the Imperators' elaborate pagodas. The few aristocrats Reive saw this morning were on foot. Most rickshaw drivers refused to work this close to the feast; they had already retired to their own ritual preparations below. The remaining cabinet members milled about rather desperately, their snatches of conversation shrill—

". . . said she *loved* the work I'd done on the hecatombs ten years ago and *of course* there'd be a seat for me—"

"—stole it right out of my hands!"

". . . so I explained then that *I* wasn't actually a *Disciple*, only *curious*, but you know how they are . . ."

This subdued mood extended to their passage into the gravator. Reive even got a seat this time; but she had grown so blasé that she sat with her eyes closed, humming to herself.

The trip went quickly. There was little conversation, no proselytizing priests or disciples. The fretful cabinet members eyed Reive distrustfully where she sat alone on a marble bench. When the gravator finally stopped they stood aside fastidiously and permitted her to leave first. Reive mistook their caution for respect. She did not notice how one of them made the sign against Ucalegon as she passed, or how another pointed furtively at her eyes.

Outside, Reive was startled to see the same sort of crowd that she usually found below during one of the lesser festivals. Men selling pappadams and fried cuttlefish, girls sitting cross-legged on the ground in front of steaming pots of black tea and kehveh. Several grubby-looking moujik children wearing discarded janissary's uniforms were hawking banners, black and red and with the toothéd wave that symbolized Ucalegon blocked on them in vivid green. There were *galli* from the Daughters of Graves dispensing prayer wheels and blessings for a small fee, and one of the white-skirted Disciples of Blessed Narouz's Refinery shouting in the 'filers' dialect, seemingly to himself. A solitary Aviator stood broodingly, the sleek black mask of her sensory enhancer covering her face as the crowd parted around her, priests and diplomats alike falling silent in her shadow. Someone had set up a little stall selling figures of the Compassionate Redeemer made of marzipan, its evil spade-shaped head and gaping mouth bright pink, its long saurian's tail dusted with golden flecks of opium sugar. With a start Reive recognized a hermaphrodite from Virtues, a pasty-faced morph who had never been very popular either with clients or her own kind. Pushing aside a plump *galli*, Reive hurried away before she could be seen, head bowed as she stared resolutely at her feet.

She ended up on an unfamiliar spur of the main boulevard. There were no strollers here, not even any of the omnipresent replicants walking the countless Orsina bastards. But the boulevard did not seem empty. Sculptures lined the broad avenue, stasis anaglyphs executed by the adolescent prodigy Karvo Solicitas. Their subject matter was uniformly morbid, scenes of executions and torment, the sort of thing made popular during the current regime. Reive stared at them bemused and walked on. In the distance the palace glowed white and gold in the simulated sunlight. She squinted, trying to see if the ceremony had started yet.

"You find Karvo's work dull?" a voice croaked beside her.

Reive jumped and looked around nervously, seeing nobody. Finally she glanced down. A very small man, a dwarf actually, stood gazing up at her with mild round eyes of a vivid, childlike blue.

"Um—yes, we, uh—" she said, glancing back uneasily at the sculptures. "Very dull!"

"I've always found him insipid myself," the dwarf confided. He gazed up at her as though she had said something quite insightful. "This whole mania for torture: idiotic, don't you think? The banality of evil and all that." He began to walk with a peculiar rolling gait toward the next little square, looking back at her expectantly.

"Yes, of course," she said, and followed him.

"Now this at least demonstrates a more mature grasp of the sculptor's art," the dwarf said thoughtfully. He pointed to three monolithic pandoramas, multidimensional images of men and women illuminated in ghastly greens and blues. As they watched the huge shapes moved with painful slowness, contorting themselves in baroque and tormented poses.

At the last image the dwarf halted. The moving figures froze, then one groaned the name of the piece.

"*Mormo*," it said, and resumed its posturing.

"*Mormo*," the dwarf repeated, as though Reive might not have heard. "Late Kendall Browning—one of his last, as a matter of fact, before that tragedy with the poisoned apples. Always unwise to eat fruit with the Orsinate. Now I think that *Mormo* approaches the truly horrifying, not just the horrible. Don't you agree?"

Reive grimaced. The pandorama showed the gigantic figure of a man devouring another, smaller man whose piteous screams were blunted by the sound of the giant's teeth cracking his ribs. Time had caused the pandorama to suffer some fallout, so that the image fizzed and popped and every few moments the sound faded. Reive quickly looked away, and caught the dwarf staring at her with an intense expression shaded with something like approval.

"Strong stuff, eh?" he remarked, and began walking once more.

"Ye-es," Reive replied, trying not to look back at the gruesome scene. They strolled for a few minutes in silence, Reive relaxing when they came to a fountain that smelled strongly of lime blossom.

"You're new here," the dwarf said a few minutes later. Reive was splashing water on her face. She glanced at the dwarf, then wiping her cheeks she nodded.

"Interesting eyes," he said. He pressed his fingers to his forehead and bowed. "Rudyard Planck, always a pleasure."

Reive stared at him, suddenly recalling Ceryl's warnings. But the dwarf only stared at her with a slightly amused expression. Finally she said, "We are Reive."

"Reive," the dwarf repeated. He had hair of a dark reddish hue, like brick dust, and wore beautifully cut trousers of azure velvet and a vest trimmed with brilliant green piping. Around his neck dangled a heavy gold chain hung with the heraldic eye and letter ☾ of the pleasure cabinet. Something about him— perhaps the way he walked, with a hint of a swagger, or maybe it was that lurid green trim about his vest— struck Reive as being not so much the mark of a dandy as of a potentially dangerous individual playing at being one.

"Well, Reive, it is always a pleasure to talk with a fellow art lover."

His voice dropped ironically. He bowed again and for a moment held her hand. His grasp was surprisingly solid for one so small. "I have to go now—some tedious business about our new Military Commandant Imperator—but I hope to see you again soon."

Reive nodded dumbly, waving after him. She waited several minutes, until the little figure was lost to sight among the crowd gathering in the distance. Then she followed him down the boulevard, until at last she stood on the promenade that fanned in front of the Orsinate's palace.

Beneath her feet the pale marble glistened, still damp from having been hosed earlier. Blue lightning whipped about the twin statues atop the palace, sending shivers of light across the dome. The air crackled, the scent of ozone nearly overpowering the scents of frangipani and lemon, ginger blossom and expensive cologne. Most of the vendors seemed to have moved here, and Reive was surprised to see many other commoners as well. The inevitable 'filers, of course, they would be at any public ceremony of note. But gynanders too, and biotechnicians still in their yolk-yellow smocks; somber women from the Chambers of Mercy and a small knot of moujiks glaring suspiciously at the splendor around them. She even glimpsed a solitary *rasa*, shuffling past in a faded set of clothes that no longer fit, its face set in that horrible rictus all *rasas* had, its sunken eyes flecked with luminous phosphorescence. Everyone looked uneasy, as though they had been plucked from their own levels and whisked up here, which was close to the truth of it. The Orsinate never wasted a major ceremony on their own staff. A few gaping moujiks and socially ambitious gynanders, the usual complement of eager 'filers—by the time they all returned to the tedium of their own levels, even the dullest execution or promotion would seem extravagant.

But this looked to be an extraordinary ceremony, even for the Orsinate. Anticipation shimmered in the air like heat. Reive could hear it in the whispered gossip of the *galli*, see it in the wide eyes of the courtesans and vavasours calling to each other eagerly from the palace steps. To keep the peace, members of the Reception Committee roamed about in their pin-striped suits. The entire Urban Cohort had been deployed. Reive ducked behind a column as a watchman rolled past, huge and shining as one of the Aviator's aerocraft. Its immense metal head swiveled back and forth as it surveyed the promenade with its seven glittering eyes, and the pavement groaned beneath its weight.

When it was gone Reive stepped back onto the boulevard, subdued. The air had grown uncomfortably warm, the reek of the unseen ocean so thick she tasted it in the back of her throat. She thought of Ceryl, and looked around, foolishly hoping she might see her in the mob. But she saw nothing but seething faces and the occasional banner with Ucalegon's fangéd wave thrust above the crowd. Her head thrummed; her eyes watered from the smoke drifting up from the vents. From the palace steps she could hear nervous laughter. Snatches of song trilled from a wireless.

"Welcome the Healing Wind!"

Someone jounced into her. A young coenbite,

one of the novitiates who performed the ritual vivi-
sections and other research functions in the Chambers
of Mercy. Her eyes were wild, her hand stippled with
blood where she clutched a jagged piece of plastic. A
crude version of the Orsinate's heraldic emblem had
been painted on it, but with a lurid red line streaked
across the eye. Beneath it swirled the gaudy whorls
that symbolized Baratdaja the Healing Wind. "Death
from Outside!" she shrieked.

Reive shoved her way past, ducking as the
coenbite swung the sheet of plastic like a scythe. Behind her a man screamed and someone else laughed;
but Reive was gone, forcing her way toward where
the promenade ended in a cul-de-sac in front of the
palace.

The crowd here was marginally more subdued.
There were more priests—lesser functionaries from
the Church of Christ Cadillac, wearing the chromium
skullcaps of their faith; a number of indigo-clad *galli*
from the Daughters of Graves, whistling and bowing
before three huge cutout images of the margravines
dangling from the front of the palace; several dozen
Disciples of Blessed Narouz, their pale skirts cutting a
wide white swath through the jumble of blue robes
and silver chrome. Near the front of the crowd was a
small group of coenbites, their yolk-yellow robes
bloodstained and torn from their ecstasies. Reive hastily retreated behind the *galli*, who seemed more intent
upon a large hubble-bubble that they circled, giggling
and smoking earnestly.

"Will you join us, holy child?" a *galli* called out to
her. He made two circles with his fingers and brought
them to his face like spectacles, then indicated Reive's
eyes. His laughter was not unkind.

Reive smiled shyly and shook her head. The *galli*
shrugged and turned back to the waterpipe. The gynander felt a pang that they had not been more insistent—she could have been persuaded to join them.
She wished she had been able to find Ceryl in the

crowd. She wished she had stayed to talk with that other hermaphrodite, back by the gravator.

Everything here was overwhelming, almost frightening. She had been so young during last Æstival Tide, only four years old and still in the hermaphrodites' creche on Virtues. All this clamor brought back her fear—the sight of the margravines, more beautiful and terrifying than she could imagine; the anticipation at the Lahatiel Gate, waiting for the huge doors to open onto the strand Outside; the charnel-house stench of the Compassionate Redeemer, masked by the smell of burning roses. She hugged her arms close to her chest and walked off by herself, staring at the palace gates.

From here she could pick out figures on the steps. Diplomats nodding coolly to each other. Emirate delators wringing their hands. Beside the lower entrances the Hierophantic Guard stood at attention, incense braziers burning at their feet. On an open colonnade near the main entrance, the Toxins Cabal had gathered to drink kehveh from tiny egg-shaped cups, pompous with their vocoders and lingua francas bleating and blinking. The pleasure cabinet spilled onto the patio, and Reive tried to spot Ceryl's drab suit among the luminous gowns and greatcoats. Over all of it the eerie blue lightning flickered with the faintest crackling sound, as though someone tapped softly but insistently upon the domes arching overhead.

More and more people arrived. Diplomats and counselors and the entire Linguistics Cabal, myriad Orsinate bastards with their replicant guardians and court favorites in yellow mufti. Reive saw the dwarf Rudyard Planck at the very edge of the colonnade, shaking his head as a tall woman bent to whisper in his ear. Then suddenly a tinny fanfare blasted from the wireless speakers. Reive stood on tiptoe to see the Imperators parading from the palace gates. All seven of them, their yolk-yellow formal robes and scarlet sashes swaying about their legs. The last one, Sajur

Panggang the Architect Imperator, wore a malachite band around his neck and emerald mourning bands on his wrists. They walked slowly to the front of the colonnade and stood there, acknowledging the cheers of the crowd with restrained nods.

It grew very quiet. The Toxins Cabal put down their little porcelain cups and stood in attentive silence. The members of the pleasure cabinet grew still, and turned their heads toward the main gate. Reive glanced back at the huge crowd gathered on the promenade. Banners hung limply above them, and thin streamers of dark smoke. Directly behind her the *galli* and Disciples and pontifices of Christ Cadillac seemed unusually alert, considering the abandoned hubble-bubbles and splintered remnants of candicaine pipettes that surrounded them.

Suddenly the air throbbed with a hollow wailing siren, as though the monstrous sculpture *Mormo* had been given voice. The echo died, then blared again. On the steps the diplomats and cabal members turned to the main gate, their faces taut. The crowd around Reive moved forward, but only a little; as though afraid to get too close to the palace. One of Blessed Narouz's Disciples jostled the gynander. When she protested he looked down at her, then with a low cry moved away, making the ward against Ucalegon. As the siren wailed a third and final time, Reive hugged her arms close to her and wished she was back in her little room on Virtues.

Beneath the lapis-crowned arches of the main gate a woman stepped forward. She wore the dress leathers of an Aviator, crimson and black. Her sensory enhancer was pushed back onto her forehead like a crown. From her black-gloved hands rose a black standard, a huge triangular pennon emblazoned with a luminous silver moon. Across the moon was flung a pointed shape, like a spear or javelin, and flickering silver letters spelled out the motto of the defenders of the Ascendant Autocracy:

NASNA

Oderint dum metuant

Let them hate, so long as they fear.

A moment later the Aviators marched through
the gate.

Against the palace's pale walls their gleaming
leather jackets glowed deep crimson, like the inside of
a beast's mouth. The creak of their leathers echoed in
the silence, a raw wind from the stars, and their
metal-soled boots clashed like hail against the marble.
From their brows their sensory enhancers rose like
crowns of black glass and steel and sent darts of reflected lightning slashing through the air. The crowd
gathered on the colonnade shrank from their ap-
proach, and Reive could hear all around her murmured imprecations to Blessed Narouz.

She shuddered. Without the enhancers to cover
them, she could see what usually was hidden in those
faces, something dreadful that the Aviators had
glimpsed and now carried behind their eyes. Many of
them were horribly scarred; but they refused surgery
to correct their deformities, preferring to bear them
into the fastnesses of space as grim reminders of their
human origin. The bottom half of one woman's face
had been blown away. Steel and raw bone gaped beneath her upper jaw, and livid red tubes coiled about
her neck. Her eyes as they gazed up at the NASNA
standard were cold and dead as the dome's false sky.

There were not many of the Aviators—Reive
counted forty—but they seemed to fill the entire colonnade. The air that drifted down from them smelled

of smoke and burning metal, and, very faintly, of charred meat.

Reive felt sick. She looked around to see if there was a way out of the crowd. Beside her two women from the Toxins Cabal whispered to each other. One of them caught Reive's eye and stared back at her, the vocoder in her throat blinking yellow. She wore thigh-high boots of sullen yellow plasteen and a soiled fez. A grub-white puppet clung to her shoulder. It glared at the gynander, then very slowly opened its mouth to display a hideous pulpy throat.

Reive swallowed. But when the woman with the puppet continued to stare she took a deep breath, then asked, "What is it? What's happening?"

"Don't tell her, don't tell her," the puppet hissed.

"A promotion ceremony," the woman replied. She gazed at Reive curiously, as though trying to recall where they might have met. The vocoder in her throat pulsed deep crimson as she slapped the puppet's muzzle. "The new Aviator Imperator has been named by the Autocracy. The margravines are going to invest him."

"A promotion," Reive repeated, and looked away.

On the colonnade, the Aviator's standard-bearer turned to face the main gate. Above the huge doorway graven letters began to glow, gold and then brilliant adamant, until the Ascendants' motto shone out over the crowd like a fouga's watchlights:

Let Us Raise A Somewhat Loftier Strain!

From the ground at Reive's feet came a loud hiss. She gasped and stepped backward, then felt the chilly mist rising from enhancement ventricles in the pavement. A heavy sweet incense, like that used in the rites at Church Cadillac—myrrh, she thought at first, or pangloss. Laughter and curses as the narcotic fumes enveloped the crowd. Reive tried to hold her breath but gave up, gasping. The sweet scent burned the back of her throat, the chemicals flooding her system so quickly that her fingers felt numb and her eyes teared. But after a few breaths she felt amazingly elated; it *was* pangloss. All around her people beamed and nodded. The *galli* laughed and hugged each other. Even the dour Disciples of Blessed Narouz grinned and removed their fezes. Reive found herself beaming at the woman with the puppet, the puppet itself silenced by the euphoric incense but still glowering. When the gynander looked up again the crowd on the palace steps was cheering wildly.

Three figures strode across the plaza, tall and thin and wearing identical suits of video-gray sharkskin, severely cut. Conical crowns upon their foreheads made them seem even taller, crowns of gold bound with chrome and steel and embossed with the twin sigils of the Prophets Rayburn and Mudhowi Sirrúk. Reive screamed along with the rest of the mob, pumping her fists in the air. The scent of pangloss grew thicker as the crowd shouted three names, the voices of the Aviators ringing above the others until the domes thundered with the sound—

Shiyung and Nike and Âziz Orsina.

The Seraphim of Araboth: the Orsinate.

One by one the three sisters bowed, their crowns winking in the harsh light.

"Which one is—" Reive choked, grabbing the woman next to her; but then one of the figures on the plaza stepped forward, arms upraised. Sapphire lightning danced above her as she smiled.

"Shiyung!" the woman beside Reive screamed, the puppet whickering on her shoulder. "Shiyung!"

Reive nodded mutely. Of course. She should have recognized her from the nightly broadcasts—the ghee-yellow skin, the enormous slanted eyes, the mouth so thin and delicate that a particularly intricate form of calligraphy bore her name. Gazing upon her now, the gynander's eyes filled with tears. She was so exquisitely beautiful, so *good*.

Shiyung Orsina. Not the ruler in name of Araboth, but the beloved of the people, the idol of the Aviators and the Children of Mercy, the lover of all those princes and women and soldiers whose ashes now mingled with the fine sandalwood powder she brushed upon her shoulders each evening, before she took into her bed the next of her countless lovers. She stood before them with her arms upheld triumphantly and let the lightning play in the air above her head, laughing as the crowd cheered her and the Aviators shouted *"Shiyung!"* until finally Âziz stepped forward and with a tight little smile took her sister's hand. Nike remained a few feet away from them, gazing distractedly up at the domes. Âziz cleared her throat. Then,

"Greetings, Seraphim! Cherubim and Thrones and Dominations, Virtues and Powers and Principalities!"

Her heavily amplified voice rang out, and the cheering subsided.

"We are here today to celebrate a triumph—to celebrate two triumphs. One of them a military conquest, and the other a scientific victory, no less than a triumph over death itself."

Her words were swallowed by a tremendous roar from the Aviators. Âziz looked startled and glanced at Shiyung. But her sister only smiled. Nike remained standing by herself, nodding thoughtfully.

"A triumph over death itself," Âziz repeated. For an instant Reive thought she glowered at Shiyung; but then Âziz continued, "You will recall that, nearly a year ago, our military forces set out to retake the ancient capital from those barbarians who have held it from us for nearly four hundred years . . ."

Reive recalled no such thing. She had thought the last military expedition was to the Archipelago—or was it the desert?—but then janissary forces went out on maneuvers so often that she had lost count. As for the ancient capital, she could remember only vague rumors. A great weapons storehouse had been there once, but the entire city was guarded by monsters, feral mutated creatures far worse than anything the Ascendants had created in their laboratories.

But these, of course, were rumors. Now it seemed that Âziz was telling them the truth of the matter.

". . . have always known the Capital City to be of unparalleled strategic importance, in addition to the ancient weapons holdings there. Now those weapons are ours: thanks in large part to the bravery and cunning employed by someone who is well known to all of you.

"Single-handedly, this brilliant military hero entered that ghastly place, after his accompanying battalion was slain by traitors within the City itself."

The gynander stood on tiptoe, striving vainly to see this military paragon. Âziz's voice rang out like a clarion, so full of pride and wonder that Reive's scalp prickled.

"There, in the ruins of the ancients, he feigned madness and battled hordes of ghouls—"

Âziz's voice dropped, and she drew a shaking hand to her cheek—

"—there, he was slain by an assassin's bullet."

Âziz lowered her gaze. Behind her the other two margravines stood soberly, Nike staring blankly at the mob, Shiyung so pale beneath her conical crown that it seemed she might faint. In the long silence that followed, the Aviators stirred, their heads moving restively as though seeking the assassin within the crowd, and Reive cowered beneath their probing eyes.

At last Âziz raised her head again. "But we were *not* defeated. By sheerest fortune, a janissary troop and Aviator battalion had been dispatched from Araboth, and arrived just hours after our hero's death. Our troops found no resistance from the cowards and monsters within the City. Those troops are there now, having found and restored the ancient armories and reclaimed the Capital as part of the Ascendant Empire.

"As for the man who made all of this possible— *his* tragedy has been turned into the greater victory. As you well know, my sister, the margravine Shiyung, has long toiled in the Chambers of Mercy, where she has made it her duty to learn all that our Sciences can teach her of the mysteries of life and death. As a new Capital will be born under the Ascendants' rule, so from Shiyung's hands a still greater hero has emerged, our new Aviator Imperator!''

At this a terrible wailing cry raked the air, as the Aviators shrieked and raised their black-clad hands, fingers curling and uncurling in their raptor's salute while lightning flickered in the domes. For a full minute their outcry drowned all other sounds, until Reive felt deafened by it and covered her ears, staring at the ground and trying to keep from weeping with fright.

Then abruptly the Aviators were silenced. Reive looked up warily and saw that Âziz had stepped back on the platform, a helpless expression on her face. Shiyung paced forward, making calming motions toward the Aviators. She stopped and stood with her hands at her sides, her beautiful face lifted so that indigo shadows edged the planes of her cheeks and her eyes were lit by the lightning playing overhead. Behind her Nike and Âziz were silent.

It had grown so quiet that Reive could hear the breathing of everyone around her, the woman with her wheezing puppet, the nervous whispers of the *galli*. On the colonnade the Aviators slowly raised their fists. As though moving in a dream, one by one the margravines returned their salute, and turned to face the main gate.

In the great doorway behind them something appeared, a shadow that resolved into cadaverous figures framed by the gold and lapis columns. The figures paused in the doorway: six aardmen stooping beneath the burden of a long palanquin of jet and steel. About their necks gleamed the monitors that all the Orsinate's personal geneslaves wore, thorns of steel and glittering ampules forming a corona about their anguished faces. Saliva fell from their muzzles in long streams. Even from the boulevard Reive could smell them, carrion and the acrid scent of chemicals draining from their sedative ampules, the cloying smell of the jasmine oil that had been laved onto their flanks. As they waited they tossed their heads, and one howled as the long barbs on its collar tore its neck. Then they stalked onto the plaza, their sloping shoulders raw beneath the palanquin's weight. Reive could feel the woman next to her whispering an imprecation to Blessed Narouz, and somewhere in the crowd a man cried out as the aardmen staggered to the very edge of the raised colonnade.

The palanquin that they carried was tall, set with columns of metal wrapped with shining spikes that branched up like the limbs of a stricken tree. In the center of the litter stood a man. He held two of the columns for balance, and swayed as they bore him forward. Reive shook her head—was this a prisoner? Then she saw that he was not bound. What she had thought were cuffs about his wrists and ankles were actually some sort of enhancers. His face too was covered by a sensory enhancer, its blank black surface whipped with reflecting light. A tunic of crimson leather hung to his knees. One hand was sheathed in crimson leather, but the other was not. It was at that second hand that Reive stared, a hand so pale it had a greenish cast. It was large, with tapering fingers, the skin shiny as though it had been burned and the grafts had not taken well. Blue light winked from a ring as the man raised his hand to adjust his enhancer. He was a very tall man, but somewhat stooped, as though he had for a long time been trapped in some enclosed space. It was an Aviator's enhancer that covered his face, and on his breast shone the Aviators' blighted moon.

When they had reached the end of the plaza the aardmen halted. They lowered the palanquin clumsily, their huge-knuckled paws fumbling over its narrow struts and spars. The margravines watched in silence, though Shiyung's eyes glittered and she smiled rapturously. Several children in the Orsinate's cortege began to cry.

The aardmen crouched beside the litter and glared up at the man, their vestigial tails switching. He turned to face them, but it was impossible to see what he looked like, because of the enhancer covering his face. After a long moment he stepped to the ground. His legs moved stiffly, as though he were unaccustomed to walking. Reive wanted to look away but could not. A sibilant rush came from beneath her feet. The heady incense of pangloss faded; the ventricles began pumping a chill mist that smelled of ozone and adrenoleen. Reive's heart pumped as well, louder and louder until she realized that she was shouting in time to its beat. When she looked around, her head ringing, everyone else was shouting as well.

Slowly the man paced the length of the plaza, until he stood before Shiyung Orsina. The crowd erupted into roars and cheers, and the Aviators began chanting a name.

Reive shivered. Every atom of her being pulsed and her mouth had opened to cry out, but now no sound came. She felt horrible, and deathly cold, as though she had been imprisoned within one of the cells where the *rasas* were regenerated. The adrenoleen made her eyes water. On the colonnade Shiyung cried aloud, her hands sweeping through the air. Reive could not hear her words but the margravine's tone was exultant. As Shiyung laughed the light bounced from her crown in waves of gold and blue.

With short, jerky motions the Aviator greeted her, his fingers curling and opening in the Aviator's salute. The cheers subsided as Shiyung straightened, her face suddenly composed into an austere mask. Clumsy as the aardmen, the Aviator fell to one knee, then rose, took her extended hand, and bent his masked head to mime kissing it.

At that Shiyung smiled—a radiant smile, a smile of utter triumph. She waited until he got to his feet again, then turned, presenting him first to her sisters, then to the other Aviators, and finally to the crowd.

Through all the cheering, Reive still could not make out his name. Her head throbbed as though she had been bludgeoned. The woman beside her was weeping.

Shiyung turned to the Aviator, stood on tiptoe as though she were going to kiss him. Instead her white hands grasped the enhancer covering his face. With a swift motion she removed it and held it up for the crowd to see. Then she smashed the enhancer upon her knee. Eddies of blue sparks fell about her legs. Behind her the man's head remained lowered as Shiyung dropped the shards of the broken mask and raised her white arms. She cried out again, her voice so thin and cruel that the gynander trembled.

An awful dread filled Reive, a sense of such horror and foreboding that not even the rush of adrenoleen could quell it. As the Aviator stepped forward, the remains of his enhancer crunched beneath his boots. Reive could hear the woman beside her whispering a name. When he reached the edge of the plaza the Aviator slowly raised his head.

His face was gone. In its place was a curved plate of red metal. Across its smooth surface reflected lightning streamed like blood. No mouth, no nose, earless, hairless; an unbroken plane of crimson metal, like the face of the most primitive kind of replicant. Only from within this mask two eyes glowed. Human eyes, so pale they were nearly transparent, as though every earthly thought and hope had been flushed from them. The mask was horrifying in its utter impassiveness, all the more so because of the dreadful orbs that stared out from it, like the eyes of a cadaver animated and made to look upon its image in a mirror. Beside Reive the woman babbled, and she heard other horrified voices—

". . . a *rasa*! She made *him* a *rasa*! . . ."

". . . died but rehabilitated him. In her labs—a game, just like a game to—"

". . . revenge, she never forgave him for breaking with her and now look at him . . ."

Reive turned wild-eyed to the woman beside
her—

"But who is he? Who did she do this to?"

—and the puppet shrieked a name,

"Tast'annin, the Aviator Imperator Tast'annin!"

Everywhere Reive heard the name taken up, the
Aviators pounding their feet in unison and shouting
until the very columns of the palace shuddered. Reive
clutched the woman beside her to keep from being
trampled in the crush of people seething forward to
glimpse him—

Tast'annin: the Aviator Imperator Margalis
Tast'annin.

The madman who had once been their greatest
military commander; the Academy student who had
been Shiyung's lover and the victor of the Archipelago Conflict.

But his own recent history was a lie. He had been
no hero in the Capital. Captured and tortured by that
City's keepers, he had been released, insane, and then
had sought to betray his Ascendant masters by seizing
the City for himself. He had died ignobly; but the rest
at least was true—the Ascendant janissaries arrived to
conquer a city already in flames, and had borne him
back to Araboth as a prize for their mistress.

It was all a joke to her. Seeing the corpse of her
lover brought to her on a stinking pallet—his head
blackened with his own blood, brain tissue a gray lace
across his shattered scalp—had she felt any sorrow,
any remorse for him at all?

"Margalis," she had whispered, and bent to
touch the pulp of gray and white beneath his eye.
"My dear Margalis."

And she had laughed, softly at first, and then
more loudly, until her serving girl had fled at the note
of venomous triumph in her voice.

Her vengeance had been carefully worked out.
She had made him a *rasa*, a living corpse subject to
her command—the ideal creature, she had thought,
to be Military Imperator. Now Shiyung stepped back

so that the Aviator Imperator could bow. His voice, heavily amplified and bloodless as a stone, echoed across the boulevard as he greeted the crowd. Beside him Shiyung stood straight and shining as a young girl, her sisters impassive behind her.

The crowd grew momentarily quiet, listening to the *rasa*'s hollow tones. Then, his brief salutation complete, the Aviator Imperator raised his empty face and gave Shiyung a final salute. His hand glowed white as a corpse-candle as it formed a raptor's claws, while all of Seraphim roared.

Only Reive remained silent, staring frightened and confused at the figures on the colonnade.

Because she knew that it was impossible for any *rasa* to feel or express a human emotion, or retain anything but a fleeting memory of its former self.

But—somehow, impossibly—the eyes that stared at Shiyung from within this Aviator's shining metal mask radiated an unmistakable and terrifying hatred.

Chapter 4

A DREAM IN THE
WRONG CHAMBER
~~~~~~~~~~~~~~~~~~~~~~~~

Nasrani Orsina had disappeared.

After Hobi stumbled from the gravator he'd turned to say something to his guide. But he saw only the gravator dropping, and a large pale hand waving from behind its sliver of amethyst window. In an instant that too fell from sight. The boy stared open-mouthed, his face reflected in the chromium awning above the gravator entrance. When the machine did not return, he shoved his hands in his pockets and dispiritedly walked home.

The dank air from the Undercity had saturated his clothes with the smells of mud and mildew. After the darkness of Angels the lights of Cherubim hurt his eyes, too bright and too many of them. He kept his head down and his eyes half-shut, ignoring the hissing of the ventricles at his feet, the distant booming sound of cheers from the level above. He was trying to remember everything about the nemosyne—her face; the feel of cool glass beneath his cheek; her faint ozone smell.

He did not notice the new posters tacked to the wall near his home. EMBRACE UCALEGON: WELCOME THE HEALING WIND! one said; and another DEATH TO THE HERETICAL TYRANTS! He did not notice where a glass brick had fallen from the base of one of the neighboring houses, or where a stream of water like a silvery filament trickled from the gap left in the wall.

Inside, the replicant Khum greeted him in a hollow voice, reminding him that he was supposed to attend an investiture on Seraphim. Hobi shook his head impatiently, waving the replicant away from him, and headed for his room. When he glanced back he saw that he'd tracked some black stuff across the chamber's white-tiled floor. He stooped to touch it, raised his fingers and sniffed.

Earth. In the hallway's glaring night-lights it looked very black and foul. He grimaced and wiped his fingers on his trousers.

"Clean this up, Khum," he ordered, and went into the main room.

His father was not there. Sajur must have gone directly from the ceremony to whatever celebrations followed. In the hall behind Hobi, Khum stood obediently, his bronze muzzle raised as he intoned in his harsh voice, "Sajur Panggang has requested that you join him immediately in the Four Hundredth Room. Âziz Orsina has called an inquisition to celebrate the Investiture of the new Aviator Imperator."

Hobi made a face.

"Fine." He hurried down the hall.

But as he passed his father's study he paused. For the first time in months, the door was ajar. Not only that, it had been *propped* open with a chunk of malachite. Hobi stared at the polished green stone, trying to figure out what obscure message it might hold for him. Then he entered the room.

It was as always; the Architects buzzing and clicking as glowing scrolls of numbers and architectural renderings moved across their screens. Beneath the mercury lamp on his father's desk several spent ampules of amphaze were scattered. Hobi picked one up and sniffed it, then glanced at the monitor on the desk.

There was a message on the screen. The violet letters flickered the way they did when an urgent missive from the margravines was displayed; but there was no sign of the Orsinate's emblem, no flowing script or crabbed hand to indicate Shiyung or Âziz's signature. Only this, spelled out in capitals—

ONE TREMBLES TO THINK OF THAT MYSTERIOUS THING IN THE SOUL, WHICH SEEMS TO ACKNOWLEDGE NO HUMAN JURISDICTION BUT, IN SPITE OF THE INDIVIDUAL'S OWN INNOCENT SELF, WILL STILL DREAM HORRID DREAMS, AND MUTTER UNMENTIONABLE THOUGHTS.

"Huh?"
Hobi frowned, leaning forward until the letters blurred in front of him. He read it again, then a third time. He was reaching for the handles of the imprimatur to record it when the message disappeared, replaced by a violet string of numerals.

He swore, switched the imprimatur on anyway, but of course the message was lost. He tried to recall what it had said—something about dreams, horrible thoughts—and felt cold.

A warning—for his father? But there had been that open door.

From his father?

He cursed again, more loudly, and glanced at the other screens. He thought of what Nasrani had said of his own education—*"I had the finest tutors"*—and wished that he had learned to understand the meaningless figures and renderings that the Architects produced without end as they maintained the city.

But it was too late for that. He lingered another minute, tracing the edges of a monitor, then left.

Hobi's bedroom was at the end of a long corridor, behind the bathing chamber and the rows of steel cabinets where the replicants recharged during their offtimes. It was a large bedroom, larger even than Sajur's, but looked smaller because of the clutter. To reach his bed Hobi had to step over mounds of clothes and unwatched 'files, and pull aside a curtain of raw silk that drooped from the ceiling in silvery folds. Hobi hated seeing the walls or ceiling or floor of his chamber. He hated it because no sooner would he grow accustomed to a particularly nice line of molding, painted lemon-yellow perhaps, or an airy expanse of billowing muslin or a mosaic of black and white rubber on the floor; no sooner would he find himself waking and turning expectantly to gaze upon an ochre stucco wall but he would find that while he slept the silent and efficient Architects had changed it. Black industrial girders would have replaced the muslin (later bright orange bricks would replace the girders), the stucco had given way to a mirrored surface so sleek he half expected it to be wet, and instead of the rough but comforting sisal flooring his feet would fall upon fine soft sand.

"Can't you stop it? Can't you *say* something to them?" he had demanded of his father. But Sajur Panggang only shook his head, sighing.

"I don't control the Architects, Hobi, you know that. I read them and keep them running, but they take care of themselves."

Hobi would stalk off in a fury, to glare at the new walls of exposed artificial wood and dig through the sand to discover the naked flooring beneath (he never did). But gradually he did find a way to fight back. Gradually *things* began to fill Hobi's room. Empty Amity decanters and bottles of wine, jacquard robes filched from his father's closets, heaps of prosthetic arms bartered from a friend who knew a friend who knew a moujik, candle-ends, expired lumieres, broken light bulbs, computer circuitry, chessboards, empty candicaine pipettes and morpha tubes, tobacco tins and snuff envelopes, more pidgin-lettered posters torn from the walls outside (PRAY THE HEALING WIND! BLESSED NAROUZ SAVES!), 'files of military formations and the atrocities of the Archipelago Conflict and one (black market) 'file showing scenes of a place Outside called the Zaragoza Mountains.

All of it heaped around Hobi's bed in an attempt to give some sense of permanence to the room. His mother had detested it, of course—

"Clean this up! It's filthy, it will make you ill—"

But his mother was dead now, and his father had never (to his son's knowledge) set foot inside the muddle that was Hobi's room.

Hobi settled into it like a tapir in its lair. Lying in bed he would let one hand fall to rest upon a stack of 'files, or fondle the desiccated stalks of a tiny and utterly illegal bamboo he had tried to grow from a stolen cutting; and it would comfort him.

Now he kicked his way through the clothes and broken vials. Dead bamboo crackled beneath his foot. An immense book lay open on one side of the bed, an ancient atlas he'd stolen from his father's library. Hobi shoved it onto the floor and flopped down on the bed, closing his eyes.

From somewhere far overhead he heard faint cheering, and smelled the faintest breath of the sea. He thought of the Undercity and Nasrani's hidden children, of the festival a few days hence. He thought of the hole he had seen, that gaping mouth of the underworld; of his father hunched over the ancient monitors in his office. He thought of these things, and of the nemosyne. Slowly he brought his hand to his face and inhaled, breathing in the smell of that livid darkness, the unmistakable raw taint of earth.

• • •

The new Aviator Imperator had finished speaking. As the throng on the boulevard cheered and the assembled Aviators gave him a final salute, the *rasa* turned and walked stiffly back to his palanquin. Ceryl was close enough that she could hear the grating sound his legs made as he moved. The aardmen stumbled to their feet, waited until the Aviator had climbed back onto the palanquin before raising it once more. Then they all waited as the three margravines passed, Âziz first and then Nike and Shiyung last of all. As she walked by him the *rasa* raised his head and gazed at her, but Shiyung ignored him. The margravines disappeared inside the doors of the palace, the Imperators close behind them; then all the rest of the Orsinate's entourage, cabals and cabinets and diplomats all crowding the entrance and talking excitedly. The aardmen remained standing beneath their heavy litter as though confused, growling softly as the last members of the Linguistics Cabal shoved their way inside.

On the colonnade Ceryl remained silent, staring at the aardmen. She was afraid to walk past them— not afraid of the aardmen, but of what they carried. She saw the *rasa* Aviator Imperator there upon the palanquin; but she remembered Margalis Tast'annin. Several years earlier, the supposed details of his affair with Shiyung had been broadcast nightly on the 'files. The official word was that the affair ended when Tast'annin was sent to the front to command the Archipelago Conflict; but a professional courtesan who had been an intimate of Shiyung's told Ceryl that the break had been the Aviator's desire, and not the margravine's. His subsequent posting to the Archipelago had been intended as an exile of sorts, but of course he had triumphed there. Afterward there had been his long sojourn back on the HORUS stations, and then the disaster in the Capital.

He had been a handsome man, rumored to be brilliant and even charming. Certainly his arrogance matched that of the Orsinate. Seeing him now, all vestiges of his humanity gone save for his corpse's hand and his revenant's eyes, made Ceryl's throat tighten with fear. *This* was what happened to those who fell out of favor with the margravines. She waited until almost all of the others had filed into the palace, waited for the aardmen to bear their terrible burden inside. But still they remained, snarling at each other, while the Aviator stood in silence, waiting.

And now Ceryl had no choice but to go: she was the last person on the colonnade, save for the Aviator and his bearers. She gave a little gasp and darted in front of them, head down. The aardmen's snarls grew louder as she passed but she did not look up. She fairly ran to the gate.

Only when she reached the portal she stopped, her heart rocketing inside her chest. Very slowly she turned to look back.

Within his palanquin the Aviator stood, staring at her. For an instant his eyes met hers. As from some unfathomable depth she saw a spark within them, a brilliant flash of gray, then nothing but that dead gaze in its crimson metal cell.

Ceryl turned and staggered inside. The aardmen wailed as she fled.

The crowd on the boulevard began to break up.

"You're a morphodite?"

The woman from the Toxins Cabal sounded doubtful. On her shoulder the puppet snorted, shaking its narrow head and sneezing. Cold air flowed up from the ventricles now, an astringent odor, not unpleasant. All around them people were stretching and rubbing their eyes.

"Yes," Reive replied reluctantly. She didn't feel like talking. Her ears still rang with the Aviators' shouts and the harsh voice of the *rasa*. "We're—we have a friend—just visiting—"

The woman continued to stare at her, her gaze darting from Reive's breasts to her groin, then back to her face.

"But you are a morphodite?"

Reive glanced around nervously, thinking perhaps the woman was actually a member of the Reception Committee. But she continued to stare at Reive, so intently that the gynander finally realized she must be confused because Reive's face was not hidden beneath the customary layers of thick bluish-tinged powder.

"Yes," Reive replied, her own relief apparent when the woman brightened. "We are a gynander—visiting here, only visiting—"

"Who could care?" shrieked the puppet. The woman struck its nose and it slunk behind her neck. She turned back to Reive, adjusting her fez.

"I think I've been to one of your scryings," she said. "When Nike Orsina had that nightmare about the runcible spoon—"

Reive shook her head. "We don't think so." She'd never attended an inquisition with the Orsinate, and started to say so when the woman cut her off.

"I'm *certain* of it. I had dreamed about a flying boat the night before," she insisted. "Nike said it was a *gorgeous* dream, that was the word she used. We're very close, Nike and I. All the margravines are my good friends, actually. I *never* miss one of their dream inquisitions." She leaned forward, peering at Reive's eyes, then made a little grimace of distaste. "Although I had forgotten about your—um—*eyes*. But I'm sure it was you."

Without looking she reached for a tiny metal purse hung about her neck, the pleasure cabinet's sigil dangling from it on a silver chain. She withdrew a long narrow card and shoved it into Reive's hand. "Here: tonight in the Four Hundredth Room. Twenty-seven o'clock. Nike will remember, she'll be pleased I found you. Bring a guest if you'd like—"

This last said airily, as though unknown hermaphrodites were always welcome in the Orsinate's sanctum. Reive nodded stupidly and stared at the card.

Tatsun Frizer, it read in small neat letters printed on a thin sheet of allurian. When she tilted it the scowling image of Blessed Narouz appeared, his hawkish profile silhouetted against the flaming refineries of Archangels. She raised it to her face and sniffed: petroleum. She slipped the card into her pouch.

"This evening, then," said Tatsun Frizer. She gave a last puzzled look at Reive's face, then headed for the palace, her yellow boots making a slapping sound against the pavement, her puppet peering back at Reive and flicking its tongue licentiously.

The gynander stared after them, lifting her eyes to take in the sweeping columns, the lapis-crowned gates and golden statues surmounting it all. She took a lock of her hair and pulled it, until tears filled her eyes, just to make sure she was awake.

An invitation to a party given by the Orsinate! Let Drusilla hear about *that*!

She dismissed a fleeting thought for Ceryl and ran back to the gravator, heedless of how this might look to the few surly aristocrats still arguing over matters of protocol and invitations or the lack thereof. She dodged servers as they rolled about the boulevard, sweeping up ashes and broken pipettes, and at the gravator entrance bumped into the vicar of the Church of Christ Cadillac and didn't even say *Excuse Me*. If only she could get back to Ceryl's chambers, find some new clothes and be gone before Ceryl returned. . . .

But when she reached her chambers, Ceryl was waiting.

"Where have you *been*?" she exploded. "I ran back here as soon as I could—"

Reive sank onto the divan. "We attended the Investiture," she said sullenly. She raised her head, adding in a haughty tone, "We have been invited to a party this evening. With the Orsinate in the Four Hundredth Room."

She dug into her pouch and held out the allurian calling card.

"Tatsun Frizer and the Orsinate and the Four Hundredth Room," Ceryl read, disgusted. "Lovely." She tossed the card onto the floor and stared at Reive coldly. "So you went to the Investiture."

Reive nodded once, her mouth tight.

"And did you have a lovely time there? A wonderful time, watching the wonderful margravines parade their latest victim in front of the mob?" She spat the last word and crossed the room, yanked open a cabinet and poured herself a glass of brandy. Once back in her own chambers, her fear had disintegrated into anger. "They sicken me—it *all* sickens me. And three days from now is Æstival Tide and we get to watch some *more* torment, when they loose their damned monster onto the beach. Well, you know what? I'm sick of it, *all* of it. Sick, sick, sick."

Reive huddled deeper into the divan and watched her through slitted eyes. It was very unwise for someone to talk like this. Ceryl seemed to read her mind: she turned and glared at her, downing another brandy. "Oh, pardon me. I forgot—bad form to talk treason in front of houseguests."

She stared at the bottle on the counter, then poured another brandy and drank it. Afterward her tone was calmer, but her voice still shook as she spoke.

"Reive—I'm sorry. It's just—I was worried, that's all. It's the time of year, it always puts me on edge. And—well, just thinking about the *timoria*. Do you have any idea how many people died ten years ago, during the last Æstival Tide? Do you?"

She began pacing the room and went on before Reive could answer. "Two *thousand*. Out of a total population of, say, twenty thousand. Several hundred trampled to death on the strand when the Gate is opened, another hundred fed to the Compassionate Redeemer for *their* pleasure. Then of course Shiyung ordered that boat race, and of course all the contestants drowned. A boat race! No one here has ever seen a boat in her life! And then the hecatombs, and the babies sacrificed—it's madness, absolute madness!"

She stopped and stared at Reive. The gynander only shrugged, then reaching from the divan snatched back Tatsun Frizer's card from the floor. Ceryl sighed, defeated.

"What am I doing, talking to you? Look at you— you're just a—a child, really," she said. She paused in front of the brandy bottle, then shoved it back into the cabinet. "Every ten years a few of us recall the last time, and maybe we get angry, or frightened, but nothing ever happens. Nothing ever changes. Four hundred years of Orsinas. I don't suppose it will ever end. I guess I'd better decide what to wear to this evening's atrocity."

She disappeared into her bedroom, reappeared a moment later holding a long sleeveless tunic of brilliant jade-green satin. Reive's mouth hung open in surprise, but Ceryl only shrugged and started across the room.

"Well, it's the damn Feast of Fear, right? Might as well wear green." She stopped abruptly and looked at the gynander. Her voice dropped.

"You won't say anything, about—about my dream? Reive?"

Reive shook her head slowly. "We had forgotten about it," she admitted. Ceryl smiled wryly.

"Well. That's just as well." She gazed with distaste at the tunic in her hands. "I guess if we're going to make it by twenty-seven o'clock we'd better get dressed." At Reive's expression she added, "I can't let you go alone. Whether or not Tatsun Frizer invited you. It would be like throwing a baby to the Redeemer."

Reive nodded, tipping her head so that Ceryl

wouldn't see her smile, and reached for her cosmetics box.

By the time they reached Seraphim Level, Ceryl's mood had shifted from aggrieved resignation to barely concealed anxiety. A dream inquisition in the Four Hundredth Room! That would mean all three margravines, and most of the pleasure cabinet, and she, Ceryl, having to convince them of the innocence and beauty and originality of some dream she'd never had. Not to mention carefully worded praise for the afternoon's Investiture, and feigned delight at the pleasures of Æstival Tide still to come. Twice she had stopped, breathing deeply while reciting a calming verse a *galli* had taught her. She wondered what would happen if she just didn't show up for the inquisition.

But then, of course, Reive would go on alone; and at *that* thought Ceryl's breathing became a tortured gasp and she hurried after her companion.

Fortunately the gynander seemed subdued. Ceryl had watched, intrigued, as Reive carefully removed mascara and rouge and powder. She had never seen a hermaphrodite's face unpainted; the effect was unsettling. Like most people, Ceryl thought of the hermaphrodites as *she* or *her* or sometimes *it*. But, as Reive blotted off the last traces of rouge, for the first time Ceryl noticed how strong her jaw was; how her mouth without its carmine pout was in fact thin, and might even seem cruel were it not for a certain perplexed twist of the lip. And her eyes, with no penciled brows arching above them, were, despite their color, quite gentle. She no longer had the childish mien associated with the hermaphrodites. Except for the lack of eyebrows and her rounded shoulders, she looked like a young man or thoughtful boy. In fact, she resembled one of the unsmiling busts of Orsina ancestors that lined the corridors of the Seraphim's palace. Ceryl had nearly commented on this peculiar resemblance, but decided it would only make the gynander conceited. Instead she sat in silence while Reive painted her face chalk-white, with only a small green whorl upon each cheek as a token of Æstival Tide.

Now Ceryl wished she *had* said something. With her face dead-white save for those green spirals and her eyes and mouth unrouged, the gynander looked disturbingly corpselike. There was little foot traffic headed for the palace, and only a few rickshaws. In one of these another hermaphrodite sat giggling on the lap of a drunken diplomat, and stared back amazed as they passed. Ceryl glanced at Reive, but the gynander didn't even look up as the rickshaw rattled by; only stared straight ahead with her cool emerald eyes.

The truth was, Reive was nervous, even frightened. Everything looked different than it had that afternoon. Servers had spent the last few hours adorning the boulevards for the upcoming festival. The water frothing in the fountains was now green, lit by hidden lanterns. Some of the sculptures had been replaced with bizarre representations of the world Outside—trees of steel and iron, grotesquely twisted and covered with thorns; huge skeletal figures of winged creatures with gaping mouths and dripping talons; naked figures of men and women cowering before the holographic image of an immense wave, its curling edge flecked with blood. There was the inevitable holo of the Compassionate Redeemer, its lamprey's mouth opening and closing in eerie silence while the ventricles at its feet pumped out the choking scent of charred roses. And seeping into everything the smell of the sea, thick and rank and warm, growing heavier as the air pressure dropped Outside. Some of the other guests wore linen masks over their mouths. Reive regretted not having bought one for herself—the briny smell nearly choked her, like having viscous water poured into her nostrils. Silently she wandered along the boulevard, twisting her head to stare at the marvels the Orsinate had arranged for the festival.

But as they approached the palace Reive stopped, shaking her head in disbelief. Turning to Ceryl she cried, "What have they done?"

It seemed that all of Dominations Level had been moved up here. Scores of biotechnicians and aardmen were still at work, dragging huge cages from the freight gravators, swearing and shouting and snarling beneath the dim violet lights of Seraphim's false evening. Trees—real trees, live trees engineered in the laboratories of Dominations—had been set in concrete tubs to form a sort of forest, palms and oaks and conifers lined up neatly in rows, but so close their limbs had tangled or, in some cases, broken off to fall in heaps on the pavement. Reive and Ceryl passed through them slowly, and drew closer to each other as they walked.

Because it was one thing to view these things in the brightly lit corridors and workrooms of Dominations, or shoved into the background of one of the dioramas where exhausted jackals and dire wolves panted on the cement floor. But to see them here, beneath the dim purple lamps in the domes above, with the humid breath of the unseen ocean thick in your lungs, the smell of the sea mingling with the ticklish scent of firs and the acrid musk of frightened animals—it suddenly made Seraphim Level seem endless.

Because, vast as it was, wherever you were inside of Araboth you knew that there was an end to it— that the Domes were there, hidden behind heat fences or murals or refinery smoke, but *there*, protecting you from the world Outside.

But the effect of these shrubs and trees and vines crowding the boulevard and the very steps of the Orsinate's palace was perverse. Rather than make the place appear smaller, the shadows and rustlings and myriad smells made it all seem *huge*. Ceryl could no longer tell where the domes were, hidden behind tan-

gled branches and leaves. Even the constant under-
current of hisses from the ventricles, of the whir of
servers out on errands, was drowned by a ceaseless
soft stirring, as though some errant wind moved
among the stolen forest.

Only the smell of the sea remained the same; and
Reive shuddered, imagining it somewhere just out of
sight, lapping against the gravator entrance or smashing through the bulwarks surrounding the refineries.

"This must be what timoring feels like," she murmured. "If you do it right. Or what it's *really* like,
Outside . . ."

In the shadows they could glimpse other visitors,
silent and subdued as Reive and Ceryl themselves,
gazing at the eerie menagerie, the black trees shot
with gold and violet where the faint light from the
domes trickled through their branches. Once Reive
stumbled, flailing as she grabbed at Ceryl's hand—

"What—!"

The gynander's eyes widened and Ceryl steadied
herself against a tree. They could hear other voices
crying out, and croaks and screams from the imprisoned animals, then ripples of nervous laughter.

Reive caught her breath, then said, "The ground!
Did you feel it—it shook, it all *shook*—"

Ceryl bit her lip, waited until her breathing
slowed. "It was the gravators," she said at last.
"Bringing all these cages up here—they're so
heavy—"

Reive stared at her as though she were mad. "The
gravators? No, it is the Wind Outside—"

Ceryl grabbed the gynander and covered her
mouth with her hand. "Stop it!" she hissed. "Do you
want to cause a panic? Get us *killed*?"

Reive glared at her, pulling at Ceryl's hand. "We
felt it! The storm, what Zalophus warned us of—"

"Reive," pleaded Ceryl. She tipped her head to
indicate where several members of the Toxins Cabal
were talking animatedly and glancing at them.

"Please—at least until we get back home this evening—"

Reive gave her a sulky look, but then she nodded. Ceryl took her hand and they walked more
quickly toward the palace.

They stopped in front of a betulamia, a sentient
tree whose slender branches plied the air gently, as
though underwater. At its base squatted a square
metal tub of mauve Catherine Wheel poppies. When
Reive touched one, its gold-tipped petals contracted,
then spat out a number of tiny bright red seeds that
crackled and fizzed as they flew through the air. From
within their cages gibbons howled and mandrills
boomed, and somewhere out of sight one of the Children of Mercy shrieked with laughter as a dire wolf
howled, a long anguished sound.

"Have they—have they brought them *all* here?"
wondered Reive. She looked around, too embarrassed
to admit what she was afraid of finding—Zalophus
caged within one of those steel tanks, the Children of
Mercy prodding him with their electrified lances.

"No," Ceryl said. She plucked one of the spent
poppy blossoms and gazed at it sadly. "Not everything
—just some of them, who knows how they choose
them—for the festival. I wasn't up here for the last
one, of course, but I've heard of things like this. It's a
—like one of the dioramas brought to life. For the
Orsinate's pleasure, and their guests. So they can pretend to cheat Death, and play at being Outside."

Reive plucked a bit of tamarack and brushed her
cheek with it, its bristles surprisingly soft and pungent. "Outside," she whispered, and let the tamarack
fall through her fingers to the ground. From behind
them echoed a recording of the Compassionate Redeemer's ululating cry.

"We'd better hurry," Ceryl said without enthusi-
asm. As she walked, poppy seeds exploded beneath
her feet, releasing their sulfurous smell. Reive followed, gazing wistfully behind them. The noise and

scents from the menagerie faded as they approached
the palace.

"What's that?"

The gynander pointed to where a smear of white
shimmered overhead, like a lantern reflected upon
the convex surface of the domes.

Ceryl glanced up, then shrugged. "I don't know.
The moon?"

The moon. Reive tried to recall what the moon
was: something to do with light. They were quite near
the palace now, closer even than she had been at the
Investiture. She smoothed her pantaloons, then
rubbed her scalp anxiously. She wished she had
brought some of her amber pomade when she'd left
her own level. Ceryl's clothes were so drab; but Reive
had found a scarf of russet gossamer and tied it
around her coiled hair, and dusted herself with silver
ash until her skin had a dull gleam like pewter. Beside
her Ceryl looked quite splendid. The jade-green tunic
set off her pale skin, the brass-and-malachite fillet
glinted from beneath her short glossy hair. Despite
her fair hair and skin, her plebeian blue eyes, Ceryl
was striking-looking. Reive could even imagine that
someone might think her beautiful—not the Orsinate,
however, whose tastes ran more toward the deliberately bizarre, even deformed. For a moment the gynander regretted not having worn more outlandish
makeup, the better to impress the margravines; but
now they had reached the very steps of the palace
itself, and Ceryl was whispering nervously beside her.

"The sentries—"

Overhead several fougas circled lazily, their spot-
lights lancing the violet air with adamant. Glass bowls
lit with rose-scented oil lined the entrance to the palace. The vicar of the Church of Christ Cadillac, resplendent in azure robes and chromium mitre, stood
on the lowest step of the palace, a ritual urceole in her
hands. As Reive and Ceryl passed she spattered them
with seawater from the silver pitcher and murmured

a ward against the world Outside. When Reive turned to stare at her she was jerked forward by Ceryl.

As they walked up the steps they were greeted by several guards in knee-length blousons of yolk-yellow linen, jade-green sashes across their breasts in honor of the festival. "Brave the Healing Wind," one called out to Ceryl, and another smiled and winked at Reive. All the guards were human save the last, a forbidding scholiast with many-jointed arms and an eyeless face guarding the arch that led into the palace. Ceryl held up the Orsinate's heraldic eye; the scholiast scanned it, then, "Ceryl Waxwing," it whispered, and Ceryl passed through the high-arched doorway. Once on the other side she gazed back anxiously at Reive.

On the steps other guests paused to receive the vicar's blessing. The fougas' watchlights swept the boulevard. The gynander hesitated in front of the scholiast, then held out Tatsun Frizer's card. The scholiast ignored it. Instead it took her hand and stretched out her palm, pricked it with a tiny needle that shot from its metal claw, humming as one of its optics scanned her face. A moment while it read her retinaprint and biogene.

"Reive Orsina," it intoned, dropping her hand. She took one final look at the silent plaza and hurried inside.

Ceryl waited a few feet down the hall. She looked relieved as Reive ran up to her. "It didn't question you?"

"No: it said our name, and then 'Orsina'—"

"It must think you're a special guest—which you are, I suppose. Well, we'll see. It's down this way. . . ."

Inside, the palace was less imposing. The halls they hurried down were simple in appearance, almost utilitarian: faux marble floors and walls of a creamy white, with white arches and columns leading to this wing or another. Busts and holoimages of long-dead Orsinas gleamed or flickered in odd corners, but otherwise the hall was empty. Unseen scholiasts whis-

pered the names of the different chambers—Toxins
Cabal Salon, the Uropan Ambassador's Suite, the Architect Imperator's Drafting Room. As they passed this
last door it opened, and a tall man and a dwarf
emerged and followed them down the hall, whispering urgently. Ceryl's hands went numb as she recognized Sajur Panggang, the Architect Imperator, and
the puppeteer Rudyard Planck. Sajur walked slowly,
his long legs slicing through the white hallways like
well-oiled shears. Beside him Planck bounded like
some macabre toy, brick-colored hair tossing, his tiny
feet patting against the marble floor. Ceryl started
walking faster, but behind her Reive paced oblivious,
staring at the smooth arched ceiling and humming
tunelessly to herself. When they reached the glass
atrium with its garden of crystal orchids Ceryl hurried
up the stairs, turning down this corridor and the next.
Still Sajur and his grotesque companion followed
them, until they all reached a dead end where a tall
red-lacquered door stood open.

Ceryl hesitated, wondering if she and Reive could
disappear inside before introductions became necessary. But it was too late.

"Serena, is it?" the Architect Imperator said
kindly, making a steeple of his hands and bowing
slightly.

"Ceryl Waxwing," she replied, bowing in return.
Sajur Panggang smiled and shrugged ruefully.

"My pardon—I am so very bad with names—my
wife was the one who remembered—"

He grimaced apologetically and adjusted the emerald mourning cuffs on his wrists. Ceryl wished that
she had worn something a little more ostentatious.
The Architect Imperator had indulged his whimsy for
archaic clothing with a plain black suit and narrow
tie, a woolen muffler tied around his long neck and
his black turban of office. An enormous and no doubt
artificial tourmaline of very pale green winked from
within the folds of black silk neatly wrapped about his
brow. Beside him Rudyard Planck bobbed like one of

his own ugly creations. He too had eccentric taste in clothes: beneath a thick wool cape his shirt had been torn to shreds and then repaired with brilliant green silk and green thread, a vulgar shade that did nothing to complement his tallowy complexion. Like Tatsun Frizer he followed the current fashion for exotic shoes, in Rudyard's case heavy fleece-lined boots that came up to his thighs. Ceryl looked up to see Reive smiling at him and the puppeteer grinning back at her. Hastily she began introductions.

"Sajur, may I present Reive—"

She faltered, realizing she had no other name for the gynander. Reive ignored her and continued to gaze at the dwarf. Ceryl grit her teeth and said, "Reive, this is *the Architect Imperator*."

The gynander only looked sideways and nodded. The Architect Imperator laughed, as Ceryl blushed and went on, "Rudyard, this is—"

"Oh, we've met, Waxwing, we've met—!"

"You have?" Ceryl stammered. "How? I mean—"

Gently Sajur Panggang took her by the elbow, murmuring, "Perhaps we shouldn't block the doorway, Ceryl. May I escort you inside?"

Ceryl choked, shaking her head, then nodded furiously and let him lead her into the Four Hundredth Room. Behind her Rudyard Planck murmured what sounded like a suggestive remark, and the gynander giggled. She tried to look back at them, but the Architect Imperator's grasp upon her arm was quite strong as he led her toward the center of the room.

She stumbled after him, glancing about discreetly to see who else was there. Tatsun Frizer, of course. The opera star Kai Kaeng. A number of thugs from the Reception Committee, trying to pretend they were guests and not security personnel. A false hermaphrodite with an open-front tunic, preening before the real thing. A tall Aviator wearing a floor-length coat of sable over his scarlet uniform, standing by himself with his back to the crowd. Another Aviator walked up beside him, hesitating before placing his hand on his arm. The first Aviator turned to him, facing Ceryl. His blank metal face reflected Ceryl's own and his eyes stared out at her, raw and wet and the color of oysters.

"—didn't realize Waxwing had such good taste as to adopt this lovely and clever young thing—"

Dully Ceryl nodded as the dwarf rattled on. The *rasa* continued to stare at her. She made a small nervous sound, then forced herself to look down at Rudyard Planck laughing as he twiddled one end of Reive's scarf in his blunt fingers. When she glanced up a moment later, the *rasa* was walking toward Âziz.

"Excuse me—" murmured Sajur Panggang. "I'll find you later, Rudyard. Ceryl—"

He was gone before Ceryl could say goodbye. She looked helplessly at the dwarf.

"What a charming young friend you have, Ceryl," he croaked. He tugged at Reive's scarf. "Although she might be chilly later. I hear Nike's chosen a wintry theme for this evening. I trust you'll be scrying for us tonight, my dear?" He reached up to trace Reive's navel, drew away a finger frosted with silver ash. "I don't think I've had the pleasure of hearing you before."

"If we are asked." Reive dipped her head modestly. Rudyard laughed and started toward the center of the room, taking Reive by the arm.

"Well, *I* certainly look forward to hearing you. Ceryl, may I get you a drink?"

Ceryl shook her head, following them. She inhaled, then sneezed. *Lovey's Prescient Chypre*, Nike's favorite scent this year, its overtones of frangipani and licorice so cloying it always made Cheryl's head ache. She tried breathing through her mouth and elbowed past another actress, a wraithlike soprano with an eyepatch who was having her first success with the current vogue for sadist opera, with its graphic (and vulgar) depictions of the Third Shining, when the War between the celestial stations of HORUS and the Balkhash Commonwealth erupted into the holocaust that blasted the prairies into black adamant and destroyed the isthmus connecting the continent with its antipode.

"—then it was like the entire *stage* tilted, and of course I just went *flying*, I've never felt anything like it in my life, the whole *place* seemed to be moving, and all week I've had the most *gruesome* headache, and now of course they tell me Shiyung isn't even going to *be* here tonight—"

The soprano turned to greet Ceryl, *Lovey's Prescient Chypre* practically dripping from her bare shoulders. Ceryl smiled grimly and plowed on.

With a crowd inside it, the Four Hundredth Room seemed little different from any other place used for a dream inquisition, except for the wood-paneled walls. Ancient carpets on the floor, walls hung with aluminum tapestries, electric lights shining from within sconces shaped like cupped hands. A duo playing therimin and bass viola sat in a corner, nearly hidden by automotive statuary. In front of them a young *galli* in indigo robes and grass-green sash sang in a pure child's voice an immeasurably ancient song—

> *"The keeper of the city keys*
> *Puts shutters on the dreams.*
> *I wait outside the pilgrim's door with insufficient*
> *schemes."*

Ceryl pinched the bridge of her nose, wondering how Reive had disappeared so quickly. Someone handed the *galli* a wineglass; without stopping his song he smiled and bowed.

"The black queen chants the funeral march
The cracked brass bells will ring
To summon back the fire witch to the court of the Crimson King."

"Ceryl. You made it."

Ceryl started as Tatsun Frizer prowled up behind her, blessedly without her puppet.

"Y-yes." She looked past Tatsun and spotted Reive on the other side of the room with Rudyard Planck. "Oh, damn—"

Tatsun followed her gaze and raised her eyebrows. Her vocoder blinked pale rose as she cooed, "That morph—she is a friend of yours?"

"The gynander? Yes—Reive, that's her name— *Reive!*"

From across the room Reive gave Ceryl a tiny wave. Rudyard Planck raised a glass half-full of virent Amity in a mocking toast.

"She's *very* attractive," said Tatsun. Ceryl looked up, surprised.

Tatsun sniffed. "Oh, don't worry, I wouldn't *dream* of stealing your little paramour. *Excuse* me—"

"She's *not*—" Ceryl began heatedly, but Tatsun tossed her head and stalked off. For a few minutes Ceryl just stood there, watching as Rudyard offered Reive more Amity and the morphodite bowed gracefully as she accepted it. The last guests straggled in— two more actors from the pleasure cabinet, a diplomat leading an aardman on a silver chain, the usual hangers-on and uninvited guests, eager for the opportunity to ingratiate themselves with the Orsinate and so inadvertently increase their chances of dying at their hands. In the dim corner where the musical duo piped and droned, the margravine Âziz sat and drummed her fingers on her knees, looking uneasy, while at her shoulder the Aviator Imperator Tast'annin stood like a great hooded gyrfalcon, his black-gloved hands caressing the back of her chair.

At sight of him Ceryl froze. She realized he knew nothing, cared nothing, about her; indeed, knew it should be impossible for a *rasa* to truly care about anything. If he had seemed to stare before, surely it was because she had been standing next to Sajur Panggang. But still he terrified her. His gaze was more acute than any *rasa*'s she had ever seen, and his hands twisted menacingly within their leather gloves. . . .

Ceryl hugged herself, pushing back a fear as strong as the one that came upon her during her nightmares of the Green Country. Of course it meant nothing—the *rasa* Imperator; this oddly self-composed gynander who had scryed her dream, taken over her life, and within days managed to get invited into the Orsinate's sanctorum; Reive's sudden and inappropriate friendship with the rakish Rudyard Planck; the reports of tremors and structural failures throughout the city.

And then there was her dream; and all of this on the eve of Æstival Tide itself. Even as she stood, her bare arms prickled with cold and fear, she could sense it all Out There, whatever *It* was—poisoned ocean, devouring sunlight, monstrous typhoon—gnawing at the Quincunx Domes, or else circling Araboth like one of the Orsinate's regenerated thecodonts grown to massive size, seeking a way to grind the city between its Luciferian teeth.

I'm going mad, thought Ceryl. *I should consult a seer;* but then she recalled that the present bizarre confluence of events derived from her doing just that.

She bit her finger. Maybe she should leave, go back to her chambers, lock the doors and refuse to come out until Æstival Tide was over. Just leave, like that, and let Reive flounder through the evening as best she could.

But then from down the hall she heard Nike's booming *hoo-ha* laugh. A moment later she listed into the room, followed by a rather worried-looking serving girl. Âziz started in her chair; the *rasa* withdrew his hands and stepped back silently, drawing his sable coat around him. Âziz stood and went to greet her sister. Ceryl took a deep breath, then quickly made her way to where a trio of young boys were pouring wine from glass kraters. She drank hers too fast, scanning the room for Reive and shivering. The dwarf had been right. It was starting to get cold—another chance

for the margravines to show off. All around the room
guests ostentatiously tugged at capes and mufflers,
garments made from the pelts of suricatas and mar-
tens and lynx specially bred on Dominations for the
pleasure cabinet. The smell of the sea, ever-present
even in this sanctum, was overlaid with a sudden
burst of scent—the odor of fir trees, so thick and so
obviously chemical in origin that Ceryl's throat
burned. She swore beneath her breath and rubbed
her bare arms. Now that Nike had arrived it would be
ill-considered to be seen leaving the room, especially
if one wasn't properly dressed. She grit her teeth and
wished she could find the gynander.

Too late she glimpsed Reive on a divan on the far
side of the room, sitting between two other
morphodites. One had painted her face in complex
pyramidical patterns; the other had small darting pig-
gish eyes within a geisha's mask and wore a towering
blond wig of corkscrew curls. Ceryl recognized her as
a former favorite of Nike's, now gone to fat.

The blond morph lifted her head, the wig teeter-
ing on her brow, and stared at Ceryl. Echion, that was
her name. As Ceryl watched, she leaned over Reive
and whispered to her, still looking back at Ceryl,
while Reive sipped at her wine and stared about the
room with her long green eyes. Whatever Echion was
saying seemed to dismay her somewhat. When Nike
bounced past with Âziz, the two hermaphrodites
looked up. After a long moment, Reive tore her gaze
from the margravines and stared across the room at
Ceryl. Ceryl motioned frantically for the gynander to
join her, but instead Reive looked back at Echion. She
glanced up once more at Nike and Âziz, then nodded
slowly. Beside her Echion smiled.

That smile turned the wine to vinegar in Ceryl's
mouth. She put down her glass, and had started toward Reive when Âziz clapped her hands.

"Well! This *is* an exciting group—Kai Kaeng, you
look so dashing!—"

The soprano with the eyepatch bowed and blushed.

"—and I know we are all honored to have our new Aviator Imperator with us this evening—"

Strained yet enthusiastic applause. The *rasa* bowed stiffly, ruddy light spilling from his face. Then Âziz was beckoning them all to come close, to form the customary circle so that the inquest could begin.

Ceryl made one last effort to get across the room to Reive. She pushed through the crowd, nodding coldly at Tatsun Frizer, when a small strong hand grabbed hers—

"Sit here with me, Ceryl," Rudyard Planck rasped cheerfully. His blue eyes glittered as he tugged her toward the middle of the room. "Here, Tatsun, you too."

"Oh, but—"

Tatsun Frizer laughed, her vocoder sparking green and yellow. "I know just how you feel," she oozed, shaking a finger at Ceryl. "Morphodites are *so* fickle. Best surrender gracefully and scold her when you get home." She settled beside Ceryl, pulling a heavy silken throw from a divan and draping it over her knees. "Isn't this *enchanting*? I can't imagine why Shiyung isn't here. Nike said they were going to have it chilly here tonight, but I never *dreamed* . . ."

Tatsun Frizer prattled on. Ceryl thought of snatching the throw from her lap. It was freezing now. On the other side of the circle, Nike sat resplendent in a fox-fur coat, the thick pelts flaming about her pallid face. Every few minutes she leaned over the serving girl, who would hand her a morpha tube or a small agate kef pipe. Next to her Âziz sat stiffly, two brilliant splotches, like crimson thumbprints, on her cheeks. The Aviator had removed his long sable coat and draped it about her shoulders. There was a spurting sound as more of the pine scent was pumped from hidden vents. The lights dimmed to a cool blue, and from the ceiling snow began to fall.

"Oh, *great*," Ceryl swore, shuddering. All around

the circle people applauded and laughed delightedly, holding out their hands and exclaiming as the snow hissed against their skin.

Rudyard Planck patted her knee. "My dear, would you like my cape?"

Ceryl glanced down to see if he was joking, but the dwarf had already begun to peel off the heavy woolen garment. "No, no," she said hastily, "thank you—"

"Just a taste of winter," Âziz was saying. Beneath the Aviator's sable coat, she wore only a simple gray tunic and trousers, her dark hair pulled back through a gold ring. "Once upon a time, this would have been the first day of summer, and I thought, Why not celebrate our freedom from the tyranny of the seasons?"

Beside her sister, Nike nodded happily, tapping her feet and waving her kef pipe. Âziz lifted her face so that the snow glistened on her brow. She stayed like that for a long moment, snow frosting her dark hair.

Then, "Enough," she said softly. The snow stopped, a few last flakes falling as people murmured their disappointment. Warmer air flowed from the vents, and another heavy dose of *Lovey's Prescient Chypre*. Ceryl tried her best not to gag. Beside her Tatsun breathed deeply, eyes closed, and murmured the seven names of Blessed Narouz.

"We have a number of interesting guests this evening," announced Âziz. "Margalis Tast'annin, whom many of you already know of course."

Faint applause. Rudyard Planck snorted softly.

"Sajur Panggang and his little friend Rudyard Planck . . ."

(A few snickers: Âziz's dislike of the puppeteer was well known.)

"Kasim Havid, the ambassador from the Medaïn Desert . . ."

Kasim tried his best to smile; like the other ambassadors he had been hostage in Araboth for a dozen years or more.

". . . even several guests who are strangers to my sister and myself." Âziz's voice rose sharply. Ceryl cowered, pulling Rudyard Planck's cape up to her chest.

Nike beamed groggily around the circle as Âziz explained, "My sister's trusted augur Echion has informed us that we have a new mantic here tonight, a visitor from the lower levels."

Murmurings from the guests. An untried hermaphrodite was always a minor occasion. Ceryl shut her eyes. This was it, then. She thought of her dead lover Giton, of her failed effort at timoring. She should have been kinder to the morphodite; she should have killed her immediately.

But maybe this would be one of those inquisitions you heard about, where everything was wonderful, and Nike and Âziz would be so taken with Reive they would take her into their private cabal of mantics, and Ceryl could disappear on Dominations among the vivariums, this time forever. It was such a pleasant thought that she never wanted to open her eyes again, but of course she did. Rudyard Planck was staring at her, his blue eyes wide with concern. He cocked a thumb to where Reive crouched beside Echion, looking as though she wanted to bolt.

"She's never been here before, has she?"

Ceryl nodded miserably at his hoarse whisper. The dwarf swore. "They'll eat her alive. Who's the fat toad with her?"

"Echion," Ceryl whispered. The dwarf nodded.

"That's right—damn her, one of Nike's panderers—"

From across the circle came several indignant *ssshhes*. Âziz raised her head and frowned slightly. The dwarf fell silent.

Nike began speaking, her husky voice slurred.

"Delightful . . . see all these familiar faces . . . most important . . . dreams during this time . . ." Her head fell forward. At her side, the serving girl anxiously snapped a candicaine pipette in two and waved the pieces beneath the margravine's nose. Nike started, let out a long *whoosh* of breath, and turned to her sister.

"Âziz?" Nike furrowed her brows. "Um—is there something . . . ?"

Âziz sighed and let the Aviator's heavy coat drop back from her shoulders. "As my sister was saying," she began in a ritual fashion, "our dreams are especially important during Æstival Tide, when the world Outside encroaches so closely upon our own. We are blessed here in Araboth to have dream-mantics of great subtlety and perception, to help us chart those dangerous territories we sometimes plumb in our sleep."

Nike nodded happily at her sister's words. Âziz glanced at her and said, "Nike? Would you care to go first?"

"Me?" Nike tittered, then shook her head. "I am afraid—dreams—can't recall—"

"Of course not, you sotty cow," hissed Rudyard Planck. Ceryl stared fixedly at the margravines, ignoring angry stares and whispers of "Shame!" and "Heed the margravine!"

Âziz's expression seemed to align her with the dwarf in this matter. She turned from Nike, just as Sajur Panggang suggested, "Perhaps the margravine Âziz would share with us *her* dreams?"

Âziz shook her head. Her face looked drawn as she said coldly, "I prefer to keep my dreams to myself for the moment."

There was silence all around the circle.

Ceryl's heart began to pound. This was the part of the inquisitions that she most hated. Either some eager volunteer would call out her dream—actors and artists in particular were prone to such reckless folly—or else the margravines would choose someone at random. Ceryl tried to compose her face into a disinterested mask, as if to show that *her* dreams were reassuringly commonplace. She let her eyes focus on Âziz's left shoulder, to indicate she had nothing to hide from the margravines; but then, horrors! Âziz seemed to find this interesting. The margravine's eyes narrowed, she leaned forward, staring directly at Ceryl, and said, "Now, you there—Shiyung's healer—"

But then another voice sounded, softer than the margravine's but no less commanding. "I would have *my* dream read."

The voice was so low that for a moment the terrified Ceryl thought she had willed it into being; but then she saw Âziz turn slowly to the dark figure at her side.

"Of course, Margalis."

The soft voice went on, "I'm not sure of the protocol, I've been away so long. . . ."

He stood and walked to the center of the circle, which was not the way it was done at all. But not even Âziz motioned for him to sit again; others in the circle bowed their heads or looked nervously at the margravines. Across the room Reive glanced around cautiously, unsure of what was happening.

Ceryl could not look away from the Aviator. Within his seamless face his eyes gaped black and ragged, the pale irises swallowed by the dim light. Ceryl swallowed, feeling faint. Rudyard Planck murmured something reassuring and squeezed her knee. More than anything, she wished *not* to hear this thing's dream. But already the *rasa* was speaking.

"I dreamed I stood in a great pit . . ." he began. His voice was so low that everyone in the circle moved forward to hear him, as though huddling around a fire in the darkness. "It was night, and there were scorched clouds running through the sky. All around me were flames. At my feet were the bodies of children, contorted into horrible shapes—they were children I had slain—and the ruins of machinery. There was a wind blowing, a very cold wind. I could feel it picking through my clothes, it was the kind of wind that gets into your bones, and I felt it inside me, as though my ribs might crack from the cold.

"Then I looked up, and for a moment the clouds broke, and I could see the stars. Who knows?—perhaps I might have seen the pallid lights of HORUS, or the ruins of my own command station, if only I had known where to look. But it had been a very long time since I had seen the sky, and I no longer recalled the configurations of the stars. I gazed up there for a very long time.

"When I looked down again the bodies of the children seemed so small to me, so—fragile. And suddenly the horror of where and what I was overwhelmed me and I began to weep, knowing I had murdered them. And then I woke. And when I woke I wanted to weep still, but I could not. And that was when I knew it was only a dream. Because you see, I had dreamed that I was a man.

"And, of course, I am no longer a man. But when will I be rid of this dream?"

His voice rose when he began to speak of the stars, and when he said *But when will I be rid of this dream?* the words came in a sort of brazen shriek, like the clamor of some great engine grinding against stone. Ceryl shivered, while beside her Rudyard Planck covered his ears. Tatsun Frizer whispered the names of Blessed Narouz. Reive sat bolt upright, her eyes wide as though bewitched. Âziz stared resolutely at the floor.

Only Nike seemed unperturbed. Without a word she held out a hand to her white-faced serving girl, who gave her a candicaine pipette. The margravine snapped it and inhaled. She shook her head, as though snow still clung to her hair.

"Well, isn't that interesting," she began, when another voice cut her off.

"This is not a true dream," the voice said, clear as a child's.

Oh, god, no, thought Ceryl.

You *never* accused someone of lying at an inquisition.

Tatsun Frizer pawed at Ceryl's knee. "Isn't that

your little *friend*?" she whispered in disbelief. Ceryl pushed her away and watched, horrified, as the gynander walked into the circle.

"No?" The Aviator's terrible eyes fixed on her.

"No," replied Reive. Her hair had fallen to her shoulders in loose, oily-looking coils, and her cheeks were flushed. She looked like a demented child, not the mannered scryer one usually saw at inquisitions. Âziz raised her eyebrows, beckoning a serving boy to refill her wineglass, and leaned over to say something to Sajur Panggang. Echion smiled very slightly.

Please, please stop, Ceryl prayed. Very faintly she could hear Rudyard Planck whispering her name. She glanced at Nike, still holding the broken ends of her candicaine pipette. The margravine was staring at Reive entranced.

The gynander continued, her voice oddly toneless.

"It is not a true dream, because you are no longer a true man. It is the last memory of your last life. Somehow it has entered your regenerated consciousness. Because it is not a dream you will never be free of it."

The Aviator stared at her, motionless. Finally his voice rang out, so loud and deep that Tatsun Frizer gave a little shriek.

"You are right! It is not really a dream, because I am no longer a man." He nodded at Âziz and Nike. "This is a very clever creature you have here, Margravines. Perhaps it will scry *your* dreams for us?"

Âziz coughed, wiping her mouth with her hand and pushing away the serving boy as he offered her a towel. She nodded slowly, and stretched her long hands out toward Reive.

"Yes. Of course." Her eyes narrowed. "My dreams of late have been so—*unusual*—that I did not trust them to our usual seers. But *you* appear to be a rather unusual mantic, strange child."

Murmurings and excited glances from the crowd.

Âziz smiled a twisted smile and crooked a finger at Reive. "Come here, then, child. What's your name?"

Reive blinked and looked around the room, as though just waking up. She glanced back at Echion, who nodded, and then across the room at Ceryl, who pretended not to see her. Âziz watched her patiently, still moving her hands to beckon her closer. Warily Reive crossed the circle to stand before her.

"Our name is Reive."

"*Reive.*"

Âziz drawled the syllable, wrinkling her nose. Relieved laughter from the circle. "Well, *Reive.* You're quite a talented thing. I'm surprised we haven't met before."

She reached to touch the gynander's chin, tilted it so that Reive gazed back at her. Âziz drew her breath in sharply.

"Your eyes." Reive struggled to look away, but the margravine's hand held tight to her. "Where did you get such eyes?"

Reive's reply was so low it could scarcely be heard.

"We were born with them, Margravine."

"*Born* with them?" snapped Âziz. She let go of the gynander and turned to her sister. "Gynanders are *generated* on Dominations! They never have such eyes—"

Nike nodded. She said thoughtfully, "Shiyung has eyes like that—"

"Enough!" Âziz's voice cut her off. She turned back to Reive, regarding the gynander's slim figure in its filmy costume. Raising her eyebrows Âziz reached to stroke the edge of Nike's fur cape.

"Here, Reive—you look cold."

Âziz tugged at the cape; it slid from Nike to the floor, where she pointed at it, staring all the while at Reive. At first the gynander did nothing; then with a slow nod she took the cape and wrapped it around her shoulders.

Âziz stared at her through slitted eyes. "Very

striking. I have not seen you here on Seraphim before."

"We have only been here this week."

"Are you Echion's guest?"

Reive looked uneasy, finally shook her head.

"No."

All around the circle people were whispering and glancing at each other. Many of them were staring at Ceryl. She coughed and looked around the room fiercely, trying to avoid the gynander's eyes. Now Reive was staring at her. The powder on one cheek had been smeared, so that the green whorl there looked like a bruise. Beside Ceryl, Rudyard Planck whispered, "Don't worry, there's help if you need it."

"Come now, Reive, you must be *somebody's* guest," Âziz said sharply. "*I'm* not angry, I'm sure you didn't intend to insult our new Aviator Imperator, and I'm sure he doesn't feel that way. Margalis?"

She glanced at the Aviator. He shook his head, but it was impossible to tell what the gesture meant. Âziz went on, nonplussed. "See?"

Reive pulled the furs tight across her chest. Suddenly she pointed.

"Her."

Ceryl gasped. She had indicated Tatsun Frizer.

"She gave me an invitation—this afternoon—at the Investiture—"

Tatsun Frizer cried out and shook her head.

"A charming place to meet, I'm sure." Âziz smiled coldly at the stammering Tatsun, then turned to Reive. "And of course you wanted to come here this evening—"

Reive nodded. "Yes, Margravine . . ."

"She is fearless," Rudyard Planck whispered to Ceryl. Tatsun Frizer was silent now, her face bright red and teary-eyed.

"She's insane." Ceryl closed her eyes and turned her hands so they faced palm-upward, and murmured the soothing verse the *galli* had taught her.

On the other side of the room the gynander and

Âziz faced each other, the margravine still smiling that tight twisted smile.

"Well," Âziz said at last. She traced the outline of Reive's cheek, her finger smearing the rest of the gynander's makeup. "We don't normally allow uninvited guests into the Four Hundredth Room, especially at the beginning of Æstival Tide . . ."

She paused and looked across the room at Tatsun Frizer, who gibbered in protest.

"*But,*" the margravine continued, "seeing as how your scrying satisfied the Aviator Imperator, I am curious to hear what you have to say about *my* dream." Her face grew taut as she drew her hand back from Reive. Her voice dropped to a whisper. "I have not slept well for many nights, Reive. I would be very—*pleased*—with you, if you could discern the meaning of this dream. . . ."

The gynander nodded silently. Ceryl found she couldn't keep her eyes shut. Watching Reive, her own terror was almost overcome by pity—the gynander was trembling, her face smeared with powder and green kohl. She stared unblinking at Âziz as the margravine began to speak in a halting voice.

"It is two weeks now, I have not slept because of this dream. . . ."

From the air vents wafted a soft odor, something redolent of lavender smoke and new leather. The faces around the circle grew more relaxed as the incense filled the room and the margravine recited her dream. Ceryl inhaled deeply, her thoughts drifting. She smiled, recalling Reive's spindly figure declaring *This is not a dream* to the new Aviator Imperator. It would make a good story to tell, tomorrow, the stuff of *tanka* parlor gossip and much speculation among the pleasure cabinet. An unknown gynander appears and within a week is the margravine's new favorite. The parallels to Ceryl's own situation were obvious. Perhaps Reive would be given her own chambers on Thrones, or be brought up to Seraphim, there to tend to Âziz's nightmares. Or even stranger things might happen.

This is the game that moves as you play it. . . .

But then something broke Ceryl's reverie. The pleasant droning in the background had stopped. Âziz, after speaking for some minutes, had suddenly fallen silent. In front of her Reive stood stiffly, eyes half-closed, her hands clenched. Ceryl rubbed her forehead. Had she fallen asleep? She looked up in time to see Âziz take a handful of white powder from a raku bowl and toss it on a tiny cast-iron brazier. A harsh scent cut through the lulling incense. Rudyard Planck fidgeted and Tatsun Frizer looked around anxiously, as did most of the other guests. Only the Aviator remained unmoving, staring at the gynander.

In the center of the room Reive seemed to sway a little. With one finger she touched her temple, then sneezed and looked around, blinking. Âziz gazed at her through slitted eyes and continued.

"And then I was standing at a window in the gondola. In front of us the domes seemed to be cracking. For a minute I thought they were shattering, but then I realized it was just the skygates opening. The fouga started up through them. I was afraid for a moment, because I had never been Outside—I never *have* been Outside—but then I was excited, to think of what I'd see there—"

Ceryl choked. Her whole body felt as though it had been grasped by giant pincers. She hunched forward, gripping her knees, her face absolutely white.

Rudyard Planck tilted his head. "Are you all right?" he whispered. "You look sick—come, I'll help you outside—"

"No," said Ceryl. Dimly she could hear the margravine, going on and on, a voice she knew she would never stop hearing, ever—

"Ceryl?"

—because all of this, now, was like a dream—

"Ceryl?"

—and she had to see how it came out.

"Oh, my god," whispered Tatsun Frizer. "The margravine's gone mad . . ."

From the expressions of others in the circle, she was not the only one who thought so; but Ceryl could only hear Âziz—

". . . the fouga going higher and higher. And when I looked down, I saw this—this *crack* in the ground beneath the domes—and I knew in a moment I would see something, something—"

A rush of images in Ceryl's mind: the bluish lights of the vivarium; the shadows of the trees on the boulevard; her lover Giton's face beside hers in bed and then Reive in that same bed, Reive there now with her green eyes glowing . . .

". . . and I knew if I looked out the window I'd see—"

Âziz hesitated. The room was deathly silent as the margravine reached for another handful of white powder. Nike stirred, looking around in vain for her serving girl, who had crept to the door. Ceryl tried to count the number of steps it would take to join her. Rudyard Planck pointed a thumb at Reive and whispered, "Waxwing, I think maybe your friend is getting a little too—"

"I *knew*," Âziz repeated more loudly, her face flushed, "if I looked out the window, I would see—"

"*The Green Country*," Reive announced in a voice shrill as a kite's.

All around her was a sudden sharp intake of breath, as though the Four Hundredth Room had become a wheezing bellows.

"The *what*?"

Âziz's hand had stopped in midair above the raku bowl. White powder sifted from her fingers as she stared at Reive.

"The what?" Âziz said again.

Oh, Reive, no, thought Ceryl.

"Oh, dear," said the dwarf.

Ceryl gazed at the gynander. Dimly she could see dark-clad figures rushing from hidden doorways of the Four Hundredth Room, hear voices and someone beside her frantically repeating her own name. A woman was shouting. She remembered a plain of endless verdure, and that sense of exhilaration, of doors opening everywhere . . .

"The Green Country," repeated Reive.

She turned her pinched face to gaze one final moment at Ceryl, a look of love and triumph and utter hopelessness. From across the room the *rasa* stared at her, his gloved hands clenching and unclenching. Âziz was screaming something to the dark figures swarming like fire ants around the gynander's slender form, their prods and whips singing. And then Reive was gone, a prisoner of the Reception Committee.

Chapter 5

THE *RASA* REPENTS
~~~~~~~~~~~~~~~~~~~~~~~~~~~~~~~~

"I must see her."

Sajur Panggang nodded wearily. In the library
across from him sat Margalis Tast'annin, a friend very
long ago when they were both young and students at
the NASNA Academy. Their friendship had long since
ended, weakened by the wearying decades of Sajur's
rise in Araboth and Margalis's decline into obsession
and then madness as he became the most powerful
military commander on the continent. Sajur had always assumed Margalis would die a violent and terrible death. Now it seemed that even death was not
enough to destroy him, at least not as long as Shiyung
Orsina was alive. The Architect Imperator leaned back
in his favorite chair, an oaken Morris chair grown
black and hard as ebony with the centuries, and
tapped his chin with one long finger.

He had left the Four Hundredth Room immediately after the gynander's revelation. Not a prudent move on his part; but he had been overcome by his own reaction to Âziz's dream. That part about the crack in the Undercity—at once he felt elation and a sort of greed. To think of the margravine being foolish enough to admit to such a dream! It was too perfect. In Araboth's enclosed world, such fears worked like a virus, seeping into the populace and spreading until others would be felled by that same nightmare of the Undercity crumbling and the dome caving inward like a bad fruit.

There were already fearful rumors everywhere. Every level of the city had felt the tremors that now shook Araboth four or five times a day. Early this morning there had been reports of a conflagration on Archangels, with hundreds of *rasas* immolated in moments as one of the refineries blew. The resulting shock waves had been felt as high as Thrones Level, and here on Cherubim a greasy pall hung in the air, a smell like rancid oil and rotting cloth.

And now news of Âziz's dream would spread throughout the city. The Architect Imperator smiled at the thought. A margravine having an apocalyptic dream on the very eve of the Feast of Fear! If only his sisters hadn't exiled Nasrani. He was the only one who had anything like a sense of diplomacy, and of course his youth had been spent in training as an Architect. But Nasrani was lost to his arcane longings as meanwhile the city was slowly being teased open, rivet by rivet, fiber by fiber, the joists and beams and hidden underpinnings of Angels painstakingly prised apart like the corpse of an aardman within the Chambers of Mercy. And all the while the margravines fretted over half-baked plots and imaginary threats by bastard pretenders to the Orsinate dynasty.

None of them would ever know the truth, because no one but Sajur communicated with the Architects, and not even Sajur ever ventured to the

Undercity. He glanced up at the *rasa* sitting across from him and shook his head very slightly.

"I understand, Margalis. Really I do. But, well, you must see how it is right now. Âziz is in a state over this, I know it seems petty to you but they get worked up over these things. She takes her dreams very seriously—"

The *rasa*'s harsh voice cut him off. "Oh, but so do I, Sajur. So do I. That is why I would like to see the hermaphrodite."

Sajur reached for his glass. He stared into the emerald liquid, nodding as though he were trying to think of a way to arrange such a meeting; but in truth it could not be done. For the sake of their dead friendship he wished he could help Margalis; wished he could do something as simple as offer him some of this very fine Amity, or show him the new windchamber he had installed in Angelika's old dressing room. But these things were lost on a *rasa*. Sajur sipped his Amity and sighed.

"I wish I could. But it would do no good for me to intercede for you—Hell's teeth, Margalis, you're their chief of staff now! *You* know what it's like. They listen to no one except each other. Once the Reception Committee's taken someone, well it's all over. And Âziz has made up her mind about this. Sedition, treason, the old sad song. And, well, it's just a morphodite after all, not worth dirtying your hands—"

He finished awkwardly. The hands that rested on the edge of the library table across from him were encased in black leather gloves. On one finger a heavy ring winked in the light, a gold ring set with a blue stone and circled by letters spelling out *NASNA*. Sajur imagined that one of those hands lay quite calmly: the one with the Academy ring—a peaceful hand, a *tamed* hand in its steel and glass and plasteen sheath; while the other twitched restively. In truth both hands were as ominously still as the Aviator Imperator himself.

"My memories—my memories are incomplete,"

the *rasa* said slowly. "The morphodite at this evening's dream inquisition somehow saw the truth of
what I told her—it was not a dream at all, but a fragment of my earlier life. I would ask her how she knew
this. I would see if she could help me—*remember*—
other things."

His voice ended in a hollow whistling breath.
Sajur knew that Shiyung had gone to great pains to
revive Tast'annin's voice, the long hypnotic drawl that
could charm a rector at the Academy as easily as it
could command a phalanx of Gryphons in maneuvers
over the Medaïn Desert. But the man's voice was
gone. The empty sound that boomed at him now was
as cold and dull as the voice of a Gryphon itself. The
voice of something meant to obey, twisted within this
tortured husk of a commander.

"I'm sorry, Margalis," Sajur said gently.

On the divan the *rasa* that had been Margalis
Tast'annin raised his empty face. He had been the Ascendants' greatest soldier, the most brilliant student
ever to graduate from the NASNA Academy. A tall,
proud man, his shoulders stooped a little from having
forever to look down upon those who answered to
him. Sajur remembered him as a youth, reckless and
with that sharp tongue ready to lash out at the slow,
the unwitting, the men and women doomed by their
birth on the wrong level in Araboth, the wrong creche
in the desolate Outlands, to a lifetime of service to the
Ascendants. Tast'annin had been a bold if frightening
figure even then, with his gold-straw hair gone early
to gray and his colorless eyes that reflected whatever
the sky showed them—the sky that only the Aviators
saw now, and the mongrel slaves bred to serve them.

That power to command remained in the hooded
figure that sat and stared at Sajur Panggang. The
metal mask hid what Shiyung had been unable to sal-
vage from the decomposing corpse. Though there
were the eyes, of course, she had managed to save the
eyes. A whim of the youngest margravine who, while
not truly soft-hearted, liked to be thought so. And

See patterns

perhaps she had believed it would somehow make him seem more human.

This final conversion had been her idea. Tast'annin had been rehabilitated before, of course, he was too valuable a commander to have blinded or lamed in battle. But each regeneration had left his mind frailer and more prone to madness—Sajur thought of a particular kind of dog that Shiyung had bred for several years, thirty generations compressed and refined in the nucleovats, until the elegant structure and slender muzzles she so loved had collapsed into whimpering heaps of bones slung in a sack of flesh, drooling and twitching at their mistress's ankles.

She was determined that no such thing would happen to Tast'annin. After the Archipelago Conflict there had been months of delicate surgery, that business with his ears for instance; but still there had been something they could never quite repair. A certain mental brittleness, a tendency to see patterns where there were none. As though he always heard a strange high-pitched sound the rest of them were deaf to, a sound that would gradually drive one quite insane.

This time he would not fail them. Shiyung had ordered the final conversion after the janissaries found his corpse in the abandoned capital. His activities there had been a sort of treason, of course. He had been betrayed by the Capital's Governors, betrayed and then handed over to the half-human aaradmen who had tortured him, unmanned him, but then, in a characteristic fit of pity, freed him. Once on his own again he had made his way to the ruins of one of the Capital's great landmarks, an ancient and malign Cathedral. There he had planned to conquer the Capital for himself, seizing control of its ancient armories and enslaving its people.

But he had failed. Within hours of his defeat, Ascendant janissaries had captured the City and borne

Tast'annin's body back to Araboth, where his treason was revealed to the Orsinate.

A lesser man than Tast'annin would have remained dead, his body thrown before the Lahatiel Gate to be torn apart by the mob. But the Orsinate understood that treason itself was not necessarily a bad thing. It bespoke a certain amount of ambition, and vision, and the Orsinate recognized that vision at least was often in short supply among their staff. And then there was the matter of Tast'annin's relations with Shiyung. Many years ago, of course, but even Âziz acceded that sentiment was not without its place in their (admittedly full) lives.

So Margalis Tast'annin was brought back to Araboth. Rather, his body was brought back; the process of retrieving Tast'annin was a longer one. This time there would be no chance of him succumbing to anything so rustic as a bullet or an aardman's jaws. There would be no question of the frailty of the flesh, because there would be no flesh.

Very little, at least. The *rasa*'s degenerated form was hidden now in its metal sheath. They left him a hand—Nike's idea, she was an admirer of the cinematic arts and had noticed this was a popular conceit in ancient films—and they left him his eyes, because Shiyung insisted. His mind of course remained his own, although the biotechs improved his aggression responses and enhanced his already acute intuitive skills. Only his memories were imperfect. Certain things he could not recall with any certainty as being dreams or actual events. He spoke, for instance, of the existence of *dark gods* as though such things were commonplace. But the Orsinate felt this was a trifling weakness in a military commander.

They might have reproduced his body, or given him another, younger one, instead of the metal shell that now sat watching the Architect Imperator drink rather more Amity than he should. But it had not been Shiyung's idea to end the affair with Tast'annin.

And with Shiyung, sentiment was not combined with a forgiving nature.

The Aviator Imperator lifted his head. The gassy blue lanterns sparked the mask's smooth crimson surface with violet and ultramarine. "Never mind," he replied to Sajur. "Perhaps it is not important."

Sajur looked relieved. The Amity made it easier to imagine this was the old Tast'annin in the room with him, and not a corpse enhanced with liquid bio-circuitry. "Would you like to watch some 'files? I've got last year's graduation from the Academy, Salih Mukheyat gave the address. Or some of Nike's collection. Let's see—"

He jumped up and crossed to where a stack of 'files leaned against one of the Architect's secondary monitors. "Let's see. 'The Story of the Last Chrysanthemum,' that's quite nice. Or 'The Broken Will,' Nike said that's considered George Owlden's masterpiece." He rummaged through the 'files, holding each to his ear so it could whisper its title. "Hmm, *Khibel ab Mejnun*,' Khibel the Fool—"

"Thank you, Sajur. Not tonight." The *rasa* stood, leather clothing skreeking against his metal limbs. "I will let you sleep."

Sajur's voice quavered a little, drunkenly. "Are you quite sure?"

Tast'annin shook his head. "Yes, Sajur. It is late, I'll leave you with your 'files and—"

He inclined his head toward the crystal decanter winking in the dim light. "Another time, perhaps, we'll watch 'Khibel the Fool.' "

Sajur walked with him to the door. "I'm sorry Hobi wasn't here to see you. Khum said he went out with—a guest—this afternoon. I know he wanted to offer his congratulations. . . ."

"Give him my best."

Tast'annin let the man hold the door for him. Outside, the deep indigo light that demarcated evening gleamed above the pagodas and spires of Cherubim. The *rasa* stared up to where the central

Quincunx Dome curved, a great gleaming black hand cupped over the sleeping city. He raised his own hand in imitation, palm down, and turned away.

"Good night, Sajur."

"Good night, Margalis," the Architect Imperator called softly. He raised his hand in farewell, but the *rasa* did not look back.

Shiyung winced as the eyra screamed again. She had miscalculated something in the final stage of the great cat's compressed gestation. When she pulled it from the vat the epidermal layer of its skull had not completely formed, and the pink skin had sloughed from it like icing from a too-warm cake. The creature lay at her feet, shrieking, while nucleic starter pooled around it. Delicately she lifted one foot and stepped over the steaming liquid, reached down and gently prodded its chin. Its screams became a dull moan, and then silence.

"Damn."

It was the third one that day. Shiyung was impatient and had difficulty waiting the correct amount of time when indulging her hobby. Now she turned and walked to the door, sidestepping other damp places on the floor of her laboratory. "Me-suh," she called softly. "Me-suh, I think I'm finished for today."

Her replicant assistant appeared, a copper woman with snaky hair and a pronounced list to one side. Robotic engineering had been an earlier passion of Shiyung's. "I'm going to try another breed of big cat tomorrow, Me-suh. Maybe a tiger. I think there's something wrong with this strain."

Me-suh bowed, her bad shoulder scraping the wall, and headed for the dead cougar. With a sigh Shiyung started upstairs.

The message chamber showed a call from Nike, her sister yawning as she mumbled something about a ruined inquisition. Shiyung grimaced and replayed it, then went through the other calls until she found one from Âziz.

"—thought I'd tell you first it's nothing, absolutely *nothing*," Âziz's aggrieved voice scraped through the air. "An idiot morphodite, she's been detained of course, but of course there are all these *rumors* now, and then there was that explosion on Archangels, so I think we'd better—"

Shiyung rolled her eyes, switched off her sister's peevish voice, and went into her bedroom. Another great cat, a caracal, sprawled upon the bed, like ghee poured upon the black coverlet. It meowed throatily when it saw Shiyung. Shiyung wrinkled her nose as she pushed it to the floor: really, she needed a less fulsome hobby. But the rewards of bioengineering were greater than those of robotics. She couldn't control the actions of her great cats and half-human creations, and she derived a perverse satisfaction from that. As the youngest of the Orsinate, Shiyung had always prided herself on being unpredictable—refusing to use human servers; taking the side of the moujiks during the Medifac Insurgency when she was only nine years old; attending mass at the Church of Christ Cadillac and even driving one of their ancient vehicles into the flaming wall during the sect's communion rites. In the last few months she had been fascinated by what she heard of an eerie new cult formed by the *rasas,* and she had even entertained thoughts of having another natural child. She would be more careful this time, and choose a father whose genotype was not so similar to hers. It was a shame that baby had been deformed, but at least the Children of Mercy had been glad to have it, if only for a little while.

It would be interesting, she thought, to have a living child. Children were so *spontaneous.* Her great cats and geneslaves were beautiful but lacked that element of uncertainty, their wild instincts bred out of them centuries before.

"Right, Bast?" she murmured, stroking the caracal's proud jaw. Someone had told her once that she looked like a panther, a biotech she'd slept with during Æstival Tide.

"Green eyes and a cruel jaw and velvet hands," the woman had whispered to her over a hubble-bubble on the beach. Shiyung had to look up the word and its image to see what a panther was, but after that she began toying with the genus *Felidae* in her laboratory. For a little while the biotech had assisted her, but then she'd grown rather too demanding and Shiyung had her put with the other Chosen during the Hecatombs.

But Shiyung's passion for predators remained. She'd filled her chambers with caracals and ocelots and servals, and was disappointed when they didn't kill the birds and squirrels she made for them. Then for a while she'd gone in for canines, jackals and fennecs and even an aardwolf, technically a different strain but so unusual. But the cats still offered the most visually pleasing effects, and recently she'd begun to try to revive their aggressive instincts, with mixed results.

"Ah, Bast," whispered Shiyung, pulling the caracal back beside her. She reached for one of the camphor cigarettes kept in a silver holder at her bedside. As she lit it a bell chimed and the foyer scholiast's voice echoed, "You have a visitor."

Shiyung exhaled. The caracal sneezed and slid from the bed, taking the woolen comforters with her. "Who is it?"

"The Aviator Imperator Margalis Tast'annin."

Shiyung smoked in silence for another minute. Finally she said, "Show him in, please." She put out her cigarette and crossed to her armoire. She had just dropped her laboratory robes and stood before the mirror in a white silk chemise when Tast'annin appeared in the door.

"Forgive me, Margravine. I'll wait until you're dressed."

Without glancing at him Shiyung pulled a flannel

kimono from the wardrobe and shrugged into it. "Oh, please, Margalis, I think we're past all that now. *Especially* now."

She turned. She was alone with him for the first time since she'd pulled his brain from the crucible and begun the complicated procedure of bonding it to its metal form. He wore not the NASNA Aviator's uniform but a simple robe of black jacquard. As he entered the room she glimpsed glints of white and crimson light glowing within the silken folds. "Thank you for seeing me, Shiyung."

She sank into a chair near the curtained window and regarded him critically. It was unsettling to hear that hollow voice echoing from a mouthless mask. "It's late, isn't it? Although of course you don't get tired now. Not that you ever slept very well."

He shrugged. The robe rippled along his shoulders and she saw the sleek line of metal there, melting into the crimson curve of his neck. "Sleep. It's interesting that you should mention sleep—may I sit?—because it is a dream that brought me here."

"How interesting." She motioned at the bed. The *rasa* sat. At his feet the caracal blinked, then growled softly, and Shiyung smiled with false ingenuousness. "I had no idea that *rasas* could dream."

"Not my dream. Âziz's."

"Ah." Shiyung made a chucking sound and the caracal curled at her side. "I heard about that. Âziz called me. Oh, Me-suh—"

The server appeared in the doorway. "Some iced vitro for me. Margalis?"

For a moment his translucent eyes flickered from gray to dark blue. He said, "No, thank you."

"Of course, forgive me—you have no mouth." Shiyung wrinkled her nose and covered her face, a naughty child stifling a laugh. When the server returned with the tumbler of blue ice she sipped it, staring at the *rasa* through slitted eyes. After a few minutes she leaned forward and asked conspiratorially, "So tell me, Margalis: what is it like? Is it different, really? Can you still feel things? I mean—"

She gestured at her thighs with one slender hand, pulled aside her kimono. "Like that, what's it like now?"

A strained sound from the *rasa;* then, "Nothing. I feel nothing anymore. At least I don't feel it physically. But of course I *remember* many things."

Shiyung gave a small disappointed sigh and let her kimono drape back across her legs. She took another sip of her vitro. "It must be painful for you. Remembering things."

Tast'annin tipped his head so that she saw the mask's smooth contours, crimson threaded with silver in a pattern that appeared only when it caught the light at a certain angle. His eyes glowed dangerously. "It is worse than any torment I could have imagined," he said at last.

For some minutes they sat without speaking. Shiyung sipped her drink. At her feet the caracal snored softly. The *rasa* seemed deep in thought, at least his posture assumed pensive lines as he stared at the floor with its simple grass carpeting. Finally he looked up. Tast'annin's ice-pale eyes stared out at Shiyung as he said, "There was a hermaphrodite at the dream inquisition this evening. An interloper of some sort. She correctly scryed my dream—my memory—and then Âziz asked her to read hers."

"Yes. She told me." Shiyung was bored. Her pleasure in Tast'annin's plight had not been as acute as she had hoped. She felt neither glee nor the rarer thrill of remorse and pity; only a detached vicarious curiosity that Tast'annin seemed unlikely to indulge. "Âziz had a little fit and had her locked up."

"I'd like to see her."

Shiyung raised an eyebrow and finished her drink. The faintest note of something—pleading, maybe, or anger; it was so hard to tell when he had no face—had crept into the *rasa*'s nearly uninflected voice. "Âziz?"

"No. The hermaphrodite. The one she's imprisoned."

"Hmm."

Shiyung set the tall tumbler on a night table and stood, stretching. Her kimono fell open on a swath of buttery skin and she did not bother to close it as she walked to the window. She was thinking again about the child she had given birth to fifteen years before. Another one of her whims. She and Nasrani had been sharing a bed, and she had decided it might be interesting to have a natural child. Only something had gone wrong—the physicians warned her about it, and with her dabbling in genetics she had known there was a chance of something like this. Too many Orsinas together over too many centuries. When the child was born she couldn't bear to look at it, the tiny penis and behind it the pink vulva, and witch's milk oozing from its breasts. The last report she'd had of it, from the Chambers of Mercy, was that it was a true hermaphrodite, the first to be born of natural parents in many years. She hadn't bothered finding out the details of its final disposition.

Now, thinking of this morphodite who had so upset Âziz, she wondered what had happened to that other one. Perhaps it had been cruel of her to give it to the Chambers of Mercy. Perhaps—her heart beat a little faster at the thought—perhaps there were reparations to be made. Perhaps Blessed Narouz (or Christ Cadillac, or Prophet Rayburn) had sent this other morph just for this purpose, to permit her to make amends. It might be a noble thing for her to do, to save this gynander. Especially at Æstival Tide. Shiyung was very fond of doing noble things under the right, usually public, circumstances.

She pulled the draperies back, displaying a dizzying view of Araboth: the cobalt reaches of the dome above, indigo and rose-pink and viridian sweeps of light below, darkening from level to level, until at the very bottom an inky blue gleamed, as though reflecting back the fastnesses of Seraphim.

She looked up at the domes and pointed. "You can see the stars tonight. There—?"

Tast'annin stood and stepped beside her. He placed one hand on her shoulder. It was warm, warmer than any human hand would be, and vibrated so that her shoulder tensed beneath it. "Yes, those are stars. Some of them, at least. There, and—"

He pointed to the faint light salted across the dark curves of the dome. "There. That is Orion."

"That star?"

"No. That set of stars. A constellation. The Hunter."

"And that?" She pointed at a glorious sweep of color trailing from horizon to horizon. "The Milky Way?"

He made a small sound meant to be laughter. "That is the reflection of the palace lights in the dome."

"Ah."

Behind them the caracal continued to snore. Shiyung let the curtains fall back across the window and turned to Tast'annin. "Why do you want to see her, this hermaphrodite? Why didn't you go to Âziz?"

The *rasa* shrugged. "I knew she would refuse me, at least tonight while she's still angry. And who knows, tomorrow the hermaphrodite might be dead."

Shiyung nodded thoughtfully. "Probably. Was she pretty?"

"Childish. But yes, she was attractive."

Shiyung settled onto the bed and motioned for the *rasa* to join her. "But that's not why you want to see her."

"No," he admitted. "It's not. She said something tonight, about Âziz's dream. She said it symbolized the Green Country."

Shiyung was silent. She bunched up a corner of the woolen comforter and released it, glanced up to see the *rasa* staring at her with those eerie bright eyes.

"Well," she said after a moment. "Rather careless on her part, I'd say. No wonder Âziz had her locked

up." She nibbled her lip thoughtfully. "I wonder why
Âziz didn't tell me. I mean when she called, she said
the morph had been detained but she didn't say why.
So my sister has dreamed of the Green Country."

She stood and paced the room, nudging the caracal as she passed it. It sat up, startled, then stretched
and slunk beside its mistress.

The Green Country. Of all the superstitions that
haunted the city, the most potent. Not even Âziz
would have been able to keep from succumbing to
some fear when she heard that particular twist given
to her dream. It must have been a very stupid
morphodite, to just spit out something like that. Very,
very stupid.

Or—

And here Shiyung slowed her pace and stared at
the mirror that hung across from her bed. A chrome
crucifix dangled above it, with a tiny plastic automo-
bile hanging from the cross's horizontal bar. Beside
this hung a polyimage of Blessed Narouz and a vial of
petroleum, a moujik prayer wheel, and a plastic bas-
relief of Nefer-ka' ehlvi.

Or, thought Shiyung as she flicked the prayer
wheel so that it spun with a loud whir, *perhaps the
morph has the true Sight.* The Final Ascension had been
predicted for centuries now, mostly by those who suf-
fered under the tyranny of the Orsinate Ascendants.
Recently there had been Signs that were difficult to
ignore, even by an Orsina, and especially if one listened to those on the lower levels. The *rasa* cult, for
instance—surely *that* was evidence of something, the
dead seeking some kind of revelatory meaning in
their hopeless, horrible existence. And these shakings
and tremblings of the ground; and last night an explosion in one of the refineries. And of course the usual
claims of publicity-seekers that they had heard the
Redeemer waking early from its decade-long sleep, or
seen the mad geneslave Zalophus flying like a fouga
beneath the domes.

Her sisters scoffed at these tales—at least Âziz

scoffed; Nike nodded absently and took more morpha
—but Shiyung considered it a point of honor to pay
attention to such things. No mongrel cult was too
rabid for her to partake in its rites at least once; no
moujik witch so deranged but that Shiyung wouldn't
take a vial of her spittle and carry it back to Seraphim
to display on her wall or in one of her curio cabinets.

"Did she have a name, this morphodite? Do you
remember what they called her?" She turned back to
the *rasa*. Her cheeks were flushed and her eyes glistened as she hurried to sit beside him.

Tast'annin nodded. "Reive."

"Reive? Just that? No other name, no number?"

"Reive, that's all she said. Very young and thin,
with very black hair. I think she wore—"

"No, that's all right, I can find her. Reive." The
caracal nudged her knee and Shiyung took its head
between her palms and squeezed it absently, until it
whined. "Me-suh! Come here, I need you to locate
someone for me—"

The snaky-haired server creaked back into the
room, its linen covering flapping across its copper
torso. Shiyung explained, "A hermaphrodite named
Reive, detained by the Reception Committee this evening. By my sister Âziz."

"What crime, mistress?" Me-suh's voice came
out in a low croak.

"I have no idea. Sedition, probably. Or—well, I
don't know. There was a disturbance at that dream
inquisition in the Four Hundredth Room. Run her
name through the main file."

The server nodded and creaked back out again.
Shiyung tapped her foot on the floor and hummed to
herself. After a few minutes Me-suh returned.

"She is on Cherubim, mistress. In the Howarth
Reception Area."

Shiyung clapped and plucked at Tast'annin's
sleeve excitedly. "Did you hear that? Howarth. That's
right below here, it will only take a few minutes—"

Howarth was where political prisoners were received.

She stood and went to the armoire, flung aside coats and robes and lumen-accented tunics until she found matching trousers and blouse of a deep burgundy shade. She dressed quickly, then pulled her dark hair back so that it fell in a shining line past her shoulders. Finally she tugged a dark hood around her face. Watching her the *rasa*'s eyes closed for a moment. When they opened again she stood by the door, waiting.

"All right, Margalis, we'll go visit your little friend."

He slipped beside her and the door hissed shut behind them. For a moment Shiyung looked at him with shining eyes.

"I stayed home this evening to work—everyone else is always sleeping this late. It's nice to have company for a change."

He stared at her without answering, and then followed her down the hall.

Centuries earlier, the tenth Orsinate dynasty had designed the Howarth Reception Area as quarters for political prisoners, men and women of considerable rank who surrendered or were captured during the unsettled months after the Third Shining.

None of the hostages ever returned to the Balkhash steppes or the jeweled shores of the Archipelago. A few of them eventually married into the Orsinate. Others became tutors, and a few even escaped to the lower levels. But most spent their lives and died in the Reception Area so that now, despite the quite-comfortable accommodations and the attentions of the Reception Committee, it was rumored to be haunted. Several guards claimed to have heard the click of mah-jongg tiles interspersed with soft laughter and the sound of something being poured onto the floor. Reive had only been there a few hours, but al-

ready she had seen the blue-tinged silhouette of a
young man cross her room and pass through the wall,
enter and cross again, as though pacing the outlines of
a chamber that had long since been walled off from
this one.

The Reception Committee treated her well, since
she was a guest of Âziz Orsina. The margravine dis-
dained vulgar privations—they weakened her guests,
most of whom were destined for the private torture of
timoring. And for successful timoring, one must have
some reserve of strength to call upon. So the Reception Committee brought Reive yoghurt and brandied
loquats and a tiny roasted quail, and watched politely
while she ate on her bed.

"You can go. We won't kill ourself," the gynander sniffed.

The two guards shrugged and smiled, opening
their mouths to show where their tongues had been
removed, then tugging amiably at the long yellow
sashes that hung from their waists.

"Fine," said Reive, and turning back to her quail
ignored them.

A minute later the steel door opened and a tall
hooded figure strode in, followed by another figure in
a black silk robe.

"Thank you, but we'll see to her now," the first
announced. At sight of the *rasa*, the guards nearly fell
down in astonishment. When they heard Shiyung's
voice they bowed, grunting and pounding the floor
with their palms, then fled. The figure in the silk robe
closed the door after them, staring out through the
metal grate into the hallway. Reive gazed up silently,
her mouth full. She choked when she recognized
Shiyung Orsina and the *rasa* Imperator.

"Aghh—" The remains of her quail fell onto the
mattress. The margravine shook her head and put a
finger to her lips. Then, smiling conspiratorially, she
carefully removed the empty plates from the bed and
sat beside Reive.

"We're your friends, Reive," said Shiyung. She

turned to the *rasa* and beamed, but Tast'annin only stared at Reive with cold blue eyes. Shiyung shrugged and continued, "I understand there was some—confusion—at a dream inquisition this evening. But you can tell us what *really* happened."

Reive swallowed, stammering, "We can?" She tried not to wince as the margravine put her arm around her and shook her gently. She smelled of nucleic starter and amber. Reive thought she looked less beautiful than she did on the 'files.

"You can," the Aviator intoned.

Reive's voice quivered as she gazed at the *rasa*. "You—we saw you this morning. The Investiture— and your dream—"

Tast'annin stared down at the morphodite. The Reception Committee had removed the smudged makeup from her face. With her blank, sharp features and her long legs swinging from the edge of the bed, she looked like an effeminate young boy. He had never understood the vogue for hermaphrodites, found them slightly repellant in fact, with their soft round faces and vapid eyes. But this one seemed more alert than most—flippant even, despite her obvious fear. He spoke to her gently enough.

"I am—I was—Margalis Tast'annin. A NASNA Aviator First Class, now Aviator Imperator to the Orsinate."

Nodding, Reive turned to the margravine. "And you're Shiyung."

The margravine smiled, tossing her hair back so that Reive could see her earrings, solid gold and so heavy that her lobes had distended a full inch from wearing them. The letter ☽ and the Eye of Horus: the Orsinate's insignia. "That's right."

The young one, Reive thought. She wondered if those earrings hurt. *The crazy one.*

Shiyung looked at her expectantly. "We'd like to help you, Reive. Is there anything we can do to help you?" She put her finger to the gynander's chin and tilted Reive's face toward her.

"Is there more to eat?"

Surprised, Shiyung drew back. Tast'annin made a small noise that might be laughter. "Those quail aren't very big," Reive said defensively.

"Ye-es," said Shiyung. She frowned. "But—well, I was thinking more along the lines of, Could we perhaps make you more comfortable? Somewhere else?" Her voice rose suggestively.

"The margravine would like to rescue you," explained the *rasa*. "If you remain here her sister is likely to have you executed in the morning."

"Oh!" Reive sat up very straight. "We didn't know. We thought—" She gestured at the neatly appointed room with its comfortable chairs and oil paintings and elegant china. "We thought she had forgiven us."

Shiyung narrowed her eyes. "You haven't been among us for very long, have you, Reive?"

"N-no." She flushed and toyed with her hair.

"But you're a pantomancer, surely you are aware of the significance of a dream of the Green Country?"

The gynander nodded slowly.

"We've known that dream," she said. She glanced at the *rasa* staring at her sideways, like the cormorant in Zalophus's tank, his eyes glittering feverishly. She turned to Shiyung. "We have scryed it twice now."

"*Twice?*"

Reive cowered on the bed. "Yes." It was as Ceryl had warned her, she would be executed at once, or used as one of Âziz's *timorata*—or, worst of all, given to the Compassionate Redeemer in the festival's propitiary rites.

Shiyung turned to the *rasa*. "She says she's scryed it twice."

"So I heard."

Shiyung clasped her elegant white hands, looking around the small room as though she expected it to disappear in a mist. "But—this is incredible! The same dream, *that* dream, twice? Margalis, this could—what does this *mean*?"

Tast'annin shrugged, his kimono sliding to reveal the ribbed metal cage of his chest. "It could mean nothing. Or it could mean this morphodite is lying. Or it could be a harbinger of evil things not predicated by your Architects. What do *you* think it means?"

Shiyung bit her lip. "The 'file of Fasidin the Depraved says that to dream of the Green Country is to dream of the *el-bajdia,* the engulfing wilderness. It is a terrible omen." She reached for the gynander and pulled her toward her and for the first time Reive clearly saw the margravine's eyes: wide and childlike and an alarming shade of emerald. "Come, Reive— we'll talk someplace safer."

The gynander cast a final, longing look at her empty plate. "If anyone passes us you're to keep your head down and say nothing," whispered the margravine. The three of them left the Howarth Reception Area and hurried down the private gravator that would bring them to Shiyung's chambers.

Shiyung's quarters were larger than any Reive had ever seen, larger and hotter and filled with animals, great soft-bellied cats that skulked about the corners and seemed as intent as Reive upon finding something to eat. On the walls hung antique tapestries in somber shades of brownish-red, like dried blood or dung. The room smelled of sandalwood and damp fur, and a faint breeze blew down from vents in the ceiling.

"But why would you say these things about my sister?" Shiyung asked softly. She sat very close to the gynander and stroked her thigh absently as she spoke, tracing the imprint of a bruise on Reive's white skin.

"Because it's true," Reive said sullenly for the tenth time. "We saw the Green Country in her dream. It is in her eyes as well, you have only to look to see it. Please, can we please have something to drink?"

Shiyung pursed her lips in annoyance, then clicked her fingers. Her server listed into the room, and the caracal moaned softly. "Me-suh, bring us some of that aquavit and whatever else there is—fruit or something."

Frowning, the margravine stood and paced. Behind Reive stood the *rasa,* so silent that the gynander held her breath, to see if she could hear him breathing; but she heard nothing. His pale eyes glittered as he watched her, and it seemed that his irises bloomed a deeper blue as Shiyung grew more agitated.

The margravine stopped and gazed sharply at Reive.

"Now I can tell you, morphodite, that my sister Âziz would be the last person in Araboth to have that dream. Unlike me she has no interest whatsoever in theological matters, and she is not—shall we say— superstitious. Now I would have thought this was a more commonplace dream, an omen perhaps of unrest during the upcoming holiday. But I find it very interesting that you interpreted it so differently, especially on the eve of Æstival Tide. There are *many* interesting things about you. For instance, how is it that you came to this level without a sponsor? You were not on the guest list for that inquisition—"

"We were invited—" Reive tugged at the small mesh purse hanging about her waist and pulled out Tatsun Frizer's allurian calling card. "See?"

Shiyung took the card and read it, then tossed it aside. "Frizer. She's in Blessed Narouz's Refinery. How do you know her?"

Reive started to explain about that morning: the walk along the boulevard, the Investiture, and the woman with the puppet who had given her the card. But as she started to speak Tast'annin's face trapped her, like the black mirrors set by moujiks to capture the souls of the dead. "We—we don't know," she stammered.

"She will not harm you, Reive," the *rasa* said softly. He moved closer to her and placed one gloved hand upon her knee. He stroked her leg gently, as Shiyung toyed with her caracal. "If what you said was true—if Âziz really did have a prophetic dream—why that is quite an unusual circumstance, and you must understand better than we do what that portends. Don't you, Reive?"

His voice had grown soft, its monotone and the scent of sandalwood lulling her so that her eyelids drooped and she let herself sink backward into the pillows. She said nothing, her mouth shaping a silent ☽ as the *rasa* continued.

"You read my dream without any difficulty—perhaps a *rasa*'s dreams are not so challenging as those others—and so now I will tell you something, Reive. I think you were right. I think Âziz *did* have the dream of the Green Country."

Shiyung made a small noise, whether of disapproval or restrained excitement the gynander couldn't tell. Tast'annin's hand upon her thigh tightened, squeezing more and more forcefully until Reive cried out. But he did not seem to notice, only went on speaking in his calm toneless voice.

"You must understand, I have seen before what happens when people do not pay attention to their dreams. Âziz and her clever siblings have been supporting research in distant places, facilities in the wilderness where it was thought safe to perform some rather cruel acts—upon children, among others. I daresay Shiyung has forgotten all about that little project of hers—"

Shiyung blinked her calm green eyes and shook her head. "Children? Which one was that?"

"The Human Engineering Laboratory. The Harrow Effect, that was what they called it. A method of inducing multiple personalities and then using the subjects in emotive engram therapy. Psychic vampires, capable of reading the emotions and memories of others. They would make ideal spies and terrorists for the Orsinate, perhaps even help them to escape their servitude to the Ascendant Autocracy. Only the

subjects were so unstable that they often went mad
and killed themselves, or induced suicide and madness in others."

Shiyung furrowed her brow, her little mouth
pursed into a frown. The *rasa*'s voice rose slightly.

"See, Reive! She doesn't even remember. But *I*
recall when Shiyung was so excited about the Harrow
Effect that she couldn't—well, she couldn't do much
of anything. She and her sisters had great plans—the
Human Engineering Laboratory would be a testing
ground, they would go on to have child farms where
they would raise entire armies of disassociated terrorists, ready to kill and be killed without a single
thought. Certainly without a single thought from the
Orsinate. They would seize control once more of the
ancient capital—ah, see, Reive, she remembers *that*
part—and install a new Governor there, someone
chosen expressly for that purpose from the highest
ranks of the NASNA Academy. And of course, eventually the Orsinate would move there, at least one of
them would—the youngest, perhaps, she was known
for a certain recklessness that sometimes passed as
foresight. She would not be afraid to go into the wilderness and live in the ruins, once the ruins had been
cleaned up a bit—she may be feckless, but she is also a
fastidious young woman."

The *rasa*'s voice had grown quite loud. When he
fell silent its echo filled the room like a bell clanging.
Beneath his fingers dark welts had sprung up on
Reive's leg. She covered her face with her hands, biting her lip to keep from crying out again. Abruptly he
let go of her. With a cry she backed away from him
until she bumped into the wall.

From where she reclined against a stack of pillows, Shiyung stared at Tast'annin, her needle-thin
eyebrows raised above guileless eyes. "I *had* forgotten
about that project," she said. "Whatever happened to
those people?"

"They are all dead," the *rasa* replied. Reive huddled against the wall, shivering. How could the mar-

gravine stand it, listening to it—*him*—talk like this? The sound of his voice was enough to drive Reive mad; and the way he looked at Shiyung . . . Reive crossed her hands across her chest and prayed the *rasa* would forget about her, forget she had ever come here.

The *rasa* crossed the room to stand above Shiyung. With one gloved hand he reached to caress her hair, letting it slide between his fingers in a long black stream. "Or most of them are, at any rate. A few escaped; at least one that I know of. It's ironic, isn't it? That little diversion of yours caused so much misery and destruction; and yet you don't even remember it. . . ."

Shiyung closed her eyes, arching her neck against the *rasa*'s hand. "I remember it now," she said, her voice thick with a dreamy petulance. "I got the idea from the dream inquisitions, it all seemed to tie in somehow. . . ."

The *rasa* stared at her with his bloodless gaze. "It *does* tie in," he agreed. Shiyung's hair gleamed within the fingers of his leather glove, jet against ebony. "I like it when things connect like that: I have a rather jesuitical predilection for order. The Academy does that to one," he added.

Shiyung gave a small sharp gasp. Not, as Reive first thought, because of what he had said, but because the *rasa*'s hand had moved slowly, almost lovingly, from her hair to her neck. His fingers lay across her throat, dull black against her moon-white skin.

"Margalis," Shiyung choked. At first Reive thought she was teasing, but then she saw that one of the *rasa*'s hands had tightened around her throat; the other was pulling her up by her hair, until she staggered to her feet.

"*Mar-ga-lis—*" she said again, thickly, swallowing the name so that Reive could barely hear her.

"Wait—" the gynander said hoarsely, clutching her hands in her lap. "No—we—please, *no*—"

The *rasa* stood beside Shiyung now, like a shadowy figure manipulating a life-size puppet. With his gloved hand he tugged her head back, her hair flowing through his fingers like dark water. His other hand clenched her throat until a rivulet of blood sprang from between two metal fingers, sending a fine red spray upon his robes. The margravine's eyes bulged, her mouth twisted as she stared at Reive, hands slapping frantically at the air. Reive fell back against the floor, gasping, and still it went on, the *rasa* tightening his grip upon Shiyung's throat as he tugged slowly and steadily at her scalp.

And then, with a sound like shears cutting through very heavy cloth, he yanked sharply at her head. Reive shrieked and covered her mouth. The *rasa* let go of that cascade of ebony hair, pushed the head forward until it lolled crookedly upon one shoulder so that she stared dully at the gynander. The emerald irises were swallowed by watery red. A fine line of spit ran from the corner of her mouth to her chin, joined the thin stream of blood that trickled from between dark bruises upon her throat. Gently the *rasa* shook her by the shoulders; a sudden gout of blood poured from her mouth to splash his boots.

"There," said the *rasa*. He pulled the corpse heavily across the room and propped it against some pillows. He moved Shiyung's hands to her breast, then crouched to spread her hair in a jet fan across her shoulders. "You could almost imagine she is a real woman."

The gynander clutched her stomach, Shiyung's name catching in her throat. Shiyung's caracal crossed the room, nosed at the corpse and growled plaintively. It grew unbearably hot. Sweat pooled beneath Reive's breasts and trickled onto her stomach. There was a faint sound, like a far-off explosion. The tapestries on the wall shivered as though a figure moved behind them.

The *rasa* stood, his limbs creaking, and let one hand linger upon Shiyung's cheek. Finally he said, "I must go now."

death → free will

Reive choked back a scream. "*Go?* But where will you take us, what—"

"You must stay here." As he stared down at her Reive saw her own face reflected in that horrible blank mask. "If you try to flee they will only find you that much sooner. Here you might have time to get something to eat."

Reive's teeth chattered so that she could barely speak. At her feet the caracal licked Shiyung's eyes. "B-but if we stay they will blame *us*, they will think we killed her—"

The *rasa* shook his head. "You must admit, it does seem rather strange—your apocalyptic reading of Âziz's dream, and then your escape from the Reception Area, and whatever are you doing here in Shiyung's chambers?"

Reive began to weep, as the *rasa* went on, "But they would not blame me, even if I stayed. Because, you see, a *rasa* has no volition of its own: no will to love, or hope, or seek vengeance. It would be impossible for me to kill the margravine, or anyone else."

"But then how . . . ?"

The Aviator Imperator gazed down at the shivering gynander, the corpse with its long black hair spilling onto the pillows. He raised one hand to his face, and by a trick of the light glancing from his sleek mask it seemed that he had a mouth, and that mouth smiled.

"But how could I kill her, when by my own admission such a thing is impossible?" He stepped over Shiyung's body to the door and paused there, his blue eyes huge and brilliant. "Perhaps, after death, we are controlled by a will even stronger than our own."

For a long moment his gaze lingered upon her.

"Dreams are dangerous things, Reive Orsina," he said, and left her alone with the corpse of the margravine Shiyung.

Chapter 6

THE BEAUTIFUL ONE
IS HERE

~~~~~~~~~

In the darkness she sleeps. The darkness moves about her, touches her steel breasts, the chromium arc of her mouth, the downcurved lapis petals that are her eyelids. There is a secret to waking her, a little joke really, if only the darkness knew.

The woman had named her Nefertity, *The Beautiful One Is Here*; but the name could also be read as *Great Fortune Comes*, or again as *I Am The Million Years*, or even as *The Beautiful Ones Are Here*. She had not yet known great fortune, nor had she lasted a million years, at least not this shell of metal and plastic and shining magnetized wire. Had she remained outside as her siblings had, those other gilded husks wherein the dreams and memories of the Last Days had been encoded, she would have been lost like they were, or melted into streams of hissing metal and mercurial

misogyny

— Marryat cult

thought, the glories and songs and warnings of the *fin de millénaire* so much poisonous gas choking the fiery air.

But she was the Beautiful One. She was beloved: she had been saved. The woman had kept her in a stone-and-steel bunker with her, alone, while outside the years spun by in a silent fury and inside the woman's hair grew white. The woman's name was forgotten now; but once other women, a million women, five million, had known her name and sang it and tapped it out upon their monitors, upon their breasts, upon the sleeping faces of their daughters.

But the woman died four centuries before, of old age. One of the few women of her century to do so—many more succumbed to plague, or childbirth, or the gynocides, or were executed as political prisoners, or herded into research facilities where their wombs were used to give birth to the Ascendants' nightmares.

And so now only Nefertity might recall the woman's name; but the Beautiful One is sleeping. As she sleeps she dreams of the woman in the bunker, the woman eating krill paste and halvah with her fingers and afterward leaving a sweet smear across Nefertity's mouth. In another time or place, mice or flies would then have crept across the nemosyne's sticky mouth to feed; but the woman had long since eaten them. Decades passed and the woman lived on, alone in the bunker with her books and her 'files and the gorgeous machine she had stolen when the American Vatican fell to the recusants. And through all those afteryears she alone spoke to the Beautiful One, whispered her secrets, warned her of the enemy, shared with her 'files and books and paintings and programs and films and holos and songs. Into Nefertity's cold and boundless heart the woman poured all her dreams and memories, like shining sand into a glittering pit; and Nefertity swallowed them all, she embraced them, she recalled them, she recorded them, she devoured them. The woman would die one

neo=Medieval period

day but Nefertity would not. Nefertity would remember, Nefertity would never ever forget.

And so the woman brought them on, raging as she strove against madness and age and illness, struggling to recall for the nemosyne's databanks all those other women whose histories would otherwise be forgotten. The woman groaned and mumbled, dragging them by hair and breasts and hands, pummeling them as she tore volumes and photographs and tapes from her shelves, until one by one they all fell into the maw of the Beautiful One—

The Venus of Willendorf, the Animal Wife, the Bog Woman, the Iron Age Princess, Queen Hatshepsut, Cleopatra burning on the Nile, Nike headless and winged like dawn, Brisingamen wearing the rainbow's ardor about her neck, Demeter's tears burning grapes upon the vine, Sappho's leap, George Sand's trousers, Mary Godwin sneezing as she molded the new Prometheus from the Mediterranean mud, Judith and Salome carrying their lovers' heads beneath plump arms, Garbo talking, Sarah Bernhardt sleeping in her coffin, Queen Victoria spinning in hers, Mary Pickford, Mary Quant, Mary Magdalene, Mary Queen of Scotts, Sei Shonagun, Lady Murasaki, Yll Peng-Si the Tyrant of the Mongolian Nuclear Republic, Sylvia Plath, Gracie Allen, Hedda Morestein, Anne Frank, Indira Gandhi, Fasa Manh-Tul, Kyra MacDougal, Gertrude Stein, Artemis, Astarte, Inanna, Kali, The Norns, The Fates, The Grey Sisters, the Supremes, Margaret Thatcher, Magda Kurtz, Lizzie Siddal, Kwan-Lin, Loretta Riding, Nefertity . . .

A thousand of them, a million—

And when she died the woman left the nemosyne in her case, and on the case a set of hieroglyphs spelling out her history, and instructions for her use, and beneath that the nemosyne's name scratched into the plasteel shell—

NFRTI: Nefertity. *I Am The Million*.

The Beautiful Ones Are Here.

•   •   •

Hobi could not sleep. For hours he tossed in bed, listening for the sound of his father's return from the dream inquisition, staring glassy-eyed at the mess surrounding him while he rubbed his feverish cheeks. He kept seeing that black pit in the Undercity, hearing the chilly voice of the Architects intoning *There is a breach in the fundus of Angels* as the monitors filled with glowing letters spelling out terrible warnings he could not understand.

But mostly, he thought of Nefertity. That was what filled his mind: the golden face of the sleeping nemosyne with the twisted hieroglyphs and archaic letters across her brow. The sharp nose, the arched cheekbones tipped with silver, the chin pointed but rounded at the end (like his own, if he had only known it) and chased with silver threads like water flowing across her crystal flesh. Most of all, her eyes. Slanted eyes, even as she slept he knew they were beautiful eyes, and trapped such strange things! What face had she looked on last? When she awoke now to see *him*, would she falter and perhaps cry out?

Hobi moaned and turned onto his back, threw his arm across his forehead as he stared at the ceiling. She was a replicant. Even when designed for sexual congress (and few of them were: there were other things for that, argalæ and aardmen and even, he had heard once to his disgust, *rasas)*, even when created as robotic courtesans, replicants could not respond appropriately to their human partners, not really: because of course they were only machines. Beautiful machines, sleek and clean of line as dolphins, but no more capable of loving response than one of Shiyung Orsina's mutated animals.

Hobi knew all this, of course. He had slept with boys, more often with girls; and with one of his human tutors he had visited a brothel on Principalities, and engaged a moujik woman. All of these experiences had been, if not precisely memorable, at least satisfactory. He knew from books and 'files that there was supposed to be some more severe level of attachment involved with other humans; all the great stories said so. But one didn't see evidence of these attachments on the upper levels of Araboth. His father had been grief-stricken by his wife's murder, but when she was alive he spent a good deal of time pursuing girl children and leaving her to the ministrations of her own cohort of artistic young men. To be sure, the affairs that convulsed Cherubim and Seraphim were nearly always between men and men, or men and women, or women and women. There had been Zubin Billimoria's obsession with the *rasa* of a deformed moujik child, of course, but everyone agreed that his passion was sentimental to the point of grossness. And on the upper levels it was considered very gauche to tryst with androids.

Why then couldn't Hobi forget Nefertity's metal face, or the sound—a chime that seemed to have followed him back to Cherubim, he swore that thin silvery sound was what kept him from sleeping—he had heard when first he gazed upon her? The Beautiful One, Nasrani had called her; Nasrani the clockwork man.

Hobi closed his eyes and thought of the exile going from one cabinet to the next in his cyclorama, waking the Titanium Children and Maximillian Ur. He would find Nasrani and go with him to the Undercity, and find her once again. And somehow, somehow he would wake her.

He did not rise until the following evening. Red-eyed and smelling of brandy, he stumbled out to where his father sat in the dim main room, staring at a mercury lamp. Sajur wore the same black suit and turban he'd had on yesterday. He had removed his emerald mourning bands and lined them up neatly on the small table in front of him. His Imperator's chain of office, with its golden crucifix and opaline eye, hung around the neck of the lantern.

"Good morning," Hobi muttered. He sank onto a brocade pillow and called to Khum down the hall, "Kehveh please."

Sajur Panggang reached out to the mercury lamp and touched its glass chimney, watching the silver liquid stream toward his hand. " 'Good evening' is more like it. Are you ill?"

"A little." Hobi shivered and pulled his robe tighter around him. With surprise he noted an empty decanter on the table by his father. Next to it was a crumpled sheet of allurian tissue from one of the computer imprimaturs, flickering gold and purple upon the marquetry tabletop. Âziz's stationary. He'd last seen it after his mother's death. "Has—did something happen?"

Sajur sat in silence for a few minutes, tapping the edge of the crucifix against the mercury glass and humming a tune that had been popular last Æstival Tide. Tomorrow the gamelan orchestras would be banging it out again, as the crowds waited for the Lahatiel Gate to swing open. Hobi cleared his throat and started to ask about the Investiture, but thought better of it.

At last the replicant Khum returned with a salver of kehveh. Sajur Panggang's demitasse steamed at his elbow unnoticed. Hobi spooned sweetener into his and sipped it, eyeing his father uneasily. Outside, Cherubim's residential canyons glowed crimson and gold, and the nuclear CLOCK read near midnought, but still Sajur had not switched on any lights save that single glimmering lamp.

Finally he turned to his son and said, "You weren't at the dream inquisition."

Hobi looked surprised. This wasn't normally something his father would care about, certainly not enough to send him reaching for the Amity and sitting in the dark. "No. I'm sorry, I just—"

"There was a gynander there. A new one, someone from the lower levels. She scryed Âziz's dream—"

He hesitated and stared at his son. Hobi suddenly felt cold. He had the terrible feeling that his father was going to announce, "—And I know where you went with Nasrani Orsina."

Instead his father said, "And she said it was the dream of the Green Country." He paused and turned again to gaze at the flowing interior of the mercury lamp. "Âziz Orsina: she said Âziz dreamed of the Green Country."

Hobi swallowed his kehveh. Despite the sweetener it tasted bitter and he pushed the cup away. "The Green Country," he repeated uneasily. "But—Âziz? The gynander must have been drunk."

Sajur spread his hands as though warming them. Now it almost seemed that he was trying not to smile. "They had her imprisoned, of course. The morphodite. I wish they hadn't, at least not yet. I—"

He looked up at his son. The lines around his eyes looked as though they had grown less taut since yesterday. "I would have liked to have spoken to her first. It's—rather an unusual thing for a margravine to dream of, just days before Æstival Tide. Don't you think?"

Now he really *was* smiling. Hobi looked away hastily and gulped his kehveh. The Green Country. He stared down at his demitasse, so that his father wouldn't see his face. "How could she? Âziz, I mean —how could *she* have dreamed it? And—well, what happens now?"

"Now?" Sajur shrugged and held his empty cup up to the mercury lamp. The silvery light made the porcelain glow like melting ice. "I guess we wait and see if the story gets out to the 'files. There'll be riots, if it does. The entire city is at fever pitch already, anticipating the festival. I've never seen anything like it, in other years. You've heard the rumors, of course."

Hobi's stomach knotted. "Rumors?"

"Yes. Some sort of tremors shaking the lower

levels. One supposedly caused a refinery explosion on Archangels. I've heard they've even been reported up here."

His father smiled, so unexpectedly that Hobi shivered. His father took no notice. With both hands he removed his turban, pausing to glance critically at the artificial tourmaline nearly buried within the folds of black silk. He removed the stone, dropping the turban, then carefully placed the tourmaline on the floor. Hobi watched him, too stunned to do more than stammer.

"The Green Country—that's supposed to be a prophesy, right, a storm or something. The domes—the domes failing. Are we—are we safe here?" he babbled as his father stared ruminatively at the tourmaline.

Sajur shook his head. "Safe?" he repeated. "*Safe?*" He lifted his foot, then very slowly crushed the tourmaline beneath the sole of his boot. It made a grinding noise, then suddenly exploded into gray powder and flying chips of glass. The Architect Imperator raised his head.

"Of course we're *safe*. The Architects monitor everything, and I monitor the Architects, and the Orsinate monitors me. How could anything possibly go wrong?"

He turned, reaching for the little gold crucifix that hung against the mercury glass lantern.

"Father—" Hobi choked; but Sajur ignored him. He smiled, wider and wider, tapping the crucifix against the glass until suddenly it shattered. Volatile spirits flamed up in a flash of silver and blue, and just as suddenly were gone. The crucifix lay in a hissing pool of liquid on the marquetry table.

Hobi stared at him, his heart throbbing so painfully that he thought he would faint, but his father did not look up or even move his hand from the caustic mess, only continued to smile and stare, until at last he said, "One trembles to think . . ."

From the room down the hall came the *click* and

whir of the Architects where they had been left to their mœbius loops, abandoned to their terrible employment.

The Architect Imperator had gone quite mad.

In the vivarium Zalophus dreams. It is a dream of open seas, of waters full of leaping fish and creatures with claws strong enough to rip through the wings of any animal foolish enough to let its flight bring it within inches of the roiling surface. There are many of these animals in Zalophus's dream, just as there are more fish here than he has ever glimpsed in all the centuries he has been imprisoned in the vivarium. The fish and the flying creatures spin and toss, and when Zalophus heaves himself through the air they fall into his gaping mouth. Then he smacks back into the ocean, and feels himself sink down, down, through the blue and churning water until it grows cooler around his huge body and he feels the current that will lead him back to *them*, back to those others like himself, his dark and massive sisters. He has lost them, the pod left behind as he chased a great eel through the arctic night. He has lost them and now, five hundred thousand years later, he is still searching for them.

But he has never really seen the open sea. Not this sea, at least; not this Zalophus. Through his dreams he sounds and bellows, and sometimes through his waking days as well, calling through the watergate to where the Gulf pounds against the silent shore that encircles Araboth. *Come back, come back,* he thunders; but his sisters do not hear him. It is as the gynander told him: they are millennia dead, and there are no others of their kin left to answer him.

Now something else shakes his sleeping as well, though this is harder for the zeuglodon to comprehend. Not the smell or taste or rush of water along his sides and fins but another thing, a smaller thing that is more frightening, because it has nothing to do with water at all.

It is a sound. It is a voice: a human voice. The great carnivore cannot understand what it is saying, but he knows it is speaking to him. It reminds him of the voice of the gynander who lured the siren into his tank one evening; or rather, the gynander's voice reminds him of this other dream-voice, high and fluting and plaintive. It is a voice beseeching him. He understands that it is desperate, it is pleading, but he cannot understand what it is saying or what it wants. He cannot really understand its desperation, except insofar that it is a kind of hunger, a yearning akin to his own awful dreaming of the open sea. It cries and begs beneath the waves of that other, larger and less complicated mass of memory; it weeps and pleads without ceasing.

The voice maddens Zalophus. In his sleep he turns, scraping his head against the side of the tank, and moans so loudly that the walls of the vivarium shudder. But the voice does not sleep. It *cannot* sleep, because it is part of the oldest geneslave. It is the sliver of consciousness of the other thing that went into the creation of the sentient zeuglodon, the thing that had been a man before some researcher centuries before decided to make of it a new thing, a new creature. It moans and pummels inside of Zalophus as the whale moans and thrashes inside its prison; and like Zalophus it will never be free.

But now the dream of Zalophus changes. The sea falls away and suddenly there is another element all around him, the terrible air that he feels so briefly when he throws himself from the water and for a few seconds is surrounded by a vast glittering desert. Only now this other element is everywhere; and the whale moans in terror, because while the sea is still there it has changed. It is not the smooth unwavering field he flows through but something new, something brilliant that hurts him, slashes against his brain and stabs his puny eyes.

But even as Zalophus rolls over and over in his sleep, that other stab of memory, that tiny voice, welcomes this new and hurtful thing: because what has frightened Zalophus is *color*, a rush of remembered blues and violets and golds and greens that the other thing, the thing that was once a man, recalls.

And the memory of the man rejoices. As suddenly as the terror flooded Zalophus, it is gone. The voice inside him is abruptly silenced. Across the glowing grid of the whale's thoughts there rolls the image of a vast and shining plain, a surface smooth and gleaming and alive even though it is not the sea. It stretches forever, from one horizon to the next, an immensity of hills and fields and prairies and mountains gleaming beneath a sun that is not deadly, a sun that flickers not silver-gray but golden, where rains that are not poisonous sweep the blue-washed sky. Everywhere that plain shines and gleams in a way that baffles the zeuglodon. And if Zalophus had only understood what it was that he glimpsed, the sad monster would have known to name these colors, known to name them *green;* would have seen the silvery rains and known they were the massive storm system whorling above the western ocean, the storm that battered the coast year after year, growing stronger through the decades as the coast fell away like splintered shale; the storm they called Ucalegon.

Zalophus does not know this. But that other thing, that mote of human consciousness trapped within him—*it* sees and understands. Ucalegon the Prince of Storms is coming; Baratdaja the Healing Wind is shrieking northward across the peninsula. Beneath the domes of Araboth the Ascendants dream of blood and steel, the Architects of grids of light; but Outside the Green Country grows nearer. Somewhere within the ancient whale's brain that jot of humanity sees the Green Country, and it understands and remembers. The tiny imprisoned voice exults, to have glimpsed it thus for one last moment; and then is forever silenced.

• • •

If Hobi had been a more patient young man, he might have waited for Nasrani Orsina to return. If he hadn't been so frightened by his father's madness, he might have recalled that it was unusual for more than a few days to pass without a visit from the exile. Nasrani and the Architect Imperator were both grand masters at the intricate and ancient word-game *tanka*, which involved creating an image in five words. Not surprisingly, Sajur Panggang was adept at verbal landscaping—

> *Sanguine tapestry,*
> *moldering leaves:*
> *Autime—*

Never mind that he had never seen *real* leaves moldering anywhere, save within the vivarium. Nasrani did not share his friend's sentimental disposition but preferred a type of verbal portraiture, often scabrous. For example,

> *Drooling imbecile,*
> *his clothes*
> *smell—*

An unkind reference to a member of the Reception Committee who had annoyed Nasrani during his brief incarceration. Nothing save an event of truly calamitous proportions—say, the murder of one of Nasrani's sisters—would have canceled the weekly *tanka* game, with its bursts of rude and delighted laughter and the scent of Amity heavy in the air. If Hobi had been a patient and prudent young man, he might have waited—although, as it turned out, he would have waited in vain.

But Hobi was not that sort of young man. In twelve hours Sajur Panggang had not moved from his chair by the ruined mercury lamp. The replicant

Khum brought him tea and whiskey and cardamom-flavored cakes, but Sajur only sat, snoring loudly or else waking to finger Prophet Rayburn's crucified image among the slivers of broken glass. He did not hear Hobi when the boy spoke to him; he did not fight when his son and the replicant tried to move him, only let his body grow slack and slumped back grinning in the chair. Hobi finally left him alone, sickened and terrified. He tried to tune into the 'files for news of the inquisition or reports of executions, but the 'files had been locked: the screens showed only the calm eyes of the Architects and the words *Sorry out of service*. Tomorrow it would be Æstival Tide; the 'files should be showing preparations for the Great Fear, the immense Lahatiel Gates being oiled and primed to open, the prostitutes and imperial courtesans and myriad cultists costumed in hideous array for the timoring rites and mad rush into the sea.

But without the 'files Hobi couldn't see any of this. He felt like a prisoner, although he really was not —the doors were not locked, he could come and go as he pleased; but Hobi was afraid to leave. No one called; there were no visitors. Khum brought him lunch and poured endless glasses of brandy; his father snored and grinned, until Hobi thought he might go mad as well. Once the entire chamber trembled. The brandy in Hobi's glass rocked back and forth, and one of Sajur's holographic anaglyphs glittered into view and just as quickly sputtered into black again. Too stunned to move, Hobi waited for nearly an hour, certain that this was it: the breach he had seen on the monitors only a few weeks ago had finally spread to the very domes, and the entire city was going to come crashing down around him.

But nothing happened. Sajur did not speak, or seem to notice. There were no aftershocks, no emergency bulletins on the still-dead 'files. Nothing. Finally the boy got up and stumbled to his room. He reached beneath his bed and withdrew a small silver flask, the last of the Amity he had hidden away. He drank it, sitting on the floor and leaning with eyes closed against the bed.

So. His father had gone mad. Terrifying as the realization was, it was neither unusual nor even unexpected. Each year a score or so of the Orsinate's inner cabal went insane, varying from Musach Alvin's unsuccessful attempt at flying from a third-floor balcony to Shiyung Orsina's increasingly ridiculous involvements with bizarre religious sects. As a blood relation of the Orsinas, Sajur Panggang was practically doomed by birth to some form of mental anomaly. Fortunately Hobi was too young to consider even momentarily the notion that he himself might be similarly affected one day.

What Hobi was more concerned about was the fact that the city was very probably falling into ruin, even as he gulped the last burning mouthful of Amity. In other circumstances he would have gone to his father for help. Now the only person he could think of turning to was Nasrani, but god knew where Nasrani was to be found. If he were to go to the margravines, they would either laugh at him or, worse, believe him; and upon discovering his father's failure to halt the destruction, Hobi would no doubt be imprisoned and executed along with Sajur. One thing Hobi was certain of: the margravines would do nothing to aid the failing city or its people.

That was when he thought again of the Undercity, and Nasrani's hidden children. The exile had said that the nemosynes knew things; that if only they could find a way to wake Nefertity, she might be able to help them relearn all the secrets lost to the centuries of the Long Night.

Hobi stood—unsteadily, the flask falling to the floor with a soft *chink*. He had that terrific clarity that Amity brings to an empty stomach and a head primed for dreaming. He knew what he must do. He had to find the nemosyne again; find Nasrani too, if he could, but Nefertity was most important. Just because Nasrani had never been able to wake her didn't mean that Hobi couldn't try. He was not unlettered in certain kinds of stories that his mother had been fond of, ancient tales that involved quests and tasks and very often the salvation of certain individuals, usually women, who through no fault of their own had come to be imprisoned in cells of glass or stone or even unfamiliar bodies. And while Hobi knew that Nefertity was no such thing, and the near-certain demise of Araboth a matter of considerable gravity, still he was rather a young boy, with a passionate (if shy) nature; and there had been all that Amity.

He dressed, choosing his clothes with care. A white shirt of heavy sueded silk that made his chestnut hair look darker, his fair skin even more pale. Moleskin trousers of a color so deep it could not (and was not) termed evergreen or viridian, even though there were forbidden hints of those shades in its nap. Hobi of course knew that they were *green* trousers, as did the furtive moujik tailor who had designed them for him for a timoring several months ago. He had planned to wear them when he joined his father and the margravines on the viewing platform for the opening of the Lahatiel Gate. Instead he would wear them for this final secret journey.

Because he was leaving; because there was really no reason for him to stay. His father was mad and would surely soon be dead, his mother was dead, indeed it seemed quite evident that soon *everyone* he knew, from that moujik tailor to the margravine Âziz, would be dead. If he could somehow find Nasrani, he would warn him and enlist him in his endeavor. But otherwise he had his mind made up:

He would go back to the Undercity, find the nemosyne, and if he could not wake her, he would carry her with him, until they found some way to escape the coming holocaust.

Some way to get Outside.

•   •   •

It felt strange to be taking the gravator alone. Even though he had been there once before, only days earlier, the trip to the Undercity had grown fixed in Hobi's mind, as though it were a beloved memory from his childhood. The little fountain with its statue of the *timorata* bubbling spearmint water; the heavy crimson drapes; the grinding of its gears as the chamber dropped level after level through Araboth's glowing spectrum—periwinkle, scarlet, violet, every possible shade of purple deepening to the eternal night of the Undercity—all these things had in the last few days knit themselves around the boy's heart, so that now the touch of those drapes against his cheek, the slant of wine-colored light as they passed through Principalities—all had become entwined with the calm and frigid face of Nasrani's sleeping nemosyne. The amorphous terrors that had paralyzed him were gone, now that he had left Cherubim.

The trip to the Undercity could have lasted forever but in fact was over in a very few minutes. He jumped when the gravator announced its arrival on Angels. The doors fanned open, and a rush of fetid air greeted him as he approached them. He waited for a long minute, until the gravator repeated its announcement, somewhat peevishly, and the doors started to creak shut once more. Before they could close on him he jumped outside.

Immediately darkness engulfed him like a freezing wind. Hobi clapped his hands to his pockets and cursed: he had forgotten a lumiere. He started to sprint back into the gravator, but groaning like an old server it already had begun its slow ascent. He swore again, desperately; then heard from somewhere nearby a rustling sound, too loud to be something stirred by one of the ventricles—*were* there vents down here? When he held his breath the noise stopped. Heart pounding he waited to hear it again. But now there was only silence.

He thought he remembered which way to go. To the right; and yes, he found a wall there, damp and foul-smelling. His feet sank into some soft cold stuff as he walked on, one hand always on the wall. He tripped over chunks of concrete and once or twice splashed through shallow puddles. Always he kept one hand on the wall—that way, he thought, he could find his way back.

Once he stumbled. His foot hung in the empty air for what seemed like minutes, as he cried out, flailing, certain that he had fallen into the abyss that was shattering the Undercity like a porcelain cup. But it was nothing, just a gap in the walkway. He waited a few minutes, panting, and went on.

After a while it began to seem that it was not so dark here as he had first thought. At first he thought his eyes played tricks on him, making it seem as though there was a dimly lit doorway here, a glowing heap of embers there. But soon he discovered that there really *was* light, of a sort. A few feet in front of him something glowed like the remains of a fire nearly dead. He stopped to look at it more closely, and then in a spurt of bravery decided to walk over and investigate. When he removed his hand from the wall he had a horrible feeling, a vertiginous sense that he was going to pitch into some bottomless void. The impulse to fall back against the wall was nearly irresistible, but he bit his lip and stepped forward.

It was not the ash-heap he had expected, but a pile of stones, or broken concrete. They glowed a faint and ruinous green, not a solid color but pocked with different shades, here nearly yellow, there with a bluish sheen. He thought of the corpse-candles that were used in the rites of the Chambers of Mercy, tapers made from the organs of *rasas* destroyed illegally for such purposes. Hobi bit his lip, then touched one of the stones. His hand came away wet, and it too glowed. There was a foul odor of putrescence. He recalled the stories he had heard of *rasas* down here, and shuddered; but surely not even *rasas* would venture to the Undercity.

He wiped his hand on his trousers, leaving a long

streak that faded into the darkness after a few minutes. He looked around in a futile effort to get his bearings, and for the first time noticed that there were other scattered heaps glowing in the distance.

"Damn," he whispered. He glanced down at the pile at his feet. It struck him suddenly that it might not be the artless heap he had first supposed. He nudged it with his foot. It didn't budge. When he looked up again it seemed that those other dim pyramids might be beacons of a sort, or markers; but he could discern no order among them, only scattered fragments of light, dull green or blue like the veins of an odorous cheese. It seemed that his eyes finally were adjusting to the darkness. He could perceive immense shadows that must be buildings, and smaller shapes that were the ruins of skyscrapers or maybe autovehicles. Dark as it was, some faint, almost imperceptible light trickled down from the levels above. His eyes aching, he turned and stumbled off once more.

As he picked his way back to the wall Hobi tried to imagine what would use such primitive means of illumination or navigation. He had grown up hearing stories about naughty children and recalcitrant servants who fell or were pushed from their warm havens on Cherubim, and tumbled to Araboth's primeval footing so far below. In the stories the children did not die, as they surely would if they were to actually slip from behind the protective barricades that ran along the outermost perimeters of each level. In the stories the children eventually found themselves in the Undercity, and it had always seemed to Hobi that it would be infinitely preferable to die. Mutated monsters were supposed to live there, creatures carelessly disposed of by the bioresearchers or dilettantes like Shiyung Orsina. Aardmen with too many eyes; hydrapithecenes that somehow flourished out of water; morphodites so hideous that even the jaded appetites of the Orsinate and their cohort had no use for them. All of these things (and betulamiæ whose treelike trunks had sprouted feet, and argalæ that snapped and clawed at their patrons, and things that went unnamed because gazing at them you were struck speechless) ended down on Angels, there to breed in the unkempt earth and ruined skyscrapers and abandoned refineries. Hobi had never questioned the veracity of such tales. Aristocrat's children *did* fall sometimes, which was a shame because there were always too few of them, and servants and other hapless persons *did* get pushed, more often than you'd think. It had just always seemed so impossibly far away. The Undercity might as well have been Outside.

But here he was, inching forward through the green-pocked darkness of the Undercity with some demented notion of going Outside, trying not to think of what might have gotten here before him. In the surrounding night he heard that faint susurrant noise, like water percolating through the ground or an animal moving among the glowing piles of rubbish. Beneath his hand the wall's surface changed from something slick and steel-smooth to rough brick or stone, all of it thick with algae or moss that came away in heavy foul-smelling wads when he pulled his hand back. He breathed through his mouth now, wishing he'd brought something to cover his face; wishing he'd waited for Nasrani to show up again. But then he would recall his silent grinning father, and the face of Nefertity, the dull flickering of her glass and metal atomies; and that would make him move more quickly through the muck.

Beneath his hand the wall abruptly gave way. Hobi stopped, gasping for breath, then reached until he touched something metal. A heavy beard of mold and fungi hung from the corners of the door, just as he remembered it. He traced its outline until he found the small metal plate where Nasrani had inserted his key. He breathed deeply, leaned forward until his forehead touched the cold dank door, then pushed with all his might.

Nothing. It wouldn't budge. He tried shoving against it with his shoulder, kicking it, pushing it again and again, until his clothes were soaked with mold and slime and he began to shiver from the chill. Finally he stopped, his head pounding with frustration. It had been madness for him to come here alone, no key, no lumiere, nothing. His eyes strained to make out anything of the door or what lay beyond it, but there was only darkness.

He stepped back and took one more deep breath. He stretched his hands out before him, lowered his head, and started to make one final lunge, when—

"Mmmph!" Hobi cried out. Something struck his back and he toppled, flailing helplessly at the rubble-strewn ground. A moment later and someone straddled him, someone large and heavy and reeking of decay. The smell made Hobi gag and he wept uncontrollably, his eyes streaming as its hands played across his face until they covered his mouth.

"Greet your Mother," it said. Its voice was utterly toneless. A cold tongue snaked inside his ear, and icy hands pushed his face into the ground. "Greet your Mother, once-born."

"Aaagh!" Hobi shut his mouth and struggled as the thing atop him pushed his face into the ground. The horrible thought seized him that it was his *real* mother the thing meant; that what he had watched burn at the Reisling Gallery a year before was not her corpse but another's, and this was all part of some awful plot against his family by the Orsinate.

"Your *Mother,"* it hissed again. It grabbed him by the hair and pulled him up, then jammed its fingers into his mouth to pry it open. Hobi retched at the touch of rot and slime on his tongue. "Show some respect for your *Mother—"*

This time when it slammed his face to the ground his mouth was open. He choked, tasting dirt. The thing relaxed its hold a little, and gasping and sputtering Hobi finally pushed it from him. It seemed to be satisfied; he heard it step back, its feet splashing fetid water on him.

"Wha—" Hobi began, sobbing with fear and disgust as he tried to see what it was that had struck him. The unseen creature made a gurgling noise and cut him off, its glottal voice slow and measured.

"No questions. How did you get here?"

Hobi pointed vaguely, wiping his mouth and spitting. Filth dripped into his eyes as he strained to see what was there. Something as tall as he was, but wraith-thin. He dimly made out long lank hair, glowing with the same greenish phosphorescence he'd seen on the little pyramids, and a fish-white face. Something about it, the hair perhaps, or its voice, made him think of it as female. Abruptly one hand struck out at him like a snake, grabbing his chin. Its fingers were long and had very sharp nails. They felt pulpy, and seemed reluctant to touch him.

"How did you get here?" it whispered, its nails digging into his skin. Hobi cried out as he felt blood trickling down his neck.

"The gravator—ow, I swear! the *gravator*—"

The thing gave a bubbling sigh. Its arm flopped to its side. "No respect for your Mother," it murmured thickly, "no respect at all. What were you doing there?"

"I was—I was trying to get in," Hobi coughed. "To see what's inside."

"How do *you* know what's inside?"

It was just a few inches from his face. Its eyes were pale sacs flecked with green, sagging within hollows as though someone had scooped the flesh from its face. Hobi felt his insides bunch together.

A *rasa*. The stories were true: corpses walked in the Undercity.

When it spoke again he felt its breath against his cheek, cold and smelling of decay. "Are you one of the fallen?"

"*Fallen?*" Hobi's voice quavered so that he marveled the thing could understand him. "No! I just—I just came to visit, that's all."

The *rasa* thought about this, then shook its head. Its skull bobbed precariously on its narrow neck.

"You came to see Mother?" it asked suspiciously. Hobi flinched as it stretched its hands to touch his face. He realized that it could not see well—not that anything could see well in that infernal void.

"*Mother?*" But they were getting nowhere like this, so he quickly added, "Yes. Of course, yes, that's right. I came to see Mother."

The *rasa's* fingers flicked across his cheeks. It seemed satisfied by his answer, and drew back from him. "Come then," it said, and turned away into the darkness.

For a moment Hobi thought of fleeing. But then he thought of what might happen if the *rasa* called others of its kind after him in pursuit. He groaned softly and followed it.

After a few minutes he could think of nothing but trying to keep from losing his way, as the *rasa* led him through black alleys and under moldering arches. There was a constant sound of water underfoot, as though just beneath the broken earth an underground stream ran along with them. The *rasa* moved quickly, in a sort of shambling crouch. It was surprisingly strong, pushing aside a great steel door that blocked entry to what appeared to Hobi to be nothing more than a huge pile of broken concrete and twisted metal beams. When Hobi tried to follow, he got wedged between the rubble. For a horrible moment he thought he was trapped, pinned between a huge girder and a half-fallen brick wall. But then he got through, his trousers ripping and his chest grazed by broken bricks as he slid after the *rasa*.

They were in a sort of tunnel, a clear space no wider than ten feet across. Perhaps because the tunnel was empty of wreckage, it felt more open than the noisome spaces outside. And it seemed brighter here, too. Hobi blinked, then rubbed his eyes. No: it really *was* brighter. The tiled walls bulged outward, as though they were inside a huge culvert. Flowing from the curved ceiling to the floor were curtains of fungi, long beards forming glowing draperies that emitted enough light that Hobi could read broken letters set mosaic style into the wall.

ALLE PLAZA

EWAGE STATION

" 'Ewage station'?" Hobi pronounced, trying to recall why this was familiar; but ahead of him the *rasa* waited impatiently. He hurried after it.

The tunnel was straight and seemed endless, though they didn't go very far into it. After a few yards water started pooling up, growing deeper every few steps until it came to Hobi's knees. He was shivering so much it was hard to walk. The *rasa*'s sickly sweet odor had dissipated into another smell, no less choking to Hobi for all that it was more familiar. It was a scent that dredged up queer memories, the sort of dimly lit memories you have of things that happened when you were drunk or drugged or very young: and that was how he realized the smell had something to do with Æstival Tide. It filled his nose and throat and mouth like bad water. After a few minutes he realized that's exactly what it was: water. They were in the ancient sewage tunnel Nasrani had told him about, the tunnel that led Outside. What Hobi smelled was the sea, unfiltered by the domes.

The realization brought him to a dead stop. Ahead of him the *rasa* splashed on, pausing now and then to peer off to the left, as though looking for something.

The sea. What if the thing was bringing him Outside? Hobi put out one hand to steady himself against the wall. It sank into the luminous muck. When he drew it back in disgust his fingers glowed slightly, a rotten corpselike blue. He would die down here. Or, worse, he would live, become like this creature a mad thing living in the cracks between Araboth and Outside, like the ones who did not return from Æstival Tide; like all the half-human things that hung about the tattered edges of Araboth.

"Once-born."

The *rasa*'s voice rose urgently. Hobi turned to look behind him. In the near distance the tunnel's mouth gaped, black and cold—he could hear the wind hooting down after him. He turned back to where the *rasa* waited beside an opening. Dread seeped into him like the black water oozing up through his clothes. There was nothing to do but follow it. Perhaps Nasrani would worry about him; perhaps after a few days they would mount a search down here.

But tomorrow was Æstival Tide. Nothing would be done then, or for several weeks thereafter while Araboth's inhabitants recovered from the *timoria*. He could only follow the *rasa* and hope to escape, or hope somehow to make his way Outside by the time the Lahatiel Gate opened. He rubbed his arms against the chill and continued down the tunnel.

The *rasa* waited for him at the opening. It stared at Hobi with its sunken eyes, then splashed its face with some of the fetid water pooled at their feet. "Greet your Mother," it said. Reluctantly Hobi bent and flicked a few drops onto his cheeks.

"Now," the *rasa* announced, and faster than Hobi would have thought possible it slipped through the doorway and out of sight. He followed, stumbling over a few broken steps. This passage led up. It was damp and narrow and utterly dark, save for two endless smears of phosphorescence that ran along each wall. When Hobi extended his hand he found the streaks were just at arm level. He drew his hand back uneasily, wiping it on his torn shirt. He didn't want to think about what hands had been there before his.

From somewhere ahead of him echoed the soft

splashing sound of the *rasa*'s footsteps. Every now and then it paused and called back to him in low urgent tones. Hobi stumbled after it in silence. His knees ached from the cold and from bumping into the wall as the stairway twisted upward.

"Hurry now! Mother won't wait—"

It seemed they neared their destination. The *rasa* fell back to walk beside him, crowding Hobi so that he turned sideways to keep from breathing in its suffocating reek. Its long dank hair flapped in the boy's face as it slouched along, its sharp nails leaving vivid green tracks on the walls.

"Here," it panted, and stopped beside a narrow doorway. The *rasa* drummed softly on it with its nails, and the door swung inward.

"We are here," it announced, and went inside. Following it Hobi gasped.

It was the chamber where Nasrani had taken him before; but it rippled with a light so brilliant Hobi had to cover his eyes. When he peered through his fingers he saw no candles, no lumieres or electric lanterns. But blue and yellow and green light flashed from the cabinets that hid Moghrebi and the Anodyne Physician, Maximillian Ur, and all the rest. Slowly Hobi dropped his hands from his face, and stared.

Nefertity's case was open. Inside it the Beautiful One glowed, a thousand colors coruscating up and down her arms and along her cheeks, radiating out in bands of cobalt and viridian, yellow and gamboge and emerald.

"Mother," the *rasa* whispered, and stepped forward. Hobi did not move.

The room wasn't empty. Even with their backs to him he knew what they were. *Rasas,* a dozen of them, their bodies nearly luminous in the spectral light. Some could have been no more than children when they were regenerated. One had the proud carriage of an Orsina, despite skin soft and gray as wet paper. Like the one that had brought him here they wore only rotted shreds of clothing. Their staring green-shot eyes were fixed upon the nemosyne.

"Mother," the *rasa* murmured. A few feet from Nefertity's case it slowly lowered itself to a sitting position. "Mother, I have come, and brought you a once-born boy."

Hobi stared at Nefertity, then slowly walked through the figures seated around her. None of them looked at him; it seemed they did not notice him at all, save perhaps as an unaccustomed warmth passing through the room. Their eyes stared unblinking at the light pulsating from the nemosyne, their soft fingers tapping upon the floor some arcane rhythm that he did not recognize. The rasa who had led him here called out to him, "She speaks. Sometimes she wakes like this, and tells us things. They are stories of the Last Days, they are Mother stories." Then it too fell silent.

Hobi stopped in front of Nefertity. Her incandescent sarcophagus made a loud humming sound. Not the sound of a machine at rest, but more like the sound of someone, a woman in fact, singing softly to herself. Behind him in the clammy darkness he heard other things: voices whispering to themselves, fingers tapping their obscure tattoos. Hobi shaded his eyes as he stepped forward. The light streaming from the nemosyne made his head throb. It was she who was making the humming sound: and he realized now, now that he was near enough to touch her, that she spoke, chanted almost, and it was in time to this ancient litany that the corpses drummed their fingers—

> "Yet sharper pain,
> more savage even, struck her heart:
> she withdrew from the company of the gods,
> she went to the cities of men and their grasslands,
> disguising her beauty for a long time.
> And no one who saw her recognized her,
> no man, no deep-girdled woman, no one . . ."

"Nefertity," whispered Hobi. He stepped closer, stretched out his hand to touch her face. The light that had nearly blinded him grew less harsh. He could see once more the outlines of her cheekbones, the bright lines drawn under her closed eyes as though with kohl, her lips moving as they formed each word and the words spilled from her like grain.

". . . They asked her, where are you from, old woman,
you who are from another age?
Why have you bypassed our city?
There are women here who would befriend you.
There are mothers and daughters who would share with
you their ways.

And the goddess replied,
'Hello, good children of the feminine sex,
hello, mothers and daughters of the suffering earth.
I greet you,
whoever you are.' "

"Mother," whispered the first *rasa* where it knelt before her.

"Mother," murmured the others.

"Nefertity," breathed Hobi, all his fear devoured by anguished longing.

Mother stories, he thought; and an image came to his mind: his own mother leaning over him in his bed, her hand cool and smelling of opium sugar as she stroked his cheek and murmured a story to him, a mother story, of course; and if Hobi had only known he might have realized it was one of the same stories that other lonely woman had told to her nemosyne daughter centuries before. Mother stories: a trick to wake the sleeping princess: and gently, tentatively, as Nefertity's lips moved and her voice crooned on, telling its sleepwalker's tale, Hobi leaned forward and kissed her golden mouth.

"Ah," sang the replicant. With a sound soft as a spider's feet tickling across its web her eyes opened, and gazed out at Hobi: grass-green, emerald-green, green as the sea and the sirocco sky.

"Ah," she repeated, a note like a door chiming open. From within its glowing sarcophagus her crystal hand moved, slowly, until it brushed his cheek.

"At last," she murmured, blinking those emerald eyes.

> *"The Beautiful*
> *One*
> *Is*
> *Here."*

"Where is my Sister?"

The shock of seeing her move sent Hobi scuttering a few feet backward. Behind him the *rasas* had fallen silent.

"Where is my Sister?" the nemosyne said again. Now that she was fully awake her voice was surprisingly deep, and gentle—he had never heard a replicant with such a lovely voice. The door of her case clicked shut as she stepped forward, her legs moving smoothly and her head turning back and forth to survey the room. The light streaming from her faded until she shone pale white and yellow. The joints where her metal limbs met her torso gleamed blue, her eyes glowed that supernatural shade of green. She was like some beautiful toy, and in spite of his fear Hobi grinned to see her. A few feet from her cabinet she stopped and looked around, her gaze sweeping the room, taking in the darkened cabinets, the silent fearful *rasas*. She turned and pointed at Hobi.

"Where is my Sister?"

Hobi swallowed, unclenched his hands. His voice came out in a croak. "Who was your sister?"

Nefertity tipped her head. She was nearly a foot taller than Hobi. She stepped forward, reaching for him. At first he recoiled, then with shaking fingers reached to touch her hand. It felt as though mercury flowed inside it, something warm and heavy yet viscous. Her fingers closed around his and drew him toward her, until he could feel the air around her crackling.

She said gravely, "Sister Loretta Riding of the Order of Divine Compassion. I do not see her here."

Hobi tried to pull his hand back but the nemosyne wouldn't let go. *This is it*, he thought. *Now my stupidity will be truly rewarded.*

"I think she's dead," he said. "I—I'm sorry. It's—it's probably been a long time since you were with her."

Slowly Nefertity released his hand and looked away. "Twenty-one fourteen," she murmured. "Has it been long?"

He whistled, shaking his head. "God, yes!—it's—it's been *very* long." He pulled the hair back from his face, trying not to look rattled. "Your sister—what was she? A scientist?"

"Loretta? No." The deep whispery voice sounded infinitely sad. It had been centuries since the Ascendants lost the artistry to create things such as this, capable of such eloquence and mimed emotions. Hobi listened entranced as she went on.

"My Sister is—*was*—a cultural archivist backed by the American Vatican State. I was her lifetime project—the NFRTI, the National Feminist Recorded Technical Index. The entire archives of the Library of Congress's Women's Wing and the AVS's feminist collective have been recorded in my files." She hesitated. "But there were others like me—"

Her gaze swept the dim chamber and settled on the tall cabinet housing Maximillian Ur. She pointed, cocking her head toward Hobi. "They are here?"

"I don't know. I don't think so."

Behind Hobi voices stirred, and he looked back. The first *rasa* had crept forward.

"Mother," it whispered imploringly. "Mother, speak to us."

Nefertity regarded it solemnly for a long moment. "I recognize that voice. This person activated the random memory chips,'' she said at last. ''At the sound of a human voice requesting me to speak, I am programmed to enter a random recitative mode. From my files—stories and poetry and plays.''

''But not interactive,'' Hobi said slowly.

''No,'' she replied. ''But it is not difficult to access my interactive mode. Sister Loretta devised it that way, and all the women knew—''

Hobi nodded. ''A kiss. Like in the story—she programmed you to respond to a kiss.''

Nefertity gazed at him and raised her hand. ''That's correct.''

He went on, excited, ''And no one knew— That's why Nasrani was so frustrated!'' He stopped, suddenly embarrassed; wondering (as he was sure the nemosyne must be) how it was that someone as unworthy as himself had been so lucky when Nasrani after so many years had failed.

Nefertity touched Hobi's cheek, staring at him with her cool jade eyes. ''You started the interactive program again. You woke me: the kiss.'' It might have been a reward, the way she pronounced the words.

''I didn't know—I mean, I didn't *mean* to—''

''Sister Loretta programmed it. It was a joke with her. She called me the Sleeping Beauty. The others, the military modules and the biological and archaeological nodes, all responded to more conventional commands.''

''But why? I mean, why did they make *you*?''

''To save the records and stories; to make sure the stories and folktales would not be forgotten. Because of the Long Night; they feared a second Long Night. And so they made us.''

Nefertity crossed the room to Maximillian Ur, her long silver legs gleaming through the darkness. ''Units for science, for agriculture, for the arts as well as the military. You have not found them?''

''No. Not that I've ever heard. You're the only one. Nasrani—Nasrani Orsina—''

She touched Maximillian Ur's case and glanced at

the boy. "He is the new archivist?" Her tone was hopeful.

"No. Nasrani was the one who found you; at least he says he did." Hobi glanced uneasily at the *rasas* crouching in the shadows. "I guess *they* found you, too."

Nefertity shook her head, seeming not to have heard him. "But where are the others?"

She gazed down at the *rasa,* then back at Hobi. "Are *you* the new archivist? Sister Loretta said that help would eventually come. If it's been so terribly long my files must be updated."

A wave of sorrow swept over Hobi. "I—I don't think there are any more archivists. Not in Araboth, at least."

The nemosyne was silent. She stared at Maximillian Ur's blank grimace behind its swollen glass. For several minutes the room was still, the boy and the *rasas* alike waiting anxiously as the nemosyne stood, the soft *tchk* of her circuitry the only sound.

At last she said, "There was another Long Night, wasn't there? That is why Sister Loretta is gone. That is why there are no archivists left."

Hobi nodded sadly. "There was another Long Night. And—and some other things happened too."

"And they are lost, the others like me." Her emerald orbs inside their eyesockets flickered with golden lightning. "They divided us among the remaining churches and governments and reservations, to be sure that some of us would survive. Some of us were imprinted with a program-memory of our archivist. I was—I am—Loretta Riding. But the others . . ."

Hobi would not have believed a replicant's voice was capable of displaying such grief. He felt horrible now for waking her, and wondered if somehow he could manage to switch her off, return her to her sleeping state before Nasrani returned once more and saw her like this.

"Mother," the *rasa* whispered. It slipped next to

Hobi and raised its head, its ruined eyes wide and hopeful. "More stories now?"

Nefertity lowered her hand to touch its head. "Is this all that remains?" she asked Hobi. "The others like you—they are dead?"

"Oh, no! These are just—*rasas*. Regenerated corpses. You know," he added lamely.

"Regenerated corpses," the nemosyne repeated slowly. She looked past the *rasa* at the others in the darkness. "All of them? Dead? But that is a terrible thing to have done! Why have they come to me?"

Hobi shrugged. "Well, no—I mean, they're not really dead, not anymore—" He looked at the floor, ashamed. "I'm not sure why they're here, really."

The nemosyne drew her hand back from the *rasa*. Her voice was cold. "What happened, then? Was it more bombs? Or the nuclear tides? What happened?"

Hobi felt hot, in spite of the dank room. "I don't know," he muttered. "No one knows."

"Europe? Africa? The L-5 colonies?" The boy shook his head and shrugged. "All of it gone? You remember nothing?"

"Nothing."

"Where are we now?"

"Araboth. Araboth—it had another name once, that's what Nasrani said. Texas."

"Araboth." Motes of light glittered in front of her face. "Texas. Not Chicago?"

The boy looked away, defeated. "I never heard of Chicago."

"Mother," the *rasa* interrupted, and tugged at her hand. "Tell us again. Stories. The Frankenstein monster."

"Little Red-Hood," whispered another.

"Amelia Earhart."

"The Woman in the Moon."

"Stories," the nemosyne said slowly. She turned and walked to the center of the room. A slithering sound as the pallid forms followed her, staying just outside her nimbus of shimmering light. "I have been telling my stories to corpses."

Her eyes flashed as she pointed again at Hobi. "You have forgotten all the rest of it. The cities, the space stations. The wars, the gynocides, the Bibliochlasm?"

Hobi bit his lip. Her words frightened him. These were forbidden things, things that had to do with the First Days, the lost days; things to do with Outside.

"Yes," he admitted. He glanced about the room, trying to see where the door was, praying for Nasrani to appear, or for the nemosyne to be distracted long enough for him to escape. "Yes. We have forgotten all of it."

Nefertity nodded. Her body pulsed a deeper blue now, and her voice had grown louder. "But there are women and men perhaps who might want to remember? Who might have need of me?"

Hobi swallowed nervously. "I don't think so. I mean, it might be better if you just stayed here. At least until Nasrani comes back. He would know."

"Please, Mother," the *rasa* beseeched her. In the darkness its eyes were wide, almost childlike. "More stories. Please. We waited, we waited."

The nemosyne gazed down at the *rasa*, at the other white soft figures crouched in the shadows. Her jadeite eyes glittered, and she nodded as she extended her arms.

"Yes," she said, beckoning them to her. "Yes: come closer."

The first *rasa* looked back at the others, then slowly they dragged themselves forward, until all huddled in a semicircle at the nemosyne's feet.

"Yes," whispered Nefertity. There was a loud humming; when she spoke again it was in a clear high voice, the voice Hobi had heard when first he entered the chamber. "Let the dead listen to me, and learn, and remember if no one else will—"

And she began to recite.

"I was, being human, born alone;
I am, being woman, hard beset;
I live by squeezing from a stone
The little nourishment I get.

In masks outrageous and austere
The years go by in single file;
But none has merited my fear,
And none has quite escaped my smile . . .

"Now I will tell you the story of 'The Dreaming Child,' by Isak Dinesen, the Baroness Blixen . . ."

As she spoke a single great sigh rippled through the dim chamber, soft and comforted as a child's. But as Hobi gazed up at her it seemed to him that the nemosyne's features looked less lovely than they had before; that within her crystal body her adamantine heart did not burn as steadily as when she had slept, and dreamed that Sister Loretta Riding was alive.

Chapter 7

IF YOU HAVE GHOSTS

~~~~~~~~~~

If you have ghosts
then you have everything.

—Roky Erickson

Sajur Panggang was on Principalities when he heard the news of Shiyung's murder.

"The margravine Shiyung," a moujik guard told him, his face swollen from weeping. "How can this be, Your Grace, I cannot understand it. . . ."

The Architect Imperator turned away, so that the guard would not see his expression. "The Prophets tell us that there is little we can truly understand, my brother," he said softly, his mouth twisting into a smile. "Only the Architects can understand all, only the Architects. . . ."

He left the guard sniveling on his watch and wandered along the Mulla Nasrudin Promenade. The stench of the medifacs was nearly overwhelming here, but the Architect Imperator seemed not to notice. He crossed the promenade heedless of the clots of offal beneath his feet, the clouds of mucid steam that belched from the grates beneath his velvet-soled boots. Those moujiks who saw him, in his black suit with his turban of office slightly askew, pressed their fists to their heads and bowed, and afterward marveled that the most powerful of the Imperators had been so moved by the margravine's death that he ventured thus onto the hellish rim of Principalities, that his grief took him to the immensity of the Lahatiel Gate itself.

The truth was, the Architect Imperator had awakened some hours after his son's departure, to a scene of quiet domestic wreckage—broken glass, empty bottles, the replicant Khum's confusion at being left without commands. He had spent several minutes wandering around the house, not, as one might expect, checking the progress of the Architects but looking for a particular robe he had worn ten years before during Æstival Tide, a robe his wife Angelika had given him for the festival. He finally found it in the chamber that had been Angelika's dressing room, the robe wrapped in tissue paper scented faintly of lavender. He put it on, smoothing the sumptuous folds of forest-green jacquard and striking poses in front of a tall mirror. He was mindful that the color made his pallor stand out rather too severely, and that in his present state—unshaven, hair awry, a streak of blood on his chin where he had rubbed it with his cut hand—he looked more than a trifle deranged. Then he set out for the gravator that would take him down to Principalities.

Beneath the Lahatiel Gate he finally paused. Hundreds of feet above him the barricade gleamed a blinding argent. Scaffolds swayed precariously where a few unfortunate moujiks still worked, polishing the steel ribs and spars in preparation for the *timoria*. But it was not the sight of the Gate that had drawn Sajur Panggang here, but what lay beneath it.

"Your Grace."

Another moujik guard. This one obviously had not yet heard of Shiyung's death. An obsequious smile creased his flat face, and he bowed so low that his stained violet sash trailed the ground. "Your servants are honored—"

"Yes, yes, thank you." The Architect Imperator gave him a small smile and waggled his fingers. He looked distractedly about the cavernous space, and began walking toward a barred doorway to one side of the Gate. The guard's face fell. He hurried after the slender man, pulling at his sash in dismay.

"Your Grace! It is not safe within there, it is too near the festival, it is starting to wake—"

The Architect Imperator turned to regard the moujik with bemused hauteur. "I know quite well the status of the Redeemer's slumber," he said, his voice mild. "I wish merely to inspect it, and make certain that the temperature of its chamber is not dropping too quickly. You have noticed some disturbances in the last few days?" This last with a slightly raised eyebrow.

"Why, yes, as a matter of fact, we were speaking of it yesterday—"

Sajur Panggang nodded, smiling that absently ironic smile, and walked on. "You might check the 'files," he called back gently; "I believe there is unfortunate news regarding one of the margravines—"

There was no human guard at the door leading to the cage of the Compassionate Redeemer. Sentries from the lower levels had proved unreliable. They would succumb to morbid curiosity, their subsequent terror rendering them incapable of carrying out their duties. More often they simply refused to go near it. The ranks of Seraphim and Cherubim had slightly more fortitude in confronting the Redeemer, steeled by their long indulgences in timoring and the other rarefied abominations of the upper classes. But even they usually fell prey to an unanticipated sickening when, upon the occasion of the Great Fear or some reckless and spirited party-visit to the Redeemer's pen, they peered through the tiny viewing-glass and glimpsed the monster in its suspended state.

No such qualms beset the Architect Imperator. He had grown inured to such horrors, as he had grown insensible of the reek of Principalities' human smelting chambers and abattoirs. Now he simply peered into an opticon, permitting the Redeemer's robotic sentry to scan his retinafile and pronounce his name with chilly efficiency. An instant later the gate clanged open and Sajur Panggang slipped inside, dabbing delicately at his forehead with a handkerchief.

A narrow hallway, dimly lit, led a few yards to where a single steel-and-glass chair stood before a small window. The chair creaked as Sajur settled into it, the cracked leather seat emitting a smell of dust and roses. Even from here he could feel the oppressive heat of the Redeemer's cage. The glass window in front of him was so thick that he had to press his face against it to see anything, and even then it was with some difficulty that he made out the figure below. This was no failure of design on the part of the Architects. It was better for most visitors to doubt that they had had a clear glimpse of the cage's inhabitant; better that they fall back, choking, when at Æstival Tide they saw the blind colossus lumber from its cell onto the summer sands.

Sajur had no such reticence about viewing the Compassionate Redeemer. Orsina blood ran in his veins, no matter how diffuse, and for centuries the Redeemer had been the Orsinate's *enfant gâté*, their demonic familiar, the terrible rector presiding over the hecatombs every ten years, and in between times awakened every year or so and fed during public sacrifices. Sajur gazed upon it now with a sort of hunger, a yearning fired by a fraternal sympathy. Were they both not the Orsinate's prisoners, toys kept hidden away until the perfect moment arrived, when their exquisite chains might be tweaked by their captors? This was what had brought him here, here at the end of all things: the desire to look for the last time upon another monster, and feel something like sympathy. He sighed, a sound of pure regret.

As if sensing him the Redeemer stirred. Its blind head snaked upward and twisted back and forth, trying to pinpoint him, then sank back to the stone floor. Sajur drew back, his heart racing. He had not thought it would be this far into its cycle, already roused from æstivation by the temperature dropping within its cell. In a few hours an inch of ice would have formed on the thick glass window; the Redeemer would be fully awake and making its obscene ululating cry. Gazing down upon the creature's vast bulk the Architect Imperator allowed himself the luxury of a small grimace. It was truly an exquisite and hideous thing; as though by serving as the Orsinate's lictor it had become the physical embodiment of all their transgressions. Body of an extinct saurian, an alioramus, gorgeously scaled in silvery-gold and green, its deceptively slender legs with their curving dewclaws powerful enough to sprint across the scar and disembowel a man before he had a chance to turn away. Its long graceful neck ended in the head of an olm, broad and flat and eyeless, the color of cream stirred with a petal of gentian, and feathered with an olm's vestigial gills. Its yawning mouth was nearly perfectly circular, twice the height and breadth of a man. A lamprey's mouth, ribboned with rose-pink flesh without and within—long venom-tipped tendrils that whipped at its prey and stunned it, and then twitched the stupefied unfortunates into its maw. Circular rows of triangular teeth lined the inside of its mouth, layer upon layer like a manticore's, leading deep into its throat where hollow filaments fastened upon the body and sucked the nutriments from it. The Redeemer had no stomach proper. Digestion took place within those individual tubules and the drained bodies were excreted within a few minutes, slack and bloodless, bones crackled to bits. As Sajur Panggang stared, the fleshy tendrils dangling from the creature's mouth quivered, lifted into the air like so many blind worms and writhed toward the wall where he sat. At the sight his nose prickled and he pulled back from the glass; too late he realized he should have worn a protective mask. An overpowering scent of myrrh and roses filled the tiny room, so warm and sweet it clouded the senses, made one only want to crawl toward whatever it was emitted that smell and drown luxuriously as the odor filled one's nostrils.

Coughing, Sajur covered his mouth and stumbled from his chair. The Redeemer seemed to follow him, its head swaying as rose-pink tendrils weaved in front of him, tapped tentatively at the glass, and left carmine smears a few inches from where his head had been. The Architect Imperator lurched down the hallway and out into the shadow of the Lahatiel Gate, gasping as he slammed the door shut and not even pausing for the human sentry who ran up to him, white-faced and gibbering something about his health. He stumbled until he reached the Imperators' gravator and punched in the grid code for the palace, and then collapsed.

''Orsina.''

The voice tore through his room as Nasrani Orsina cracked the door open. At first he had ignored the sentry's announcement; then lay in bed trying to ignore the voice calling his name—softly at first, then louder and still louder, until Nasrani covered his ears and knelt on his bed, praying for it to stop.

But it did not stop. He finally crept from his room, more frightened now of what might happen if he did not answer it.

"Nasrani," the voice cried. "I must see her."

In the doorway in front of him stood the *rasa*. There was no breeze, of course, but still his black robe stirred so that Nasrani could see the outlines of his legs beneath the flowing silk. Legs far too slender to support that tall frame; too slender and too sharp—the edge of one metal joint had slashed the cloth.

"Margalis." Nasrani tried to keep his voice steady, affecting an air of cheerful surprise. "It's late. Or early," he added, and rubbed his forehead.

Outside the window of his chamber on Coventry (the exiles' wing, an adjunct to the main palace presently occupied only by Nasrani and the former ambassador from Antarctica, who spent her days snorting morpha and her evenings weeping over polyfiles of blue ice) the nuclear CLOCK read thirteen-five, too early by several hours for upper-level visitors. Nasrani coughed delicately. "Can we talk about this over kehveh a little later?"

"No."

Tast'annin pushed aside Nasrani as he strode into the room, hard enough to send the exile careening against the wall. "You had her before I left. You have her now. If you don't take me to her I will kill you."

Nasrani slumped against the wall, trying to catch his breath. From the corner of his eye he watched the *rasa* stalk to the window, staring down to where the receding levels of Araboth gave way to the abyss that yawned beneath Archangels.

"What is it, Margalis?" he whispered. "What have you done?"

The *rasa* stared down at his metal hand. Without the glove it glittered brightly, a lethal sheen upon its fingertips. "I have killed your sister."

Nasrani drew his breath in sharply. "Âziz?" He started for the window but the *rasa*'s gaze stopped him. Nasrani wrung the edge of his gown.

"No. Shiyung."

Nasrani shook his head. "Impossible."

"No: true. I snapped her neck and left her on the floor of her chambers. If they have not found her yet she is there still."

Nasrani stared in disbelief. Shiyung dead. He re-

membered her as a child, skinny as a rail, shrieking
with laughter as she tricked him into playing some
impossible game with her. And then each night, the
four of them sharing a bed, forgotten by their parents
(they shared a mother and three fathers between
them) as they lay side by side by side by side, Nasrani
spinning tales into the darkness like a web to snare
their nightmares. And, long after, just himself and
Shiyung, another impossible game of hers, over too
quickly.

And now she was dead.

Nasrani sobbed, an awful sound like laughter
catching in his throat. The *rasa* stared unblinking,
then said, "Tell me where you've hidden the
nemosyne."

Nasrani's voice came out in a braying cough. "I
knew you would."

"The nemosyne, Nasrani."

The exile tore at his face with his hands. "I told
her when you broke with her, I told her you were a
madman and she should have killed you then—"

"She was a fool not to." The *rasa* turned once
more to the window. "Or perhaps not. Perhaps even
then she had this in store for me. I would rather have
been dead. I wish I could die now."

Suddenly he screamed, a thin, high shriek like a
saw cutting through a sheet of tin. Nasrani trembled
and fell back against the wall; but still the *rasa* wailed,
longer than any human could have, until Nasrani
clapped his hands to his ears and stumbled toward the
door.

"*No!*"

The awful shriek turned into a shout. Nasrani
staggered, reaching for the switch that would summon help from the palace. The *rasa* strode to his side
and slashed at the wall. There was a flurry of sparks,
the smell of melted plastic.

"No one will come help you, Nasrani." His eyes
swept over the cowering exile and he lifted his head
disdainfully. "They will all be in Shiyung's chambers

by now, discovering the body. Perhaps Nike will think to call you. . . ."

Smoke curled from the tips of the *rasa*'s fingers. He held them in front of his eyes, watching the thin gray trails turn to white and then disappear. The hollow voice cried, "You are all still children playing, aren't you? You have your petty disagreements, you take sides and banish each other to your little rooms, but this is all just a game to you." He turned and paced across the room, smashed his metal hand against the glass. A single crack flowed across the pane, like a flaw in the heart of a crystal. "All of this, this city and everything Outside—you mold it and burn it and twist it to your liking. People too: you contort us as though we were your friend Planck's puppets, and then act surprised when we turn against you."

Nasrani leaned against the wall. The *rasa*'s anger seemed to calm him; if a dead Aviator could be undone by emotions, perhaps he could be undone, period. The color drained back into Nasrani's face.

"They will regenerate her," he said, groping in his pocket until he found a pipe and a leather pouch. He stuffed a wad of kef into the bowl, lit it, and inhaled noisily. After a minute he glanced up at the looming shadow.

"As a *rasa*," the dark figure said. "You would wish that on her? Your own sister?"

Nasrani's hands trembled as he tapped kef ash onto the floor. "How did you—how *could* you?" Tears spilled from his eyes again. "A *rasa*—it's impossible—"

"How did I kill her? Let us just say that I have not been myself lately."

Nasrani sniffed. His rubbed his bloodshot eyes with an anguished expression. "Why do you want to see the nemosyne again?"

The *rasa* turned from the window. Below and all around them the daylights began streaming on, gold and blue and red, cascading down each level in sheets of light until the entire vast ziggurat shone and danced like a pyramid of blazing glass. For a few minutes they watched in silence.

Then, from the palace came a high piercing wail. Abruptly the daylights paled as overhead flames of white and blue swept the domes. Distress lights. Nasrani blanched. He had not seen them since the mass executions following the Archipelago Conflict.

The *rasa* said calmly, "You said that you believed the nemosyne knows things. Well, I have—*seen things* —that I would ask her about. You said that she had many secrets. Now I have secrets too."

Nasrani joined him at the window, gazed up at the warning flares, the silhouettes of janissaries pouring like black water from their barracks.

"You really did it," he said softly. He turned to the grim figure beside him. "You killed my sister. And now you want me to take you to the nemosyne."

"Yes." The *rasa*'s voice betrayed nothing of entreaty, but the pale eyes were clouded. "I must see her. I am—haunted by something. From before— from before I died. *Someone.* I want to question the nemosyne about her."

"And Shiyung?" Nasrani fairly shrieked. "What of her? You kill the margravine—my *sister!*—and you expect me to lead you around now, do whatever you wish—"

"Yes," the *rasa* said softly. From a pocket in its silken robe it withdrew a black kidskin glove and carefully pulled it over its shining metal hand. "I do. And you will do it, because you have no choice."

Nasrani's expression folded into defeat. He patted his pockets until he found his pipe again and smoked another bowl of kef. Outside the sirens wailed on; the distress lights arced back and forth across the domes. The *rasa* stood silently and waited, until Nasrani looked up and snapped, "I have never been able to speak with her. The interactive mode is dormant; she does nothing but go through her random access files and read from them. There is a way to activate that portion of her memory, though I have never learned it. But there are other things down there, I have seen them in the room with her—"

He laughed harshly. "Angels in the Undercity! *I* cannot speak to her, but those foul things cluster around her, and she hears them! And she speaks to them! Stories, poems—" His hands fluttered. "They call her Mother, and she answers. But she won't respond to my questions. I have no reason to believe she will answer yours."

The *rasa* only nodded. Nasrani suddenly turned away, his eyes watering. He ran a hand over his face. "You didn't have to kill her," he choked. The *rasa* tipped its head back so that the brilliant light outside the window flashed blindingly against its mask. "She could have left you dead but she didn't, she—"

"I care nothing about your sister," the *rasa* hissed. "I want the nemosyne. Which one is it? One of the military units? A meteorological display?"

Nasrani wiped his eyes, then suddenly laughed shrilly. "Is that what you think? That you'll have another monster to command? No, Margalis! She's useless, utterly useless—women's stories and songs and bankrupt histories, that's all she's good for. . . ."

"Then why do you hide her? Eh, Nasrani—"

He grabbed the man's arm. Nasrani felt the metal claws beneath the thin sheath of leather, their grip tightening until he gasped and then moaned. A dark stain spread across his sleeve.

"I must see her." Nasrani whimpered. The *rasa*'s touch was cold and foul as an open grave. "I need her to find the others, to see if any of the other units survived. I need them to track someone, someone Outside. *Take me to her now*—"

He shoved Nasrani from him. The man fell to his knees, groaning and trying to stanch the blood soaking his robe. "Yes," he gasped. "I'll take you, of course I'll take you . . ."

The *rasa* nodded and extended his hand to help the man to his feet. "We will go then," said the Aviator Imperator. His shadow filled the narrow doorway. "To the Undercity; to find the Mother of Angels."

"Zalophus—oh, Zalophus, *please*—"

At the end of the zeuglodon's tank the gynander stood, panting. She had run all the way here, past the first shift of biotechs and vivisectors on their way to the Chambers of Mercy, past the white-masked guards who hurried from the gravator as she rushed past them on her way down to Dominations. They all seemed too intent on their own business to notice her; news of Shiyung's murder had just reached the Orsinate's security staff. For the moment she was safe.

It was all too much, as though Ceryl's dream had grown to envelope the city and all within it; and Reive was in it, too, she could not escape no matter how quickly she fled. Only here did she feel she might somehow outrun it, that huge green serpent coiling about the domes and squeezing them until she could feel the floor beneath her buckling, the very walls bulging in upon her until she thought she would scream—

But that was just her heart pounding, her chest straining so that it felt as though stones bashed her insides. She stopped, panting, then began running again; because if she waited more than a moment, the Wave would overtake her.

Now Reive was in the main vivarium chamber, where biotechs padded on their morning rounds, drawing blood and brain tissue from the palingenic dolphins, checking the stress monitors on the gentle manatees, who wept like women when their calves were taken from them. A few of the workers eyed her curiously, but it was too early in the shift, there was too much to be done, to worry about a white-faced morphodite running aimlessly among the tanks.

"Oh, Zalophus, hurry, please—"

Her teeth chattered and she skipped from foot to foot like a child playing. "*Zalophus!*" she wailed.

An explosion; then a small island reared from the dark green surface. A single huge black eye stared at her, and teeth like a row of shinbones clashed as his voice boomed and filled the chamber.

"Oh, happy day, child of the morning, you have come to play with me?" Zalophus rolled onto his back, his huge fins splashing at the water so that a wave rolled over the side and soaked Reive.

"Zalophus," she gasped, spluttering. "Oh, Zalophus, you must help us—"

"Of course," the great whale crooned, "come here and I will sing to you, little thing, I will tell you about my sisters, and the icelands where they are waiting for us—"

"No, Zalophus! We need you, you must tell us where we can go to hide!"

Zalophus righted himself and stared at her with huge rolling eyes. "You have brought another siren," he said hopefully. "That is so nice, sirens make such sweet companions."

Reive shook her head, shivering. "No, we haven't. Zalophus, they will kill us, they think we murdered the margravine."

Zalophus snapped his jaw. "A margravine would be just as nice."

"No! She's not here, they—" Reive wrung her hands. "Zalophus, you know all the levels here, you've been beneath the domes. Tell us where we can go, where they won't find us. Tell us, please—we will come back, we will sneak here at night and bring you whatever you want—"

Across the cavernous chamber a woman taking blood from a rorqual looked up and stared at Reive. Zalophus rolled over to shrewdly regard the gynander with his other eye. After a moment he said, "One of the margravines had a baby once. I heard them talking about it. A monster, a heteroclite. She sent it to the Chambers of Mercy; but the vivisectors did not kill it, they said it would bring ill luck. I remember, I *world is waking — fear of world*

heard them talking. I think you must be that monster. Come closer to me so that I can see you better."

The gynander ignored him, then lowering her voice she took a step toward the tank. "Zalophus, the Aviator Imperator has gone mad. None of us will be safe, not even you. If you tell us of a safe place to hide for now we will find a way to free you—tomorrow, at Æstival Tide. We will find a way, we promise."

Water raced down the zeuglodon's snout as he raised his head to stare at her. "There is a way, little thing," he groaned, a sound like crumbling stone. A summer smell filled the air. "Last night I dreamed of the other one, the little man they killed to make me. He told me that the world Outside is closer now, closer than it ever has been before. When I woke I sounded to the deepest depths and it is true, heteroclite child: the world is waking and moving in its sleep."

Reive shook her head. "There's no time," she said desperately. "We have no time for your stories now, you must tell us of a way to escape."

"Come with me." Zalophus rose until his head hung above the dark water, a green-whorled sun blotting out the false daylight. "Come with me, little thing, and I will show you the new world. There is a crack where the water valves run into the Undercity. Each day it is widening. Soon it will be big enough for me to enter, and then I will find them, then my sisters will come to meet me—"

"There is no way out! You have no sisters!" Reive shouted. The woman bending over the rorqual looked over in alarm. "They have been dead for a million years! I hope you starve here—"

She turned and ran from the vivarium. The zeuglodon watched her leave, then rolled onto his back, sending another wave rushing from the tank onto the concrete floor. A moment later he disappeared, sounding the depths of his prison to where the chink in the walls was widening, and warm water poured in through a black mouth opening onto the world.

In a chamber on the vivarium level, Âziz Orsina sat gazing at the body of her sister Shiyung. Tubes and wires ran from the corpse to a series of vats and monitors, alembics and computers controlled by the Architects' rehabilitation nexus. It would be days before Shiyung could be restored as a *rasa*, certainly not until after Æstival Tide. Âziz wondered what effect this would have on the lower levels. Shiyung had always been the favorite of the moujiks and the biotechs, as much for her prettiness and childish enthusiasms as for her occasional sallies down to visit the toilers in the refineries and the vivariums. It didn't matter that Shiyung never did anything besides smile and share an occasional pappadam with carefully selected drones. The others, the rest of the work force, would see her in person and later that evening on the 'files and puppet shows. They would see her, forehead daubed with blue and black to show solidarity with the Church of Christ Cadillac, smiling as she ate fermented beans with the refineries' human supervisors, the *rasas* in pale ranks behind her, and still later they would watch as, her lovely white face flushed with excitement, she torched the pyres for the public burnings.

How would they react to Shiyung as a *rasa*?

Âziz nibbled her fingernail and pushed her hair from her face. Beside her the biotechnician she'd chosen for the project watched nervously, making a great show of adjusting and readjusting the levels in the chemical bath that lapped at Shiyung's pale form.

"You can't do it any faster?" Âziz asked for the fourth time.

The biotech sighed, shaking his head. "We're already losing some resolution on her now, Margravine, doing it this quickly." He gestured vaguely at the tubes curling up from the tank and into the brightly lit reaches of the lab. "There's going to be some failure as it is, with her long-term memory, and her—"

"I don't care," snapped Âziz. She stood and paced to the other side of the tank, staring at her sister's white face. Already the skin had grown slack; Shiyung's mouth had drooped into a grimacing leer. "The festival is tomorrow. I need her by then. I need *something* by then."

The biotech opened his hands in a hopeless gesture. "Margravine, there's no way—"

A rumbling shook the room, sending the lamps swinging wildly. Âziz started, grabbing the edge of a table until the shock subsided. She glared accusingly at the biotech. In the tank Shiyung's corpse rocked back and forth, nucleic fluid sloshing onto the floor.

The biotech steadied himself, his face white. "That's been happening lately," he stammered. "We don't know why—here and in some of the other labs near the rim—"

Âziz looked as though she would throttle him. She pointed at her sister's neck, where a reddish bruise shaped like a half-moon creased the swollen flesh. "Do something about that," she spat, and stalked off.

Back on Seraphim Âziz returned to the Four Hundredth Room. Nike lay on a divan, gazing at a polyfile projected onto the ceiling—another work of Karvo's, one that drew quite wittily upon ancient ecclesiastical motifs. It showed three *galli* in red and yellow cassocks singing, the sweetness of their voices marred somewhat by their expressions, which were rapt with horror. A disembodied hand appeared and one by one slashed the throats of the *galli* with a bright blue scalpel. In the past Nike had found the work moving; but in the wake of Shiyung's death it seemed rather hackneyed, sentimental in fact, and when Âziz entered the room she switched the sound off and turned to her, musing.

"I was thinking we should revoke Karvo's privilege," she said, gesturing at the ceiling.

Âziz nodded wearily. She crossed to the divan and sank onto it. "Petra," she called. A yellow-haired girl appeared in the doorway. "Bring me some warmed valerian, please. I've got a terrible headache."

After the girl left she turned to her sister. "He says he can't do it any faster and we won't have her before Æstival Tide. Well, not before it starts, at least. There's some trouble with decay, memory loss, I don't know." She raised her hands hopelessly, dropped them into her lap as the yellow-haired girl returned with a steaming samovar and two porcelain cups. She placed them on a table and left. "Now if this had only happened to Nasrani, Shiyung could have done the regeneration herself."

Nike nodded, still staring with a frown at the silent images flickering across the ceiling. The last *galli* had fallen, lying atop a white rug with his fellows, their blood and their bright cassocks lurid against the calm background. "I can't believe I ever thought his work was subtle. I *am* going to revoke his privilege."

Âziz made a disinterested noise, stirred her valerian and sipped it, wincing. "You know there's going to be an uproar if she's not there when we open the Gate. She's too popular, especially these last few days. With all these reports of structural problems, *she's* the only one of us they would trust—we've *got* to try to have her *rasa* on hand, something to make them believe she's still alive, still there to sympathize with them. But news of the murder has already gotten out, and with all this other confusion . . ."

She closed her eyes and inhaled the steam. After a moment she said, "I just need a little time to think of something, something to distract them. I don't want any riots this year, things are bad enough with these damn tremors and that fire yesterday. We need *something*." She looked thoughtfully down at her cup. "Perhaps we could forgive Nasrani."

Nike clicked off the polyfile and stood. Yawning, she crossed the room to where her sister sat. "That would be nice. I wanted him at the next inquisition anyway." She picked up her cup of valerian and stared at it, then cleared her throat and asked delicately, "You've taken care of them? The guests from last evening—"

Âziz shrugged. "I've ordered that they be rounded up. The Committee Head told me most of them are already in the Reception Area—"

"Sajur?" Nike raised an eyebrow.

Her sister shook her head impatiently. "We can't detain Sajur. We've never arranged for his successor." She tapped one front tooth with her fingernail and mused, "Although there is a woman, an ethical mathematician, who might be suitable. . . ."

Nike nodded. "So we can't detain Sajur. What about that woman, what's her name—Waxwing. The biotech. The one we traced the morph back to?"

"She's to be detained with all the rest. Friser, the Ambassador, Planck—Sajur's going to be distressed about him." Âziz finished her drink and put the empty cup on the tray, dipped her fingers into a small bowl of borage water and flicked them dry.

"Sajur." Nike licked her lips and settled on the divan beside her sister. "What has he to say about all this? Have you seen him?"

"No; there's no answer in his chambers. But what is there to say? An unknown morph, a murderous interloper from the lower levels, what else can one expect? We make some new appointments to the appropriate cabinets and as soon as possible call another inquisition. Perhaps tomorrow night, that would be appropriate. . . ."

Nike drummed her fingers slowly on the edge of the brass divan. "But your dream." Her dark eyes when she raised them to her sister were clouded. "The morph said—what if what she said were true?"

"The Green Country? The storms?" Âziz sniffed and poured some more valerian. Nike watched her, then pulled a morpha tube from her pocket, tipped its contents into her cup, and drank it in a gulp. "Sajur says it's impossible for a storm of that magnitude to be undetected. The Architects, the weather stations . . . HORUS would have notified us of anything strange."

Nike shook her head. Already her pupils dilated and her voice grew slurred. "But we lost the NASNA Prime station last fall, and the others in the Net took such a hard hit from the Commonwealth. We needed someone stronger up there to oversee the repairs. We never should have sent Margalis to the Capital," she finished angrily. "He should have stayed on HO-RUS—"

"He would have been immolated with the rest of his substation if he had," said Âziz; but her sister ranted on.

". . . knew it was a mistake—that whole business with the Capital was a fiasco!"

"You went along with Shiyung at the time," Âziz remarked dryly. "As I recall you agreed with Margalis that the old weapons centers should be reactivated. You seemed to think Shiyung would do a very good job of administering the place, once Margalis had taken over as Governor. You seemed quite eager, in fact, to have Shiyung gone from here."

Nike sputtered but said nothing. There *had* been a brief resurgence of a petty childhood rivalry about the time of Tast'annin's failed venture to the Capital. Finally she spat, "All the same! Personnel wasted on *that* instead of keeping up the celestial surveys—there could be a storm out there *right now* and we'd never know a thing—"

She stopped, and walked unsteadily to the window. Her voice shook as she went on. "The 'files said that a retaining wall on Virtues collapsed early this morning. The warning systems didn't go off. The Architects did *nothing*—I accessed the scrolls from yesterday, they didn't even record it." She turned to her sister, her face suddenly pale. "Âziz, it's like in the prophecies of Fasidim and the story of John Bingham's wife. It's—it's the sort of thing they say will happen, before the city falls—''

Outside the distress lights still slashed the domes with white and blue. Three fougas rose from their hangars, trailing the long incantatory pennons advertising the start of Æstival Tide. Âziz raised her cup and smiled, but her eyes were bitter.

"Don't be absurd," she said. "A dream, it was only a dream."

"*The* dream—the morph said it was the dream of the Green Country! The Architects are failing us! What if—''

"Listen to you, Nike! You're talking about Mrs. Bingham and listening to a *hermaphrodite*! I can't believe this—you sound as crazy as Shiyung. There'll be no need to regenerate her at all, just pop her crown on your soft little head!''

Nike bit her lip and stared at the floor. Her voice was whining. "But *why*, Âziz? Why would a morph kill her? *How* could she kill her? It doesn't make sense. *None* of this makes sense. The Architects have blinked off, there've been reports of cracks in some of the vivariums, a tremor on Principalities. Malva Circutus from the Toxins Cabal told me that on every level below Thrones there's been some kind of tremor, and now they're saying it's the storms coming. If the lower levels hear about your dream . . .''

Âziz glared at her, stood and walked to the window. For several minutes she watched the fougas drifting up and down, their turquoise banners rippling and snapping in the air rising from the refineries. Her mouth grew tight.

"They should be towing funerary pennons," she said at last. Her head snapped up and her eyes blazed angrily. "I don't know how or why that unfortunate did it, and I don't care. Shiyung is dead, and we can't let these other rumors go any further. We have to find the right way to deal with this before the Gate opens, or we'll have a revolt on our hands. I want to see that morph now. And the one she's been living with. Shiyung's healer, Ceryl Waxwing."

She pressed a button on the windowsill and summoned the yellow-haired serving girl. "Tell the Head of the Reception Committee to bring the gynander Reive here, and the biotech Ceryl Waxwing. And get some 'filers: I want 'filers here for the sentencing."

She turned back to Nike. "The morph's a political enemy. She murdered Shiyung. I don't know how she escaped from her cell, or how she did it, but she did. And the other one's a collaborator. We'll 'file the sentencing and have it broadcast constantly until tomorrow: Shiyung's murderers, political collaborators. If we can't have Shiyung there when we open the Gate, we'll have those two instead, as a designated sacrifice. And Nasrani—we'll reinstate him. We'll give them to the Compassionate Redeemer, have Nasrani perform the honors. If the crowd gets unruly we open the Gate before the appointed hour. *That* should satisfy the lower levels." She bit her lip thoughtfully. "Maybe we won't have to regenerate Shiyung after all. . . ."

Nike ran a finger along the edge of the window. "But these rumors of structural damage—you don't think we'll be setting our own pyres if we go through with the festival, opening the Gate to Ucalegon?"

Âziz leaned against her sister. "It was only a dream, Nike," she whispered, stroking her hair. "And the Architects are guarding us. Nothing will happen, because it was just a dream."

Nike sighed and nodded, her eyes heavy-lidded from the morpha. As the distress lights glowed beneath the central Quincunx Dome, she let her sister take her in her arms, and waited for the Reception Committee to arrive with their guests.

Ceryl Waxwing tapped her foot and stared anxiously out the window as Rudyard Planck poured himself another glass of brandy.

"There's no point fretting about Reive, my friend," the dwarf announced. He held his snifter up to the light and sipped from it, making admiring noises. "This is very fine, I believe this is one of the vats I had drawn myself, after the success of my Generation Twelve puppets. They're probably going to send us *all* to the Reception Area—Âziz won't stand for this business about her dream getting out—so you might as well have another glass of this wonderful stuff and enjoy it while you can. Though last time I visited the Reception Area they had some quite fine Amity—"

Ceryl had drawn her breath in sharply at the words *Reception Area* and now whirled furiously, as though to knock the snifter from Planck's hand. But for some reason the sight of the red-haired dwarf perched atop the granite table, sipping brandy, stopped her.

"You're probably right," she sighed, defeated. She strode to the table and poured herself a glass. Her eyes watered as she swallowed it, and Rudyard Planck reached up to pat her thigh.

"There—have a bit more, don't gulp it this time, and try to relax. There's worse things than prison," he added, eyeing his brandy doubtfully.

"What?" demanded Ceryl. Her hand shook as she unstoppered the decanter and filled her snifter again. "Dying? That might be worse."

The dwarf shook his head, pursing his lips. In the confusion after Reive's detention he had urged Ceryl to leave the Four Hundredth Room with him and return to her chambers. He glanced down at the table, where a polyfile showing a young boy pierced by myriad steel spikes hovered an inch above the granite surface.

"I see you indulge in timoring." With a little moue of distaste he turned the dial at the base of the polyfile stand, so that the image flickered into random darts of light.

"Not really." Ceryl shook her head wearily. "I tried once. It—it made me sick."

The dwarf looked up at her and nodded approvingly. "I never could see the charm in it myself. A disgusting practice. This vogue for resurrecting ancient torments, pleasures of insane Roman emperors —madness, pure madness. Proof positive of the decadence of our times. Crimes against nature. I find them abhorrent. That's why I'm rather unpopular around the pleasure cabinet." He smiled wryly and turned back to Ceryl. "At least with dying one can always hope for rehabilitation, if you're important enough to *them*. But once you're in the Reception Area: well, usually you just stay there. Or else—"

His voice trailed off and he finished his brandy in thoughtful silence.

Or else they give you to the Compassionate Redeemer. That was what he was going to say, Ceryl knew that. She swallowed her brandy defiantly and poured herself a third glass. Rudyard Planck raised a small gingery eyebrow.

"That will make you sick, my friend. It's a shame to waste good brandy—"

"I'm not wasting it," Ceryl replied hotly. "You said to enjoy it. Well, I'm enjoying it. I'm having the time of my goddamn life. Reive's been drinking it like—"

She stopped and drew her snifter under her chin. On the table beside a holograph Reive's mysid drifted in its globe. Somehow they had never gotten around to finding a suitable hiding place for it. The sight of the tiny creature brought tears to her eyes.

"They'll kill her, won't they?" she said, almost in a whisper. "They won't even try her probably, just— just execute her. She's just a child, really. No more sense than—well, than that thing."

She pointed at the mysid and wiped her eyes. "A gynander, there'll be no reason to rehabilitate her. Not like—" She grimaced, gesturing at the door. "That one. You know. The new commander."

"Tast'annin? The *rasa*?" Rudyard frowned. "I hope not. I wouldn't want one of my *puppets* to be rehabilitated if it meant that. No," and he took a last sip. "I'm afraid our friend may soon be enjoying the most sublime timoring of all: with the Compassionate Redeemer."

Ceryl's breath froze in her chest as she recalled her own treacherous dream. "Will they question her?" she asked, trying to hold her hand steady as she placed her empty glass on the table.

"About you, you mean? I daresay they already know everything they want to know about you and your relationship with that unfortunate morph." He sighed noisily and eased himself onto the floor. He ran a plump finger along one eyebrow and began to pace. "Rather presumptuous of her to read Âziz's dream like that. Not to mention the Aviator Imperator's."

He stopped in front of the window, peering over the sill to watch a fouga nosing down through the blue air toward the sentry hangars.

"Why did they regenerate him?" Ceryl joined Rudyard, watching the dirigible on its long slow pass down this side of Cherubim.

"Our new commander? Surely you've heard that old gossip."

The dwarf shook his finger at her, but his voice was kind. "Margalis Tast'annin was probably the most brilliant Aviator to come from the NASNA Academy in the last century. His mother was Penelope Métanira—you must have heard of her, the greatest mystical poet since Hanna Vollmann. I suppose that's where he got this odd—*way*—of his. Rather a melancholy temperament for a military leader," he mused. "There was a peculiar business at the Academy when he was there, another student's death under mysterious circumstances. But our Margalis graduated with honors, did his time in the Provinces and the Medaïn Desert—but you *must* know some of this! He was an extraordinarily handsome young man, that golden hair and blue, blue eyes—I've seen the 'files—a hero of the Archipelago Conflict, and oh, what else? Single-handedly wiped out the Commonwealth's submersible fleet; or that's what *they* would have you believe."

He gazed out the window, across the ultramarine fastnesses that hid the Palace. "After that he became quite enamored of Shiyung—of course you knew that, everyone did—and of course *that* ended, and he was practically exiled, sent to command the HORUS substations, and then Shiyung had that insane plan to retake the abandoned capital of the old United States, Âziz was the only one with any reason at all about that, and—"

At Ceryl's raised eyebrow he sniffed, "Oh, of course: how could *I* possibly be privy to all this? My dear friend, if one must be a dog, then be a rich man's dog. It helps that my mother was Angelika Panggang's stepsister. Anyway—"

He stared moodily across the room at the door. "Anyway, his mission to the Capital failed. Failed dreadfully, despite all this fanfare about Triumph and Victory Is Ours. Some horrible mishmash of death-cults and geneslaves and vengeful barbarians. From what I heard, he was tortured; escaped; went mad. Set himself up as some sort of cannibal king presiding over barbaric rites. And then, of course, he died. And *then*, of course, he was regenerated.

"And for one of his nature . . . Well, Margalis Tast'annin has a sensitive, one might say almost a *visionary*, temperament for a military commander. And that makes him a very dangerous man. *Made* him a very dangerous man. Now I suppose he's a very dangerous *rasa*. Mad as a rutting mandrill, crazy as Nasrani and the rest of them, but more, I would say, *ascetic*. Quite attractive, to a certain kind of person."

He lowered his voice. "*I* heard that when he broke with Shiyung she tried to kill herself. Raced toward the edge of a furnace during a refinery tour. Some moujik grabbed her at the last minute. That was when they sent him to HORUS."

Ceryl turned her back to the window. "How horrible."

She stalked to the table and slopped some more brandy into her snifter. "You know, they killed my lover. Giton Arrowsmith. Supposedly it was an accident but I think they wanted him dead. He was always too outspoken in his criticism of them." She returned to the window, swaying a little as she peered down at Rudyard.

"Is that when you tried timoring? After he died?"

She sipped her drink, her eyes glazing over, and finally replied, "Yes. I wanted—I wanted to know something. About death. What it's like."

"And?"

She shook her head. "Nothing. They die, is all. They suffer, we watch." She tipped her chin toward the door. "Like them. Nike and Shiyung and Âziz. We suffer and *they* watch."

The dwarf nodded pensively. After a moment he sighed, and said, "Well, I'm sorry for your friend Reivé. Sorry for myself, too," he added, giving a sharp laugh. "I hoped to spend more time with her. I like morphodites."

A soft sound at the door. Ceryl jumped, glanced down at the dwarf, her eyes wide and terrified.

"Ah, well," murmured Rudyard Planck. He raised his glass mockingly as the door opened. A small figure darted into the room.

"Ceryl!"

Not the Reception Committee; not the inquisitors.

Reive.

Ceryl raced across the room, hugging the gynander and then dragging her into the bedchamber. "Reive! I thought they took you—"

"They did," the gynander gasped. Rudyard Planck tiptoed to shut the front door and hurried after them.

"Âziz *can't* have let you out," he said flatly. "You escaped—?"

"The Aviator." Reive trembled so that Ceryl held her tight, stroking her thin hair and murmuring wordlessly. "He came and Shiyung, Shiyung— Oh, Ceryl, we didn't know where to hide, where else to go—"

From the next room came the hushed *click* of the door opening again, then the pad of feet across the floor.

"Reive Orsina. Ceryl Waxwing."

Their shadows blotted out the light from the doorway. The Reception Committee, six of them in their dark suits and white linen shirts. Each carried, almost casually in a white-gloved hand, a slender electrified cudgel, and the man who had spoken waved a tiny canister of nervetorque. Reive began to sob.

"You won't need *that*," Rudyard Planck pronounced. He drained his snifter and replaced it fastidiously on a table, then walked up to the man with the nerve gas and gave him a little shove. "If you know who I am, then you know—"

"Shut up, Planck," one of the others spat. She strode forward and glared down at the dwarf, then at Reive. She held up an allurian scroll, cleared her throat and read, "Reive Orsina, Ceryl Waxwing." Pausing, she glanced balefully at the dwarf, then added, "Rudyard Planck. Âziz Orsina cordially invites you—"

Rudyard turned to stare at Reive. "Orsina, did she say? Reive *Orsina*?"

"Damn it, Planck!" The woman pushed him so that he tripped and fell against the granite table. When Ceryl gasped the woman whirled to face her. "You're Waxwing? You're wanted with the other one, for—" The woman turned to the man with the canister of nervetorque. "What was it?"

"Collusion," he said, almost sadly. Ceryl was surprised to see that he had tears in his eyes.

"Collusion on what?" demanded Rudyard Planck

breathlessly as he stood, rubbing his chin where blood welled from a gash as long as his finger.

"Murder," the man said, and now he really did brush a tear from his cheek.

"Murder? But who—"

The woman cut Ceryl off by pushing her toward the door. "The assassination of Shiyung Orsina. Chain the morph while I get this one—"

As she struggled Ceryl twisted to see Reive staring bleakly as the man wrapped metal loops around her hand and neck. At her feet Rudyard Planck gazed at the gynander with an expression of nearly ecstatic disbelief. Then Reive turned to Ceryl and said, quite clearly, "The *rasa*—he believed me—it is Ucalegon—"

"But that's impossible—how could she—" She turned to see the first guard with her cudgel poised above the mysid's globe. "No! Leave that, it's—"

As Ceryl flung herself at her the guard turned, her cudgel smashing through the air onto Ceryl's head, again and again and again. Ceryl heard screaming, felt something snap inside her neck, like a bit of plastic cracked between the fingers. Then she felt nothing, only that same dreamy sense she had had in her dream, of the world falling endlessly away beneath her like tarmac beneath a rickshaw's wheel, and before her a plain of exultant green.

It was late evening in Araboth. The Architects had finally switched off the distress lights. Faint music drifted down from Seraphim, snatches of songs popular during Æstival Tide in earlier decades. Fougas cruised through the periwinkle air towing pennons with the arcane sigils of the Feast of Fear—waves with ravening teeth, a bleeding sun. The Orsinate's guard could already be seen, resplendent in their festival garb as they paraded around the palace, night-lights glinting off suits of shining yellow plasteel and leather face-masks. Pyres flickered around the rim of the upper levels, sending eddies of white smoke into the perfumed air as the Seraphim and Cherubim tossed intricately folded paper encised with prayers for the dead into the flames. On the lower levels a festival air prevailed as moujiks and morphodites, biotechs and 'filers, began preparing the feastday meals of sugared pumpkin seeds and cardamom custard, tripe soup and jellied krill and unripe peaches rolled in cayenne, and the nine-layered *pilau* known as Breath of the Redeemer, with its confits of tamarind and prickly pear, and the crisp-fried tentacles of sea-nettles. And on Archangels the enslaved *rasas* began their own somber rites, carrying the mummified remains of Blessed Narouz to a balustrade overlooking the Lahatiel Gate.

A few people wondered that such preparations for the festival would be carried out following the death of a margravine. Many more still had not heard the news of Shiyung's death. It seemed the evening 'file broadcasts had been interrupted by one of the tremors shaking the lower levels. Still, there were rumors among the Toxins Cabal on Thrones, and even in one of the 'filers' pods on Powers, that there had been an assassination attempt of some kind. The Aviators had mutinied, under the command of the corpse that was their leader. Âziz had stabbed her sister Shiyung. Nasrani Orsina had killed all three margravines, serving them shark poached in a broth of speckled-fly mushrooms.

Nasrani Orsina had done no such thing. Clad in blue and gold robes and wearing the heavy conical crown of the Orsinate, as the nuclear CLOCK clanged the evening hour he hurried to the small gravator that serviced Coventry wing. Behind him the *rasa* moved silently, like a great dark insect on hinged steel legs, black robes flapping about him like wings and only his eyes betraying the man within.

"Embrace the Fear that feeds us." The robotic sentry whispered the traditional Æstival Tide greeting as Nasrani waited impatiently for it to scan him. "Nasrani Orsina. Pass." A moment longer while it read the *rasa*'s cold blue eyes, then, "Margalis Tast'annin. Pass."

Inside tiny red lights blinked across the ceiling. There were no views of the lower levels as this gravator dropped, only the chill black walls of its shaft and occasional glimpses of flickering lights and the leaping flames of the refineries. Nasrani settled into one of the cramped seats (no extraneous comforts for exiles) and gingerly rubbed his bandaged arm. The *rasa* stood beside him, staring out the narrow window.

Finally Nasrani spoke. "They'll find you, you know. If you go back with me now I'll argue for you—"

"They won't." The *rasa*'s voice might have come from the sentry's black cylinder. "They think the gynander did it. The one at the inquisition; the one who scryed Âziz's dream."

Nasrani let his breath out and shrugged, defeated. "Yes, I heard about her. Âziz told me: she said it was—" He looked at the floor. For an instant Shiyung's image hung there before him, her long legs cool against his, her green eyes laughing as she drew him closer. He cleared his throat. "She said it was the dream of the Green Country."

"Yes. That is one reason why I want to see the nemosyne."

Nasrani plucked at a thread on his robes. He sighed and removed his crown, wiping his forehead where sweat had beaded beneath its weight. He tried to smile. "Still the inquiring skeptic, Margalis?"

The *rasa* turned to Nasrani. His eerie mask reflected the exile's face, distorted so that it was as though Nasrani gazed upon his own skeletal image, all hollow eyes and grinning fleshless mouth. He shuddered and looked away.

The *rasa* said, "I have seen things you would not believe, Nasrani Orsina: the fruits of your family's poisonous tree. Now I have become one of those rotting fruits. And so, it seems, will your sister Shiyung. Your

rasa – human voice

ancestors invented the timoring after the Architects shared with you their secrets for rehabilitating corpses, so that you could indulge your passion for death without having to die yourselves. Although you do die eventually, don't you? Even the Orsinate dies, although you are scarcely more than ghosts yourselves, your blood has grown so sick and weak . . ."

He took Nasrani's hand. The exile gasped as he felt the steel fingers slice through the soft leather glove, the metal biting into his own palm until he cried out and looked down to see blood staining black leather and spilling onto the floor.

"Oh, but, Nasrani," the Aviator said as he tightened his grip upon the exile's bleeding hand, "Nasrani, Nasrani . . ." as though nothing had happened, as though Nasrani were beside him at a dream inquisition, and not inside a gravator plummeting to the Undercity.

And suddenly that hollow voice took on a new tenor, a tone that was bright with wonder; and Nasrani looked up, terrified at what this might mean, that a *rasa*'s voice should sound so human. "While I was out in the world I saw things that would take your breath away, things that even an Orsina would find sublime. *Children*—"

And here his voice dropped to a whisper, a hiss that made Nasrani's hair stand on end—

"I saw *children* butcher each other like animals, because your viral rains had turned them into ravening beasts. I took counsel from a cadaver, a hollow skull who spoke more wisely than ever your diplomats and cabinet did. And I saw a girl who could kill with her mind; and now who among your family can do that?"

Abruptly the *rasa* dropped Nasrani's bleeding hand. The exile snatched it away, moaning beneath his breath as he wrapped it in a handkerchief. He blinked away tears, then forced a smile. "Now, Margalis," he began, trying to sound composed, "you know that we have scientists and researchers who—"

Science — twists

"Science?" The *rasa* turned to him, his eyes scorched pits in his empty face. "*Science?* You do not understand! I helped bring a *god* to birth in that accursed City, and all your science was for nothing there! What has your science done, but scald the earth and poison the seas, make howling beasts and tormented scarecrows of men and children and devise new ways to torture them, all for the pleasure of a family of inbred aristocrats! Did your *science* give my body back to me, my life and heart and soul? *No!* It twists everything, it can only hold up a charred skeleton to the image of the live thing it once was. But—"

His voice grew softer, and his hands as they groped the air were more graceful than any *rasa*'s Nasrani had ever seen. "But I have glimpsed something stronger than your science, children lovelier than your most precious *timorata:* a boy who embraced Death and his sister, who defeated It. *They* had no need of laboratories or Architects or gabbling aristocrats."

"In the Capital?" Nasrani breathed. The gravator jerked, throwing him against the wall, then dropped another level. "You saw this in the Capital?"

The *rasa* nodded. "Yes: the place they called the City of Trees. Those two children were stronger even than I was, at the end: else they would have died, and I would not."

"Where are they now?"

"I do not know." The *rasa* stared out the window, to where violet lights bored through the murk of Principalities. "When your sisters did not hear from me for many months they feared—rightly—their plans had gone wrong, and sent their own janissaries to seize the City. Their troops arrived mere hours after my death. All I have learned since my—*recovery*—has been chaos and lies. But I do not believe those children are dead."

His pale eyes flickered and he looked out the window, as though seeing something besides the grim substrata of Araboth. "I know she at least is not," he murmured a moment later. "That girl is bound to me now, somehow, through my death perhaps. She is alive still, I know she is. I do not sleep now, it is all like a constant dreaming and I see her, she is out there, somewhere, and I must find her."

He leaned forward and placed his hands conspiratorially upon Nasrani's knee. The slashed remnant of one black glove fell to the floor as the *rasa* gazed into the exile's eyes and Nasrani gasped.

Because now it was no trick of the light that made him imagine features upon that sleek black mask. Somehow—whether by some perversion of the biotechnician's rehabilitative work or through the will of the Aviator Imperator himself—through some macabre machination the cold smooth metal had begun to form itself back into the semblance of a man. Like hot tar that bubbles and can be stretched and pulled about, the crimson mask rippled, seethed, was still. As Nasrani watched in horror a mouth appeared, the metal seeming to ooze as it outlined thin lips and shining black teeth that clashed as the *rasa* stared at him, grinning.

"What is it, Nasrani? 'Bad Science'?"

"N-no—" the exile stammered. On his knees the *rasa*'s fingers twitched. He glanced down to see that its steel fingers had cut through the fabric of his trousers as though it had been paper. He looked up to see the smooth planes of the *rasa*'s mask protrude and sink as cheekbones appeared, a jaw, a pointed chin— the perfect simulacrum of the face of Margalis Tast'annin, cast in liquid flame. Eyes bulged beneath sharp metal brows; a metal blade protruded and shaped itself into a nose like a kite's bill.

"Do you think your sister would love me now, Orsina?" the *rasa* whispered. "Or—I forgot, she is a corpse too, of course she would love the dead—"

Crying out, Nasrani pushed him away and scrambled to his feet, his crown rolling across the floor.

"Sentry!" he shouted, yanking at the gold cord by the gravator door. But before he could touch it the *rasa* had sheared the cord in two, and grabbed him by the throat with his other, human hand.

"No, Nasrani," he said, and drew the man back down beside him. Nasrani whimpered. The Aviator dabbed at his bleeding hand, then with a smile withdrew his finger and traced the outline of Nasrani's babbling mouth in blood. "I still need you. To find the nemosyne. And then—and then I think I will need you to help me leave Araboth for good."

Nasrani cried out. "Leave the domes! I can't—we could never—"

The Aviator grinned. Blood trickled from his lip, and a silvery tongue like a steel serpent darted out to flick it away. "But we must. I was too hasty up there; they will realize soon that the gynander did not kill her. I should have brought her with me. She *knows* things. When I told her my dream, she recognized in it the germ of a memory that haunts me. There is much I could learn from her, I think." He fell silent and stared broodingly out the window.

"From a morph?" Nasrani's voice was shrill. "They're all quacks, those pantomancers, quacks or half mad—"

"Not this one. She has the Sight. Âziz was frightened enough by what she said to have her imprisoned. I freed her, but then I lost my head. . . ."

The *rasa*'s voice faded. In the silence Nasrani could hear faint wails and the roar of the Architects' Conciliatory Engines grinding through the dim avenues of Archangels. The gravator slowed, then picked up speed again.

Nasrani licked his lips and said, "My sisters don't believe in the predictions of pantomancers. At least Âziz does not. She fears treason, that's all. She is a fool. They are all fools." He bent to pick up the Orsinate's crown. His bleeding hand left sullen streaks across its lapis sides. "The gynander is right: Ucalegon will destroy us."

"Then you believe her."

"I know that on my brief forays Outside I saw

things that my sisters would deny were possible." His voice rose angrily. "I could have helped them, and their precious Architects: but they didn't believe me. It should have been enough, that I went Out, and made it back inside—"

"We are here." The gravator lurched to a stop. As the door jerked open the *rasa* turned to Nasrani. "If you try to betray me I will kill you here, and do such things to you afterward that you will beg to be recast as a *rasa.*" Without a word Nasrani nodded and followed him outside.

The Architect Imperator sat watching the fougas outside his window, the bright banners with their weeping sun and devouring wave. He had returned from his encounter with the Compassionate Redeemer, his raucous laughter rousing his idle replicant; and then spoken with the Architects. The breach had spread to the intake valves beneath the Gate on Archangels; the sump pumps on Angels had been crushed beneath the weight of the ocean as it flooded the first tier of the filtration system. One of the Architects had run a meteorological survey and it was as he had hoped, one of the scores of storms that battered the coast each summer was building to the east. By the following day, Æstival Tide, the winds Outside would be strong enough to rip the hair from a man's head. When they opened the gate to free the Compassionate Redeemer and loose the throngs upon the beach to watch, the change in pressure would be enough to send fault lines rippling through the domes like fire through straw.

The Architect Imperator turned from the window and walked to the wall. He pressed a switch hidden beneath an oil portrait of his dead wife. A sweet smell filled the room, a smell of orange-flower and jasmine. There was the sound of soft laughter.

In the middle of the room darts of light flickered, red and green and gold, then slowly coalesced into the image of a woman sitting on a white high-backed chair. She was laughing, her gray eyes flashed mockingly, and though no sound came from her mouth as she spoke, he could still hear her saying, "By the time you need this you'll be so old you won't be able to see it clearly."

Of course he was not that old at all, and she had been only a few months older than the polyfiled image when they'd murdered her. Without taking his eyes from the image he reached and switched it off.

He would go and tell them now, he decided. It would be the final commission of his duties. As he gathered his things he thought, briefly, of his son, and wondered where he had been these last few days. From his pocket he withdrew a small piece of paper neatly lettered with green ink, and with a tiny silver butane lighter he set it aflame and watched it turn to white ash. Then he walked down the hall to where the cylinders and monitors hummed contentedly to themselves. His last words to the Architects were a series of commands, and a final order to destroy all records of Araboth's construction.

After he left the fougas drifted out of sight. The empty room grew dark and the smell of burned paper gradually faded away, though the scent of orange-flower and jasmine lingered a little longer.

The Reception Committee brought their new guests to the Four Hundredth Room. Theirs was not to be the first sentencing that evening. The other guests in attendance at the dream inquisition had all been sent to Principalities, as volunteer donors for the medifacs. Tatsun Frizer screamed and called upon Blessed Narouz, then fainted loudly, resulting in her being borne down immediately via vacuum capsule. As the Committee brought Ceryl and Reive and Rudyard Planck to the Four Hundredth Room they passed Echion in the hallway, shrieking as she was led to the special chamber where she would be administered excitatory hormones, the better to prepare her for her role in the Feast of Fear. When she saw her, Reive began to cry.

"Don't worry," soothed Rudyard Planck, ignoring the Reception Committee's baleful glances as he gazed up at the gynander. "Sajur Panggang will be there and he'll intervene for us. Tomorrow we'll all be drinking sake with Nike on the beach—"

Reive nodded miserably as her guard tugged at the chain about her neck. Behind her, in the arms of two of the stronger Committee members, Ceryl moaned. Across her forehead a swollen purplish bruise showed where the cudgel had smashed against her; she had been unconscious ever since.

The Reception Committee shoved their way through a 'file crew crowded around the door to the Four Hundredth Room. Their monitors and catoptics were trained upon a small dais that had been rolled out for Nike and Âziz. The margravines sat in ornate chairs of bronze and steel, decorated with the automotive motifs the Orsinate was fond of. There were two other chairs, conspicuously empty, beside them. At Âziz's feet crouched the yellow-haired serving girl Petra. The margravine stroked her hair absently, murmuring; but her face held a cold expression and her gaze lingered upon Reive. Beside her Nike yawned, her pupils dilated from morpha, and sucked at a bulb of kehveh. Both of them wore simple shifts of white linen and their conical crowns of office, and over these heavy capes of shining black and yellow rubber. Everyone looked miserably uncomfortable; the room was so hot that condensation trickled from the metal arms of the margravines' chairs.

Once inside, the Reception Committee shuffled about, adjusting their ties and their guests' chains and maneuvering to avoid the catoptics focused upon them. Âziz tapped one sandaled foot upon the marble floor and tugged at Petra's hair until tears welled in the girl's eyes. Another girl tiptoed about the perimeters of the chamber, adjusting the vents until jets of cool air hissed into the room.

The Head of the Reception Committee cleared his throat.

"May I introduce your guests," he began. The catopticians turned, their machines whirring, and began to 'file the prisoners. They hastily switched their focus back to the dais as Âziz waved the Head away impatiently.

"I know who they are." She stood and held her arm out. Petra wiped her eyes and assisted her from the dais. The catopticians scurried to 'file them, the crew leader speaking softly but excitedly into a vocoder as he followed the margravine across the room. Âziz shoved Petra away. She stopped in front of Rudyard Planck and peered down at him, frowning.

"Rudyard Planck. This is a surprise. Now, if your patron Sajur Panggang were here—"

The catopticians tripped over each other as she did a graceful turn, her long pale hand indicating the empty beds and divans at the far end of the room.

"—but, he is not." Her tone as she turned back to the dwarf was questioning, but Rudyard only shook his head, his ruddy face gone quite pale.

"I—I don't know where he is, Margravine, but there's something you should know, surely we can wait a little longer—"

"We cannot," snapped Âziz. On the dais Nike smiled absently and waved at the dwarf. The vents made a popping sound; the flow of cool air stopped, and a barely perceptible tremor shook the room. The two serving girls exchanged frightened looks.

Âziz strode to where Ceryl moaned in the guards' arms. "What's wrong with her? Is she ill?" She tipped Ceryl's chin back with one finger. Ceryl groaned and her eyes rolled open, then closed again. Âziz dropped her finger; Ceryl's head flopped against her chest. The margravine grimaced. "Wake her up, I want her to understand the terms of her sentencing."

She turned to Reive. The gynander had composed herself, and stared back at the margravine with clear green eyes. She looked at Ceryl, limp in the arms of her guards, and blinked to keep the tears from spilling. She gazed back at the margravine. Hatred like a philter ran through her entire body, hot and strong. Very slowly, she smiled.

At that smile Âziz suddenly went cold.

Shiyung. She looks just like Shiyung.

She remembered her sister's bastard, dead at birth . . . Or no—there had been something wrong, they had sent it down to the Chambers of Mercy because it was sick, there was something wrong with it, it—

It had been a hermaphrodite. Âziz caught her breath and gazed back at the gynander.

The Four Hundredth Room had grown very still. Reive could hear Rudyard Planck beside her, his breath coming in quick agitated gasps, and next to him Ceryl groaning as one of the Reception Committee pasted an amphaze tab to her temple. Alone on the dais Nike sucked noisily at her kehveh bulb, then dropped it to the floor and slumped back in her seat, eyes closed as she welcomed her morpha dreams. A few feet away the 'filing machines whirred and clicked as Âziz stared at her prisoner, and the prisoner, her smile a rictus of pure loathing, stared back.

An odd feeling had come over Reive, a sort of vertigo; as though she leaned over the restraining wall that circled the palace and looked down upon the receding levels of Araboth to the lugubrious depths of the Undercity. At first the margravine's face frightened her—like the *rasa*'s, utterly blank and unlined, as though no emotion had ever touched her deeply enough to leave a mark upon that white skin. But now something had changed. The margravine's mouth remained set in that grim smile, but her eyes flickered with something else—fear, Reive realized.

She's afraid of me . . .

And suddenly she thought of the sentry by the Seraphim's gravator, scanning her retinafile and saying, *Reive Orsina: pass.* And the sentry at the palace reading her genotype: *Reive Orsina.* And the mad zeuglodon's thick voice booming, *One of the margravines had a baby once . . . I think you must be that monster . . .*

In the arms of his captors Rudyard Planck struggled. After a moment he gave up and sank to the floor, the cuffs biting his wrists as the guards tightened their hold on his chains. He winced. The floor of the Four Hundredth Room was warm—more than warm, *hot.* It would be just like Âziz to roast the place before a sentencing. But even the margravines looked uncomfortable. Could it be that this was an *unanticipated* change in temperature? Such a small thing; but it would fit into the complex and seemingly meaningless pattern he had seen these last few days, a pattern that seemed to be disclosing a single fact:

The margravines were no longer in control of the city.

Twisting around he stared up at Ceryl, her eyes huge and black from the amphaze, her expression witless. A single 'filer had his optics focused on her, and swiveled to get Planck looking at her. The dwarf mouthed an obscenity and turned away.

In front of him the margravine and Reive were still staring at each other. A sly curve had broadened Reive's smile, and the dwarf noted suddenly that Âziz looked distinctly frightened. There was something odd about the whole scene, something weirdly familiar. He craned his neck, trying to see back to the dais where Nike still sat by herself, dreaming. Those two empty chairs: Shiyung would have been seated there, and once upon a time Nasrani as well. . . .

It struck him then. Shiyung. The expression on Reive's face was like that of the youngest Orsina—the same mocking smile, the same intense light in her eyes. And those eyes—she had green eyes, emerald-green eyes slanted as a cat's, and she didn't wear tinted lenses to disguise them.

Like Shiyung Orsina; like Nasrani.

"She's one of them." The words came out before he could stop them.

"Huh?"

Ceryl's voice sounded sharp, but that was just the amphaze. She had no idea where she was. Several men and women in dark suits and narrow ties were supporting her; her head throbbed, but other than that she felt no pain. When she tried to move her hand it didn't respond; it seemed she couldn't move at all. She remembered something about a dwarf.

". . . one of *them*!" the voice whispered, more loudly this time. One of the Reception Committee kicked him, but the dwarf ignored her and hissed until Ceryl looked over at him, blinking.

"Damn it, *look* at her, Waxwing! Where the hell did you find her, she's one of their bastards!"

Several 'filers had turned to check out this new confusion. Âziz shook her head, half hearing the whispered accusations behind her but too stunned by the thought of what this might mean: a true Orsina, the child of siblings as she and Shiyung and Nike and Nasrani had been: a true heir. In front of her the gynander gazed at her with Shiyung's eyes in her pointed face, dirty hair uncoiled about her shoulders, small breasts and tattooed thighs and that tiny penis half-glimpsed inside her gossamer trousers. A morphodite, heir to the Holy City of the Americas. Âziz started to laugh.

"Well," she said quickly, straightening herself and adjusting her conical crown so that the light flared from its twin crosses. "I wouldn't have expected an assassin to scare easily."

Clicks and whispers as the 'filers all turned to Âziz.

"Assassin, Margravine?" one called out from the back of the room.

Âziz nodded, her smile gone. Get this over with quickly, get them out of here and into the holding area by the Gate. "Early this morning," she began, glancing back at Nike asleep on her throne; *"early this morning—"*

Nike jumped, glanced around and nodded anxiously. Âziz gave her a curt look, then continued.

"Early this morning we discovered the body of our sister, Shiyung Orsina, in her private chambers in the Alkahest. She had been murdered, her neck snapped. The murderer and her accomplices have been detained—"

Gasps and a few angry shouts from the 'filers. Âziz swept her arm out toward Reive and Ceryl and Rudyard Planck, but looked over her shoulder and whispered to the head of the 'filer crew, "No names, no names." Then, sternly and facing the optics, "These three are hereby sentenced for the murder of Shiyung Orsina, also for collusion, also treachery and theft—"

"We did *not*—" Rudyard Planck said hotly, before someone kicked him.

"Theft," Âziz repeated. On her throne Nike adjusted her rubber cape and nodded. Âziz coughed, then said, "But even criminals and assassins may beg for forgiveness. We have heard their pleas; we will show them mercy, and allow them to save their eternal souls through the ministrations of the Compassionate Redeemer."

Ceryl's mouth twisted as she tried to gasp. Rudyard Planck shouted, "No!" The 'filer crews murmured excitedly. Only Reive continued to stare at Âziz with that same cold smile, although she grew pale and her hands trembled.

"There," Âziz announced. She turned to the head of the 'filer crew and waved at him dismissively. "That's it, that's all, tell them to stop. *Now.*"

Muttering and staring balefully at the three prisoners, the 'filer crew started to leave. One spat at Reive as he passed her. Another stopped in front of Shiyung's empty throne and held out her optic, before the crew head came after her, barking at her to leave. Âziz stared after them with a satisfied expression. Nike smiled and waved goodbye.

"Damn it, Âziz, you *know* we had nothing to do with this—" Rudyard Planck exploded, heedless of the guards tugging at his bonds. "That morph, you *know* who that morph is—"

Âziz turned to him, smiling; her eyes glittered as she said, "I do indeed: the murderer of our sister."

"Couldn't—done it," said Ceryl. Her voice was thick, almost unintelligible. Âziz and Rudyard Planck both looked at her, surprised; her captors jerked her chain but still she went on. "Too small—look—her. Didn't—hear she said—*rasa*, Aviator—where's *rasa*?"

Âziz's face grew tight but she said nothing. On the dais Nike sniffed and stood, grabbing the arms of her throne as she was unbalanced by the weight of her heavy rubber cape. "Where *is* Margalis?" she asked. An empty morpha tube rolled out from her feet and she giggled, then looked at her sister. "Âziz? We should tell him, because—*you* know."

"It makes no difference what you do now."

Reive's voice came out clear and high as a child's. One of her captors raised his hand to strike her, but Âziz shouted, "Enough!" and gestured for him to leave.

"Go, I want you all to go now! They are guests no longer, they are now prisoners of the city. I have summoned a guard from the Aviators—"

The Reception Committee looked aggrieved. "*Go,*" repeated the margravine fiercely, pointing at the door.

"She doesn't seem too afraid of this murderer," a guard muttered. On his way out he kicked Rudyard Planck. Âziz remained with her arm outstretched commandingly. From down the corridor echoed the clatter of boots on marble. The Reception Committee dropped their hold on the steel chains that bound their prisoners, adjusted their ties, and shuffled toward the door.

As she watched them leave, Reive cried out, "We know who we are! We know—"

Rudyard Planck looked at her, frightened. "You know—" he said, and stopped.

The gynander only tipped her chin and stared at Âziz through slitted eyes. "We know now. We have the Sight, we have seen what is to come. *We* may have scryed it, but it was *your* dream, Âziz."

The margravine stepped forward until she stood in front of Reive. She bent to take the gynander's face in her hands.

"You are a fool, whoever you are." What little color was left in Reive's face bled away and her gaze faltered; she looked like a child being punished. "There will be no storms, hermaphrodite, because *we* control the weather. We control everything in Araboth."

She let go of the gynander and turned to stride across the room. She stopped in front of a tall column and gazed back at her sister. Nike looked confused, then raised a triumphant finger and pulled up the hood of her cape.

In the doorway several tall figures appeared, gleaming in their crimson leather uniforms. "Enter," Âziz called out to them. She glanced at her prisoners, then back at the Aviators. "I was just telling them that there is nothing to fear from the weather— what's a little rain?"

The margravine pressed a switch hidden behind the column and flicked her own hood over her head. A sound like flames licking at the walls; then a brackish scent filled the room. A moment later fine mist began to fall from tiny jets in the ceiling.

"See!" Âziz crowed. Nike adjusted her cape, holding out her hands to catch the moisture. "Nothing to fear from the weather, nothing at all!"

One of the Aviators stepped forward and raised her hands in salute. Rain caught in her silver hair and glittered like sun on steel. "Margravine—"

Âziz turned to her. "I want them in the holding

area on Archangels. The prison by the Lahatiel Gate. They're to speak to no one."

"Yes, Margravine." The Aviator gestured; the others followed her. But before they could reach the prisoners a tremor shook the room. Nike cried out and grabbed a chair. Glass tapers rattled in their sconces and one shattered as it struck the wall. For an instant the rain ceased; then there was a gurgling from overhead and it poured down heavier than before. Âziz's mouth was set in a grim line as she pulled her cape about her shoulders. Only the Aviators seemed not to notice, their booted feet steady upon the marble floor, their eyes fixed on the margravines.

"Take them," whispered Âziz.

Ceryl whimpered. Rudyard Planck's ruddy face went white, and he struggled as the first Aviator lifted him in her arms like a child.

"No! Margravine, please, Sajur Panggang will tell you—"

Only Reive remained impassive, her smile gone, her dark lashes trembling above pale green eyes. "It is coming," she whispered. She lifted her head to stare at Nike. The margravine clutched the edges of her cape and shivered in the chilly artificial rain. "There is nothing you can do now to stop it, it is—"

"*Now!*" shouted Âziz. "Have them shriven in preparation for their meeting with the Compassionate Redeemer."

"As you wish, Margravine."

The leader of the Aviators stared at the dwarf still struggling in her arms, then with her head motioned to her followers. They stepped forward and not ungently took hold of Ceryl and Reive. "Please don't fight," one said. Ceryl collapsed against his chest. In her captor's arms Reive turned to gaze at Âziz. The rain glistened against her breasts, where the ward against Ucalegon gleamed brilliant yellow and blue against her white skin.

"The Wave will take you all," she said. Then they bore her from the Four Hundredth Room.

Silence for several minutes. "That's it, then," Âziz said at last. The door remained open; rain pattered against the walls and ran down through the little diamond-shaped grates set into the floor. Nike nodded, still steaming in her cape. Her sister began to pace, finally paused and tripped another hidden switch. The ocean-smelling rain tapped against the floor, then stopped. Warm air blew up through the grates. Sandalwood essence oozed down through ventricles in the ceiling. "There: all done."

"What did she mean, 'She's one of them'?" Nike's voice was still husky with morpha, but her eyes were brooding. She crossed the room to her sister and took her arm. "Âziz? What did she mean?"

Âziz turned away. "Nothing. They're desperate, they were just talking."

Nike shook her head. "No. I heard them. That morphodite—she looks like Shiyung. And Nasrani—she looks like both of them. She's their child, isn't she, the morphodite they were supposed to have killed—"

"What would you have done?" Âziz shook her arm free and glared at her sister. "I didn't know, I had no more idea than you did, until today. She's a bastard, and a monster—you saw her, a hermaphrodite! They would say it was an evil thing—*if* they knew. It's best we do this, Nike, she should die before anyone else has a chance to learn about her."

Nike hissed softly. "It *is* an evil thing, Âziz! That was a tremor just now, it's as she said . . . She has the Sight, she scryed your dream—even if she *did* kill Shiyung—"

"She's a scheming little morph, that's all! How could *she* kill Shiyung?" Âziz laughed coldly. "You saw her, a skinny thing like that—"

Nike's eyes widened. "Then who did?" Her cape squeaked as she hugged it close to her and suddenly her eyes widened. "Margalis! *He* did it—you knew it and—"

"*I* will take care of Margalis. Shiyung was spending far too much time on the lower levels, Nike, you saw that. They were starting to think she belonged to them, and she was starting to believe it. It was time for a change, Nike. She'd been turning us against Nasrani. We need to speak with him now, it's been too long. We can't have these squabbles go on forever.'' Âziz tossed her head, the black hood of her cape falling back onto her shoulders. ''And Sajur, I want to see him as well, I think we should ask him about—''

''About what, Margravine?''

The two sisters whirled. In the doorway stood the Architect Imperator. He wore a morning suit of striped gray wool with a high white collar. The black turban of his office drooped over his forehead, but the Orsinate's heraldic eye had been ripped away. In its place gleamed a brooch of Angelika's, a glittering piece of ancient computer circuitry in clear plastic, set with zircons and emerald glass.

''Greetings, Nike.'' He stumbled as he walked into the room. There was a small gash at the corner of his mouth where he had cut himself shaving, and blood spotted his white collar.

''Sajur!'' Âziz frowned. Then she composed herself and walked to meet him. Behind her Nike stepped gingerly. A cloying steam rose about their feet, where the cold rain had pooled and was now heated by the vents. ''I was going to call you—we need to discuss a few things. Tomorrow's opening ceremony, for one—''

Sajur waved her away. Nike gasped: his white shirt-cuffs were soaked with blood, and blood dripped from his wrists to the slick floor. ''No need, Margravine, no need at all. It doesn't hurt, Nike, I drank quite a bit first, did a bit of morpha—''

He grinned, straightened himself unsteadily to face them. When he raised his hand to straighten his turban a long red smear marred the soft fine cotton. ''I am performing my final duty to you, Âziz.'' He covered his mouth as he coughed. There was more blood. ''I have sabotaged the Architects. There is a chasm beneath us now, on Angels—a fissure the length of the Undercity. The domes are already starting to buckle under the stress. Tomorrow, when the Lahatiel Gate opens—"

He smiled and flicked his fingers, *fffttt!* A fine spray of blood spattered the margravines' black rubber capes. "You shouldn't have killed Angelika, Âziz. It was ungrateful of you, after all I've done."

His voice almost sounded pleading. "And she won't let me sleep, Âziz, I see her at night, she comes to me . . ."

He choked. Blood splattered his trousers. "Don't bother calling your damn Aviator watchdogs, I—" Shuddering, he crumpled to his knees. "—dying anyway."

"The domes! The domes!" Nike shrieked. Âziz slapped her and turned back to the man slumped on the floor.

"How do we stop them, Sajur?" she shouted. "Dammit, tell me! The program, how do we revert the program?"

The Architect Imperator smiled and gazed at the ceiling. "Nothing to be done," he murmured. "Set them and left them . . . strange things, uncontrollable—ideas of their own, now."

His voice faded to a soft gurgle. The bloodstained turban slid from his forehead to the marble floor, and he rested his cheek upon it. For one last instant he stared up at them, his dark eyes glazing over. He whispered, "But you'll see *lots* of weather, Âziz . . . bring an umbrella." He closed his eyes and was still.

The two margravines stood staring at the corpse of the Architect Imperator. Then, "We'll die! I told you, she was right, it's all going to come down!" Nike screamed and whirled to run from the room. Before she reached the door her sister grabbed her.

"Don't be an idiot! He's lying, he was drunk and half-mad, Nike, listen to me, *there is nothing to worry about!*"

There was a dull grinding overhead. The hissing

of incense from the ventricles abruptly stopped. The smell of burning petroleum filled the air, and a sound like crackling paper. As the margravines slowly raised their heads, hail began to fall in the Four Hundredth Room.

Book Two

THE FEAST
OF FEAR

Chapter 8

SHADOWS OF THE
THIRD SHINING
~~~~~~~~~~~~~~~~~~~~~~~~

The doors opened onto the Undercity.

"I've forgotten my lumiere," Nasrani said. He leaned against the wall of the gravator, cradling his bleeding hand, and looked as if he were about to faint.

"There will be no need," the Aviator replied. "Give me your hand."

Nasrani shook his head and started for the door. "No, please—" he stammered. "I'm all right, I can see fine—"

The Aviator stepped beside him. His hand when it enveloped Nasrani's was warm, then hot, so hot that the exile cried aloud. There was a small hissing sound, like a fly caught in flame, and the stink of burning cloth. The exile choked, reeling backward, but the Aviator caught him. When Nasrani looked down at his hand, the bleeding had stopped and the skin glowed a translucent red.

"We will have no need of light," said the Aviator. As the doors began to slide shut again he grabbed them and pushed them apart. The wood and metal buckled and bulged outward. Nasrani covered his face as splinters of glass and wood flew everywhere.

"Don't!—you're destroying it, we won't be able to return—"

Metal gears shrieked and ground futilely against each other; then there was silence. Tast'annin stepped into the darkness. When he turned to face Nasrani the exile caught his breath. The *rasa* glowed softly, a dull crimson glow like the Flames of the Eternal in Blessed Narouz's Refinery.

"Do not be afraid," he said, his voice echoing in the void of Angels. "Come, Nasrani."

The exile stumbled after him, stammering, "You ruined it—the other gravators—wait—"

"There will be no need," the *rasa* repeated. Above him reared the immense shadows of the Undercity, the faint and distant glimmerings of blue and gold and crimson where the refineries and medifacs burned far overhead. From beneath their feet rose a heavy smell, an odor as of things newly exhumed from the earth. Nasrani gagged and covered his mouth with his sleeve. The *rasa* waited for him, a ruby taper burning in the endless night.

"Where is she?" he asked after a little while. "I will go before you if you tell me the way."

Nasrani coughed, nodding. "Augh—that smell! I will show you, this way—"

He began to feel his way very slowly, the *rasa* beside him silent, his feet making almost no sound upon the broken earth. The labyrinth of walls and buildings the exile had used before to guide him had changed. Smooth surfaces crumbled beneath his outstretched hands, great blocks of metal and concrete sheared away at his touch, plummeting into unseen chasms just a few feet from where they walked. Nasrani trembled and chattered to himself, stopping to stare about him in wonder, as though he'd forgotten where he was. More than once the *rasa*'s hand roused him, so hot that it singed his torn shirt.

"Something has happened—something terrible has happened," Nasrani said again and again. The ground felt different than it had on his earlier visits— soft and friable, as though it had been churned by the passage of an immense nematode. Into this raw earth the remains of familiar buildings had been swallowed, and other things disgorged. A huge smooth dome of glass, miraculously unbroken. Beneath it rows of emaciated human figures embraced blocks of steel, their empty eyesockets staring up at Nasrani and Tast'annin as they passed. Wrecked autovehicles and boats bulged from the ground, their hulls scorched and fused together to form one great misshapen machine. Where before there had been only a smooth expanse of dead earth and concrete now erupted a heap of broken forms of wood and metal. From them spilled bones, bones and skulls and sleeves of deep blue and scarlet, trimmed with metal brocade. The *rasa* paused to stare at them. Where his hand brushed the edge of one uniform a tiny spiral of smoke rose, and a crackling sound.

Nasrani stopped and gazed overhead. An eerie red glow suffused the darkness. In the distance clouds of black smoke seemed to billow and rise, obscuring the silhouette of the monstrous ziggurat looming above them. An uneven but ceaseless current of sound swelled beneath it all, a rush like running water, punctuated by soft retorts and sudden explosive roars, as of huge buildings being pried apart and thrown to the ground. Beneath his heavy clothes the exile sweated and shivered; his wounded shoulder ached and his hand throbbed almost unbearably. He wiped his face, squinting as he struggled to see something of the rest of Araboth—flames leaping from the refineries on Archangels, and a white pulse that might have been distress lights from Seraphim. And closer he saw other flames, and pallid greenish globes that bobbed in the distance but never seemed to grow any nearer. Another smell choked him, along with the fetid reek of decay; a smell of burning, of acrid chemicals and gas. He coughed and stumbled, and nearly fell into a narrow crevasse that slit the earth at his feet like a razor tearing through skin. When the *rasa*'s hand touched his shoulder he jerked back. It was burning hot, as though it had been cast into a furnace.

And suddenly Nasrani realized that was exactly what had happened. The Undercity was burning. The *rasa*'s metal form was heating like an ingot thrust into the heart of a forge. Nasrani stopped, weaving in the near darkness.

"I can't—we can't go on," he gasped. His eyes were wild. "Margalis—the Undercity is burning, if we go on we'll die from the heat. I don't understand," he whimpered.

"Look." The exile shrank as the *rasa* gripped his shoulder with one fiery hand. "Can you see—there, at the base of that shattered pyramid?"

Nasrani swallowed. He nodded, peering where the *rasa* pointed. "Yes," he whispered. "I see, Margalis, but—what is it?"

The *rasa*'s eyes glowed, brighter and brighter until they were like two holes of flame. In the distance they heard a hollow rasping. "It is a rift, a chasm at the bottom of the city. See—? Boiling up there, that is water, it is the sea coming in from Outside. That smooth wall behind it is one of the conduits that supplies the vivariums. The fulciment of the entire city is rupturing."

Nasrani stared at him. "What do you mean?"

"There!"

The Aviator pointed at the pyramid, gleaming dull gold in the murk. The steady rasping grew louder and louder, until suddenly a terrific *crack* rent the air. For an instant the pyramid flamed brilliant white; then like a heap of ashes it collapsed and sank all at once into the darkness.

"How can it—" Nasrani staggered forward as the *rasa* shoved him.

"We have no time!" Tast'annin cried harshly. "We must find her quickly, the city is falling around us—"

Nasrani stumbled and halted, hugging on to a broken steel post. "Margalis—Margalis, please, listen to me. I don't know where we are. It's changed—if what you've said is true, if the city is collapsing around us—it's all different. The landmarks are gone —there used to be an alley, there, and a, a sort of archway—"

Tast'annin looked over his shoulder, nodding. "It is still there. See—the arch has fallen, it is caught on that narrow landing—"

Nasrani shielded his eyes, then exclaimed, "It is! I see it—the doorway is still there, behind it—"

He picked his way through the rubble, the *rasa* at his side like a flickering crimson shadow. Every few minutes the ground beneath them shuddered, and once where Nasrani's foot had been a moment before a fissure tore the earth apart with a noise like rending cloth. Nasrani shouted and nearly fell; but the *rasa* caught him, and then he was running the last few yards to collapse within the ruined doorway.

"My keys—I forgot the keys," he gasped after a moment. The stone and metalwork felt wet beneath his fingers. His trousers were soaked. Warm water streamed from a crack above his head, spilling onto the ground and running off into the rift spreading slowly across the earth. Tast'annin stood above him and shook his head.

"We won't need them. This is the entrance?"

At Nasrani's nod he raised his arms and took hold of the broken edges of a lintel. The door crashed inward. Silence, broken only by the gurgle of water.

"Where is she?" The Aviator's harsh voice hung in the empty air. Nasrani got to his feet and followed him into the room, shaking his head in disbelief.

At one end of the room the ceiling had caved in.

Beneath twisted spars of steel and piles of plaster he saw Maximillian Ur's cabinet, smashed into a heap of wood and glass. A few feet away the replicant's bladed arm twitched rhythmically, its fingers curling and uncurling around a shard of metal.

"No," Nasrani whispered. "My children—no—"

Slowly he circled the room, the ruined cabinets and crumpled banners adrift in pools of black water. In one corner the shattered body of the Anodyne Physician sat upright, her head askew, one side of her torso crushed so that her ruined circuitry glittered coldly, a frozen explosion of glass and wire. "No known remedy," her clear voice repeated over and over. "No known remedy, no known remedy . . ."

Weeping, Nasrani stooped over her, yanked a golden filament. The Physician's head rolled into her lap and she was silent.

"All my children?" he murmured, and turned to where a girder had fallen and covered Moghrebi's gilded case. His voice rose to a shriek. "*All?*"

In the middle of the room a pile of wreckage hid where the Titanium Children had slept, where Apulieus had laughed and the Mechanical Baboon chattered with her brazen cubs. There was nothing left. Only, pinned beneath a corroded metal beam, something stirred and moaned piteously.

"Yes?" Nasrani cried, hurrying to kneel beside it, but then drew back. "Aaah—the miserable thing!" he spat.

It was a *rasa*, or had been—its arm had been sheared from its body and lay beside its shoulder. There was no blood, only a watery ammoniac fluid. The creature murmured to itself. It could not lift its pale head, only twist to gaze at Nasrani with one bleary eye. The man grimaced and turned away. The other eye bulged from its socket, black and swollen as a grape. It stank of ammonia.

"Mother," it whispered. "Mother, please—"

Nasrani looked back down. "Mother? The nemosyne—is she here? Did she escape?"

The *rasa* moved its head feebly. "Mother is gone —the once-born took her, gone, gone. Please . . ."

Nasrani stood and wiped his hands in disgust. The thing mewled, trying to move. The *rasa* crossed the room, pushing Nasrani away, and knelt beside it.

"Which way?" he asked. His voice was almost gentle.

The *rasa* stared at him, then whispered, "There is another door—a tunnel—"

Tast'annin glanced over his shoulder, turned back to the creature silent now, twisting feebly beneath the weight of the twisted beam. He stretched out his metal hand until it covered the *rasa*'s face, then with a quick motion snapped its head back, severing the spine. The *rasa* twitched and was still. Nasrani made a hoarse sound and looked away. The Aviator stood, gazing down at the wretched corpse.

"It said she escaped. It said she went into the tunnel," he said at last.

Nasrani stared at him dumbly, shaking his head. His face was streaked with tears. "All of them," he said again.

"No." The *rasa* shook his shoulder and pointed. "There is an opening. A tunnel, it said."

"But she couldn't—how could she? She has never moved, she never woke for me—"

Tast'annin pulled him through the wreckage.

"Then she has awakened for someone else," he said, and ducking beneath a broken column he entered the passage.

It happened almost before Hobi realized it. His ears popped; one of the *rasas* swiveled its head to stare at the ceiling. Nefertity continued to recite in her clear child's voice the story she had begun many hours before—

" '. . . Were you ever happy, when you were a man, since you left the womb, unless you were trying to get back into it?' and she gave me a virgin's look of disdain.

" 'Will I be happy now I am a woman?' I demanded.

" 'Oh, no!' she said and laughed. 'Of course not! Not until we all live in a happy world!' "

Hobi yawned, as much because his ears ached as because of boredom. The nemosyne had been reciting from her memory 'files, stories and poems she chose seemingly at random. This was how she had enthralled the fallen *rasas,* those poor creatures starved for any kind of companionship, even the chilly voice of a nemosyne chanting oddments of useless data.

At first he had thought he could listen to Nefertity speak forever. Now he knew that even wonderful things—maybe *especially* wonderful things—are best enjoyed in small doses. All around him the *rasas* sat in perfect silence, unmoving, their glowing eyes fixed on the shining figure in front of them. Hobi scratched his nose, thinking that perhaps he might take a walk, just across the room of course. He had just started to his feet, his legs prickling from having been still for so long, when suddenly the floor tilted beneath him.

"Wha—" the boy cried, and was knocked to his knees. There was a horrible crashing noise, hollow hooting cries from the *rasas.* The candles went flying; burning wax spattered his face and then it was dark, except for Nefertity's cool blue glow.

"Mother—" someone whispered, and said no more.

"Perhaps I will continue this later," Nefertity pronounced softly. But Hobi could no longer see her. Something heavy struck his head, knocking him to the floor. For a moment he thought he had been blinded.

"Nefertity," he choked. His arm hurt when he raised it, but he *could* raise it, and now when he moved his head he could see, too.

The ceiling had fallen in upon the room. The replicants in their cabinets, the *rasas* who had been listening to Nefertity: all were buried beneath twisted beams and plasterboard and heaps of rubbish that seemed to smoke, but that was just the dust and plaster. A few feet away he saw the *rasa* that had brought him here, pinned beneath a girder. Across the room the Anodyne Physician's case had been shattered and she was speaking solemnly to herself.

"Oh, my god," Hobi whispered. He stumbled to his feet, biting his lip against the pain, and tried to get his balance without touching anything. He was afraid that if he breathed too deeply the whole room would disintegrate around him. The ceiling was completely gone. Where it had been were only the exposed guts of the ancient building, a horrible mass of wires and steel beams and metal joists, writhing and rippling as though made of windblown silk. "He did it, he really did it. . . ."

"Who did it?"

Hobi turned to see Nefertity, standing calmly amid the ruins like a shining beacon of glass. On the floor beside her two *rasas* lay side by side, faces white as plaster save where greenish fluid trickled from one's mouth, giving her a grotesque harlequin's smile.

"My father," Hobi said, dazed. He stepped toward the nemosyne, abruptly stopped. The floor shook ominously beneath him, and eddies of fine dust cascaded down from the broken ceiling. He froze, gazing desperately at the nemosyne only a few feet away.

"I can't move." His voice cracked; dust in his throat made it hurt to speak. "It will all come down— my father did this, he programmed the Architects to destroy the city—"

"How do you know this?"

"I overheard them." He was practically babbling now. "A few days ago—in his study. They said there was a—a breach, somewhere down here. I didn't un-

derstand. . . . He was indoctrinating the program,
he ordered them to do this—"

The nemosyne stared at him, her emerald eyes
serene. Pale blue light pulsed about her hand as she
raised it and reached for him. "I will go with you,
Hobi. Let us leave this place now."

He stared at her in disbelief. "Go? We can't go—
it's falling to pieces around us—"

A distant explosion. The room shook again, and
one of the *rasas* whispered a name. Nefertity looked
down at the broken creature, then back at Hobi, her
hand still extended toward him. "We can leave the
city," she insisted gently. "Perhaps we will find the
others of my kind, Outside."

Hobi swallowed, shut his eyes, and breathed
deeply. He thought of the tunnel that had brought
him here, the overpowering smell of brackish water.
He remembered how only a day before he had
dreamed of this, madly: to find the nemosyne again
and leave Araboth, venture Outside and die there if
needs be.

"Hobi." Nefertity's voice was soft. He opened his
eyes to see her in front of him, her crystalline hand
upon his shoulder. "Hobi, it's time."

And at that word *time* he heard it again—the
same sweet high chiming that had rung in his ears the
first time he saw her. He nodded dumbly, glancing
around until he saw the door at the far end of the
room, the entrance to the tunnel. Part of the wall had
collapsed beside it, the door itself hung open; but he
could see the faint green glow of phosphorescence inside, hear the distant purling of water.

"That way," he croaked. He began to pick his
way through the rubble, stepping over an unmoving
rasa and averting his eyes from the sight of the Titanium Children crushed and splintered into arrows of
golden glass. Beside him Nefertity walked in a nimbus
of azure light, her hand upon his shoulder firm and
cool. Once the floor shifted beneath them, sliding so
suddenly that Hobi cried out and nearly fell. But the

to the sea

nemosyne caught him, and as in a dream he walked the last few steps until they stood within the doorway.

Nefertity's hand slipped from him and her voice came soft in his ear. "Do you know the way?"

Hobi shook his head. "No. But I think the tunnel leads out—at least once it did, it was a sewage tunnel. I think it might lead to the sea."

"Ah." She stepped before him into the gloom.

For a moment the boy remained, and gazed back into the room: the banners torn and furled about broken beams, the pale, nearly luminous bodies half-buried beneath the rubble, and Nasrani's ancient toys shattered where they had been sleeping.

"No known remedy," the Anodyne Physician murmured. In the darkness a *rasa* whispered, and something moved, slithering across the floor. Hobi bit his lip, and turned to where Nefertity waited for him.

"This way?" she asked.

He nodded: there was no other way to go.

They walked in the eerie darkness, Hobi running his hand against the damp wall and Nefertity gliding noiselessly beside him. Her aura deepened from azure to cobalt and then faded to a pale sapphire, barely enough light to see by; but her adamant heart shone brilliantly, a golden orb flashing in the darkness. The tunnel pressed close around them, dank and cold. Hobi's feet slipped through shallow water, and he heard water rushing very near to them, as though an adjoining tunnel served as a conduit or sluiceway. Other sounds echoed from far away: soft roars and crashes, sudden cracks and booms. And always the sound of water, seeming to grow louder now, as though the sluiceway had opened onto a river. Hobi hugged his hands in his armpits, shivering, his jaw clenched, but after they had been traveling a little while he relaxed. He was cold, true, his feet nearly numb from sloshing through chilly stagnant water; and he had seen what no one else in Araboth had, the breach in Angels that would send the whole thing crashing down in a day or two.

But oddly enough he was no longer afraid. He almost felt elated, if it hadn't been that his feet were damn near frozen he might have run down the narrow passageway instead of slogging through the muck.

"You are tired," Nefertity said. They had come to where the passage opened onto the larger tunnel. Hobi leaned against the archway, panting.

"Tired?" He looked up into those huge depthless eyes, the silvery whorls and deltas of her face. Suddenly he grinned. "No, I'm not tired—just trying to figure out which way to go."

She nodded. Splinters of gold and green flecked the air about her face, and without thinking Hobi reached to touch her cheek. It grew warm beneath his fingertips. When he drew his hand back the imprint of his fingers remained, azure petals glowing against her quicksilver skin, then slowly faded.

How can she be so beautiful? he thought. His chest felt tight with a longing so intense it made him dizzy. Something warm brushed his forehead. He blinked, saw the nemosyne staring at him, her eyes wide, reflecting nothing, her voice sweet and heartless as a bird's.

"Do you know the way?"

He started to say no, then stopped and nodded.

"Down there," he said, and pointed away from the direction he had first come with the *rasa*. "I don't know where it goes, but *that* way leads back to the Undercity, the gravator—" They started to walk once more.

For a long time they went without talking. The sound of rushing water grew louder, the water splashing about their feet rose higher, until it reached the tops of Hobi's knees. Around Nefertity the water glowed. When Hobi looked down he could see tiny shapes darting about her legs, tiny black fish like feathers streaming through the water as they followed her. He could no longer hear the boom and crash of the Undercity's foundation shifting. He could no longer hear anything but water. It didn't seem quite so dark. Algae and fungi still blotched the curved walls above the waterline but did not glow, only covered the ancient tile like a dark stain. The air was warmer here, too. It flowed through invisible vents and stirred Hobi's long hair matted on his neck, and carried with it the overwhelming reek of the sea.

And, absurdly, as that smell grew stronger, he grew more frightened. A few feet in front of him Nefertity moved effortlessly, the water streaming from her silvery thighs. As though sensing his fear she turned to look back. Hobi coughed, wiping his face with his wet sleeve and trying to compose himself. He asked, "What was she like? The woman who made you?"

The nemosyne waited until he caught up with her. "She did not make me. Others made me; she programmed me. She was my archivist."

"Loretta?"

She nodded. The water had grown shallow again, and the nemosyne stooped to gaze into it, where a black mass pooled like ink around her glittering feet. She dipped her hand into the water and brought it up full of tiny wriggling shapes, let them slide between her fingers back into the shallows. "They will die if they keep following me," she said, gazing ahead. "Up there the water stops—"

Hobi squinted and sloshed on. Nefertity followed.

"Loretta Riding," she said after a minute. "She was a Sister, a member of the American Catholic Church." She tilted her head toward Hobi. "You know who they are?"

He shrugged. "I've heard of them. Heretics, like the rest of them—they were purged after the Third Shining."

Nefertity said nothing. Her shimmering heart dulled to bronze as she walked, the water about her

Rayburn + Orsina kill Amer.
Catholics

feet in small pools now that reflected her pale blue form.

"Purged," she said at last. Hobi nodded, embarrassed. "You killed them, then?"

"*I* didn't kill them!" His voice rose sharply and he blushed. "I mean, none of us did, really—this was hundreds of years ago. It was Prophet Rayburn—well, his father, actually—Roland Orsina—and the *TelÂl ibn Waba*, the Prince of the Plague. You know. The first Ascendants. The Chosen."

Nefertity stopped. "The Chosen."

Her voice suddenly did not sound so calm. A deeper tone cut into it, more like a woman's voice than a replicant's. When Hobi looked at her he saw that the emerald had drained from her eyes. Now they glowed dead white, like the eyes of a *rasa* just pulled from its tank.

"The Chosen: you mean the recusants, don't you? The zealots who survived the Second Ascension?"

Hobi started to agree, but the nemosyne cut him off. Her voice was husky with anger. Loretta Riding's voice, he realized suddenly—one of Nefertity's programs had been encoded with the dead woman's persona, like the palinmplants that gave some *rasas* the memories of their earlier lives.

"The Chosen! They murdered children so that only they would survive, did you know that? In Meritor, Nebraska, where they'd sent them to be away from the cities, to be safe from the plague. Loretta was there, she'd volunteered to set up a folklife program recording the children's accounts of the Holocaust. She left one day to come back to Evanston and the following week it happened. The Chosen came. They slaughtered the children and their teachers, and then they commandeered the Children's Encampment and moved in with their own children and their drudges, their deacons and their mullahs. They claimed that their prophets predicted a Second Ascension, and they were right, of course; but is that any reason to butcher children like sheep?''

The husky voice grew quite shrill. Hobi shook his head anxiously.

''No—no, of course not—'' he stammered. The nemosyne stared at him, *through* him; she had become something quite different from the beautiful automaton he had first glimpsed in Nasrani's hidden room. Tongues of light rose and flickered from her shoulders and her arms. Her body glowed a fierce cobalt, like an android's cooling in its adamant saggar. He had to look away from her, away from that face like a burning torch, those white-hot eyes piercing the dim tunnel.

She said, ''That was why she went into hiding, with me—in one of the bunkers they built after the First Ascension. She shouldn't have taken me with her, of course—I belonged to the Church—but by then everything was falling apart again. She moved her entire library into that little place. Books, videos, films, syntheses; and of course she had me, I'd recorded over ten thousand hours of material by then. And for the rest of her life she read to me, and recorded what remained. Her books, mostly, and her memories. What she recalled of the world before the First Ascension, and just after. She never went outside again.''

Hobi's feet ached from the cold. He wanted to start moving again. He wanted to run. The nemosyne was silent. Slowly her eyes cooled, until they shone a very pale green, and the angry blue drained from her limbs and torso. She could have been a reflection on the surface of the water, a rivulet of light.

Hobi shivered, rubbed his prickling arms and was absurdly grateful that he could feel them. He asked, ''What happened? In the end, I mean. How did she die?''

As she replied Nefertity's voice was a woman's voice, weary and sad. ''She was not a young woman when we entered the bunker. She was old, and she

women as chattel for geneslave experiments
—lest we forget

grew very old. For some years I cared for her, when she could no longer move easily. I prepared food from what remained in her stores, and purified the water she obtained from her ground still, and carried her when she could no longer walk; but she grew more and more forgetful, and finally one day she must have commanded me to sleep. Perhaps she knew she was going to die soon, and wanted to spare me—although of course it would only *seem* that I grieved, and if there was no one else there to see me, why then what would it matter? A robot alone in a steel bunker, mourning her dead mistress—but it must have seemed too much like one of her old stories, the idea must have saddened her. She was the kindest and wisest of women, Sister Loretta. Some people said she was a *real* saint, not one of those cowards who waited until the bibliochlasm and what came after, before they grew bold enough to speak against the Ascendants—and before we went into hiding there was much talk of canonizing her among the women of the Church.

"Those were dark days, after the Second Ascension and the Third Shining. In the west they hunted women down like horses and bred them, until they saw the monsters they gave birth to. Then they just killed them, or used them in their experiments. That was when they started breeding the geneslaves. You told me there are geneslaves everywhere now. Well, then the notion was a new and monstrous thing. Loretta organized a movement against it, and the women tried to stop it. And failed, of course; I can see now that they failed."

Again she was silent; if she had been a real woman he thought she would have sighed, or wept. Finally she said, "That was why she became so obsessed with me, with the project. 'We cannot forget,' she told me, 'but we are human and we *will* forget— but not you, Nefertity, never you—' "

Her voice grew soft, almost a whisper, and she chanted,

"Let the stars
Plummet to their dark address,

Let the mercuric
Atoms that cripple drip
Into the terrible well,

You are the one
Solid the spaces lean on, envious.
You are the baby in the barn."

She was silent. Almost Hobi could have seen her, then, standing before her inhuman muse: a white-haired woman, thin and strong as a steel wand, with eyes blue and raging and a voice scraped raw from reading, her knuckles swollen from the ceaseless effort of turning pages, turning dials, turning history into myth and myth into a woman who would not die, would not fail her, would not forget.

"A saint," he whispered, and Nefertity slowly nodded.

"But even saints die," she said at last. "And to spare me from witnessing that, Loretta ordered me to sleep; and so I slept. For centuries, I slept. Then someone found the bunker, I suppose, and took me from it. I do not remember. By then they had forgotten about the nemosynes; they had lost the means to wake me, or even the desire. If what you told me is true, they must have brought me a very great way, and then forgotten me, for me to end up in this place. But again, I cannot remember. My files have been disturbed, my random memories were accessed. But they never woke me: in all these years and years, Hobi, only you came to wake me."

She raised her hand, cool and heavy as glass, and placed it upon his. She said no more.

Hobi stared at her, embarrassed and awed and ashamed. This lovely thing, this creature of light and steel, woven with the memories of a dead Saint and the dreams of a million dead women: how could she have come to him, how was it *he* had been the one to call her from the darkness after all this time? The thought terrified him; suddenly Nefertity terrified him. What *was* she, really, this robot that was centuries old, this thing that had called him and his people murderers, monsters?

"You don't believe me." Nefertity's voice was soft as her hand slid from his shoulder.

"No! I do, of course I do—"

He turned so quickly he nearly slipped and fell into a shallow pool at her feet. "It's just—well, it's so strange, I can't understand it all. *You're* so strange." He shrugged, and looked away. "I—I don't know what to do anymore. I don't know what will happen, when we get Outside. *If* we get outside."

Nefertity nodded. "We should continue. Until we find the way out; we should go on." Her voice was cool and uninflected once more. When she began to walk again it was with an android's detached and fluid grace. "Shall I tell you some more stories, while we walk?"

Hobi followed her numbly. "Yes, please," he said.

"I know nothing, (the nemosyne chanted), I am a tabula rasa, a blank sheet of paper, an unhatched egg. I have not yet become a woman . . ."

Her words echoed gently in the darkness. Behind them, the tunnel receded into gray haze pocked green and yellow where phosphorescent algae glimmered. Ahead of them stretched pure night. The sound of rushing water had died. In its place Hobi heard a faint and regular booming, and felt the tunnel's floor quivering beneath his feet. More explosions, he thought at first, but as the air grew warmer and more humid and the smell of salt ripened with other things —soft decay, the fetor of green strands rotting on old wood—Hobi knew that they were, at last, approaching the bottommost rim of the Quincunx Domes, the edge of the world, Araboth's very brink.

They were coming to the end of all things. They were coming to the sea.

Chapter 9

BENEATH THE
LAHATIEL GATE

~~~~~~~~~~~~~~~~~~~~~~~~

They were brought to the prison on Archangels—a true prison, not the last refuge of unfortunate diplomats or Orsinate appointees fallen out of favor. Their cell was small but clean. The Architects modeled it after the oubliettes the Ascendants had developed after the First Shining, when it was important to detain political prisoners but equally important to keep them alive, in the face of radiation sickness and plague and the various viral strains decimating the continents. The translucent walls glowed soft white, as did the floor and ceiling, a color that made your eyes ache. After a short while even closing your eyes did no good: pallid amoebic shapes drifted across the inner field of vision like parasites afloat in the orb's humors. Reive had heard of a particularly nasty torment engineered by the Orsinate—a strain of bacterium was furtively injected into the eyes and temples, which then induced a softening of the brain into fatty matter within a few hours. It was better not to close your eyes, to go blind staring at the gently pulsing walls, than to wonder whether such an entozoan was probing your consciousness.

There were no chairs or beds. The floors and walls radiated heat, not an intense heat but unrelenting. Whenever Reive tried to lie down she felt as though she were being slowly parched upon a grill, and Rudyard Planck skipped back and forth across the cell hissing to himself, his face bright red and his palms glistening with sweat. Only Ceryl seemed unaffected. The amphaze given her in the Four Hundredth Room had done nothing except to rouse her for a brief while, before she subsided back into moaning and twitching restlessly in a corner. The bruise on her forehead had swelled and bulged slightly, a deep purplish-red. When Rudyard very gently touched it, it felt hot, and Ceryl cried out, her eyes rolling open for an instant to stare at him in horror.

"She will die if she is not treated," the dwarf said, looking up at Reive. Ceryl's head dropped back onto her chest. From the other side of the cell, a few feet away, the gynander stared at him dumbly. "Her brain is swelling and that bump has gotten infected."

He crossed the room to a glass door facing a bank of tall cylinders filled with dark fluid, within which swam the prison's aurible monitors, hand-sized, flat yellowish forms like paramecia or spermatozoa.

"She is dying!" he shouted at them, his hands leaving a smear on the thick glass as he pounded it. "Damn it, call someone, a healer, for god's sake—"

One of the cylinders blinked dull red, warningly; but nothing else happened. Abruptly the dwarf turned away, and began to hop across the cell again as though nothing had happened.

"She's going to die," whispered Reive. Her pale face was flushed. The mullah who had shriven them had also shaved her head, in deference to her being a hermaphrodite, and with cauterizing needles had drawn an intricate ward upon her scalp, an open hand with a mouth gaping in its palm. The mullah's excitement over shriving a morphodite had been too much: his hands shook and he climaxed while tattooing her. Now the assassin's ward bled steadily, the gaping mouth oozing a watery discharge that steamed when it dripped onto the floor. "She will be fortunate if she dies before Ucalegon devours us all." Then she bowed her head and wept.

The dwarf stopped hopping long enough to give her a shrewd look. His red hair stuck up in damp tufts like a basilisk's cockscomb. But before he could agree with her Ceryl moaned again. The dwarf turned to stare at her pityingly.

"It would be better if she died now," he murmured. He moved his hand in a gentle gesture above Ceryl's head, reluctant to touch her and cause her further pain. Reive nodded, clasping her arms about her chest. The mullah had taken her clothes, her scarf and jewelry, and she had been given a linen shift to wear, grass-green and of coarse weave. It itched terribly in the heat. "But I can't kill her. Could you?"

The gynander shook her head and looked away. Rudyard Planck bowed, tears filling his eyes. "This is terrible—to leave her in such pain like this until tomorrow. . . ."

"Better that than be given to the Redeemer."

The dwarf said nothing. Since they had been taken from the Four Hundredth Room neither he nor Reive had mentioned the Compassionate Redeemer, although the mullah who had shriven them spoke of little else. After his impulsive ejaculation he had left the shriving chamber for several minutes. He returned wearing a fresh robe and carrying a polemnoscope that he unfolded and directed toward the wall.

"This was during the Tenth Dynasty," he announced. Ceryl lay unconscious on a gurney by the door. The subdued Rudyard Planck sat next to her, his wrists chafing in their chains. From where she was strapped onto a cold steel table Reive craned her neck to watch great blobby images dance across the wall, obscuring a mosaic that showed Mudhowi Sirrúk wearing an Aviator's leathers and extrasolar enhancer. The mullah went on, "If you look closely you can see Nasrani Orsina in the corner there, waving, beneath the Redeemer's hind legs."

The polemnoscope hummed loudly. Suddenly the images came into sharp focus. Reive tried to turn away. Cursing, Rudyard Planck threatened to have the mullah castigated by the Architect Imperator.

"The Architect Imperator would not object," the mullah remarked blandly. "We met in a *bhang*-parlor once, and he confided to me that he had always been fond of that year's gala. Now, this was just ten years ago. There—where the Redeemer is crouching, you can just make out that face—well, it *was* a face—that was Grishkin Matamora. You know, the arsonist—"

And so on. Afterward neither Rudyard Planck nor Reive had referred to the mullah's diversion. In earlier years each had glimpsed the Compassionate Redeemer during Æstival Tide—Planck from one of the Orsinate's formal viewing gondolas, four-year-old Reive from a great distance, where she huddled on the strand barely two feet from the Lahatiel Gate, afraid to venture farther Outside. Neither cared to discuss the fact that along with the failing Ceryl, they were to be given to the Redeemer as a special sacrifice.

The cell's white walls did not dim as evening approached. They only knew it *was* evening when a human guard appeared, bearing a tray set with three globes of nutriment. Finally exhausted by her pacing, Reive leaned against one wall, wiping the sweat from her face and watching it steam from her palm. In her corner Ceryl lay, silent and unmoving. Reive could not bear to look at her; the thought of her dying filled her with a terrible sadness, but also with a rage so intense she thought she might go mad, or harm her surviving cellmate in her fury. When the guard arrived only Rudyard hurried to the glass wall, waving frantically as she slid the tray into their cell. But the guard tipped her head so that he could see where her ears had been sliced off and replaced with flat blue auricular disks, and opened her mouth to display a gray tongue split neatly in two like an eel's belly. The dwarf turned away, discouraged.

They drank the nutriments, grimacing at the strong fishy taste. A few minutes after they were finished the empty globes collapsed and melted into small puddles, and eventually evaporated. Reive tried to get Ceryl to drink as well but the woman only moaned and twisted her head. She would not open her eyes. The swelling on her head had turned nearly black, and Reive trembled as she held Ceryl's head in her arms.

"I would be very surprised if she lived until dawn." The nutriment had revived Rudyard Planck. He leaned on the wall across from Reive and tilted his head at Ceryl. "Though she'll be the lucky one if that's the case."

"Yes." The gynander sighed, blinking back tears. Gently she lay Ceryl back upon the floor, after carefully wiping the sweat from her face. She glanced down at the still-full globe in her hands. Impulsively held it out to the dwarf.

"Here—we are not thirsty anymore."

Rudyard Planck blinked, startled. "What? Oh, no —please—" He waved his small hands, his face turning an even brighter red. "I'm much smaller than you. Please—drink it, Reive."

"Please—"

The dwarf saw the pleading in her eyes, the need to do this one small good thing. He took the globe and drained it.

Reive crossed the room and leaned against the warm wall. She closed her eyes, trying to recall something pleasant: the smell of sandalwood in Ceryl's chambers, the taste of krill paste, the sight of her mysid floating in its glass jar. If only she could be free again, she would make offerings to all the gods; she would join Blessed Narouz's Refinery and never venture to the upper levels again.

The dwarf watched her, one hand shading his brow to keep the sweat from running into his eyes.

"I think you really are their child," he said after some time. Reive made no move to show she'd heard him. "Shiyung and Nasrani's. When I first met you, by the Karvo sculptures—do you remember?"

Reive's eyes opened, two alarming stabs of green in the opalescent light.

"Even then it seemed to me you looked familiar, although of course I didn't piece it together. Who even knew, who would remember, after all these years—how long is it?" He stared at her intently. "How old *are* you?"

"Fourteen years," she finally pronounced. The dwarf nodded.

"That would be exactly right. The same year the Archipelago Conflict began. Shiyung and Nasrani opposed it; that's how they found themselves together, I imagine, siding against Nike and Âziz. The year they sent Margalis Tast'annin to Kutaraja on his first command, the year the first HORUS installation failed."

He began to chew his thumb. "That was a bad year." He sounded depressed.

Reive stared at him impassively. "We are their only child," she said. "They should be happy to have found us."

Rudyard snorted. "Not likely! Âziz thinks she will live forever—she *will* live forever, unless someone poisons her, or Margalis strangles her as well. In three hundred years there has not been a single peaceful succession by an Orsina. Too many bastards, too many feeble-minded children. A true heir by brother and sister—even a hermaphrodite—that would be too dangerous. Better to have Nike stupefied with morpha and Shiyung as a *rasa* and Nasrani exiled; or better yet, Nasrani brought back into the fold now

[handwritten: mixed roles of women = patriarchy ↓ new age]

that Shiyung's been clipped. Âziz would never let you live. She would never let anyone live who knew about you."

The thought seemed to depress him further. He sank to the floor and stared at his feet. A bad smell hung about the cell, as of pork left uncooked for several days. Ceryl lay stretched upon the floor now. Her breathing had grown so soft that Reive could no longer hear her. She crept to Ceryl's side and cocked her head, listening.

"She's dead."

The dwarf nodded without looking up. The gynander prodded the woman gently. The body felt rigid. When she picked up one of Ceryl's arms and then dropped it, it thumped loudly against the floor.

"We should call someone—she was kind to us, and we never thanked her—"

Reive began to cry, crouching back and staring at the glass wall where the aurible monitors undulated through their viscous element. Rudyard Planck gazed at the corpse and then at Reive, wide-eyed, an expression that might have been gratitude as much as despair.

"She alone has escaped," he said softly. "Be grateful, little Reive, she has escaped—perhaps she will bless us, wherever she is—"

He shut his eyes and began to recite the *Orison Acherontic* of Christ Cadillac, pausing for good measure to invoke Blessed Narouz as well as the Prophets Rayburn and Mudhowi Sirrúk. When he finished they sat in silence, the only sounds their labored breathing and the nearly inaudible *tick* of the monitors outside the cell.

Reive slept and dreamed. At least, she thought it must be a dream. She knew that the uncomfortable parameters of their cell were designed to make sleep impossible; but how else to explain that she was once more hurrying down the corridor to the oceanic vivarium,

ravish bride

her bare feet stinging where they slapped the cool floor?

"Zalophus!"

Even as she called out she knew that it made no sound. There was no ripple in her throat to form the name, the white-clad Children of Mercy did not turn to see who it was that shouted by the zeuglodon's tank.

But Zalophus heard. The enormous head reared from the dark water and gazed at her, plankton streaming from his teeth.

"Little thing," he roared. Reive marveled that the Children of Mercy didn't hear him, either. "You have returned! Come with me now, quickly! The gates are opening at last!"

Water sluiced across her feet as he rolled onto his back, flippers waving. Reive shook her head.

"We can't go with you, Zalophus. We would drown."

The whale moaned and dived beneath the surface. A minute later he reappeared, spray frothing from his blowhole. "Come with me, human child," he sang, and shivering, Reive felt the sound within her bones. "Come with me, or else you will die—Ucalegon the Prince of Storms flies across the seas, he is coming to ravish his bride, even now the city quakes to think of him! Come with me, we will join my sisters and witness the holy act!"

Reive looked away to stare at the watergates hung with shining banners, the gaudy flags and pennons of Æstival Tide. Already the offertory pyres had been lit. The air was thick with the scent of myrrh and the scorched smell of the gilt papers covered with the names of the recently dead, long narrow scrolls tossed onto the pyres by the followers of Christ Cadillac. Beyond a narrow gap at the top of one of the huge barricades she glimpsed something shining, a sliver of light the color of Rudyard Planck's eyes. *That is the sky,* she thought. *When we next wake they will open the Lahatiel*

gospel — I was hungry & you fed
— Reive—death & rebirth

Gate for the Redeemer, and then we will see the sky for the last time.

"We cannot go," she said, turning back to him. "We are to be given to the Compassionate Redeemer. Besides, you would only eat us."

Zalophus groaned, shaking his great head. "The Redeemer! So cruel, a thing without a mind, without a thought, nothing but teeth and bowels! It has no heart and so no true hunger! Ah, Reive, it is a sin to treat you thus!" And Zalophus raced about his prison, churning the water into green froth and roaring so that Reive clapped her hands over her ears.

But at last the whale grew still. The waves lapping against the tank's lip subsided. "I must go now, little thing," he crooned, rolling to gaze at her with one enormous liquid eye. "Reive, Reive Orsina. I was alone and you spoke to me. I was hungry and you fed me, Reive."

The gynander shrugged, laughing in spite of herself. "You are always hungry, Zalophus!"

He drew up and back into the air until he smashed down into the water, then twisted and leaped once more, higher and higher, until his huge body blotted out the light and Reive stumbled backward.

"I will not forget!" he bellowed, and for the last time dived beneath the tank's surface. Reive huddled against a wall, shaking, waiting for the water to grow still again. But Zalophus did not return, then or ever, to his prison beneath the Quincunx Domes.

"Reive."

The dwarf had been repeating her name for some time now. Two guards in the Orsinate's violet livery stood waiting behind the thick glass door, idly tapping slender cudgels against their palms. One of them stared at the gynander's pale form with no less surprise than did the dwarf himself—Rudyard was suddenly petrified that Reive had died too. But finally she stirred and blinked, gazing blearily at the ruddy face hanging a few inches above hers.

"Reive, it's time."

"Time?" She sat up and looked around. The walls had changed color, from white to a glowering red. Ceryl's corpse still lay sprawled in the corner. She turned quickly back to Rudyard. *"Time?"*

He crooked his thumb at the door. "Guards." His voice was so low and hoarse she could not at first understand what he said. "For us, Reive. They're taking us."

"Taking us?" For a moment she thought of Zalophus, heard him booming *Come with me*, recalled the splinter of blue gleaming above the watergates. She thought of him repeating her name: Reive, Reive Orsina. She stood, ignoring Rudyard Planck patting her hand comfortingly. The cell door slid open onto the waiting guards. Reive shook her head, heedless of the blood dried on her scalp, the tendrils of hair left where the mullah had shaved her carelessly. She walked up to one of the guards and pointed to Ceryl.

"We want you to burn her properly. *No medifacs.* Have her pyre set on Dominations—"

The guard stared at her, eyes furrowed, and then started to grin. Reive looked at him coldly and said, "Dominations! Do you hear us? We are Reive Orsina, heir to the Orsinate! We want that woman given full obsequies and burned this morning. *Before* the Gate is opened."

The guard looked startled, glanced at Reive and at Ceryl's body and then at the other guard. Slowly they both nodded. Reive looked back at the dwarf staring openmouthed and said, "Come on, Rudyard. We don't want to keep the margravines waiting." The guards stood aside for him, then led them down the hall.

Nike Orsina stood staring at the corpse of her sister Shiyung. Of course, it wasn't exactly a corpse, because the body that floated in the narrow steel vat was not precisely dead. Tubes ran from Shiyung's nostrils and ears and anus, delicate wires had been fitted to her shaved skull and to her fingers. A corrugated black hose fed into her mouth; Nike could see it move very slightly, in and out, like a bellows. The body was immersed in a clear liquid that smelled like standing water, with a faint undertone of cabbages.

Nike wrinkled her nose and leaned away from the tank. It had been her own idea to come here, to the laboratory on Dominations where the *rasas* were rehabilitated. After she had left the Four Hundredth Room and returned to her own chambers she could not sleep. Sajur's death had frightened her, and Âziz's insane obstinacy in the face of so many terrible omens. The dream of the Green Country; the tremors that, since last evening, shook the entire city with alarming regularity; that uncanny morphodite. She kept seeing her, so young and thin, looking so much like Shiyung when she was a girl. How could anyone see her and not recognize her as an Orsina? Âziz believed that Nike did not notice things—Shiyung had thought so too, and Nasrani, before he was exiled—but Nike *did* notice, more than they knew. It was a common belief among morpha habitués that, far from numbing the senses, frequent—and in Nike's case, nearly constant—use of the drug made it possible to see and sense things outside the perimeters of normal consciousness. Nike had discussed this with Shiyung once and her sister had agreed, stating that once while under the influence of kef she had watched Nasrani's thoughts leaving his head, in the form of small orange globes. This had not been what Nike meant; but she recalled it now, gazing at Shiyung's face beneath the vat's bubbling surface.

The morphodite was Shiyung and Nasrani's child, sole heir to the thirteenth Orsinate. The first heir in hundreds of years, if one believed the histories 'filed in spools on Powers Level. It was an abomination, of course, a natural child and a heteroclite; but it would be a greater abomination to kill it and have no living heir to the dynasty. Nasrani was exiled, Nike herself had never had any interest in governance, and the demands of despotism had driven Âziz quite mad. Of Shiyung nothing remained, certainly not within that empty carapace. Nike was sure of that. If anything, since the corpse had been given to the biotechnicians for regeneration, it looked less alive than anything Nike had ever seen. Its skin was soft and pulpy; a whitish fuzz grew from the corner of one eye. The fingers splayed open like a frog's, moving back and forth as nucleic starter was pumped into the tank. It was grotesque, worse than the flayed smelting children of Archangels; worse than Shiyung's most addled experiments at geneslaves. Another sign of Âziz's madness: there was no way Shiyung's *rasa* could be presented to the multitudes as Tast'annin had been. They would riot and kill the surviving margravines rather than have such a horrifying reminder of their beloved Shiyung stalking witlessly through the city. A sudden horror seized Nike: that this was how *she* would end up someday, a gormless thing resuscitated in the bowels of Araboth and then forgotten, left to wander the lower levels with all the other doomed and deathless toys of the Ascendants.

"No," she whispered. She groped at the banks of switches on the wall beside her and turned back to the tank. The liquid churned inside it, flowing over the top and spilling through grates on the floor beneath. She muttered to herself, then closing her eyes she reached into the vat and grabbed the thick hose that covered the corpse's mouth. Nike gasped—the flux was freezing cold, viscous; the hose heavier than she could have thought possible. She yanked it once, then again and again, until finally it slipped loose. Then, teeth chattering, she snatched her hands back and looked wildly about the room for something to dry them on. She found a biotech's robe and wrapped her hands in that, and returned to the tank.

Shiyung's corpse had risen as the liquid did, and

now bumped against one edge of the vat. A milky ichor stained the nucleic starter around her mouth. Fine white threads of tissue streamed from her nostrils and a small hole above one eye. As Nike stared in horror the corpse's eyelids rolled back, to show pale irises corrupted with tiny yellow spores. It gazed up at her, its pupils mere specks floating atop cloudy green yolks; then suddenly the eyes moved to stare at the side of its tank. Nike shrieked and stumbled backward. More and more starter poured onto the floor, and before she could do anything the corpse was falling as well, pushed by the weight of the liquid bubbling up from the vat.

Nike screamed. The corpse flopped onto its side but otherwise did not move. Its flabby white limbs sprawled across the grates. Its head faced Nike; its eyes remained open, staring blindly at her. A tiny pink delta of flesh, like a kitten's tongue, protruded from one corner of its mouth. Nike turned and fled, shouting at a startled biotech in the hallway to seal the laboratory until she gave further orders. It was not until she reached the Seraphim's gravator that she stopped, panting, and tipped the contents of a morpha tube between her trembling lips.

Originally, the Lahatiel Gate was to serve in emergencies only. In the event of holocaust or direct attack by the Commonwealth, the entire population of Araboth could be funneled through the immense steel mouth and evacuated onto the shore outside. An intricate system of gravators fed onto the eastern rim of Archangels where the Gate loomed, arching up and up into the darkness, its ribs and spikes entwined with bas-relief images of ancient janissaries and war machinery, flames and floodwaters, and above all of it the Ascendants' motto picked out in letters of bronze and jet. When the Gate was open, one could see immediately outside of it a sweeping promenade that led down to the beach, copper pilasters and brazen steps long since tarnished to a moldering green and swept with sand. The sand itself was a different color here than that just a few yards away—dark, almost blackish. It always felt damp, and stained one's bare feet a rusty color, and it did not glitter in the sun as the sand did elsewhere. It might have been as the moujiks said, that the earth could not swallow so much blood.

From where she stood on the Orsinate's viewing platform, Âziz would in a few hours be able to look through that gate and down those sweeping steps to the beach, to the pale turquoise water swelling beyond. She would never have admitted it to her sisters or brother, but sometimes she wished she just could open the Gate and gaze out at that calm expanse of white and green and gold. It was a terrible weakness on her part, Âziz knew that. It distracted her, kept her from focusing on the business of ruling the city and dispatching the Aviators on their endless missions against the Balkhash Commonwealth and the Håbilis Emirate. Instead, over the years she had grown increasingly obsessed with her climatic chambers, the engines and programs that allowed her to create rain within the Four Hundredth Room, snow and sleet and even, by means of a series of brilliant lamps, a modest simulation of sunlight. And it was this obsession that had become the chink in her consciousness whereby the dream of the Green Country had burrowed, to haunt her restive nights and now stalk her even during Araboth's false daylight.

She thought of all of these things as she watched the moujik crews finish polishing the Lahatiel Gate's elaborate finials and hydrolically charged hinges. In a few hours they would gather here, all the levels of Araboth. As she was each Æstival Tide, she would be struck by how few of them there were, really. Perhaps ten thousand living humans in a city that had been designed to hold a million. And how many of that ten thousand were moujiks, tainted blood? Or sterile marabous like the morphodites? Add another thousand or so *rasas*, and the more intelligent of the geneslaves, and it still was not enough of a population to warrant the effort and energy expended by the Architects to maintain the Quincunx Domes.

Not to mention the energies of the woman who ruled it. Âziz drew one cool white hand across her brow, and sighed. Each year there were the usual complaints from the cabinets, overeducated anthropologists and demographers who claimed the hecatombs of Æstival Tide were no longer justified. What had begun in the years following the Third Shining as a method of population control, combining elements of both circus and sacristy, had over the centuries degenerated into the *timoria*, the Feast of Fear. Even with the *rasas* toiling in the infernal flames and darkness of the refineries, there was scarcely enough of a human work force left to perform those services that were beyond the nearly omniscient powers of the Architects. And so learned persons suggested that it would be better for the city, Better For The People, if the feast was annulled, or its nature altered. There was even talk of doing away with the Redeemer—its terrible appetite could scarcely afford to be whetted on those rare occasions when it was roused from its nearly endless slumber. It was a grotesque pet, really, nothing more; the margravines themselves loathed it and always had, but it belonged to the Orsinate, had been their charge through the centuries like the city itself, and Âziz could not truly imagine destroying it, no more than she could imagine a ten-year cycle without its Æstival Tide.

Because the Feast of Fear was more than an occasion for mere torment and bloodshed, sacral madness and terror. Without the overwhelming anxieties engendered by this brief glimpse of the world Outside, combined with the threat of the Compassionate Redeemer, what was there to keep the people of Araboth from rioting, even from attempting to flee the domes? The Orsinate had very carefully created the machinery of superstition and sacrifice, twisted scientific faith and religious belief in their powers to rule the city. They knew that the Architects were the true powers behind Araboth. Without them the air processors would fail. The tiny but deadly storms that sometimes erupted in the uppermost reaches of the domes would not be dispersed; the water filters would rust and decay. The surgical interventions that provided safe if unnatural childbirth and the *rasas'* morbid nativities would become impossible. The Redeemer in its carefully monitored hibernation would wake and sing its demented aria; the geneslaves would turn upon their creators. And finally the domes themselves would crumble and collapse, exposing the city's vulnerable heart to the firestorms and viral rains that raged Outside.

It was unthinkable, of course. Since the First Ascension there had been how many celebrations—forty? forty-three?—a small number, really. If each feast had been an individual, why there would scarcely be enough of them to fill a room! But they were precious individuals, like the margravines themselves, and their fates were not to be decided by monkish social scientists and religious fanatics.

Âziz gripped the edge of the balustrade in front of her. Far below the viewing platform she could sense a rumbling, not another tremor but the Redeemer turning in its waning sleep. Already the smell of singed roses sweetened the medifac's noisome air, and Âziz fought the urge to go down to the creature's cell. Soon enough, soon enough its scent would change, when, hunger appeased at last, it crept back into its cell, and the odor of burning roses faded into that of lilies (said to be the favorite of the Ascendant who had created the monster).

But Âziz's concerns were not with the Redeemer. She was thinking of what Sajur Panggang had said before he died: that he had programmed the destruction of the city. That, like their Imperator, the Architects had at last turned against the Orsinate; and—like his—that betrayal would be their last.

It did not seem possible. For nearly five centuries

the city had stood, impervious to the buffets of gales and waves Outside. Why, not even a drop of rain had ever made its way beneath the Quincunx Domes—

Though it seemed perhaps that was to change. From the floor far beneath her echoed the crash of something falling. A moujik cried out; the viewing balcony shook, and flakes of metal drifted past her. In the uneven light spilling from lanterns high overhead the flakes looked green. They fell in a slow unbroken rain upon Âziz's head.

Sudden tears seared the margravine's eyes. She bowed, pressed her head against her hands. It *could* happen, of course. Sajur was certainly dead, and frightful events had shaken them all in the last few days. There were precedents for this sort of thing— Pompeii choked by Vesuvius, Hiroshima a cindery shadow against the distant mountains, San Francisco swallowed by the no-longer *pacific* ocean. Cries echoed from far below her, and she clutched the balustrade as it swung, as beneath her feet the flooring whipped as though it were a carpet being shaken. After a moment it subsided, only to tremble again; and at this Âziz wept.

To think these were its final hours: the Holy City of the Americas, the last place upon the continent where the glories of Science still held thrall. She bowed her head against her hands and cried softly, thinking of all that would disappear forever, if Araboth fell.

But after a little while she stopped. She couldn't afford to waste time like this, sobbing like her sister Shiyung after the execution of one of her lovers. Wiping her eyes, she left, hurried past the Redeemer's cell and toward the gravator that would bring her to Seraphim's hangars, where the Aviators guarded their fougas and Gryphons.

Not all the glories of the Orsinate would perish with their city.

·   ·   ·

Before her imprisonment, Reive had never been on Principalities—she didn't count the brief excursion from the Virtues gravator to the Lahatiel Gate at Æstival Tide. The level's very name had always been enough to make her shiver, with its intimations of the Emirate's ruling legions imprisoned to languish in the fiery darkness. Now she and Rudyard Planck were hurried past tall grim buildings of blackened limestone, quarried when Araboth was still being built by masons recruited from the Eastern Provinces of Colorado and Nevada, the huge stone blocks then dragged up to Level Three by android slaveys and work teams from the Emirate. The sight of those windowless fortresses was even worse than the imagining of them. Millions of fossil shells and crinoids were embedded in the limestone, smutted by centuries of smoke rising from the refineries and the caustic airs released by the medifacs themselves. Beneath her feet the ground was cold stone, and there too she saw the imprints of shells and soft tubes, things like ferns and creatures that were all vertebrae or carapace. Reive shuddered, wondering if that was what the ocean was like, Outside, teeming with these worms and larval things, and seashells like eyes closing upon the eternal twilight.

In front of her Rudyard Planck ignored the buildings. He padded after their guards in his soft-soled boots and stared resolutely at the ground. The sound of their passage was swallowed by the roar of the medifac engines, their relentless *thud-thud* broken by the occasional shrieks of steam escaping from a huge valve. Several times deafening reports shook the entire level, and bits of rubble came crashing down from far overhead, spraying them with dust and grit. The floor would shake, and once Reive screamed as an entire huge block of stone reared up from the ground, shearing through a wooden building as though it were made of rice paper. Through the resulting gap in the floor flames streamed upward, and even their guards shouted and fled, dragging Reive and Rudyard after them.

At least, she thought, *at least Ceryl was spared this.*

Finally they reached the end of the medifacs, the last long low buildings with their hook-hung scaffoldings like gallows thrust against the gray walls. There were greasy black stains on the ground near the railing, where heaps of rubble were dusted with black ash. Tremors continued to shake the entire level, and faint cries and shrieks followed each round of explosions. A little ways down the hallway she glimpsed people milling about the dark entrances of a number of gravators.

Another smell permeated the air here. Roses, thought Reive, but something else as well—like the faint odor of carrion that rose from Zalophus's tank, or the scent of corruption that hung about a chamber where timoring had recently taken place. She felt a powerful urge to run away, to find the source of that smell for herself—and that was when she recalled the Compassionate Redeemer.

They were nearing its cage. She had managed to avoid thinking of it—easy enough when it seemed at any moment they might be killed by falling stone, or swallowed by some gaping rift. But now they were very close to their final destination, and the thought of what awaited them there made her shudder.

There really was no way out. They really were going to die. She thought of all the tales she had ever heard about the Redeemer, about executions, about Æstival Tide. She felt light-headed, almost giddy: to think that her life had come to this! A month ago she was wandering the halls of Dominations, thinking about scrounging a meal; now she was herself to be offered to the Redeemer as the festival sacrifice. She scratched her head, feeling where the mullah had nicked her scalp. She felt a wave of sorrow for Rudyard Planck, plodding along a few feet ahead of her, his collar pulled up so that tufts of red hair sprouted from it. He was innocent, really; if only she hadn't met him that day in the sculpture garden!

But then another explosion rocked the city, and

she thought of Ceryl's dream, of the margravine's and her own; and she knew that there was no escape now, for any of them. Only Zalophus—perhaps he at last had found a way out. Her eyes watered and she sniffed loudly. She thought of running away—it couldn't possibly be any worse, to die now rather than an hour later—but then she heard a guard shouting at her.

"Hurry up," he cried, grabbing her arm. "The margravines will be waiting and they can't begin until you get there."

They had reached the gravators. Reive craned her neck to see above the heads of the guards pressing close to her, protecting her from the people spilling from the gravators as the doors opened. 'Filers from Powers, heads bowed beneath the weight of their equipment; biotechs from the vivariums in their yolk-yellow smocks, trimmed with green ribbons for the festival. Low-level diplomats and cabal members, trying not to look put out that they had to travel this way, rather than on the Orsinate's private conveyances. Gynanders and marabous and slack-lipped mantics stepped from Virtues, blinking in the gloom. And, walking slowly through the crowd, *rasas* from Archangels, silent and pale, their hollow eyes glowing in the dusky light. All of them touched with green: ivy and leaves plastered to hats and vocoders, robes and trousers specially tailored with emerald brocade or grass-green trim, deep green stripes showing against the black uniforms of the Reception Committee. Even the *rasas* wore bits of finery, remnants of their earlier lives—jade beads rattling around one's neck, a pale scarf fluttering from another. Reive cried out softly and buried her face in the guard's shoulder, her small hands clutching at his back. She did not see, therefore, the doors that opened before them—great narrow bronze doors, inlaid with steel studs and spikes and guarded by a phalanx of Aviators.

Rudyard Planck was not so easily disturbed by the crowd, and so he *did* see the doors, though not for the first time. As an intimate of Sajur Panggang's he had been this way a decade earlier—although the thought of what waited there made him want to hide his head as well. As the doors swung open the guards padded in, carrying Reive and Rudyard. The Aviators turned and followed them, into a long corridor with walls and floor and ceiling of copper-colored metal, hung with electrified green-glass lanterns that shone like the eyes of great malign insects. Joss sticks were set into small brass burners, gray streams of rose scent snaking through the air. Some of the Aviators stopped and turned their hands in the smoke, raising their enhancers to rub it onto their cheeks. As they passed beneath the electric lanterns Reive heard a faint high buzzing sound, a monotonous counterpoint to the even crack of the Aviators' boots upon the floor. Perhaps inspired by the funereal atmosphere, Rudyard Planck began very softly to recite the *Orison Acherontic*. Reive could feel the floor trembling beneath the feet of her guard. Once or twice the electric lanterns flickered, but there was nothing else to hint that the Architects after their long servitude were failing their masters.

Reive found that now, slung over her guard like a naughty child, her terror had eased. A cool and resigned expectation replaced it. She recalled all she knew of the Compassionate Redeemer. Its image crudely drawn in hand-tinted images on long scrolls of rice paper; the many types of sacrificial incense that bore its name, from cheap acrid-smelling joss sticks and incense blocks to rose-stamped lozenges and those elaborate coils dusted with silver nitrate that fizzed and popped and sometimes badly burned the unwary. She was too young to remember much from the last Æstival Tide. She recalled only how she and the other morphodites from the Virtues creche were marched to the head of the Gate and made to sit in a relatively sheltered spot, where there was less chance of them being trampled or thrown down the steps in the festival frenzy. There she had sucked on a marzipan image of the monster, until its sweetness made her teeth hurt and she tossed it down the steps.

Now she turned her head so that the rough cloth of her guard's uniform wouldn't chafe so at her cheek. In the distance ahead of them a narrow orange rectangle grew larger and brighter as they approached it. Reive wished she had used her time in prison more wisely, and questioned Rudyard Planck about the protocol of offerings to the Redeemer. The rectangle blazed now, the Aviators' silhouettes dead-black against it, and resolved into a great door that seemed to open onto a flaming pyre. One by one as they stepped through the doorway the Aviators were swallowed by the blaze. A few feet ahead of her Rudyard Planck raised one small pudgy hand in farewell as his guard carried him over the threshold. Then it was Reive's turn. As she blinked and tried to shade her eyes from the incendiary light, she thought without irony how strange it was that she was embarking upon a very intense and personal experience of the Feast of Fear, and yet she was no longer afraid.

The Gryphons were housed on the same level as the Lahatiel Gate, on a long spur that hung above the sands below. A worn concrete walkway led to where the aircraft were lined up on a ledge overlooking nothing but endless blue: deep greenish-blue below, pale cloud-scarred blue above. Even with the filters the light was blinding, and Âziz bowed her head to keep from gazing out upon the sea.

It was one of the only parts of Araboth where the domes were clear enough to see through. This was to enable the Aviators to gauge the weather for themselves. A totally unnecessary precaution—a Gryphon had only to extend one of its filaments to measure wind velocity, barometric pressure, precipitation, radiation, atmospheric conditions ranging from the chance of hail to the varying levels of hydrogen in the stratosphere, possible exposure to mutagens, presence of enemy airships or -craft, and evidence of radioactivity in the Null Zones. The Aviators, however, being proud to the point of hubris, claimed to be able to determine all of these things merely by gazing at the open air.

Âziz made no such claims upon the world Outside. The sight—the very *thought*—of the ocean looming outside the meniscus made her tremble. To counteract this weakness, on her way here she had pricked her throat with an ampule of andrenoleen. If she was going to travel as an Aviator travels, she would have to control her emotions. Now, as the drug took hold of her, she could feel the blood racing through her heart, and a fiery confidence replaced the fear that usually accompanied her few visits to the Aviators' stronghold. With the Gryphons, it was most important not to be afraid. A few feet from where they stood she raised her head, teeth clenched so that a skeleton's grin racked her thin face, and squinted through the brilliance at the aircraft.

There were twelve of them. Each faced the outside of the dome, where the translucent polymer was etched with spray and salt, and the outlines of the skygates glowed cobalt against the bright sky. Once there had been hundreds of these biotic aircraft, a fleet powerful enough to subdue entire continents. Over the centuries, provincial rebellions and incursions by the Emirate and Balkhash Commonwealth had destroyed many of them. The bibliochlasm alone had resulted in a score being torched like mayflies to burn in the skies above Memphis.

But most of the Gryphons had been destroyed since then. In the dark ages that followed the Third Shining, they were lost through the ignorance of pilots who were no longer properly instructed in the command of their skittish craft. Physically, the Gryphons were quite frail, no more than a skeleton and membrane containing the crystals and fluids necessary to establish the controlling link between pilot and craft, and carry the canisters of nerve gas or virus or mutagens dispatched in the Ascendants' rains of terror. Not until the Second Ascension and the establishment of the NASNA Academy were the lost arts of biotic aviation restored. Then the first generation of Aviators were trained in the arcane methods of controlling fougas and aviettes and man-powered Condors, the solex-winged shuttles of HORUS and, most beautiful and lethal of all, the Ninth Generation Biotic Gryphons, all that remained of the imposing defense structure of the short-lived Military Republic of Wichita.

Of that squadron, only these twelve had survived. Formally, they belonged to the Ascendant Autocracy; but in truth each answered only to its Aviator —the dozen finest of the Ascendants' troops. And while their pilots were faceless and nameless, grim histories hidden behind their sensory enhancers, the Gryphons were not. Skittish and deadly by turns, it was as though they absorbed into their very fabric— half biological material and half machine—the natures of the men and women who did not control them so much as give them impetus and inspiration for flight.

And so they had been given heroes' names, and heroines': Astraea and Zelus and Mjolnir, Argo and Kesef and Tyr, Chao-is and Cavas and Hekatus, Ygg and Nephele and Mrabet-ul-tan. And like heroes between their labors they waited in restless sleep, until Need came to wake them.

As Âziz approached the Gryphons stirred, swiveling on their slender metal-jointed legs until their sharp noses faced her. Filaments lifted from their foresections, silvery threads with a pale rosy blush where microscopic transmitting crystals coagulated in a nucleic broth. They wafted through the air above Âziz's head like the nearly invisible tentacles of a sea-nettle, and for an instant she felt one brush her temple. From the front of the Gryphon nearest her an optic emerged on its long tether, and scanned her silently. She stopped, suddenly afraid.

Once when they were children Nasrani and Shiyung and an Orsina cousin had come here and entered one of the aircraft. Âziz had been with them. She was usually the bravest; but something about the Gryphons made her lose heart. At the last minute she refused to join the others as they crept into the cockpit. Instead she stood watching as first Shiyung's and then Nasrani's face appeared in the curved glass foresection of the craft, and as they waved at Âziz she yelled back, threatening to call their parents; but then Shiyung had fled shrieking from the craft. Nasrani and the feckless cousin had followed her a moment later, pale and shaken. Minutes later when they sat side by side in the gravator Nasrani giggled uncontrollably, exhilarated by the experience; but he never did tell her what had happened inside.

Now Âziz stood gazing up at the first Gryphon: a machine that resembled nothing so much as a huge and delicately appointed insect. Its sides were a silvery blue that would disappear when in flight; its solex wings were retracted, folded in upon themselves like a bat's. She could hear the soft churning of its biogenic power supply, feeding from the narrow tanks behind its legs. As she stared at it the others moved closer to her, clicking loudly. Their legs scraped the concrete, their wings rustled with a papery sound that belied their strength. She smelled the ozone smell from their solex shields, the soupy odor of power supplies. In a minute they would circle her and she would lose her nerve. Abruptly she turned to the nearest one, raised her hand and cried aloud a single word command, a name. The other Gryphons did not stop, but the one she faced obediently bent its legs and lowered a small metal ladder for her to climb.

Once inside she realized she should never have used the ampule. She felt as though her heart would explode inside her; she knew her contact with the Gryphon would be affected by the drug. But she couldn't waste time now. Outside the ledge shook precariously from another tremor, even as she crouched to sit in the cockpit and the other Gryphons clicked noisily, their legs moving up and down as they sought to keep their balance.

Inside there was barely enough room for the standard crew of three. She took the pilot's seat, cradled in warm leather as it folded about her. In front of her the windshield curved above the Gryphon's pointed nose. A simple array of instruments was set beneath the window—visual altimeter, old-fashioned computer astrolabe, a line of blinking green lights. The color of the lights seemed an evil omen to Âziz, but she refused to contemplate that either. Instead she pulled her hair from her face, stared at the ceiling with its shining meshwork like webs of frozen rain, and commanded the Gryphon to join her.

She winced as a web floated down to cover her face. It felt cool and slightly moist, and her cheeks and temples prickled as it settled there. Her nostrils filled with the smell of ozone, so strong that she sneezed. Other webs descended to touch her wrists and throat. If she had been an Aviator wearing proper flight attire they would have affixed themselves to her genitals and thighs as well, so that every gesture, every throb of need or desire, would feed back into the craft's control system, and the Gryphon would calculate all of this in a nanosecond before responding to any command.

If Âziz had been properly interfaced with her craft, it probably would not have responded to her at all; would have dismissed her as not being flight-ready. But Âziz had come armed with a few purloined commands, and these the Gryphon did not refuse.

A moment when Âziz knew nothing. There was a rushing in her head that grew to a roar, then faded. She had a nearly uncontrollable impulse to flee, but thought of Nasrani—*he* would not have fled!—and grit her teeth. Then,

OrsinaGoAltitudeDestinationTimeFlight-
NexusKesefOhFourNineteenHours-
KesefWaitingWaitingWaiting

She cringed, pressing herself deeper into her
seat's leather folds. Blood filled her mouth where she
had bitten the inside of her cheek. The barrage of
words and commands continued, along with a stream
of images burning across her mind's eye: clouds, a
slash of ocean, flames, and a face black behind its enhancer. *Kesef* was the Gryphon's name; the unknown
words cues for flight setup and takeoff. Âziz's mind
reeled as the Gryphon began another query loop—

KesefOrsinaLevelTwoWindsFiftythreeKnots-
SoutheastSolarActivityRangeOhSevenOhDan-
gerousCraftAlertKesefWaitingWaitingWaiting

An impossibly blue sky filled her mind, fringed
with green that reminded her of her dream. Her
mouth filled with the muddy taste of nucleic fluid,
her eyes burned from trying to focus on the incom-
prehensibly alien presence she was linked with. Without realizing it her hands clawed at her face, and she
felt part of the web tear beneath her fingers, fragile as
silk, and felt the Gryphon's voice grow dimmer. She
would go mad if she stayed like this—

She groped at her side until she found a pocket,
slid her fingers inside, and drew out a morpha tab. An
instant later and she had slapped it clumsily onto her
wrist, ripping a piece of the web. The image of green
mountains grew faint, then a moment later flared
back again. Another moment and she felt the
morpha's first warm calm waves lapping at her spine;
a minute later and she could breathe easily once
more.

"Kesef."

She pronounced the name thickly, was rewarded
with a spurt of pleasure that nearly overwhelmed the
morpha. She knew it wasn't necessary to speak com-

web

mands aloud, but when she tried to think them the Gryphon's presence overwhelmed her.

"Kesef—I need—meet you—hour's time by Lahatiel Gate—east face—tell no one—"

The shining vision of mountains vanished. After a moment she saw the Lahatiel Gate, the eastern face where a small balcony jutted above the beach, barely large enough for a Gryphon to land. She focused on the image, concentrating until she felt Kesef's response—

OrsinaKesefOhFiveSeventeenLockgridFive-LevelTwoSecurePathZeroClearedKesefNext-Command

"That's all!—"

Âziz gasped, tried to clear her mind of the Lahatiel Gate, flashed for a second upon the Compassionate Redeemer pacing in its cage, bit her lip, thought of nothing but blackness, whispered aloud, "Finished—finished—done—"

Her mind went blank. A jolt as she felt the seat gently pushing at her; she had been unconscious. She blinked her eyes open to see the web wafting up from her face, the others floating toward the ceiling like a fine gray mist. Her cheeks felt warm and stung as though she had been slapped. Outside grayish sunlight slanted in long bars across the ground. As she clambered from the Gryphon, struggling with the ladder as her legs wobbled on its narrow steps, the other crafts once more sent their filaments through the warm air to dart about her face. She swiped at them feebly, her head still thick from morpha, and staggered to the gravator that would bring her to the Lahatiel Gate. She did not look back to see the Gryphon Kesef unfurl its great shining wings, raising them in arcs of ebon-gold and green to feel the morning sun.

• • • •

All things considered, there had been worse things than Reive's own execution. That dinner party on Thrones, for instance, when a 'filer had gotten into an argument with a member of the Toxins Cabal, over the relative virtues of vivarium-raised *fugu* opposed to oleander shoots as a means of poisoning a guest. Or the unfortunate dream inquisition when Shiyung Orsina commanded the marabou Scintilla Foot, who was lame and had very poor vision besides, to dance the morgavella on a splintered-crystal tabletop. Or the time she'd gotten lost on Powers and gone for three days without eating.

Actually—they had left the coppery passageway and seemed to be finally arriving at the Lahatiel Gate, and she had had a good deal of time in which to reflect—the only really terrible part had been their journey through the medifacs. Even prison had not been so bad—uncomfortable but not unbearable. Except of course for Ceryl—with a pang Reive recalled her friend's face bruised and shining with sweat, and felt once again the tears welling inside her; but she consoled herself by thinking how Ceryl had never really been happy, even her pleasant chambers and her position in the Orsinate's pleasure cabinet had failed to ease her melancholy dissatisfaction with the world.

As if echoing her thoughts a rumble shook the passage, followed by a loud crash. In front of her the dwarf staggered, caught himself, and glanced back in concern at Reive. They were both walking now. Their guards had walked a few feet in front of them; it was obvious their prisoners would not escape. Reive raised a hand reassuringly to Planck and continued onward. She peered about curiously, wondering exactly where they were, and if Ceryl had ever been here. It was blessedly cooler, that was one good thing. She tugged at the front of her linen smock, feeling the sweat dry between her breasts.

"Are we near the Gate?" she whispered. The dwarf stopped to wait for her. His guard trudged on, kicking at drifts of desiccated rose petals and orris root that had been strewn along the ground.

"This is the Path of Atonement," the dwarf said dryly. The guards glared back at his sarcastic tone, but the dwarf only stared at them with cold blue eyes. "That gateway back there, with the lashes on the doors, that was the Expiation Perron, and in a little while we'll be at the Narthex of the Redeemer. And *that*—"

He paused dramatically to clear his throat and eye the guards with disdain. "*That* is where we will meet with the margravines."

Reive nodded, anxious to seem as though she understood any of this. Rudyard's words were unfamiliar to her—perron? narthex?—but the thought of seeing the Orsinate again was somewhat stimulating. She knew she should be terrified, at the very least more than apprehensive about her part in the upcoming ritual. But the truth was that everything about the Seraphim fascinated Reive, and horrible as the Orsinate were the margravines held her spellbound. The Compassionate Redeemer was another matter, of course; but then she knew little enough about it. Perhaps it would turn out not to be so horrible. Perhaps Âziz would have a change of heart, and adopt her as the Orsinate's proper heir. . . .

Such dreamy thoughts—abetted by the narcotic fumes rising from vents in the floor, and intended to calm sacrificial victims traveling to the Narthex—made the gynander lose track of time. More than once Rudyard stopped, staring blearily at his feet; once Reive distinctly heard him mutter something about the inferiority of ostrich leather when wet. The attendant group of Aviators who had preceded them had long since disappeared in the sloping corridors. Reive found herself admiring the artwork covering the high curved walls, scenes painted in metallic colors showing penitents in dark suits and white shirts bowed before tall figures wearing the conical crowns of the Orsinate.

"We really didn't kill Shiyung," she said as to herself. She paused to examine a lapis-crowned figure at the end of one panel. It gesticulated frantically at the Redeemer with one hand and made the ward against Ucalegon with the other. She sought vainly for some familial resemblance to the present Orsinate, but found nothing remarkable. "We saw *him* do it— the *rasa*."

"I know." Rudyard Planck's tone was weary, but as he stopped to wait for Reive to catch up with him his eyes were kind. "You don't seem capable of that sort of thing. Which makes it all the stranger that you're a pure Orsina. Assuming, of course, that you are."

Reive shrugged. Their guards had stopped a few yards ahead, beneath a great archway that led into an open area where several brightly clad people were milling about, occasionally peeking expectantly down the Path of Atonement as though waiting for guests. Reive turned, craning her neck to determine who else was following them. She saw nobody. It was not until she and Rudyard stood within the arch, and she could see the excited expressions on the other faces, that Reive realized the anticipated guests were themselves.

"Well!" A tall woman strode toward them, hands clasped, her wrists tinkling with bracelets of tiny glass and silver bells. She had an aquiline nose and cheeks scarified with exquisitely delicate wards against the Healing Wind. "We were afraid something had happened to you!"

She wore long white robes trimmed with gold and green, and a tall chromium mitre that marked her as Archbishop of the Church of Christ Cadillac.

"I will be performing the ceremony this morning," she explained, waving her hands in a manner suggesting she was blessing them. "Others will assist me—the mullah Alfreize Neybah and High Sister Katherine Mullany—but I'll be reading your last rites and so on and assisting at the autopsy afterward. If there is one," she ended with an apologetic smile.

Behind her stalked another, very tall woman in a pale fern-colored jumpsuit, faded and spotted with age but of very fine cut. She looked embarrassed to be wearing green. Reive recognized her as one of the members of the Committee for Ecclesiastical Freedom and Punitive Delight, often to be seen on the 'files.

"The margravines will be glad to know you're here—the ceremony can begin now, we haven't found Nasrani but he'll just be sorry he was late, that's all," the second woman said breathlessly. She frowned a little as she looked down at Rudyard's soiled clothes, then shaking her head turned to Reive.

"This is an immense honor, young person," she said. She smiled approvingly at the gynander's shaven skull. "For you, for all of us—there hasn't been a morphodite offering since Sylvia Orsina's time. We are all so grateful that we've lived to see it—not that any of us wanted to lose Shiyung," she added hastily as the Archbishop's long nose began to twitch.

"I think the margravines are growing impatient," she said, coughing gently. The floor shook again and a fine rain of dust and debris fell from the steel rafters. The Archbishop grimaced and readjusted her mitre, revealing a red line where it pressed cruelly into her skin. "This way, please."

Reive straightened herself, brushing grit from her scalp, and tried not to look pleased by the Archbishop's deference. Glancing at Rudyard she saw he was staring sullenly at the Archbishop's back, but when he saw her looking he gave her a brave smile.

They followed the Archbishop and the other woman, who turned out to be a precentor and quite beside herself at the honor she was to be accorded in chanting the Redeemer's hyperdulia prior to its release. There were other ecclesiastical types roaming about—several mullahs in moss-green turbans, more representatives of the Church of Christ Cadillac, a number of *galli* from the Daughters of Graves, even a few of the Orsinate's own Saints, parading about on stilts and wearing bright green masks of the Redeemer, as well as the entire membership of the Chambers of Mercy. But despite the crowd the space seemed empty and hushed, the stilts making even *tick-ticks* upon the floor, the other participants whispering as they looked over at Reive and Rudyard and the Archbishop. As they entered the Narthex, with its bronze arches and golden fanlights glowing high overhead and the stench of burnt roses ineffectually masked by clouds of frankincense and steaming bowls of galingale, Reive glimpsed the Quir, the leader of the Daughters of Graves, peering from behind the portable aluminum screens that protected him from impious eyes. When Reive turned to stare he winked at her and waved.

"We've never been here before," she admitted, whispering to the dwarf beside her. The Archbishop had stopped to confer with one of the Orsinate's personal hagiographers, who waved a vocoder in an agitated fashion.

Rudyard Planck looked up, his blue eyes sad. "I'm sorry you've lived to see it now, Reive. It's not a very happy place, at least not from our perspective."

"You've been here before?"

He nodded, patting an unruly auburn tuft of hair back into place and then straightening his cuffs. "Oh, yes. Once every ten years, and then of course there was the year their parents died—"

He flicked his fingers toward another doorway that Reive assumed must lead to where the margravines waited. "There were *two* major sacrifices that year. Of course we're seldom so fortunate that a successful assassination falls upon the eve of Æstival Tide."

"No," Reive agreed wistfully. The word *sacrifice* made her feel unhappy again. She rubbed her bare scalp gingerly, wincing. "They won't change their minds?" There was not much hope in her voice.

"God, no." Rudyard smiled at the Archbishop staring back at them. To Reive it looked like he was baring his teeth. "That would mean they were capable of mercy, and there has not been an Orsina capable of *that* since Simon ez-Zeyma had his twin sons smothered rather than watch them die of the plague."

"But Shiyung—"

"Shiyung was capricious and anxious to be disassociated from her sisters," Rudyard said sternly. "Not always a bad thing but certainly not admirable in itself, and *certainly* not to be confused with mercy. For example, I observed once when she had the eyeteeth yanked from—"

But the Archbishop had turned and was now quite openly frowning at them.

"—*must* go, discuss this further at the moon viewing tonight on the Fourteenth Promenade," Reive heard her say to the hagiographer. "Forgive me," she announced loudly to Reive and Rudyard in tones that made it clear who she thought should be apologizing. At her side the precentor nodded anxiously. "The scribe was inquiring after your lineage. I told him it was immaterial and any genetic anomalies, apart of course from the obvious ones, would no doubt turn up in the autopsy, if of course they're able to perform one."

Rudyard bared his teeth again, this time in a manner less suggestive of goodwill. "I still believe that if you contacted Sajur Panggang—"

"Oh!" The precentor looked startled, then smoothed the folds of her jumpsuit and gazed at the floor. "The Architect Imperator is dead. Didn't you hear? A suicide. He died right in front of the margravines."

Rudyard Planck's mouth drooped open and he blinked. "Sajur? But he would never—I can't imagine—"

Another tremor shook the level. Reive gasped and Rudyard took her arm. The Archbishop and the precentor stared at each other, the Archbishop's eyebrows raised in concern but not alarm.

"Now *that* may have something to do with Panggang's departure," she announced, turning and heading for a doorway clustered with softly chattering people. "Something else that will come out in an autopsy, no doubt. Now!"

She clapped her hands, the sound echoing like a crash through the Narthex. Several people gathered by the door jumped and looked around nervously. At sight of the Archbishop and her companions they turned and, whispering, walked into the next chamber.

"Good morning!" the Archbishop boomed. "Sister Katherine—"

A plump figure wearing the dark spectacles and green mourning dress of the Daughters of Graves stepped forward, pressing fist to chin in greeting. He was heavily scented with attar-of-roses. "Your Eminence," he said in a soft high voice, raising his hood to show a round face whitened with maquillage. "We have been waiting."

The Archbishop returned his greeting respectfully, then swept her arm out to indicate Reive. "The prisoners are here. You may report to the margravines and tell them we are on our way in."

The *galli* turned to Reive. He raised his dark spectacles to reveal a pair of bright black eyes, and gazed at her with a near-worshipful expression.

"A true hermaphrodite," he murmured, shaking his head. "We are so blessed, this offering will no doubt subdue the tumult in the earth. . . ."

His voice trailed off as the walls around them trembled, and he raised his eyes to the Archbishop. "There is talk among the lower levels of fleeing the city when the Gate opens," he confided. "A residential neighborhood on Powers collapsed two hours ago. They say two hundred died, and more would have been killed had they not already left for the Lahatiel Gate."

"Mmm." The Archbishop looked about distractedly. At her feet Rudyard Planck stared up at the *galli*, and suddenly asked, "Do you think I could have a drink? Some brandy or Amity?"

The *galli* looked surprised, glancing down at Rudyard for the first time. "Oh! The other prisoner, of course. Yes, I think I could get you a drink. I'll go tell them you've arrived."

He walked off in a haze of scent. After conferring for a moment with the precentor, the Archbishop turned to the prisoners and gestured toward the door. "Please," she suggested, and waited for them to pass.

As she stumbled through the door Reive blinked at the sudden brightness and turned to Rudyard. "Is this—?"

He nodded, stepped close enough to take her hand. Behind them the Archbishop and precentor walked slowly, talking in quiet tones. "This is the Narthex proper," the dwarf explained, waving his plump hand to indicate the rows of bronze columns, chalked with dust and verdigris, leading to a sort of balcony where a small crowd waited. "We're almost directly above the Redeemer's pen here, and that viewing balcony overlooks the Gate. When it opens you'll get quite an impressive view of the sea."

Reive gazed openmouthed at the ceiling, so high overhead that it hurt to crane her neck. Huge skylights of some tawny glass let in golden light that flowed in glossy waves down the columns and across the copper floor. It was by far the most beautiful place she had ever seen, more beautiful even than the most elaborate vivarium dioramas. Rudyard looked at her rapt expression and smiled gently.

"It is an honor, in a way," he said, and sighed. "I've only been here a few times before—twice in that one year—and so I never had the chance to grow tired of it. And you don't see the same faces here, either. Mostly religious types that the Orsinate can't be bothered with more than once a decade. Like them—" He hooked a thumb in the direction of the two walking behind them, the Archbishop's robes rustling against the floor. "If it wasn't for the circumstances you might enjoy it."

Reive nodded. As they grew nearer to the balcony a wind rose, warm and strong enough to send Reive's linen shift flapping. The dwarf explained, "They'll be starting to depressurize the area around the Gate. I heard that one year they forgot, and when they opened it hundreds of people were sucked down the steps. Quite a happy occasion for the Redeemer."

"*Now—*"

The Archbishop's voice sounded unnaturally loud. The prisoners stopped, and Rudyard squeezed the gynander's hand. "I'm sorry we didn't have more time to talk about pleasant things," he said sadly.

Reive gazed at him, her own sorrow suddenly so great she didn't think she could bear it. She wanted to give him something, something to thank him for being her friend, however briefly.

"Our own dreams," she said of a sudden. She drew him to her face, close enough that she could whisper in his small pink ear. "We have dreamed of this thing, of the Green Country, and Zalophus told us that the city is falling. But there is something else—"

She barely had time to finish before the Archbishop was there behind them, motioning for them to hurry through the portal.

"—this thing, Rudyard Planck, and it is very strange: in all of this we did not dream of our own death."

On the balcony that was the Narthex of the Redeemer stood the surviving female members of the Orsinate, surrounded by high-ranking members of the clergy and one or two diplomats. A score of Aviators ranged silently along the balcony rail, their dark masks winking in the golden light. Alone among those gathered here they wore no green, only their same somber uniforms of shining black and crimson leather. There were fewer guests than usual—Shiyung's murder had cast a pall over the festivities—and the destructive tremors that had racked the city for the last thirty-six hours had quelled some long-planned parties, though

gynander → it

others were just getting under way on the upper levels. Âziz wore full Æstival regalia—lapis crown, emerald robes encrusted with metal pointelles and star-shaped cutouts, high collar spiked with stiff hollow skewers of gold and green and sapphire-blue. Stunning raiment, created for the margravines of the Fifth Dynasty, when tailoring briefly eclipsed all other interests in the palace. The vestments were all but unwearable, and indeed Nike had refused to garb herself in anything more striking than a plain black suit, which admittedly set off her pallor and her crown to good effect. For the last Feast of Fear Shiyung had also forsworn the traditional garb, but Âziz felt that this was a mistake: the populace set great store by appearances and ritual. So after leaving the Gryphons she had spent the best part of an hour being fitted by her handmaid. She had also been careful to wear beneath it all a sturdy catsuit and boots. Since there had never been any need to travel outside the palace she had no traveling bags, but assumed the Gryphon would quickly enough bring her to the safety of one of the nearer Aviator command posts, where she could better equip herself and make plans for outfitting the Orsinate in exile.

Beside her, Nike stared out over the balcony at the throng gathering below. She was unusually silent. Âziz attributed this to morpha, and in fact Nike had swallowed so many vials that her tongue was blue and she had difficulty speaking. But the truth was she had not recovered from freeing Shiyung's corpse from the regeneration tank. For hours now all she had been able to see, floating between her inner eye and the ghostly shapes of things in the real world around her, was that bloated face and its ghastly staring eyes. And she was unable to stop brooding about the gynander. She was certain it was a thing of ill omen, but whether it would be worse to kill it or let it live, she couldn't decide. Probably Âziz was right, and the ritual sacrifice to the Redeemer would both propitiate the storm and rid Araboth of an unlucky heteroclite.

But still, the gynander was a true Orsina, with as much pure blood as Nike herself; and there were no other heirs. With the entire city shaking all around them like a jelly, it was hard to believe that anything good would come of whatever was to be enacted.

From below came a long wailing cry like that of the muzzein, taken up by the thousands of people gathered at the foot of the Lahatiel Gate. The Redeemer had stirred to full wakefulness. Braziers and incense burners circled the perimeter of the Narthex, sending up spirals of blue and white smoke, and the air was so thick with the smell of joss that Nike breathed through a handkerchief. The Quir had seated himself with two retainers and all three of them hunched over a hubble-bubble, inhaling through long transparent tubes and growing red-faced and giddy in the process. In spite of these precautions the Redeemer's scent perfumed the air, stronger now and with overtones of ylang-ylang and that civet rumored to drive pregnant women mad. The guards patrolling the crowd were having difficulty keeping people from storming the entry to the Redeemer's cage. Nike was terrified that one of the nearly continuous shocks battering the levels would send the walls toppling, and free the Redeemer to run amok.

"We should begin," she said anxiously, raising her handkerchief to talk.

Âziz nodded crossly, grimacing as one of the spikes on her collar poked her neck. "Well, we can't very well start without the sacrifice, and they've only just arrived—"

She pointed to the door. The gynander and the dwarf stood there. With her head shaven and her green shift flapping loosely about her legs, Reive looked like some bizarre overgrown infant. From here the wards tattooed upon her scalp stood out boldly, although the blood made them look crude. A sudden chill swept Âziz. She recalled her dream, the gynander's high voice as she scryed it and her wide clear eyes, green as shallow water. Perhaps this was *not* a good thing.

Of course she knew that Reive had not really murdered Shiyung. Even now, Âziz could grant her a reprieve, and condemn the dwarf as sole perpetuator of the crime. But that still left the matter of the gynander's lineage—a true Orsina, even the less sophisticated scanners had been able to deduct that from her genotype. If Nasrani had been here, Âziz might have conferred with him. But god only knew where her brother had gone—to a party with his crude friends, no doubt. But she didn't need to consult with Nasrani to know that it was too dangerous to introduce a new, unknown heir to the palace. There would be fawning admirers, and clever cabal members, and ambitious courtesans, all eager to educate a young morphodite and explain to her the many reasons it would be necessary to eliminate her aunts. Especially once word of Âziz's disastrous dream got out; especially now that the Architect Imperator was dead, and the city falling to bits without him.

No. The sacrifice must take place. The crowd would demand it, and the clergy. Âziz felt distinctly uncomfortable around the latter. She lacked Shiyung's facile enthusiasms for the new and strange, her unabashed delight in the bizarre rituals that made life on the lower levels bearable to those who lived there. To Âziz, the avatars of the city's main religious orders—the castrati of the Daughters of Graves, Blessed Narouz's penitents, even the traditionally stable Church of Christ Cadillac and the Seraphim's own Saints—all were unhappy reminders of the world's dark and superstitious past, before the First Ascension began the long centuries of purgative destruction that not only made the sterile domes of Araboth possible but absolutely necessary. Âziz had no religious feelings whatsoever. For her, Æstival Tide was a practical matter, a means of both controlling and satisfying the crowd's appetite for mayhem; nothing more.

And see where it had brought them. She ticked

away a thought, to be mulled over later, in the Gryphon. Wherever she settled next, there would be no festivals.

From across the balcony she saw the Archbishop of Christ Cadillac staring at her expectantly, her lips moving. Next to her the Quir giggled over his hubble-bubble and beckoned several of the Daughters of Graves to join him. Someone had given the dwarf something to drink, and surely that was not permitted? Âziz turned away, annoyed, to gaze down upon the crowd. She wished Shiyung were here. Âziz had never performed the opening ceremonies without her. The balcony shook ominously as she leaned over it, trying to escape the haze of incense. From below a cheer rippled through the throng, and she heard her name chanted.

"Well," she said hoarsely, turning back and nodding at the Archbishop. "I guess we should begin."

"Excellent brandy!" Rudyard Planck coughed, as the plump *galli* poured him another glass from a small flask he had hidden within his robes. "Can this possibly be Roseblood 402?"

The *galli* nodded, pleased. Rudyard Planck beamed and raised his glass to him. When he saw the Archbishop descending upon him he gulped the rest and hurriedly returned it to the eunuch.

"You're supposed to be fasting," scolded the Archbishop. "Where's the hermaphrodite?"

Reive had tried to edge toward the balcony, to see what was beneath them; but the sight of the Aviators there like so many grim statues frightened her. She ended up near the Quir, momentarily forgotten.

"Greetings, little sacrificial sisterling," lisped the Quir. He pulled the hookah's tube from his mouth with a pop. His aluminum shields had been arranged carefully around him, so that his narrow face grinned at her from every direction. "Have some kef, holiest of hapless children."

"I don't think it's allowed," Reive said, eyeing the hookah doubtfully.

The Quir raised one dyed eyebrow and gazed at the Archbishop glaring down at Rudyard Planck. "If you'll forgive what is most certainly an unintentioned slur, you and your companion are both rather *small* to be offered to our most Compassionate Redeemer. Not to mention your stature would seem to have made it a most challenging experience to garrote the unfortunate margravine. How did you do it?" He lowered his voice and leaned toward her conspiratorially.

"We didn't," Reive replied anxiously. "Is this it? Are they really going to kill us?"

For a moment the Quir sucked noisily at his pipe, his eyes watering. Then he coughed and said, "Literature pertaining to the rites of propitiation for Ucalegon and Baratdaja state that an unworthy sacrifice is not a satisfactory sacrifice. An innocent person convicted of a heinous crime, such as a margravine's murder, would no doubt rouse the storm to fury rather than placate it."

The Quir paused to readjust one of his aluminum screens, smiling at his reflection and displaying two rows of evenly filed teeth. He arched his eyebrows and tilted his head, so that his reflection stared directly at Reive with an expression of gross complicity.

"The Redeemer has no eyes and so must locate its prey by means of its body heat," he murmured, as though recalling a favored recipe. "A creature without much body mass might successfully avoid capture long enough for the crowd to demand to be released upon the strand, whereupon the Redeemer would be distracted. I have always disliked the margravines, and felt Shiyung to be a dilettante of the first water. Whoever killed her did a favor to those of us who are true believers. May the Great Mother watch over you and protect you in the hours to come. I believe the Archbishop is here."

His reflection dipped out of sight in a blur of indigo. He raised his hands in a conciliatory gesture, just as the Archbishop appeared behind Reive.

"Come," she commanded, taking Reive by the

hand and leading her to the edge of the balcony. When the flooring trembled she paused, breathing loudly through her nose, but only for a moment. "We are ready to begin."

Rudyard Planck was waiting at the edge of the balcony, his face a little ruddier than it had been and his eyes brighter.

"I always said that I could die happy if I'd tasted Roseblood 402," he announced as the Archbishop approached. He sounded rather drunk. "The irony of this would not have been wasted on my dear friend Sajur Panggang, so recently deceased. He would say that a life nobly lived allows no worthy desire to go untasted."

Reive nodded, wondering at the lack of such savory moments in her own brief career. It had grown uncomfortably hot, and her shift had rubbed her small breasts till they burned. The Archbishop joined Âziz and Nike. The margravine looked distinctly unhappy. She adjusted her mitre and whisked a handkerchief across her cheeks. Then she clapped her hands and the precentor stepped forward, followed by three of the Daughters of Graves. Beside them Âziz shook her head, glaring at Nike. She raised her arms and walked to the end of the balcony. A roar as the crowd saw her.

From where she stood Reive could finally look down upon them. Thousands of people, a tide of green seething back and forth like water sloshing in a tank. When it surged forward, the throng reached almost to the foot of the Lahatiel Gate itself, where a wedge of dour Aviators stood. And now Reive saw that there was a narrow spindly stairway winding down from this balcony to the Gate, a stairway with a worn railing and uneven treads. It began only a few feet from where she stood, and was cordoned off with a heavy velvet rope of deep forest-green, much worn about the middle.

"—when she's finished speaking you may begin the hyperdulia," the Archbishop instructed the precentor in a loud whisper. They stood directly behind Âziz and the frowning Nike, and the Archbishop gazed coolly down at the crowd. She did not smile.

Abruptly Âziz dropped her arms commandingly. The crowd grew quieter. There were isolated shouts of *"Where is Shiyung!"* and *"Avenge the margravine— Bring the Healing Wind!"* When two Aviators stalked menacingly from their posts, the vast chamber grew eerily and abruptly silent. Âziz adjusted the coder at her throat and began to speak.

"We are today, as we have done many times before, opening the Gate of Araboth to the world Outside," she began, her amplified voice tinny and shrill. It cracked when she said the word *Outside*. "As our founding Saints have advised, we will gaze upon the horrors of that world, and as they did, we will turn our backs upon it, and not look upon it again for another decade."

Scattered applause and cries. Âziz looked a little more confident.

"We will also perform the rites of propitiation against the howling storms that would destroy us, were it not for the vigilance of the Architects. And our sacrifices this year will be dear ones: they have already cost us the life of our sister, our beloved Shiyung."

Screams at this, and wailing, and many voices imitating the ululating cries of the Redeemer. And then suddenly, beneath all of this came another noise, low at first, then growing louder until it drowned the other sounds. A deep and mournful wail that grew into a shriek, a moaning aria of loss and bereavement and hunger: the song of the Compassionate Redeemer.

Âziz was silent, listening with the others. Alone in that great empty space the Redeemer sang, and she felt the floor beneath her shiver, not from a distant explosion but from the weight of the Redeemer itself as it pressed against the walls of its prison and begged for release. It was a monstrous thing, so hideous to look upon that its creator had gone mad and then been murdered by his own assistant; but it had a human voice, and its sobbing song made it seem that it had human hungers as well.

Tears filled Âziz's eyes, and she turned to take her sister's hand. Reive and Rudyard Planck huddled together, the dwarf stroking her broken scalp and murmuring gently. And then a high whining sound filled the air, like the endless note of a tuning fork, so piercing that Reive backed away from Rudyard and stared upward, covering her ears.

The ceiling was moving. So far above her that it was nothing but a silver-gray crosshatch of steel and glass, shimmering through the smoke like a meditation pattern on a 'filing screen. The Redeemer's song wailed on and on, joining with that other piercing note. As Reive stared, a silvery mote like a splinter moved above her; a moment and it had become a steel beam, twisted loose from its joinings and falling, falling, until she watched breathlessly as it passed within a few feet of the balcony with a deep whistle. It fell so slowly that Reive marked where it sliced through the pall of smoke that had drifted from the balcony to hang above the crowd. A moment later it smashed there. There followed screams so anguished she closed her eyes. Still more agonized shrieks, and howls like those of tortured animals, louder and louder until the gynander realized that this was it, the beginning of the Great Fear—the mob had already given itself over to terror. She stumbled to the balcony and gazed down.

The crowd had broken up. The huge beam lay like a silver arrow across fully a third of the floor. Figures squirmed beneath it, and the bronze floor deepened to ruddy gold beneath them. From the corridors streamed more Aviators, and moujiks in green eager even now to transport the corpses to the medifacs.

Beside her the dwarf whispered to himself, his eyes closed in prayer. Reive looked up to see Âziz staring white-faced down at the carnage. Beside her Nike was yelling, her face crimson, but Âziz turned and slapped her.

"Now!" she shouted at the Archbishop. "Do it *now*!"

The Archbishop turned and called angrily to the precentor, who stepped forward and shakily began to sing the hyperdulia.

Another explosion. Only dust and scattered debris fell this time, but the crowd surged forward to the Gate. On the Narthex the clergy's frightened voices joined the others as they struggled to leave the platform. Âziz bit her lip so that bright blood pocked it, then cried, "Enough!" She shoved her way through *galli* and distracted diplomats until she stood next to Reive and Rudyard.

"Go now," she ordered, pointing to the rickety stairway. She grabbed the velvet rope and tore it off, then pushed Reive onto the first step. "To the bottom, just go—I don't care what you do next—"

Reive stumbled, looking back terrified at the dwarf. When he nodded she began to walk very slowly down, step by step.

On the platform Rudyard Planck straightened and brushed flecks of dust from his clothes. At Âziz's hysterical prodding he raised his head and looked at her disdainfully.

"There is *no need* for that," he announced. He took a step, stumbled—the entire balcony was weaving drunkenly from side to side—grabbed the handrail and began to descend a few feet behind the gynander.

As Reive walked the crowd grew quieter, and the sounds of explosions and falling debris seemed to fade. At first the stairway moved so that she clutched the railing, fearful of being pitched from it, but after a few minutes it grew relatively still, only swaying a little from her own weight and that of the dwarf. When she glanced back at the balcony it had also stopped moving. Some of the Orsinate's party seemed to have gotten their courage back. She saw a nervous *galli* arid the precentor and Archbishop peering down at her, and behind them Âziz and Nike arguing. As she paused Rudyard Planck walked carefully until he stood beside her on the narrow stairway.

"Where does it go?" she asked; although she could see quite clearly that it led to the Gate.

"It's for the sacrificial victims." He grabbed her hand and squeezed it quickly; his was freezing cold. "In years past they sometimes had the hecatombs descend it. It's amazing it still stands. It's so they can all see us. The Gate opens, and we go out first, and then they free the Redeemer. . . ."

It did not take very long to reach the end. As they descended the smell of the crowd grew heavier, sweat and perfumes, the odor of petroleum that hung about the Archangels in the refineries, and the metallic scent of blood. Overpowering all of it was the stench of the Redeemer, so intense down here that Reive breathed through her mouth. There was no longer any temptation in the smell: it sickened her, and she almost longed for the Gate to open so that it might disperse.

And then Rudyard was at the bottom, his face very pale, and he turned to help her down the last two steps. As she walked onto the smooth bronze floor before the Gate she felt the silence behind her like a wall, pressing so close that she thought she'd scream. When she looked at the Narthex balcony it was so small and so far away that her nausea grew even stronger. She reached for Rudyard and clung to him, and together they gazed up at the Lahatiel Gate.

It rose, up and up and up, a great bronze wall so smooth and dark it seemed impossible there could be a seam anywhere upon its surface. But then it moved; almost imperceptibly it shuddered as though buffeted from outside by a terrific wind. Reive suddenly thought of Ucalegon, the monstrous storm, and how even now it might be tearing at the outside of the domes. A shaft of pure terror raced through her. The Redeemer at least was something from within the domes, something engineered by the Ascendants and protected for all these years by the Architects. But a storm? She could not even imagine it, only recall the shape of the wards traced upon her breasts and scalp, slender lines coiling in upon themselves, and a wave ringed with teeth. She should have gone with Zalophus, even if it meant being devoured by him; even if it had only been a dream.

She started to step backward, was thinking of trying to flee into the crowd, when from within the breathless silence came a tiny sound, like a child crying. Reive stopped, Rudyard's hand tight about her own, and listened as the sobbing went on, so faint and heartbreaking that she wept herself to hear it, and heard thousands of other voices catching and crying softly behind her. A gust of warm air brought another rush of the scent of burning roses. Reive raised her head, wiping her eyes to look upon the huge doors before her.

It was as if those moaning sobs were tearing the Lahatiel Gate apart. Reive's breath caught in her throat. A thread of light appeared, the color of pewter, unraveling from the very top and center of the Gate until it reached the floor. As she stared the thread glowed from dull silver to gold, and then to an angry crimson; widened to a band of streaming red that raced up what had seemed to be a solid wall. The band grew wider, the light fell in a shining band upon the floor and flowed until it met her feet. Reive cried out and stumbled backward.

"What is it?" Her voice was hoarse, scarcely louder than that gentle persistent weeping. "Rudyard, what is it?"

The fiery stream continued to widen, and now the Lahatiel Gate itself was so brilliant she could not have borne to look upon it. It was as though the wall were aflame; but while warm air flowed all around her it was not hot enough for a bonfire. The sobbing moan grew louder, rising to a steady wail that was almost a roar. Behind her the crowd moved, she could hear other voices murmuring, calling out, rising in a steady torrent that at any moment would break and roll forward, to meet that terrifying wall of light.

Because the Lahatiel Gate was gone now: a wall of flaming colors rose where it had been. And of course this was not a wall. It was Outside, it was the *World* come pounding at the doors of the city.

''No!''

Crying out, she tripped, and felt more than heard the throbbing voice of the Redeemer burst into full cry. When she stumbled to her feet again it stood there before her.

It was a moment until she could even see it, she had been so blinded by that irruption of sunlight. And when she did make out its features—spade-shaped head upon long swaying neck, weakened forelegs, tail making a skreeking noise as it switched back and forth above a gaping hole that had opened in the floor —when she did discern that this was, indeed, the Compassionate Redeemer looming above her, she was more terrified for the crowd immediately behind it than for herself. That was before she realized the Aviators had erected an obfuscating field between the Redeemer and the mob. Reive could see them as through a yellow mist, and hear them, quite clearly, as could the Redeemer and the dwarf. But for the moment they were safe where they grimaced and yelled behind the transparent wall.

And Reive, of course, was not.

''Run!'' Rudyard shrieked. She could barely see him, a small greenish blur darting behind her. She fell as he grabbed her, then staggered to her feet again. A long wailing cry followed them as she ran, the dwarf at her side, and stumbled down the steps.

''Try to keep down—can't keep the crowd back forever—doesn't take much to satisfy it—try to keep *down*—'' he gasped, and Reive tried her best, yelping when she tripped and fell down a few steps. All around her roared a wind, so loud it almost drowned out the wails of the Redeemer. Spray whipped her face as they half ran, half fell down the last few steps, and then Rudyard was dragging her across something soft and hot.

"No—" She staggered to a halt, yanking her arm from the dwarf, and looked back. The Redeemer still stood on the topmost step, its neck glowing rose-pink against the darkness within the domes. That was what struck Reive—how it seemed to be utterly black in there, so dark that she wondered how she had been able to see at all. Shaking, she turned away. And stopped.

Everywhere was a howling emptiness, a rage of color and light that pounded against her. Above them rose the Quincunx Domes of Araboth, so huge they loomed like an immense silvery cloud. The limestone steps from the Lahatiel Gate ran down to the beach like milk poured from an inverted bowl. Waves of sand ripped across the narrow strand, slashing her cheeks and scalp. Beyond the beach was water, heaving in great sheets onto the beach, white and green and a blue that was nearly sable. She cupped her hands around her eyes to protect them from flying sand and turning tried to see where the ocean ended and the sky began, finally decided the sky must be that paler expanse of gray and steely blue. Directly overhead it was the color of Zalophus's eyes. On the farthest rim of the world, where it swelled against the sea, it was dead black.

"Reive!"

Rudyard's voice floated to her. She turned slowly, feeling as though she were asleep or already dead. A hot wind raked her scalp, bringing with it the faintest scent of salt roses. The dwarf stood several yards down the strand, an impossibly tiny figure against all that thrashing gray and white. He had cut himself when he fell. Where he clutched his wrist, grimacing, blood glowed ember-bright. His voice drifted toward her in broken gasps.

"Don't stand still—it will find you—*keep moving—*"

Choking, she turned and ran, her bare feet dragging through the sand. She headed for the water, a few yards away. When she looked back she saw the Redeemer gingerly creeping down the steps, head weaving back and forth, long scarlet tongues trailing from its mouth. She turned away and continued toward the water, clutching her side where it ached from running. Her mouth was dry and sour; she stopped to cup her hands in the foaming water around her ankles. When she brought it to her mouth it tasted bitter and warm as bile, and she spat it out again.

"*Reive . . .*"

The dwarf's voice sounded even fainter now. Wiping her mouth she turned, saw that he had straggled back across the beach, heading for the foot of the steps.

"Rudyard. *No.*"

She ran toward him, though it felt as though the sand sucked at her feet with each step. Once she tripped and slashed her thigh on a broken shell. She saw what he meant to do: put himself between her and the Redeemer, lure it to him and give her time to escape. When the dwarf saw her running toward him he shouted frantically, waving her back; but Reive could think of nothing now, she was like a kite cut loose in the wind. The thought of being alone on that strand terrified her; the sight of the waves crashing behind her, that inky stain on the horizon spreading beneath the sky: all of it numbed her so that she could scarcely move. She wanted only to feel something solid against her skin, metal or carven stone or glass, anything but this awful shifting *world.* She thought she would rather die than endure this horror, but then she saw Rudyard Planck.

He had reached the base of the steps, and stood there forlornly, nursing his bleeding wrist. On the steps above him, perhaps two thirds of the way down, the Redeemer swept its head back and forth. The suckers streaming from its mouth whistled through the air, and its wail had deepened to a low, questioning moan.

The dwarf looked up, craning his neck. When he saw how near the creature was he cried out and fell backward, catching himself on the edge of a step. As Reive raced up beside him she glanced aside and saw the blood spilled across the sand, a broken line that ended at the dwarf's feet.

"Don't be an idiot," he gasped. She smacked him when he tried to fight her off, grabbed him—he was heavier than she'd thought—and pulled him onto her back.

"Hang on," she said, coughing, bent nearly to the ground. The Redeemer's cloying scent filled her nostrils like perfumed water and she could see its shadow slicing through the brightness behind her as she tottered toward the waves. Rudyard yelled something in her ear but she couldn't hear him. She had some vague notion that if she could only reach the water, they could somehow find safety.

Her back ached beneath the dwarf's weight and her feet slipped on the wet sand, so that over and over she fell, struggled back up, and stumbled forward a few more steps. Looking behind her, she saw the Redeemer stopped at the bottom of the stairs where Rudyard had been, its long suckers touching the steps and sand and then plying questioningly at the air. At the top of the broad steps, within the shadow of the Lahatiel Gate, she could just make out whitish shapes, like teeth in a great dark mouth. The figures of those waiting inside, she realized. They were pressing forward, the oriels must have been removed or else extended to allow the crowd to move farther out, until they nearly crossed into the light. Above the city clouds whipped in gray and white streams, reflected in the domes' smooth glassy surface; but the sky immediately above Reive was dark green. Funnels of sand churned up the steps, the wind made a steady keen whining in her ears, drowning out nearly every other sound. All this she knew in one quick flash;

then she was staggering on again, the dwarf clinging to her fiercely as he gasped, "Down—let me *down*!" while behind them the Redeemer shambled across the sand, moaning softly to itself.

They were at the edge of the beach now. It looked solid enough, with just a few inches of foam sluicing across the sand, and then angry blue-black water like molten glass. Reive paused, shifting so that the dwarf could clamber a few inches higher on her shoulders. The wind was so strong it seemed to suck the very breath from her mouth, and she turned sideways to gulp in deep shuddering gasps. For a moment she knew nothing but an overwhelming happiness, to be still and have her lungs full of air again, and to have spray and not sand pelting her cheeks. Then: "Reive—the waves, be careful!"

Something kicked her stomach and she went flying. The dwarf tumbled into the surf. Head over heels she rolled, shrieking in pain as her arm was wrenched, then gagging as water filled her mouth and nose and eyes. She was catapulted headfirst into the sand; something slammed against her side and she felt as though her head were being torn from her shoulders. Then just as suddenly it all stopped. She was sitting up, covered with sand and sea wrack, water streaming across her lap while the wind howled in her ears. Not five feet in front of her the Redeemer crouched over the body of the dwarf.

"*No!*"

It seemed not to hear her scream, but then she flung herself at it, coughing and weeping as she battered its sides and kicked at its hind legs. The creature raised its head, the long tendrils whipping through the air until they found her. She felt something slash across her scalp, a fiery burning on one cheek. But she had distracted it; as she stumbled backward into the water it followed her. A wave bore Rudyard Planck's body a few feet inward onto the sand, then swept it out to sea once more.

Another wave knocked her down, though this

time she saw it coming from the corner of her eye and she flung herself against the sand, so that it passed over her. A moment later she surfaced, gagging and shaking water from her eyes. Her shift clung to her like seaweed. A few feet to the right the Redeemer reared above her, its long neck swaying as though confused. Reive crouched on her hands and knees, coughing and weeping. She started to crawl away from it, but the waves came on and again she went under, and again surfaced, choking.

There was a roaring everywhere, as of some immense machine bearing down upon the strand. And now rain began to fall—it must be rain, great sheets of water pounding against the ocean and striking her slantwise on the chest. Reive tottered to her feet, swaying as she tried to keep her balance. She was so exhausted that she couldn't walk. The wind was so strong it nearly beat her back into the surf; she bent against it and took a few shambling sideways steps toward the shore. She could just make out a small form creeping across the sand, nearly lost beneath clouds of spray and whirling foam.

Even as Reive inched toward shore, the Redeemer followed her, but more slowly. It seemed confused: the wind tore at its searching tendrils so that it shrieked as in pain, and its blind head arched back and forth, back and forth, as it sought to find Reive in the fray. And still it wept, an endless moan of hunger and frustration, and crept closer to the struggling gynander.

And then, from somewhere in the furious sea behind her came an answering echo to that cry. Startled, the Redeemer fell silent. The challenging roar came again. Reive turned, too stupefied to flee, trying to shield her eyes from the driving rain. Another wave knocked her so that she stumbled back a step. When she got her balance she squinted until she could see a dark form in the distance, cutting through the water like a piece of the blackened horizon cast adrift. As she watched she heard another roar, and the figure churned closer.

The Redeemer answered it, its wail louder this time and more angry. The wind threw back a sobbing moan. The Redeemer's head pointed out to sea, twitching on its snakelike neck as though sensing something there. As Reive watched it began to walk into the water, the waves breasting against it until it was swimming, its powerful back legs kicking and its tail trailing straight behind it.

It had forgotten her. At the realization Reive began to cry. Hugging her arms she floundered through the water, knee-deep now and swirling hungrily about her legs. Somehow she made it to shore. She turned and looked back out to sea.

The Redeemer had stopped, not more than a hundred yards from where she stood. Dark waves battered at its sides, and once it dipped beneath the surface, then rose again a few yards to the left. Reive could just make out its wail above the wind, a shrill cry now and fearful. A deeper note called back to it, louder even than the gale. Reive struggled to see what was out there amid the black and churning waves, the water driving down in glassy sheets. Still the Redeemer struggled through the water, its song curdled with rage and terror.

And then a wave like a mountain erupted above the Redeemer, a wave that somehow separated from the sea until it hung in the air above the other creature's questing form. Reive heard a booming roar that all but deafened her, and from the shore another sound, a scream that seemed to split the world in two as she dropped to her knees in disbelief.

Zalophus.

Even from where she crouched she could hear the report as the leviathan crashed back into the waves, and somewhere behind her a voice that she knew dully must be Rudyard's. But Reive could only stare at the water, her hands digging into the sand heedless of stones and shells that cut her fingers until they bled, the rain streaming down her cheeks as she repeated the name over and over again.

Zalophus.

He had not lied. The city was falling.

And there *had* been a way out.

As the storm raged overhead she watched the two of them struggling in the waves, the great whale roaring gleefully as the Redeemer howled and shrieked, and its song was more awful than anything Reive had ever heard; and more marvelous too. Because it was dying; she could see that it was dying. Its tail thrashed helplessly against the waves and its slender neck wove back and forth as the great zeuglodon threw itself upon its flanks, tearing at it in an ecstasy of hunger and fury. Blinding light flickered on the horizon, and a grave rumbling that would have terrified Reive had she been capable of knowing fear. But now only wonder kept her there, kneeling rapt in the sand while the waves stormed about her and she stared out to sea.

Against the viridian sky the Redeemer's scaled body gleamed faintly, crimson and jet. It flailed helplessly and seemed to be trying to turn, to swim back to shore; but all around it the water boiled eerily white and yellow, while that other immense shadow flowed through the frothing waves, leaping so that it hung like a great black tear against the sky. She could hear the whale shouting to itself, its voice wild and jubilant as it tore at its prey and the Redeemer's screams grew higher and more frantic. Behind her she could dimly make out other cries, human voices shrieking in horror and disbelief, but when she turned she could barely see the domes through the heavy clouds of spray slamming into shore.

"Reive—Reive, we've got to find someplace, someplace—"

A small hand tugged at the slack wet folds of her shift and she looked up to see Rudyard Planck, soaked and bruised but with eyes feverishly bright.

"Hurricane!" He coughed, bending over as water

dribbled from his mouth. "Might escape—go inland—
run—"

She shook her head, turned back to look out to
sea. The roar of the storm drowned all other sounds
and the glaucous air was nearly too heavy to peer
through; but she could just make out a slender silhouette moving convulsively in the murk, and then a
darker shadow rising from the sea to engulf it. For an
instant she thought she heard a voice bellowing joy-
fully in the maelstrom, a sound like singing from the
waves; her own name carried faint as a whisper from
the frenzied throat of Ucalegon.

Chapter 10

THE WOMAN AT THE END
OF THE WORLD
~~~~~~~~~~~~~~~~~~~~~~~~~~

In the darkness ahead of them Hobi saw a curl of light, at first so insubstantial it might have been a mote dancing in his eye. But after a few minutes the speck grew to a flickering wisp of green flame, and then to a tear in the black fabric all around them; and finally it became a jagged hole that grew larger and larger as they approached.

Hobi thought he might never forget what that hole looked like. His first sight of anything other than darkness, after so many hours of trudging through the tunnel. Sometimes he closed his eyes to see if there was any difference between what he saw then and what he glimpsed when they were open. There was not, really. Nefertity's cool blue gleam had faded, until only her eyes glowed, silvery green like a cat's. She had finished reciting the long story she'd begun back in the chamber with the replicants. Hobi was unhappy with the way it had ended, and since then they both walked without speaking—though he wondered if they would be able to hear each other if they *did* try to talk. In the distance the sound of explosions continued, but too far away now for him to feel them rock the passage. The rhythmic throb of the ocean roared and shushed, echoing through the tunnel like the breathing of a leviathan. Without meaning to Hobi had begun walking in time with that relentless beat, his feet thudding against the ground. Something softer now beneath his boots—he had paused once, and stooped to find sand, sifting cool and dry as ashes between his fingers.

The air had changed too. A strong wind blew through the tunnel. As they grew nearer to the opening Hobi saw that what made the light appear to flicker were numerous fluid shapes moving back and forth across the entrance, like pennons snapping in the wind. He hesitated, let Nefertity continue on ahead of him.

For hours he had prayed for some kind of light, for an end to this night journey. Now that they were nearly there he was overwhelmed by a terror so strong that his hands shook uncontrollably, and he half crouched, grabbing his knees and squeezing until his fingers grew steady again.

"I can't, I can't," he whispered. The wind pouring through the passage was warm, almost hot; still he shivered, drew his hands up, and clasped them around his neck. His hair had matted in heavy clumps against his shoulders. He thought of turning and fleeing back down the tunnel, of leaving the nemosyne to wander out there alone. He knew he would never be able to find his way back again; knew that, even if he did, he might find nothing but ruins, all of Araboth wrecked as Nasrani's secret chamber had been.

But he could not go on. How could he go Outside, knowing what he did: that to do so would make him go mad, that he would be crushed beneath the waves of light and sound waiting out there? The hot smell of the wind sickened him, thick as it was with other things—brine and dead fish and a sweet fragrance like roses. "I can't," he whimpered again, and sank onto the sand.

"Hobi."

He looked up to see Nefertity. The light weaving down from the end of the tunnel touched her with gold and green. Her fingers as they brushed his cheek were cool. "Hobi, we are almost there. Outside. We will be free."

"*Free.*" He shook his head. "I can't, Nefertity, I can't! I'll die out there—"

"But why? I detect little radiation, certainly not enough to kill you. And there seems to be lush vegetation at the mouth of the tunnel, so the earth is not contaminated—"

"No!" He drew his knees up and covered his head with his hands. "You go—I would rather die here, or go back—"

Nefertity's eyes glittered and she shook her head. "I have seen this before. With Loretta. Too much time alone, inside. It makes human beings go mad."

Hobi gave another croaking laugh. "You've got it all wrong—it's that, there—Outside—*that's* what drives us mad. That's why the domes protect us, why we never go out except at Æstival Tide—"

"But you told me it is Æstival Tide now, Hobi. You said that at Æstival Tide it is safe to go Outside and look upon the sun. You said the feast began at dawn, whenever dawn was. So you will be protected."

She turned to gaze at the tunnel's mouth, and Hobi looked up at her in despair. Shafts of golden light made it impossible to see anything except for her silhouette; but for the first time it seemed that it was a woman's profile he saw there, the sharp edges and silver lines of her cheeks and jaw softened by the sun. Even her eyes grew softer, darker, their eerie glow melted to a gentler green. She was so beautiful that for a moment his fear trickled away.

"Æstival Tide," he whispered. He had forgotten what day it was. It seemed weeks since he had told her about the Feast of Fear, but of course it had only been yesterday. The nemosyne turned to gaze back down at him, and as the shadows once more struck her face the vision of a woman was gone.

"Perhaps once we get Outside we will be able to see your friends, and you can find your way back inside your city."

Hobi nodded. His fingers relaxed and he sighed, let his hands drop to feel the cool sand. This is what he had wanted to do, after all. Have an adventure. Find the nemosyne and leave the city. It seemed like a child's dream now, stupid and dangerous; but he had done it nonetheless, and in a way it *was* something to take pride in. And surely nothing was irrevocable— even now, revelers would be gathered beneath the Lahatiel Gate, and he could find someone there to help him, Nasrani or even one of the margravines. He pushed himself up, brushing sand from his trousers.

"All right. Nasrani will be there, and my father—"

Though in his heart he knew that his father would not be there, at least not with the margravines upon their viewing platform. "Let's go," he ended hoarsely, following Nefertity. And with each step that brought him closer to the sunlight his dread grew, until he stood within the tunnel's very mouth, blinded and battered by a hot fecund wind; and crying out, he fell to his knees, bringing his arm up against his eyes to protect him from the horror of the world Outside.

Tast'annin never tired, but there were moments when Nasrani was certain that he had fallen asleep, and walked dreaming with that fiery angel at his side. Once he woke to find himself in the *rasa*'s arms, being carried through a passageway where water gushed from a break in the wall and swirled about the *rasa*'s knees.

"Please, I can walk," he protested weakly; but the Aviator shook his head.

"It is too strong. The current would sweep you away."

So Nasrani clung to him like a child. He gritted his teeth against the heat radiating from the *rasa*, burning through his damp clothes until they steamed and filled his nostrils with the smell of sweat. At last the water fell behind them. The tunnel began a slight incline, and the *rasa* paused to let Nasrani clamber from his arms, puffing and wiping his face with his soiled handkerchief.

"Are you sure this is the right way?" he demanded, hurrying after the dimly glowing form.

"It is the only way now." The Aviator Imperator's voice drifted back, echoing sharply. "And even here the walls are failing. Soon the entire Undercity will collapse, and then one by one all the upper levels will fall."

Nasrani's breath came in short gasps. He felt an anxious jab at his heart, and patted his greatcoat vainly, looking for a morpha tube. "But why?"

His tone sounded shrill and whining. He paused to catch his breath, then called again, trying to sound calm. "Why, Margalis? Why destroy the city? Who would do this? Who *could* do this?"

"Why?" The *rasa*'s voice sounded almost amused, and he halted, turning to wait for Nasrani to catch up with him. "Because it is an abomination. Because it should never have been created in the first place."

Nasrani put out a hand to steady himself against the tunnel wall. By the *rasa*'s dull crimson glow he could see another crack forming, spinning out across the concrete like a spider's thread thrown against the air. "Don't be absurd, Margalis," he said testily. Exhaustion and hopelessness had nearly driven out his

Do the dead dream?

fear of the Aviator Imperator. "No one would have survived Outside all these years—the domes were our salvation—"

"The Orsinate should never have been saved. Better for all of us if they had died four hundred years ago. As to who could destroy the city . . ."

Tast'annin shrugged. Dark lines shadowed his face, and he looked away, down the length of the tunnel. "I would destroy it, had I the power to," he said softly. "All of them: I would see all of them dead."

Nasrani shuddered, ran a hand across his brow. "We'll see ourselves dead soon enough, if we don't find our way back to a gravator."

The Aviator started walking again. "You're a fool, Nasrani. I told you, Araboth is collapsing. Soon the Undercity will be buried, and Archangels, and the medifacs, all the way up to your precious Seraphim. If this passage doesn't lead us out somehow, you will die here."

Nasrani nodded curtly but said nothing. *I will die here*, he thought, *but what of you? Can the dead die twice? Do the dead dream?* He gave a bitter laugh, and the *rasa* turned to stare at him with its coldly human eyes.

"You are not afraid. That is good." He pointed down the length of the tunnel. Very far away a pinpoint of light showed in the spiraling void, so small it might have been something Nasrani imagined, drawn from the darkness like a minnow from black water. "I think that is where the tunnel ends. I can hear them, down there—"

Tast'annin cocked his head. Nasrani could hear nothing save the hiss and roar that had grown gradually louder the farther they went. "Yes," the Aviator said at last. "It is the end. They have left us at last, they have escaped from Araboth."

"Escaped," Nasrani murmured. A warm wind chased down the passage and dried the hair on his neck. "So will we escape, to go mad or be consumed by the sun."

"The sun is not poisonous. You know that, Nasrani, you have been Outside."

Nasrani shook his head. "Only for a few hours . . ."

He shuddered at the memory. "It smelled—it smelled of water, and something else. I don't know what. A horrible smell." He pinched his nose, squinted at the fleck of light far ahead.

"Things growing." The *rasa*'s face leered back at him. "That is what you smelled, Nasrani. Milkweed and cholla and evening primrose, huisache and mesquite and rugosa roses. You will smell them again, soon."

The thought made Nasrani's stomach churn. He stumbled on in silence, the tunnel's cracked cement floor giving way to sand beneath him. In the distance the light grew larger, until the *rasa*'s shadow staggered on the ground in front of Nasrani and his own shadow danced across the broken walls. The unbearable heat gradually became bearable—a different sort of heat, less painfully intense, wind-borne and salt-scented.

The Aviator Imperator continued tirelessly. If anything, his steps hastened as they grew closer to the end of the passage. Nasrani watched him with a sort of detached curiosity, as one might regard a replicant performing a difficult task.

Finally he called out, "Why do you want to see her? Why is it so important to you?"

The *rasa* did not slow his steps, but when Nasrani called out again he stopped and turned to him.

"Why?" Nasrani ended, a little brokenly. He looked up at the *rasa*, then shrugged and gave him a hopeless smile. Aqua light washed over them from the tunnel opening, shot with gold and darker green. Without the thrash of the festival drums, the clamor of the gamelan at the Lahatiel Gate to mute it, the sound of the pounding waves was brutally loud. Nasrani's ears hurt and he rubbed them fitfully.

"You told me when you discovered it that the nemosyne had been linked with an archaic religion."

Nasrani nodded. "Yes, that's right. The American Catholic Church. Mostly women—she had been programmed by a woman, her files are mostly women's histories, mystical nonsense. She would be of no use to you, Margalis."

The *rasa* shook his head, gazed at where the light streamed onto the sand. "Oh, but she would be," he said. "You see, I saw something very interesting in the Capital. I saw a new religion being created—or, rather, a very old one being resurrected. It was an—*unusual*—experience. And I also found the ancient weapons storehouses there. Had I not been killed in such an untimely fashion, why I might have resurrected them as well.

"And later, when I found myself back among the Seraphim, well I thought of you, Nasrani, I remembered how excited you were with your metal woman. You invited me, once long ago, to go with you to see her—in a weak moment, of course, you might not even remember. I think we were drinking Amity with your sister Shiyung, and after she had left us you were feeling rather grand. I refused, because I wanted to follow Shiyung—"

A break in his voice. Nasrani flinched and started shuffling forward again, wishing he had said nothing.

"—but now I wish I had accepted your kind invitation. So think of it this way, Nasrani—it is a few years later, but what's a few years between old friends?"

Nasrani tried to twist his grimace into a smile. A moment later he felt the *rasa* beside him again, his heat also seeming to dissipate as they left the Undercity behind them.

"There is another reason," Tast'annin said after a few minutes. "Manning Tabor at the Academy used to talk about the nemosyne network. He claimed to have deciphered computer programs, records that revealed where the original units had been deployed. I scoffed at him then, but now I realize he must have been right. He said there were military units still active in the United Provinces, and one or two that were rumored to have been captured by the Commonwealth after the Second Ascension. There was a master unit that controlled all of them, or could control them all if it was activated. The Military Tactical Target Retrievals Network. Your sister consulted Tabor at length about it. She thought it might be located in the ancient arsenal in the old capital. That was why she sent me there. I searched for it but I found nothing, there was no indication that it had ever been there.

"But I think that your nemosyne might have knowledge of this unit, if the nemosynes were truly linked at some point. If you could activate your nemosyne to search for them, you could locate the other existing units anywhere in the world. One could control them—control the military forces they control."

Nasrani's head ached; he scarcely focused on Tast'annin's words. He stared at his feet, shading his streaming eyes with his hand. A few feet in front of them the sand glittered dazzlingly white. Brilliant blue light danced at the edges of his vision.

"What difference does that make, if Araboth is falling around us?" he shouted above the din of the waves. "If you've killed Shiyung, and the rest of us are going to die anyway? What possible difference could it make for you to find this master nemosyne?"

He stopped, swaying, and with one hand clutched his stomach. Nausea gripped him; he hardly had the strength to look at the *rasa* stopped beside him. "Margalis!" he pleaded. "Don't—you can't leave me like this, you can't go—you'll die out there—" He sank to the ground, fingers scrabbling at the sand.

The *rasa*'s glittering blue eyes regarded him with utter contempt. "Ah, Nasrani," the Aviator Imperator pronounced. His voice rang dispassionately as he walked away. "Now I see that you truly are an Orsina: that is, an utter fool."

He left the exile kneeling in the entrance to the tunnel, and stepped out into the sunlight.

Hobi screamed, his voice torn from him and flung into the wind that came flying across the water. Overhead other things screamed as well, scraps of cloud or perhaps the raging tips of waves thrown against the sky. It was not until Nefertity knelt beside him and laved his forehead with water, until he dared open his eyes again, that he looked up into the sky and recognized those shrieking rags as birds.

"Hobi—Hobi, it's all right, it's only the sea—"

He tried to hear something else; strained to catch beneath the ceaseless chant of the waves another song—the grinding of the Gate as it opened, the screams of the crowd spilling down the steps onto the thirsting sand; the long moaning wail of the Redeemer awakened from its year-long sleep. But there was only this horrible sound, gentler now than it had been when it echoed through the tunnel but no less terrifying, and stabbed with the harsh cries of the gulls.

"Hobi, please. Open your eyes and try to stand— we have to leave this place, we are too near the water. A storm is building, we must go to higher ground."

He coughed, pushed her hands away, and finally sat up. When he opened his eyes the light was so painful that he cried out again, would have buried his face in his hands except that Nefertity took him and pulled him close to her, until feeling her cold steel enveloping him he took a deep breath and nodded.

"All right—I'm all right," he whispered. He wanted never to move from her, the chill kiss of smooth metal and glass upon his cheeks and arms. But she pulled away from him. He stared down at the sand beneath him, every shade of brown and white, pinked with broken cowries and wing shells and crescents of green and brown glass. A tiny object like the limb of one of Nasrani's emerald monads glistened beside his ankle. He picked it up and stared at it, still not daring to raise his face to the sun. It was the leg of some small creature, jointed like a server's leg, but hollow and light as a straw and ending in a tiny flattened fin. It came to him suddenly that it was the leg of a crustacean, like one of the crayfish or prawns he had often eaten at banquets on Seraphim. A real animal, one that had never seen the inside of a vivarium tank. Something that swam in the water flowing and receding a few yards from where he crouched, and hunted there for creatures even smaller than itself. Hobi let the leg slip from his fingers to the sand, and leaning forward he vomited upon it.

Afterward he felt better. Nefertity had stood so that her shadow blotted the sun from his face, and waited silently for him to rise. He did so, his arms flailing at the air until the nemosyne caught him.

"I can't—it's too big—"

She waited until he grew calm again. The water pulsed relentlessly against the shoreline, stretched out before them without end: blue, green, white. He did not think he could stand to gaze upon it, it seemed so raw; but he forced himself to look. Just for an instant. Then he turned and stared down the beach, to where the Quincunx Domes rose shimmering above the sea.

"God—look at them!"

He shook his head and took a step away from the nemosyne. During the last Æstival Tide he was always conscious of the city behind him, but then it had seemed more like a solid wall, a buffer between sea and sky, too huge for any detail beyond the black maw of the Redeemer's cage and the lapis-crowned figures of the Orsinate waving from their balcony. From here the domes looked both smaller and more impressive. He could see the two domes nearest him, and rearing above them the central Quincunx Dome, glittering with a dark greenish cast, pocked everywhere with irregular black indentations. A large curved rectangle in the central dome would be one of the skygates. As he stared it began to grow darker at one end, and a minute later a fouga rose from it, small and delicate as a bubble in a water-pipe, and trailing festival pennons like colored threads in the breeze.

"Hobi."

He looked back, startled. He had forgotten the nemosyne, forgotten where he was. An awful vertigo as he tried to focus on her amid all that gold and blue; then, amazingly, he found that he could do it. He could look at her, he could even walk back, dizzy but no longer nauseated.

"Hobi, look at the horizon."

He looked behind him. He hadn't noticed before the jagged green shapes spurting everywhere opposite the sea. Trees, he realized, trees and bushes. But then Nefertity took his hand and pulled him, gently, toward her.

"No, not there—the other way, the horizon, see? That line at the end of the ocean."

He turned obediently and looked where she pointed. At the rim of the world, above the unbroken line of blue and turquoise water, seethed a blurry darkness, immense as the sea itself. The whitish sky ended abruptly where it met this livid wall. He remembered looking through 'files in his father's library, hearing one of his friends describe a trompe l'oeil garden he had once visited on the vivarium level, and what he saw shimmering there.

Mountains, he thought in amazement. He turned to Nefertity. "Mountains!"

She shook her head. "No. *Clouds*, Hobi, it's a storm—"

"Clouds?"

It was the first time he had ever spoken the word aloud, and he said it again, staring at the line of black and gray advancing steadily above the waves.

Clouds. A storm. Just as the moujiks had always predicted. *Ucalegon, Prince of Storms. The Wave will take you.*

Suddenly he laughed, laughed until he had to stoop, holding his ribs as the air swam about him, white and gold and green. He laughed so long and so hard that Nefertity's eyes darkened from jade to emerald, and her body glowed in alarm as she plucked his sleeve and called out to him fruitlessly. Finally she grabbed his arm and started dragging him down the beach, the two of them stumbling through the sand. And still Hobi turned to stare back at the ocean and what loomed above it, that cinereous wall more massive than the domes, more massive than anything he could ever have imagined; he stared at it and laughed on and on and on, and the gulls banked above them, keening in the wind.

When they reached the edge of the beach he finally calmed down. Here trailers of greenery laced the sand, vines overgrown with flat yellow flowers that smelled sweet and whose hearts hid creamy spiders like pearls. Hobi took off his boots and socks, wincing at how hot it was. After a few minutes he pulled them back on again, swearing as he picked sand-spurs from his soles. Nothing grew on the stretch of sand between Araboth and the sea, but where the sand ended the jungle began. He had never before seen anything like this tangle of jade and brown and yellow, moving in the stiff wind, and the bursts of crimson and iridescent blue exploding from it as they approached.

"Those are birds," Nefertity explained. She sounded rueful. "If I were a zoological unit, I would know their names."

Hobi nodded. Already he recalled his other self—the self that had nearly been incapable of leaving the tunnel, the self that had crouched retching upon the sand—as he recalled his mother; someone precious but irredeemably lost. The air was so choked with smells that breathing was like eating—great gulps of roses and brine, a scent like carrion that turned out to be the fragrance of trumpet-shaped blossoms twining round a tree; the smell of the tree itself, heady with leaves and the spiciness of its decaying bark. He slashed at a branch with his hand, sending up a cloud of black and golden wings like sparks. Butterflies, he knew that from the vivariums. Birds and butterflies, and a dead crab's leg. He would have rushed headlong into the thicket if Nefertity hadn't stopped him.

"Higher ground, Hobi."

He turned to her, aggravated. "How do you know all this? 'Higher ground,' 'It's a storm'?"

Her wide eyes gazed at him unblinkingly. The soft whir of circuitry echoed the waves behind them. "Loretta. Before our exile I went with her when she traveled, and she always spoke to me. And I know from my programmed histories. If we are where you say we are, that is a part of the country that was plagued with hurricanes long ago. After the Shining of the Second Ascension the weather patterns changed, and it was besieged by tidal waves."

She pointed, far above them and inland, where a shadow rose in an uneven cusp against the blue sky. "There—that is high ground. We should try to go there. If we walk along the shore we may find a path inland, or running water. The woods here are too overgrown for us to pass through safely."

Hobi fell silent, nodding, and trudged after her along the strand. His first ecstatic joy was fading. Hunger and thirst made his head ache. The sun beat down on him like a block of stone. Bits of old stories came back to him, of ghouls that lived Outside, the remnants of men who had been stricken by the mutagenic rains. The thought made him hurry behind Nefertity.

Once, he stopped and looked back down the beach. It seemed they had been walking for hours, but the gleaming curves of the domes seemed no more distant than they had before. Only the shape of the shoreline had changed, and the dark silhouette of the storm clouds. They filled most of the sky above the ocean now. The wind blew stiffly in from the sea.

Great sheets of sand tore past him, tearing at his mouth and eyes and seeming to burn through his clothes.

He raised his hands to shield his face as he looked out to sea. The waves had grown bigger. They smashed against the beach, sending up plumes of froth and a dark spray of sand and broken shells. The wind had a different smell now, too. Different from the cleansing scent of the ocean, almost stagnant, as though from somewhere far away the clouds had sucked up fetid pools and carried them here. Even the air seemed heavy and moist. Hobi spat to get the taste of salt and grit from his mouth. The sun bulged from the clouds, luminous, faintly green. When he turned back to follow Nefertity he saw that the jungle of trees and cactus growing along the shore glowed with an eerie yellow light. Shells crunched beneath his feet. The bigger conches cast strange shadows across the sand, and his steps disturbed small things that raced to burrow into the scar.

It must have been several hours since they first peered Outside. The tor that was their destination no longer seemed so far away. Overhead the gulls had grown all but silent, wheeling fretfully and occasionally diving into the waves. From the trees came a constant rush of wings. He looked up to see dark shapes arrowing against the sky, heading inland. Once or twice he halted and tried to make out some sound from the direction of Araboth, but there was nothing, only the pounding waves, and the wind stinging his ears.

When he looked up he saw that Nefertity had stopped to wait for him. The ground at her feet was brighter than it was elsewhere. As he approached he saw that water poured in a narrow stream from the woods down to the sea. He ran the last few yards, stumbling to his knees in the shallow water and drinking greedily. Then he lay on his back, letting the stream pour over him until his clothes were soaked and his sunburned face soothed. He stood, flinging back his long hair so that it hung heavy and wet on his neck.

"We can follow this," Nefertity said. She pointed to where the woods opened up on either side of the stream, vine-hung trees and rosebushes giving way to cactus and small gnarled trees covered with papery, dull-orange flowers. "It might lead us up to that hill. At least we will be inland when the storm hits. If we hurry."

He glanced back at the domes of Araboth. They reflected the darkening sky, the sun a white blister on the curved surface. He knew now that he would never go back. Something inside of him had broken, a connection that had once tethered him to his parents, his dead mother and mad father, but now was gone. He felt fairly certain that he would die out here, and sooner rather than later; but if what the nemosyne said was true, if the city really was crumbling, then he would have died anyway. At least now he had seen the city from Outside, a sight only the Aviators had ever glimpsed from their Gryphons; and he had walked with a nemosyne, a creation from the First Days, and heard her speak with the voice of a woman centuries dead. Not even Shiyung Orsina had ever done all these things; not even Nasrani. His exhaustion eased somewhat at the thought. He started walking up the middle of the streambed, the wind sending his damp clothes flapping against his feverish body.

The stream coursed through a ravine that grew deeper and narrower the farther up they climbed. Nefertity walked alongside it, picking her way faultlessly among rocks and shattered blocks of limestone that seemed to be the remains of some huge building. Eventually Hobi had to clamber from the stream and join her. While shallow, the water flowed faster here, and it grew more difficult to keep his footing on the moss-covered stones. The sun passed fitfully in and out of the clouds, clouds so dark that the light seemed more like that inside the domes. The spindly trees cast shadows of an inky blackness against the green sky.

As he stumbled through prickly pear and thorny underbrush birds flew up in a flurry of squeaks and trills, and once he nearly stepped on a fistful of yellow bees clustered on a rotting log, too lethargic to fly or sting him.

Nefertity cautioned him against speaking—"You will grow too tired, we *must* reach higher ground before the winds strike." His head and body had resolved into one great pulsing ache. Several times he paused to lean over the ravine and drink, and pull bright red fruit from the prickly pears—not as sweet as those grown inside the vivariums, but something at least to fill his stomach.

"Hobi—look—"

He turned from where he crouched beside a cactus knobbed with fruit. Nefertity had disappeared. The monotonous vista of twisted greenery and dun-colored thornbushes stopped abruptly a few hundred feet in front of him. He stood, catching his trousers on a cactus spike, and pulled away heedless of the tear on one leg. His ears hurt from the wind battering at them. When he looked behind him he could see nothing but a dense web of green and brown. Ahead of him the trees fell back, so that it was mostly cactus and spare brush that had been tortured into anguished shapes by the relentless wind.

"Hobi, here—it's the top of a hill, there's something here—"

He hurried after her, sliding through a loose scree of pale limestone. He fell once, cutting his hand on something. When he drew his bloody fingers back he found a wedge of metal buried in the dry soil, bright blue and yellow, with teeth painted on it. It glowed eerily in the aqueous light, and Hobi shivered as he tossed it away.

In a few minutes he reached the top of the promontory. The wind was so loud that he covered his ears. When he tried to stand he nearly fell over, buffeted by air blasting warm and strong as from a huge oven.

Nothing grew here. He stood at the edge of a flat plateau that stretched perhaps a mile across, rimmed with stunted cactus and a few sturdy mesquite. Odd shapes littered the barren landscape, some of them big as houses, others smaller, like toppled statuary. Through it all the stream ran, a dull thread nearly invisible beneath the lowering sky.

"What is it?" Hobi shouted, but the wind ripped his words into a whisper. He turned to look behind him.

Under a range of black and umber clouds roiled the sea, so distant that he gasped to think they had climbed this high. From here all of Araboth could be seen, rising straight above the sand on a peninsula barely large enough to contain it. The small lip of sand beneath the Lahatiel Gate glittered in the ominous light, and glints of blue and gold flickered from the spires of the Gate itself. But elsewhere there was scarcely enough sand to keep the water from lashing at the foot of the domes. Even knowing nothing of its history, Hobi realized that it could not always have been like this. Erosion, or some natural disaster unmarked inside the domes, must have gnawed away at the sands surrounding the city. Otherwise how could it have been built there, with the waves coursing so near its fundament? An awful vertigo seized him—to think he had lived there all these years with the ocean lapping *right there*, with nothing but that fragile shell to protect him, and the vigilance of the Architects. He swayed, and would have fallen but for a cold hand clenching about his elbow.

"Hobi, come with me. There is shelter here."

Reluctantly he let her drag him away, his eyes fixed upon the vision of the domes like five clouded eyes set into the sand, the water churning around them and casting up long streamers of white and green beneath a somber sky.

The wind howled so loudly that they did not try to speak. An overpowering reek filled his nostrils, like water clogged with blossoms. Even with Nefertity gripping his arm he stumbled—the ground was uneven, covered with sharp stones that cut through the soft soles of his boots. But when he looked down he saw that they were not stones, but bits of metal and glass, some of them worn smooth but others sharp and rusted as though just torn from some huge machine. And they were all brilliantly colored, red and yellow and green and blue and orange, and striped or spotted or laced with intricate designs. He saw fragments of words spun across sheets of metal or plastic sticking up from the ground like severed limbs. *ILLER*, they read, or *DOL*, or *ING*. A scalloped yellow plate, a sort of canopy twice his height, rose from where it was half-buried in the ground, and flapped in the wind.

FUN!

It shouted in bold red-and-yellow letters.

Other things lay sprawled on the stony ground. Hollow images of creatures many times the size of a man, their huge misshapen ears cracked and bent, bulbous noses knocked awry or sometimes buried next to their crushed heads. Centuries of neglect on the exposed tor had caused their paint to ripple and crack, flaking venomous chips of acid-green and candied blue onto the scarred earth. And everywhere were the remains of machines, huge blackened metal arms shooting up from beneath heaps of rubble, flattened engines and broken domes of glass, a gigantic skeletal wheel rising against the turbulent sky like a charred and deadly moon.

Hobi stopped. His voice croaked thin and shrill above the wind.

"Where are we?"

Nefertity shook her head. Her translucent body glowed dull cobalt, its shining spindles and circuits shuttling back and forth inside her chest. "I don't know," she said after a moment. "The ruins of some-thing—a funfair, I think."

"A *what*?" Hobi yanked his arm from her and clasped himself. In a way this was worse than first seeing the world Outside alone: because that at least he had been prepared for, that was a nightmare he had fought and thrashed through all his life. But this? It was grotesque, all those inhuman faces with their lumpy grins, random letters like shrapnel flung against the desolate earth, immense scorpions of blackened steel crushing one another beneath the weight of a huge fallen tower. And through it all the stream coursing in its rust-colored bed. His stomach knotted to think he had drunk from it before.

" 'Fun,' " Nefertity quoted softly. She pointed at the broken canopy. Her voice shifted into its crystal-line recitative mode.

"Roundabout, coconut shies, big wheels, swingboats, rock stalls, all the fun of the fair. Midget pantechnicons bearing such legends as: 'Loades of Fun, Fun on Tour,' etc. You press the time-switch; the lights go on; everything clicks into motion. Then stops. Until you press the switch again."

She stopped. The wind rushing through the bro-ken chambers of a small building made a howling sound.

"It's making me sick," said Hobi, shouting to be heard above the wind. "Who would do this?"

Nefertity's eyes glittered, but her voice was calm. "People long ago," she said. "After the Second Shin-ing, perhaps even earlier than that. They liked to go to the seashore. Loretta used to like it, she told me. They built things there—pleasure cities. I think this was one of them."

Pleasure cities. Hobi remembered what Nasrani had told him about the city that had stood here once. Wealthy people, slave traders, gamblers. They might have climbed here, where they could look down upon the sea, and thrown their hours and their money to the ravening winds.

But he couldn't imagine who would have derived pleasure from *this*—these broken statues, and machines whose use could never have been anything but obscure. It was worse even than the Orsinate's dream inquisitions. He shivered, his teeth chattering. A whistling sound echoed across the tor, once and again, and again, then small reports that grew louder. Hobi cried out. Something struck his neck, then his face, and he drew away his hand to find it wet.

"It's started."

Nefertity turned back toward the ocean. A solid black line seemed to shimmer only inches above the edge of the promontory. Clouds of silver shook through the air—rain, Hobi realized, this was *rain!*—and a distant crashing echoed the wind screaming across the tor. In this sudden twilight Nefertity was a silvery blue beacon in the center of the world, calm and implacable as the rain lashed about her. As Hobi huddled beside her he thought he could see something out on the outermost edge of the horizon, a rent in the disturbed surface of the great ocean—something black and huge, as though the rim of the world had suddenly plunged into an abyss. He pointed at it. The rain struck him so hard that his face felt as though he had been slapped.

"I do not know," said Nefertity. Rain streamed down her body in fiery runnels. "But we should find shelter."

"*I* know what it is," the boy said slowly. As they watched the black bulge on the horizon grew even huger, and moved across the lashing gray sea, heading toward the shore. Hobi felt dizzy, almost speechless as he realized what it was that ripped across the ocean toward Araboth.

He said, choking, "I saw it—in a, a 'file once, about the Third Ascension. A kind of wave—like what you said before, the kind of wave that came after the Second Shining."

"Tsunami," the nemosyne whispered. "A tidal wave."

He nodded, staring numbly at the black ridge, the massive plateau of water rising to crush the sands below. "It's really come, Nefertity." He knew she could not hear him above the wind, he could no longer hear himself, but he went on anyway. "Like they always said—

"Ucalegon."

Nasrani had turned and fled after the *rasa* left him, back up the tunnel until the sand slithered beneath his feet and shallow water lapped at his soles. His breathing roared in his ears, and another sound, faint but unceasing. The pale green light that had filled the passage near the tunnel's mouth had faded until it was nearly too dark for him to see. That was what finally stopped him.

He stood in the middle of the tunnel, swaying back and forth. He could once again hear the murmurous explosions that rocked the Undercity, and feel the ground tremble. For the hundredth time his hands patted futilely at his greatcoat, trouser pockets, boots, searching for something, anything—empty morpha tubes, paper wrappings, ashes, lint. Nothing. He had found it all hours before, chewed it or spun it to grit between his fingers and then flicked it into the darkness. There was nothing left now, not in his pockets, not anywhere. If he went any farther back into the Undercity he would find the tunnel blocked, or be crushed by the walls caving in. Slowly he turned, and began to walk back toward where the passage opened onto the shore.

It was some time before he realized that it should not be this dark. In the distance the tunnel's mouth gaped, no bigger than the end of his thumb. Light trickled from the opening, but it was fainter than be-

fore, and had a greenish cast. His legs felt numb from
walking. To either side the walls of the tunnel seemed
to glow faintly. There was a strong smell of dead fish.

From the corners of his eye he glimpsed small
shadows flickering against the tunnel walls. When he
stopped he saw that it was only a trick of the feeble
light. There were no real shadows, only dark blotches
on the tiles. He rubbed his eyes, then stepped toward
the wall. There was something odd about it, something he hadn't noticed before, when he had been so
intent upon listening to Tast'annin ranting on and on.
His foot caught on something, and he kicked away a
soft object. There was enough light for him to see it
was some kind of clothing, a bundle of dark blue cloth
that hit the sand with a soft thud. He turned from it,
knelt and ran his fingers across the wall's broken tile,
heedless of the dank mold catching under his nails.

There were words there, written in a script all but
erased by time. Words and crudely drawn pictures.
Nasrani snatched his hand back when he saw that he
had smeared the images, patches of ruddy clay and
something black like charcoal clotted across his palm.
He drew back a little, squinting as he tried to read in
the watery light.

nnot get out.
ee da s
and now   The Wave
i c me
orror nd death fro
The S

The letters slanted down and disappeared into
the sand etching the wall's bottom edge. Behind him
he could hear a faint whistling sound. Very slowly he
lifted his eyes, and saw it drawn above the broken

lettering. A shape like a coiled spring etched upon the tile, opening into a fluid line that circled something meant to be a hill, he thought, a hill dark with small shapes that might have been people, or houses. Above it spear-shaped missiles, wavering lines to indicate flames, a horrible thing meant to be a human face, but veined with glistening tendrils of mildew. Beneath the spiral was a carefully drawn curl, opening into a hand with fingers splayed, like the claws of a stooping raptor.

'' *The Wave is come,*' '' Nasrani breathed. He traced the air above the image, leaned forward until his cheek pressed against the moist wall, and closed his eyes. Teeth had been drawn jaggedly in the mouth of the wave, teeth and a tongue that unfurled until it reached the smooth base of the hillside.

Behind him the whistling grew louder, was swallowed into a gurgling roar. Too late he turned and tried to run. But it was already there, it had found him as it would find his sisters and all the others who waited for it, arrogant or fearful or unknowing. Just as they had always said, as had been predicted for a hundred years, as it had come centuries before and would come again to claim the city they had been proud and foolish enough to build within its path. He tripped in the darkness and fell, and as he slumped to the ground he heard it, a million feet pounding up the twisted passageway, its voice a roar that deafened him, winding and turning until it found him crouched beneath its image and crushed him there, while all about the stones shrieked and tumbled into sand.

"Ucalegon," he whispered. The wave devoured him.

Chapter 11

UCALEGON

It was difficult to see what was happening from the viewing platform in the Narthex.

"Is that some kind of *fish*?" asked Nike, incredulous. Rain blew in sharp cold gusts up from the open Gate. She shivered, wishing she'd worn a rain cape or something warmer than her thin silk suit.

At her side the precentor, still upset that her rendition of the hyperdulia had been interrupted, stood smoking a camphor cigarette and gazing out to sea with an unfocused, rather sour expression.

"Someone over there yelled it was that thing you keep down on Dominations. The whale." She flicked her cigarette ash in the direction of a group huddled at the edge of the balustrade, primarily intimates of the Quir who seemed giddy from kef and champagne. The chromium mitre of the Archbishop of the Church of Christ Cadillac rose above the little crowd, a somber note amid the doomsday revelry. A moment later the Archbishop detached herself from the gathering and hurried to Nike's side.

"There is something you didn't tell me," she said angrily. Her face was bright pink and shining with sweat. She looked terrified. "This morphodite you chose for the sacrifice, what's her name, Reed—"

"Reive," Nike corrected her. She patted her cheeks with her handkerchief and looked about distractedly for her sister.

"Reive," the Archbishop went on. "She's innocent!" She inclined her head toward the group still leaning over the balustrade, calling excitedly to unseen people below as a hapless servant tried to hold a sheet of plastic over their heads. Shrieks and laughter as the balcony shuddered and debris hailed down from the ceiling. "The Quir says she told him she was *innocent*. Someone else says your sister acted in collusion with the Aviator Imperator to murder Shiyung, and falsely accused this mantic. To deliberately enact the rite of propitiation with such a sacrifice—"

She stopped, breathless, and stared out to sea. Nike stepped beside her, wiping rain from her nose and squinting as she tried once again to pick out the Redeemer's small shadow amid all that gray and silver. Black clouds moved so quickly overhead that she could imagine the howling wind was the sound of their passing. She could barely make out a dark shape leaping dolphin-wise upon the horizon before it was swallowed by immense waves.

"Zalophus," she said, turning to the precentor and shaking her head. The Archbishop stared at her as though she were mad. "The whale: a very archaic geneslave, its name is Zalophus. I can't imagine how it escaped."

"The entire city is collapsing!" exploded the precentor, ignoring the Archbishop's disapproving gaze. "You've brought this upon us, you and your sisters—"

Nike made some vague *ttt-ttt* sounds and flapped her hands in the precentor's face. "My sister is a fool," she said with surprising vehemence, and poked the Archbishop with one wet finger. "Actually, they're both fools, but at least Shiyung is a dead fool. Âziz is the one you want to talk to about all this, Your Eminence. Not only was that morphodite innocent, she was Shiyung and Nasrani's child. My sister wanted her dead. If you can find a 'file crew you might question her about it. Also about the death of Sajur Panggang, who claimed that the domes are collapsing. Please excuse me."

The Archbishop and the precentor fell back, dumbfounded, as Nike pushed her way past them. On the balustrade behind her triumphant cheers arose as the Quir's aluminum shades were hoisted above the small crowd and the rain sluiced off in shining sheets.

"May Day, May Day," Nike muttered to herself. It was something she had heard once in a cinema show about explosions on large ships. The floor shook and she steadied herself against a column, reached into a pocket and emptied a morpha tube into her mouth. She waited a moment and tapped an amphaze ampule to her throat for good measure, then closed her eyes and grimaced, waiting for the burst of clear-headedness to come. Her back molars tingled and her mouth went dry. For what seemed like a very long time there was a shrill buzzing in her ears and a popping sound. When she opened her eyes she saw that the column she had been leaning against had toppled. She looked over to see if Âziz was with the group on the balustrade and saw that the balustrade too was gone, sheared away as though it had been a bit of unwanted furze on a topiary sculpture.

"This is very bad," Nike said thickly. The high-pitched buzzing turned out to be screams, an unrelenting series of shrieks and moans that seemed to come from everywhere, above and beneath and to every side of the margravine. She started to take a step past the fallen column, her legs moving with unnatural slowness, and almost immediately stopped. There were people pinned beneath the column, some of them still moving and at least one of them screaming so loudly that Nike's hair stood on end. When she glanced down at her feet she saw that the pointed toes of her boots were splashed with blood and what at first looked like grass. Nike made a small unhappy noise and stumbled backward. Her siblings' many complaints about her intemperance finally seemed to be not entirely unwarranted. She wished she had not taken so much morpha.

"Your Grace, Your Grace—"

She turned unsteadily, her eyes tearing. Smoke was billowing up from somewhere, not the sweet-scented smoke of Æstival incense but black oily clouds with a horrible chemical tang. She could scarcely make out the small plump figure of the Quir, one half of his pallid face covered in blood as though sloppily rouged.

''Yes?'' she heard herself asking politely, but the Quir had grabbed her hand and was dragging her after him as though she had refused to acknowledge him. And indeed, when, coughing, she brought her hand to her mouth, she could feel her jaws tightly clenched, and could hear a droning humming noise that she realized, with embarrassment, that she herself was making.

"Your Grace, here, may be safer, you took a bad hit back there—"

She let her hand fall back to her side and saw that it was bright red; from the handkerchief dangling between her fingers dripped large spots of blood. She started to say something to the Quir, ask him what exactly it was the morphodite had said to him about her innocence. But then they were struggling down a long stairway, the Quir pushing bodies from their path, some limp but others lively enough to shout or howl as they tumbled from the steps. It was not until they reached the bottom that Nike could catch her breath and look around, and see that the Quir had brought her to the very mouth of the Lahatiel Gate itself.

"My sister," she gasped, pulling away from the Quir's surprisingly strong grasp and striving to peer through the haze of smoke and rain that clouded everything. "Âziz—"

It was not what she had meant to say, she had meant to thank him—she had some vague idea that his intent in bringing her here was to save her—but suddenly all she could think about was Âziz, and how if there was any way out of this hellish morass, Âziz was sure to know of it. But the Quir's expression as he stared back at her was not precisely that of a person, even the leader of a young and disagreeable cult, who had gone to some trouble to save the margravine of the Holy City of the Americas.

"Your sister has fled," said the Quir. For the first time Nike noticed that his large eyes, red-rimmed and slightly protuberant from smoking kef, were keen and possessing of a certain malevolent intelligence. He brushed a tear of blood from one cheek, leaving a brownish smear. His voice rose as he strove to be heard above the shrieking wind. "As soon as I set eyes upon that child I saw Nasrani in her, strong as steel. If I had known sooner I would have taken her in myself. We have seen now where your carelessness has led. The Compassionate Redeemer is dead, and the Healing Wind is upon us."

He gestured angrily. To Nike it seemed that he pointed where the Lahatiel Gate was flung open, one of its immense steel doors as carefully askew as a bedroom screen. The steps leading down to the beach were mobbed with people, screaming, fighting, trapped between the collapse of Araboth above and behind them and the oncoming tide before.

"The Wind," Nike repeated in a childish voice. She lifted her head, as though to see the Healing Wind coiling in the air above her; but what she saw was far worse.

In the uppermost reaches of Araboth, where for

time immemorial the domes had cast their bluish light
—periwinkle, cobalt, violet, but always blue—there
where they had always curved protectively above the
twinkling city, a hole had rent the sky.

It *was* the sky. Steel-gray, slashed with a dull poisonous green, a jagged gash larger than the Gate itself
gaped within the domes, a hole larger than the palace,
larger than anything Nike could imagine—

As she stared, black specks flew into it, like motes
swimming in a huge eye, and horrified, the margravine realized that these were *people*, people and rickshaws and buildings, all manner of things from within
the city, sucked upward by the rocketing change in air
pressure. Nike clapped her hands to her ears and
screamed—she could feel it now, something pounding at her skull, but without a sound because suddenly she could no longer hear. Everything around
her was whirling, flying, falling. In the numbing silence walls and floor gave way, and then she too was
falling only something caught her, someone—she
glimpsed the Quir, white with terror but pulling at
her desperately—and then there was an explosion,
and she could hear again, and she was lying behind
piles of broken stone and there was glass everywhere,
shining, and blood, but she was safe for the moment
and alive.

"What—" Nike coughed. The Quir, his indigo
robes torn and bloodstained, gave her a cruel look.

"Shut up," he said hoarsely. There were other
people with them, other *galli* she saw now, some of
them badly injured but all seemingly able to walk.
They were in a sort of alcove hidden behind the stairs
leading down to the beach. Rain flooded the floor,
driven through gaps in the wall through which Nike
could glimpse the mayhem outside. Waves were lashing at the steps, driving those who had survived the
collapse of the domes upward; but at the top of the
steps there was nothing but wreckage now, human
and stone and steel.

"We must—go somewhere—" Nike gasped. "Rooms—my rooms—"

"Don't be a fool," the Quir shouted. From his toneless voice she realized he too must have been partially deafened when the domes gave way. "It's like this everywhere—"

He fumbled at his waist, withdrawing a wire reticule. He pulled out a vial of petroleum that he opened and pressed to his fingertips. Angrily he flicked petroleum in Nike's direction.

"Your sister Âziz is an evil horrible woman," he spat. "It was her dream of the Green Country that opened the way to this disaster."

He pointed through a gap, to where Nike could see a swollen black hump on the horizon. As she gazed at it, the dark mass grew. It was a moment before she realized that it was not really growing larger. It was growing *nearer*.

"We could find the morphodite and make amends," she gasped, brushing a droplet of petroleum from her cheek. "Some sort of inaugural ceremony, this evening perhaps—"

The Quir raised his face to hers. His bulging eyes were very bright. "Don't be absurd. The domes have failed us. Within the hour we will all be dead."

Nike nodded, sickened, and looked out to sea again. Behind them another explosion tore through the city.

"Some of us have readied ourselves for this day," he said. He raised one hand, his azure sleeve flapping around his wrist, and beckoned to one of his followers. "I have not until today been among his faithful, but it's never too late for converts. Even at the end of all things, Blessed Narouz was able to wrest a shred of meaning from disaster. It was he who said, 'It is never too late, and there will always be enough to go around.' "

He paused reflectively. His voice had grown hoarse from shouting, and when he spoke again it was nearly in a whisper. "He was speaking of petroleum, of course, and of course he was wrong," he added. "There never is enough, and this time it really is too late. Although certain of Blessed Narouz's rites will prove useful to us now. Goodbye, Margravine."

He raised both hands and shouted something Nike couldn't understand. As she turned to see who he called to she glimpsed five or six people in indigo and green, their robes soaked and filthy with sand and oil. Some of them were in the alcove with them; others forced their way through the gaps in the wall, yelling. Several carried torches that sputtered in the rain. There was an overpowering stink of petrol and smoke. Nike started to protest, to suggest that they retire to the Four Hundredth Room to discuss the possibility of canonizing Reive Orsina, but then the ground beneath her buckled and she fell to her knees. The Quir shouted again, louder this time, and as Nike tried to get to her feet she saw one of his followers heaving a plastic bucket at her face. She screamed as it sloshed over her, burning her cheeks and hands as she scrabbled at the steps, and screamed again as one of the brands was thrust at her and the *galli* fell back, chanting and shrieking. Very dimly above the thunderous roar of flame and wind she could hear the Quir's voice, quite calm now, reciting the *Ethyl Spiritus* even as the waters rose about his ankles and then his thighs and finally engulfed him. By the time the rushing waves claimed her body there was really nothing that remained of her, save blackened bones and a twisted cone of metal wrapped about with greasy rags, and a charred morpha tube bobbing in the turbulent sea.

Âziz was surprised at how easy it was to reach the Gryphon. She fled as the first explosions swept the area beneath the Lahatiel Gate, just as Reive and Rudyard Planck were staggering along the beach with the Compassionate Redeemer behind them. Already she could tell that it had all gone wrong—Nike's refusal to

wear proper Æstival attire, the blatant rudeness of the
Archbishop and precentor, that storm raging Outside
when there should have been the more restrained
horror of a still blue sea and little waves lapping at the
sand. Instead, the Lahatiel Gate had opened upon
Ucalegon itself, and there was no way the Orsinate
could pretend to have anticipated *that*. Not even the
thin bands of sunlight slicing through the clouds, not
even the sight of the Compassionate Redeemer nosing
along the beach could placate Araboth's populace,
once they had glimpsed that storm raised like a gigantic fist ready to crush the Quincunx Domes. There was
no Scream, none of the orderly chaos of the Great
Fear; only a few moments of stunned murmuring before the throng broke into shrieks and enraged shouts
and turned to flee back into the city.

Âziz gazed out at the storm, the wind tearing at
her crown so that it tipped over one eye. *Nasrani was
right, the bastard*, she thought. She straightened the
crown and turned, slipped through the diminishing
crowd on the Narthex balcony to a small plain door
nearly hidden behind a line of toppled columns. A
steady grinding thunder rang out, as joists and beams
collapsed and storage vats burst into flame on the refineries level. For an instant it was all nearly too
much. Âziz's head roared and she would have given
herself over to the Fear like everyone else; but then
her hand found the little doorknob, the metal warm
beneath her palm, and without thinking she ran into
the passageway and let the door slam behind her.

Inside it was hot but blessedly quiet, the stillness
broken only by muted roars and the groan of the
wind raging at the Lahatiel Gate. An unblinking line
of dim yellow lights ran along the tunnel floor and
Âziz followed these, her booted feet slapping against
the ground and her breath coming in loud spurts. After a few minutes the yellow lights grew brighter and
a soft voice intoned, "Privileged area, please stop."
She stopped, gasping as the sentry pierced her hand,
and whispered, "Âziz Orsina. Pass."

Before her the door slid back to reveal another balcony, semicircular, its floor inlaid with garish mosaics. It seemed to jut out into the very heart of the storm, buckling and swaying as though made of corrugated leather. A sonic fence should have surrounded it, but the power must have failed—there was no warning hum, no flicker of blue light to indicate where the fence ended. If she wasn't careful she might plunge hundreds of feet into the crashing sea.

But Âziz was very careful. In the center of the balcony the Gryphon Kesef waited, its wings tucked tightly against its sides, its nose drawn in as it crouched against the floor. Rain gusted in sheets across the open space, dashing against the Gryphon's legs. As the margravine crept onto the balcony her boots crunched against something solid; glancing down, she saw the surface pied with hailstones like rice pearls. She cursed, sliding on the ice; caught herself and inched forward again. In a few minutes she had reached the Gryphon.

The howling wind had risen to a shriek. She could not hear herself as she shouted the command, could not hear if the aircraft responded. But a moment later the Gryphon rose unsteadily on its jointed legs, the slender metal stairs descended, and she was climbing them, clinging to the narrow struts as the wind battered her. Then she was inside.

Gasping, she flung herself into the seat. The leather molded itself around her and she felt a prickling warmth as auxiliary enhancers sent a soft surge of endorphins and nutriments into her veins. She blinked, stared up to where the webs began to descend in a gray haze; shut her eyes as they touched her face and she could feel the strange patterns tracing themselves onto her cheeks, temples, the inside of her wrists.

OrsinaKesefNineTwelveCycloneSystemGrade-
OneRescueAdvisoryOverriddenUnitRecalled-

LockgridFiveLevelTwoWaitingWaitingWait-
ing . . .

Âziz cried out. Across her mind's eye crimson
lines formed an intricate crosshatch, a grid bisected
with green and glowing blue spheres. She could hear
the fluting voice of the thing called Kesef, the
Gryphon that waited for her command; she could feel
the ground shuddering beneath it. She clenched her
mouth shut and tried to focus, concentrating until she
brought up an image, the figure of an Aviator silhouetted against the domes of Araboth. Then she willed
away the domes, tried to imagine what one of the
frontier outposts might look like, ended up with the
Aviator's silhouette and a hazy blue background. *Go
there*, she thought, then said the words aloud in a
croak.

"Where they are—the Aviators—find them—"

There was a crackle of static electricity, a blinding
light outside and then a crash. She could feel the
Gryphon fighting her, trying to override her command as it sent warning messages blaring through her
mind—

CycloneTsunamiHurricane-
GaleSamielDangerDangerDanger

—but she repeated her command, again and
again, each time the image growing clearer in her
mind, until finally with a shudder she felt the aircraft
move around her. Then it was as though the flesh had
been sheared from her face: all around her she felt the
raw wind, the rain like razors slicing against her skin;
but of course that was the Gryphon and not her, and
it was the Gryphon's voice keening like a brazen bell
as it soared from the balcony, up and up into the
whirling storm until she could feel nothing, not even
the shafts of light spearing along its wings as the gale
tossed it and the Gryphon fought to make its way
inland, while the woman who had commanded it lay

unconscious in its grasp, beset by evil dreams. She did not realize until later, when she woke, that she had unconsciously given the solitary figure of her voiceless command the stooped bearing and ruthless pale eyes of Margalis Tast'annin, the Aviator Imperator.

"They will all die," Hobi said dully.

Beside him the nemosyne stood, silent. After a moment she nodded.

"It is a tsunami, a tidal wave. On the subcontinent they sometimes killed millions in a single night."

Hobi shivered and drew away from her, until he brushed against the edge of the wall. They had found the ruins of a building, its top rounded and painted in flaking greens and yellows, the whole thing sunk like a culvert into the pebbly debris-strewn ground. The wind screamed down the opening and rain poured in, draining away down countless holes after it had soaked Hobi to the skin.

From here they could look off the eastern face of the tor, down onto the glassy surface of the Quincunx Domes. White foam churned at the edges of the city. The narrow sandy spit that had stood between Araboth and the open sea had long since been swallowed by engulfing waves. Flecks of black and gray scudded across the top of the receding water. With horror Hobi realized that these were people, the tiny figures of the revelers who had been released earlier when the Lahatiel Gate opened. He buried his face in his hands and turned away.

"I can't bear it," he whispered. Nefertity could not have heard him above the wailing wind, but she leaned over and touched him gently.

"Perhaps you can sleep, we will be safe here—"

"Sleep?" he yelled, striking at her with one hand. "How can I sleep, my father is down there, Nasrani, everyone—"

The nemosyne regarded him with cool aquamarine eyes. "It was an evil place," she said at last. "It has happened before, that the wind has swallowed an evil place—

> "All flesh died that moved upon the earth: all in whose nostrils was the breath of life, of all that was on the dry land, died.
>
> "But God said, I will establish my covenant with you; neither shall all flesh be cut off any more by the waters of a flood; neither shall there any more be a flood to destroy the earth."

Her voice chimed above the cry of the wind, and Hobi turned to her and spat, "That's another of your precious sacred stories? A broken promise?"

Nefertity tilted her head so that the rain struck sparks around her eyes. "A man wrote that," she said. She pointed to the east. "Look, Hobi. If you can bring yourself to look—that is the fall of Araboth."

He turned. Sky and ocean had become one vast unbroken plane of gray and green. In a froth of pounding waves the Quincunx Domes seemed to float, small and frail as bubbles of glass. A fouga, a tiny obloid that glowed bright blue through the silvered haze of rain, suddenly shot up from one bubble as though striving to free itself. An instant later it was gone. There was nothing else to indicate that anything had ever lived down there. The domes might have been the cast-off shell of some creature, a submarine egg-sac washed onto a crumbling lee.

"There," Nefertity murmured.

Midway between the shore and the horizon a swell black and viscous as oil detached itself from the rest of the ocean. Hobi strained to hear something, a rising shriek on the wind or perhaps a roar; but oddly it now seemed that the wind had died, and while the rain still ripped across the tor there was no other sound. Certainly nothing terrible enough to be the voice of that Wave. He shrank closer to the nemosyne, without thinking clutched at her as he watched it rise and grow larger and larger still, until it was so impossibly huge he cried out, thinking that it must tear away at the very foundation of the headland where they crouched.

But it did not: only gathered strength and power until now he *could* hear it, a noise like all the engines of Araboth screeching into life and he knew that he was hearing the voice of the Wave itself, the boundless throat of the sea shrieking havoc as it reared above the fragile domes, the ancient folly that was Araboth, and smashed it into oblivion.

He must have blacked out, because the next thing he knew he was skidding across the tor, broken glass and metal tearing through his clothes as Nefertity grabbed at him and he struck at her, shouting.

"Hobi, stop! There's nothing you can do, it's gone now, nothing—"

He ran to the edge of the plateau, where the rust-colored stream had swollen to a copper torrent plunging down the steep incline. It was like it had never been there at all. Far below, at the base of the tor, the ocean seethed in glass-green knots and coils. Of the domes of Araboth there was nothing, not a metal blade, not a fragment of shattered glass: nothing. Rain nearly blinded him and he wiped his eyes, squinting through the haze. Only a few minutes later, after Nefertity stood beside him steaming in the rain, did he see something, a long twisted bit of white that might have been part of one of the inner retaining walls, wash up on a narrow spar of beach below.

"It is finished."

He raised his head. Beside him Nefertity stared down at the angry waters, her beautiful face calm and cold as the image on a sarcophagus. Fury surged inside of him and almost he sprang at her; but then she was shaking her head, and her voice sounded strange.

"Hobi. Hobi—we're not alone."

He looked where she pointed, to where the stream disappeared downhill. He blinked and wiped his eyes again, not certain if he was imagining it; but no, there was something there, a figure—and behind it many figures—the first one tall and wearing crimson leathers. An Aviator, wearing an enhancer, his face covered with a scarlet metal mask that gleamed in the rain like a warning flare. Behind him trudged sullen forms in robes and janissaries' uniforms and the pleasure cabinet's rosy silks, only their festival scarves of green were torn and stained, and their faces too seemed to have been wiped away by the storm.

"*Rasas,*" the boy breathed. His teeth chattered as he realized that the one leading them was a *rasa* as well. He would have run but Nefertity held him. The figures paced slowly up the hill, heedless of the rain streaming around them and the gale tearing at their clothes. Their leader walked the last few steps until he stood upon the plateau. When he raised his eyes to meet Hobi's the boy saw that he was what remained of the Aviator Imperator.

"Commandant Tast'annin," he gasped. He thought he might be sick.

"Horemhob Panggang," the *rasa* said in a low voice. He turned his gaze to Nefertity. "You have her. The nemosyne. Nasrani's metal woman."

Hobi nodded dumbly. Behind the Aviator the other *rasas* had stopped. They stood, shuffling and silent. The rain where it struck some of them seemed to leave a soft impression on their skin.

"Yes," the boy whispered at last. He coughed, tried to make his voice louder but succeeded only in raising it to a croak. "Nefertity—that's her name—"

"Nefertity," the Aviator repeated. He stepped forward, until he stood directly in front of the nemosyne.

"Commandant," Nefertity said, her voice cool and uninflected. Her eyes and throat began to glow deep blue.

"I heard much about you, many years ago, from my friend Nasrani Orsina," the *rasa* went on. "He said you were more beautiful than any real woman he had ever known, excepting of course his youngest sister.

At the time I did not believe him. I see now he was right."

He bowed, the rain spilling from the cusps of his leather jacket.

The nemosyne stared at him, her gaze implacable, almost cruel. "I think it is a pity you did not perish with the rest of your people down there," she said, gesturing to where Araboth lay somewhere beneath the sea's flow. Her voice had the husky, drawling edge of Loretta Riding's.

"Oh, but I have already given one life to those people," the Aviator replied, raising his head and glancing back at the waiting figures behind him. "As have these others. Araboth's forgotten ones, The Fallen—Hobi knows about them, don't you, Hobi? Forgetful revenants, corpses who stray away from their prams when their nannies aren't looking. Military commanders who don't linger long enough in the beds of imperious mistresses."

The nemosyne stared at him before replying coolly. "Let us go free. Let the boy go, at least—there may be others who survived, let him go and see if he can find them."

The Aviator swept his arms out, sending up a plume of silver spray from his jacket. "I won't harm him. His father was a friend of mine, once. And I have had enough of killing, for a little while." He gestured at the other *rasas*. "They were in the Undercity—they were following you, the light you shed as you passed through the tunnel. They followed me, and I followed you. We made it halfway up the hill before the gale struck. They are all that escaped from the city."

He laughed mirthlessly, light glinting from his black teeth. Behind him the rustling of the waiting *rasas* grew louder. The rain was slowing. Overhead the clouds lightened to the color of verdigris, and on the eastern horizon sunlight darted from gaps in the clouds.

"I am not a military nemosyne," Nefertity said, her voice harsh. "I belonged to the radical wing of the

American Vatican. I am a folklore unit. I am useless to you. Let me go."

The Aviator shook his head. "No. You can link with the others—you were all designed to interface with each other."

"The others are gone."

"I believe they still exist." He stepped closer to her, took her gleaming metal hand in his dark and sanguine one. "Shiyung believed that as well, that's why she sent me to the Capital. The Military Tactical Targets Retrieval Network. It is somewhere out there still. HORUS was receiving random transmissions from it, before the raid by the Commonwealth destroyed their satellites."

Nefertity's eyes darkened to cobalt. Hobi could smell something faint and metallic, like ozone, as she withdrew her hand from the Aviator's.

"Metatron," she said, and recoiled. "The primary military unit—that's what they called it. Loretta said it was destroyed when Wichita fell."

"I think it is still there. Somewhere. It broadcasts on a shortwave radio frequency. If we were to find an area where the airwaves were not contaminated, we might be able to find its range. *You* might be able to find it."

The *rasa*'s hollow voice had grown low, almost wheedling. Hobi started to back away from him, when suddenly the Aviator's hand shot out and grabbed him.

"Aaagh!" The boy yelled and tried to pull away, then stumbled to the ground. The *rasa*'s hand cut into his flesh like ice.

"Let go of him," Nefertity commanded. Her entire body blazed, the mist around her glittered blue and green and gold. Behind the Aviator the other *rasas* murmured and crept forward; some of them fell to their knees. "He is innocent, let him go."

"Come with me, then," said the Aviator. "Else I will kill him—and you will be responsible."

Nefertity was silent. At the Aviator's feet Hobi

writhed, his arm held taut in the *rasa*'s grip as a single long tear of blood ran from wrist to elbow.

Nefertity looked down at Hobi, her eyes glittering. "Let him go," she cried. "Yes, I will go with you." Anger flared in her voice. "But how dare *you* harm him, how can *you* break the laws that bound you from harming your creators—"

The *rasa* grinned horribly, the splintered light making a tortured skull of his goblin face. "I am not truly a *rasa*, Mistress Nemosyne, nor am I human. Nothing commands me but myself, and, perhaps—"

He raised his hands, letting go of Hobi so that the boy collapsed, moaning, at his feet. For an instant a shaft of sunlight struck the Aviator, setting his crimson jacket aflame. His pale eyes were lost in shadow as he cried out words the boy did not understand. Then the sun was gone, the rain hissed once more upon the broken ground.

"Master—"

A thin voice called from behind the *rasa*. Hobi looked up. In the gray-green sky something glimmered, a spark that seemed to flicker more brightly and grow larger, until he saw that it was an aircraft of some kind, and as it plummeted toward them he made out the unearthly grace of one of the Ascendant's Gryphons.

"Kesef!" The Aviator's voice rose in command. Abruptly the Gryphon's wings folded back and it plunged to earth like a javelin. Hobi cried out; but at the last second the Gryphon hovered, seemed to stutter in the air; and then its six jointed legs descended, followed a moment later by a folding stair delicate as a gentleman's fan.

"What—" Hobi began, turning to Nefertity; but before he could speak something fell from the aircraft's belly. A tangle of arms and legs on the silver stairs, resolved into a single person struggling with some sort of ornate costume rife with spikes and lumens. A moment later and the stranger was on her feet, tearing at her face as though something clung there. When she turned, shaking rain from her cheeks, he saw that it was Âziz Orsina.

"Margravine!" Hobi exclaimed, and would have run to her if the *rasa* had not stopped him.

"Help, dammit, is this the frontier? Have we reached a substation?" The margravine tore the last bit of her Æstival garb from her and flung it to the ground, then turned and kicked furiously at one of the Gryphon's legs. "Where *are* we, dammit?"

From the *rasas* waiting on the hillside came a low sound, a sound that became a hiss. Âziz turned, startled. "Oh! *Oh*—"

Looking back, she saw Hobi and the nemosyne and the Aviator Imperator. She bit her lip, rubbed her chin, and then tossed her head back defiantly.

"Margalis! I might have thought *you'd* find a way out! Well, come on, then, you know the way— where's the nearest substation, we've got to get out of here—"

Behind her the hissing grew louder. Hobi shrank closer to Nefertity, as slowly the *rasas* began to creep the last few feet up the hill to where the margravine stood, glaring at Tast'annin.

"—this bloody thing doesn't listen at *all*, I thought they were supposed to respond to direct emotive input, let's go *now* while the storm's let up—"

Tast'annin shook his head. "I don't think so, Âziz," he murmured. Her eyes blazed and she took a step toward him, was stopped by a hand on her shoulder. "I think some of your—*people*—have need of you. . . ."

Behind her the *rasas* had gathered, crooning and sighing and mumbling among themselves as they surrounded the margravine. Âziz saw them and gave a small cry, tried to push her way through them but was borne off, as first one and then another grabbed her, handing her over their heads until finally she disappeared in a weaving thicket of white arms and hands and mouths.

Hobi looked away, covering his eyes. Âziz's shrieks grew louder, were nearly drowned by the sound of tearing and many soft voices crooning to themselves. The boy crouched against the nemosyne, weeping.

"It's all right, Hobi, it's all right," she said gently, stooping over him. Above her the Aviator Imperator stood, brooding in the gathering dusk. She raised her face to his and said, "We must find others for him. Other people. Otherwise he will go mad. I've seen it happen before," she ended sadly.

The Aviator nodded. "We will find them. There is a girl, a girl I left for dead in the Capital—she knows things, she can deal death with her mind. I would find her."

"Nothing but death," the nemosyne said bitterly, hugging the weeping boy to her. "You have seen where it brought them, and still you would have nothing but death."

The Aviator shrugged. "I have questions, that's all." He turned to the Gryphon and lay his hand upon the edge of its steps. When he glanced back at Nefertity a spare ray of light glinted in his pale eyes. "I have always tried to keep an open mind about these things."

The nemosyne said nothing. She waited until he climbed into the aircraft, then murmured, "Hobi, it's all right now. We will go from here, we will find another place. . . ."

Hobi shuddered, wiped his eyes, and looked up at her. "I'm ready," he said at last, his voice hoarse. He looked over his shoulder, to where the eastern horizon was banded with streamers of gold and violet and red.

"It's over," said Nefertity. "The storm is gone, it's passed over us now. That's the sky, the sun breaking through—"

The boy looked in the other direction, down the hill. He could just make out shadowy figures moving in the distance, and hear scuffling noises in the brush.

Before he could turn away a voice called down from the Gryphon.

"Come now—it's ready, I had to clear away the mess she'd made, but there's room now for both of you—"

The boy stood, wincing at how much his legs ached. Gingerly he touched the raw gash on his arm where the Aviator had cut him. "Is it safe?"

Nefertity shook her head. "What is 'safe,' now? It's not safe to stay here alone; it's not safe to have him murder you." She walked stiffly to the stairway, turned to Hobi, and bowed slightly. "I thank you anyway, Hobi, for waking me. It's better not to sleep, I think." Without saying more they climbed into the Gryphon.

He had always thought it would be exciting to fly in one of the Aviator's biotic craft; but then he had thought it would be exciting to see clouds, too, and mountains. Now Hobi knew that one grew accustomed to things Outside very quickly.

He felt queasy at first, as the Gryphon accelerated impossibly fast and burst into the air like a flame. There was only one biotic hookup, for Tast'annin. Hobi and Nefertity sat in two narrow seats behind him, and peered out a series of round windows at the tor receding beneath them in a rush of gray and brown. Then the Gryphon banked and shot out over the ocean, seeming to bounce across cusps of air like a rickshaw over uneven transway. Hobi bit his thumb and hummed nervously. After a minute or two he felt easier, and leaned closer to the windows.

Below them the ocean purled almost gently against sheer rock, all that could be seen of the precipice that had once sheltered Araboth. Of the domes he could see nothing; only a few bits of flotsam floating in the dark water. As they skimmed above the coast the rock gave way to sandy beach, nearly as smooth as the water itself. There was nothing here, either, save for uprooted trees, a torn length of white cloth wrapped around a spar, two sodden bags that almost looked like bodies . . .

"Hey!"

Hobi yelled so loudly he was surprised the Gryphon didn't halt, the way a rickshaw would. The Aviator scarcely stirred where he reclined in front of them, only raised a single finger warningly.

"Hey," Hobi repeated, a little desperately now, "I think those are *people* there—"

Beside him Nefertity leaned to gaze out her window, then without a word placed her hand upon the Aviator's shoulder. Abruptly he sat up, glanced down at the beach, then back at Hobi. Still saying nothing he settled back into his seat; but the Gryphon immediately began to descend.

Hobi held his breath, waiting for the jolt when it landed; but he felt nothing, was stunned when the floor slid sideways beneath his feet and the airy steps unfolded. "Wait here," the Aviator commanded, and climbed out.

Hobi crossed and uncrossed his legs. A gust of warm air shot up from the opening in the craft. If he slanted his head just right he could see one of the Aviator's booted feet and what might have been the ragged hem of a linen garment. Then abruptly the Aviator's grim form filled the opening. Hobi crouched back as the *rasa* climbed inside, carrying something in his arms. The nemosyne slid from her seat onto the floor, folding her long legs under her.

"Move," the Aviator said sharply, shaking his head at Hobi. The boy hunched into a corner beside Nefertity. The *rasa* lay a slight figure on the seat where Hobi had been, then silently turned and went back outside. He returned after another minute, this time with an even smaller form that he set in Nefertity's seat. Without another word he slipped back into his place. The steps slid up and disappeared. With a heart-stopping rush they were airborne again.

When Hobi was sure the Aviator was linked with

the Gryphon he leaned forward. In his seat lay a slender figure. At first he thought it was a boy, a boy with shaven head; then with a grimace he drew back.

A gynander. She was breathing heavily, with a slight rattle in her chest. As he watched she suddenly turned to one side and vomited a great quantity of water onto the floor.

Hobi leaned back hastily and turned to the other figure. A dwarf. With a spurt of elation he recognized him—Rudyard Planck, a friend of his father's.

"Rudyard!" he cried, pummeling the back of the seat. The Gryphon swooped in a long slow arc and he fell back. "Rudyard, it's me, Hobi—"

The dwarf stirred, groaning. Beside him the gynander whimpered, then suddenly shot up.

"Where are we—we don't know, let us go, please—"

Hobi fell silent, noticing her green eyes widen with terror as they took in the cramped curve of the aircraft, the dwarf coughing beside her, the nemosyne glowing like a corpse-candle in the back of the craft. Finally he said, "You're safe—whoever you are. At least as safe as we are." His tone sounded defeated, and he pointed to the *rasa*, motionless in the front seat. "That's the Aviator—this is his Gryphon, there's no way out. I'm Hobi, that's Nefertity—"

The nemosyne nodded.

"—and I know Rudyard Planck, I think, and who are you?" He tried to sound polite.

The gynander shook her head. "We are Reive," she announced, coughing and wiping seawater from her chin. "Reive Orsina."

"Orsina?" Hobi sucked his breath in, then said, "I thought they were all dead."

"We are alive."

Hobi groaned: it was too much to ask of him, really, to survive a typhoon and then be polite to a lying morphodite. He closed his eyes, pretending he was asleep.

But in a few seconds he opened them again. The

gynander was sitting with her face pressed against one small round window, staring transfixed at the ocean below and paying no attention to him whatsoever.

"Hobi Panggang," the dwarf said hoarsely, as though noticing him for the first time. "Bel's balls, you look just like your father after a toot." He reached out and prodded Hobi uncertainly with a damp finger. "Sorry to hear about that, Hobi, very sorry." He turned to the nemosyne and said, "Rudyard Planck, odd circumstances."

"Nefertity," the nemosyne replied softly.

"Huh?" Hobi shook his head and wriggled across the crowded floor until he was beside the gynander. "What's out there, can you see something?"

Reive nodded, so excited the words caught in her throat. Her finger stabbed the gritty window specked with salt and dirt, and pointed to the luminous sea below. Hobi rubbed his eyes, looked down and then behind him.

Through the small windows on the other side of the Gryphon he could glimpse green, shivering blades of green and blue as they soared above the coast and the setting sun speared the sides of the craft. Then, looking back through the window where Reive pointed he could see the ocean, so tranquil now that it all seemed a dream—Ucalegon, Araboth, the evil margravines, his father and mother and Nasrani, everything but that endless sweep of turquoise a dark and fitful dream from which he had just awakened. He might almost fall asleep again, now, with his head resting against the cool glass, only someone was jostling his elbow and crying in a shrill voice, "Look! Look!—"

—and pointing to where something moved through the gentle swells, something that even from here he could see was ponderously huge and dark. Only there wasn't just *one;* there were four of them, and they seemed to be playing, great clumsy things somehow taking to the air of this new green world just as he was, twisting in impossible arabesques as they swam in and out and between each other—

"—he was right," Reive was babbling as the Gryphon banked to the west and she craned her neck to see the last of them, four vast creatures leaping and crashing back into the sea with a bellow they could hear even from this distance; "he said they were waiting for him, he said his sisters would come and they did, oh, they *did*!"

And wondering, Hobi pressed his face close to hers against the glass, watching the great whales until they were gone, swallowed like the rest by the sea.

ABOUT THE AUTHOR

ELIZABETH HAND is the author of the novel WINTERLONG. Her short fiction has appeared in numerous magazines and anthologies, her articles and book reviews in the *Washington Post*, *Detroit Metro Times*, *Penthouse*, *Science Fiction Eye* and *Reflex Magazine*. Her third book, THE EVE OF SAINT NYNEX, will be published by Bantam Spectra in 1993. She lives on the Maine coast with novelist Richard Grant and their two children, where she is working on a supernatural novel called WAKING THE MOON.

Bantam Spectra Special Editions

If you enjoyed this Bantam Spectra Special Edition, here are some other titles you'll find of interest:

❏ The Silent City by Elisabeth Vonarburg
(29789-9 • $4.99/$5.99 in Canada)

In the aftermath of nuclear fire, Elisa is the first of a new race of humans who heal remarkably quickly. Her powers, however, aren't a gift; they come with enormous responsibility—and Elisa must face bearing the weight of the fate of all humanity.

❏ Aestival Tide by Elizabeth Hand
(29542-X • $5.50/$6.50 in Canada)

The dazzling sequel to the highly praised *Winterlong*, this is the story of a society forever protected from the presumed horrors of the Outside having to come face to face with their worst fears.

❏ Full Spectrum 3
edited By Lou Aronica, Amy Stout and Betsy Mitchell
(29191-2 • $5.99/$6.99 in Canada)

A collection of short speculative fiction on the cutting edge written by some of the most innovative voices in the field, including Ursula K. Le Guin, Gregory Benford, Poul Anderson and Norman Spinrad. "*Full Spectrum 3* may be the best original anthology ever produced."—*Locus*

- -

Available at your local bookstore or use this page to order.

Send to: Bantam Books, Dept. SF 159
     2451 S. Wolf Road
     Des Plaines, IL 60018

Please send me the items I have checked above. I am enclosing $_____ (please add $2.50 to cover postage and handling). Send check or money order, no cash or C.O.D.'s, please.

Mr./Ms._____

Address_____

City/State_____Zip_____

Please allow four to six weeks for delivery.
Prices and availability subject to change without notice.   SF 159 9/92